DON'T LOOK AWAY

BOOKS BY RACHEL ABBOTT

DON'T LOOK AWAY

Rachel Abbott

bookouture

Published by Bookouture in 2023

An imprint of Storyfire Ltd.
Carmelite House
50 Victoria Embankment
London EC4Y 0DZ

www.bookouture.com

First published in the US and Canada by Bookouture in 2023.

ISBN: 978-1-83790-168-5
eBook ISBN: 978-1-83790-167-8

PROLOGUE

Slowly, gently, he eases down the handle and slips silently through the door.

She's there, on the bed, covers thrown back. He stifles a gasp as his eyes travel the length of her body, from her long naked legs, exposed to the cool breeze drifting gently through the open window, to her chest, rising and falling with each soft breath. In the still of the hot night the only sound is the murmur of waves lapping the pebbled beach.

Her breathing changes. He stands perfectly still. Is she awake?

He waits, but she doesn't stir.

Inching his way further into the room, he creeps to the side of the bed, longing to reach out and stroke her silky flesh.

He stands motionless, watching but not touching.

ONE

FIVE DAYS EARLIER

'I'm not doing it, Jay. I don't care what you say or who you tell, I'm not climbing down that bloody cliff.'

'You owe me,' Jay whined, 'and Mum'll kill me if I lose one of my trainers. They're new.'

'It's not my fault!' Ollie shouted. 'You shouldn't have been arsing around, should you? Go get it yourself.'

The trainer in question was lodged on a rock about ten metres below them. Jay had pulled it off and thrown it at Ollie for taking the piss of him because he fancied a girl at school.

'You've got no chance!' Ollie had teased.

Ollie had ducked, and the ill-fated trainer had sailed above his head and over the edge of the cliff.

'It was your fault, Ollie,' Jay complained. He sounded about five years old, not thirteen. 'You wound me up and Mum'll kill us both. You're my big brother. She'll say you should have stopped me.'

Jay had a point. He was still a bit of a mummy's boy, despite declaring he had the hots for a girl a year older than him. Ollie, with an additional two years of sophistication under his belt, had made the mistake of laughing at him.

each moment going to stab me with a painful reminder of all that happened both before, during and after that trip? I had thought my heart was broken before I arrived, but by the time I left it was torn to shreds. We should never have come. It was a huge mistake, but somehow when Mum's aunt Helen approached me at the funeral to suggest the trip, I didn't know how to refuse. There was something vaguely terrifying about her, in her smart black suit and veiled hat.

'Nancy, I know how difficult all of this has been for you. You mustn't blame yourself for your mother's death. Whatever anyone tells you, it's not your fault. Do you hear me?'

I wanted to believe her. I *needed* to believe her. But I couldn't then, and I don't now.

I didn't know my great-aunt Helen well. The last time I'd seen her was two years earlier, when Mum first became ill – and then only briefly. I remember how direct she had been – severe, almost, with a clipped voice that left little room for argument. Now she was gripping both of my arms in her hands, staring straight into my eyes. It occurred to me that she was the only person who had looked at me properly in weeks. Even the doctor had walked past me without a word as he left the crematorium, his mouth pinched as if he was trying to stop himself from saying something.

'Listen,' Aunt Helen said. 'It would do you good to get away. I have a cottage in Trevyan, a tiny Cornish village. I've not lived there for three years, but you should go for a holiday. You're nearly nineteen – old enough to go alone. Or take Lola – just the two of you. I'll write to you, Nancy – send you all the details. But go soon. The break will be good for you.'

I hadn't known what to say. For the two years that I'd been caring for Mum I had barely left her room, and I wasn't sure if the holiday would be an exciting adventure, or something too terrifying to contemplate.

'Nancy needs it,' I'd heard Aunt Helen tell Dad in that

bossy voice of hers. 'She's lived and breathed the same air as Janice for all this time, and she must feel the greatest loss. God knows, you've been no use at all.'

I don't think I was supposed to hear that.

Although he didn't say as much to Aunt Helen, Dad told me he wouldn't hear of us going on our own.

'Lola's too much of a responsibility for you, Nancy,' he'd said. I'm not sure that's what he meant; I think he was saying he didn't trust me to take care of her. 'I'll get someone to look after the farm and I'll come too – give you some freedom while I make sure Lola's safe.'

He failed, of course, but somehow that became my fault too, and although the holiday wasn't the beginning of all that happened, it was certainly the beginning of the end.

Now the train is growing ever closer to my destination and I feel light-headed. I don't know if I can do this, but I have to try.

THREE

The roads are starting to look vaguely familiar as the taxi makes its way from the station towards Trevyan and there are a few places I recognise.

The taxi driver has tried to make conversation, and although I've done my best I think my monosyllabic responses have convinced him that I'm not worth the effort. I don't want to be rude, but my stomach is churning, my head spinning.

He has one last try: 'Are you here on holiday, or working?'

'I'm not working, but I'm not sure if it's a holiday or not,' I answer, and I see him glance at me in the rear-view mirror with a puzzled frown. I could try to explain, but I'm not sure how lucid I would sound. 'I'm sorry, but I'm not sure why I'm here at all.'

I didn't mean to say that out loud, although it's true. I don't have a plan, and it adds to my confusion. The last few weeks have demanded a bewildering array of decisions, and I feel stunned by it all.

It began about two months ago with a phone call to the care home where I work. I had been giving a foot massage to Doreen, a delightful lady in her nineties with a wicked sense of humour, when a voice called through the open doorway.

'Nancy – someone on the phone for you!'

'Do you mind taking the number, please? I don't want to leave Doreen mid-massage.'

Doreen winked at me. 'You go, lovey. It might be a man!'

I tapped her foot with my finger and got up from my knees. 'Less of that, and stop trying to marry me off!'

'You need someone, Nancy. You're way too good to be on your own.'

She meant well – they all did. Some had even tried a bit of matchmaking with their grandsons, which was always awkward for all concerned. It was impossible for me to explain why I wasn't interested in a relationship: that the thought of the inevitable heartbreak was too much for me. It was unusual for me to get a call at work, though, so in the end I wrapped her feet in warm towels and headed to the office.

The news that Aunt Helen had died and left me her cottage took a long time to sink in. I thought it was a mistake to start with, but when I returned to Doreen's room to tell her what had happened, she let out a whoop of joy. I was in a daze, the very thought of the cottage filling me with an anxiety I hadn't experienced in years. To me, it was a place that reeked of guilt, grief, despair and fear – somewhere I had never wanted to return to.

I was sorry that Aunt Helen was dead, but I barely knew her – which made it all the more strange that she'd left me her cottage. I vaguely remember her from when I was small. I think she looked after me when Mum had Lola, but then I didn't see her for years – not until Mum first became ill, and of course she came to the funeral.

The holiday she offered had ended in disaster, and I don't know if she blamed herself for what happened. Or maybe she blamed me, because contact afterwards was sporadic and any attempt I made to keep in touch was met with a rather abrupt response, which is why it seems so odd to find that I am now the owner of her cottage. And I wish with all my heart that I wasn't.

My life is simple, ordered, the biggest decision of each day being what to eat. Even that takes little effort, as it usually amounts to selecting whatever is at the top of the pile of ready meals in my freezer. When I am not working, I read or watch television. I neither need nor want more, and I cherish the predictability of each day. My colleagues try to persuade me to go on wild nights out with them, but they take it well when I refuse. They accept me for who I am.

Now my life has been disrupted. Not only must I decide what to do with the cottage and its contents, I have no idea how I'm going to feel when I walk through the front door.

The taxi driver breaks into my thoughts. 'Nearly there, love,' he says, glancing at me again in the mirror as if to check I'm not having a meltdown in the back of his taxi.

I catch fleeting glimpses of the sea as the taxi weaves its way along narrow streets, and memories come flooding back as we reach Trevyan, a tiny village just beyond the edge of a much larger town. I remember the hope in my heart when we arrived last time; the feeling that my family could be healed in this tranquil spot; the fleeting dreams of days spent together exploring the stunning coastline and the pretty local town. How naïve that seems now.

Nothing appears to have changed. A row of stone cottages painted in pastel shades line one side of a quiet lane, facing a tiny pebbled beach and the ocean beyond. No one comes here to swim because huge rocks encroach on the shore, making it almost impossible to get into the sea. It's a rare quiet spot in this tourist-mad part of Cornwall. Maybe that's why my rather aloof Aunt Helen liked it so much.

As the taxi draws to a halt, for a moment I just sit and stare at the cottage. My throat tightens, and I press my lips together.

Come on, Nancy. You knew this would happen.

I did. I had been preparing for this moment for the whole journey. It's the point I have mentally tagged: *stage one – the arrival.*

I've identified all the difficult stages I will have to get through, and this is my first hurdle, soon to be followed by my next: *stage two – walking into the cottage.*

It's just a building.

I know that. *Just a building.*

The cottage looks the same. For some reason I had expected it to be different, like a place I have never seen before. I manage to pull myself together to pay the taxi driver, tipping him far too much by way of apology for my aloofness and, staring at the money in his hand for a moment, he stuffs it in his pocket and jumps into his seat with a quick thank you. He looks relieved to be driving away. I feel a stab of panic as I stand alone on the pavement, my case by my side, watching the taxi disappear into the distance. I want to shout to the driver to come back, to take me to the station so I can flee back to a world that might not be exciting, but is one where I feel safe. It's too late.

The gate creaks as I open it, as it always did, and I wheel my case through and stand still, taking it in. It's not a big cottage, but it's pretty with its cream-painted stone walls and pale blue front door. On the end of a row, looking straight out to sea, it boasts a small cobbled courtyard with some rather decrepit-looking metal chairs and a table.

'Get on with it!' I say the words out loud as I bend down to move a plant pot.

Just as I had done eleven years ago, I retrieve the key, push it into the lock and turn.

FOUR

ELEVEN YEARS AGO

'They've left a key for us – it's under the plant pot. Lola, can you get it, please?' Dad asked.

Lola ignored him and turned to look at the sea.

'Lola!' he said.

Her attitude for the whole journey had been one of moody sulking, and I didn't think it worth the argument, so I put down my suitcase and bent to move the pot. I handed Dad the key and he took it from me without a word.

'We'll have to find a better place if it's the only key,' Dad muttered, glaring at Lola.

She was being irritating, but I was sure it was grief. She hadn't cried at all since Mum died, not even at the funeral. She just stood with her lips clenched tightly together. Dad had reached out to try to hold her hand, but she yanked it out of his grasp. I tried to take his other hand, certain that he needed the comfort as much as any of us, but he pushed his hands into his pockets before I made contact.

Unlike Lola, I felt as if my eyes were constantly leaking, and my body ached with crying. The doctors had said that with proper care there was no reason why Mum shouldn't have made a reasonable recovery from the illness that cut her down before she was even forty years old. But she hadn't got better. Instead, she had died – and I was her carer. No matter what Aunt Helen said, I knew they blamed me.

Dad turned the key and pushed the door. It stuck and he muttered something under his breath as he gave it a shove. I didn't know why he'd come really, and if a sticking door was enough to irritate him I had no idea how we were going to get through the next two weeks.

I followed him inside, and while he headed straight for the stairs, I looked around. It was much smaller than our home in Shropshire, but immediately it felt welcoming. I was surprised that this was Aunt Helen's house. She had seemed so austere on the occasions I'd met her, and I would have imagined hard lines and immaculate pale grey carpets. Instead, the door opened straight into a stone-flagged living space, on the left of which was a kitchen area lined with pale green wooden units. A scrubbed pine table just big enough for four people sat on a patterned rug in the centre, and I imagined a group of friends sitting there, eating hearty food, cooked with love.

To the right of the central wooden staircase was a sitting room with a battered two-seater brown leather sofa and an armchair covered in a cream throw. An old wood burner sat on the hearth. I thought how cosy it would feel on a cold winter's night, listening to the sounds of the waves washing the beach, curled up with a hot chocolate in front of a blazing fire, book in hand, or sitting on the deep window seat, stuffed with multi-coloured cushions, watching the sea across the lane.

Our home had a different feel. The rooms were large and draughty, and they hadn't been decorated in my lifetime so we lived with peeling wallpaper where the damp had seeped through. Dad thought the previous owners must have taken lodgers, because the layout upstairs was unusual, with a solid fire door separating one corridor and bedroom from the rest of the space. Whatever its past, no one had had the time or the money to improve it, so it was patched up haphazardly. I never thought about it much until I stood in Aunt Helen's cottage and felt it wrap itself snugly around me.

'Enough daydreaming,' Dad said as he thundered down the stairs. 'I've just been to look, and there are only two rooms. A double and a twin. You can argue between yourselves who has which. I'll take the sofa.'

I gave him a puzzled look. 'Why don't Lola and I have the twin? You can have the double.'

He walked into the kitchen and started to fill the kettle. I had no idea why, because we hadn't thought to bring any tea or coffee with us. It felt like it was something for him to do so he didn't have to look at me.

'Not sure that's a good idea. I think you both need your own space right now.'

I stared at his back. Did he think Lola wouldn't *want* to share with me? I felt a sob building in my chest, but before I could choke out any protest at his words, Lola spoke.

'I'll share with Nancy.' She didn't look at me. She was looking at Dad.

'I'm not sure, Lola,' he said.

'Don't care whether you're sure or not, it's what I'm going to do.'

With that, she picked up her bag and marched upstairs. I stood and watched, shocked at how she had spoken to Dad.

He slammed the kettle down, not bothering to switch it on. He spoke to the wall.

'It's grief making her like this. Lola's not like you. She can't cry. She bottles everything up and it comes out as rage at the world. I just happen to be an easy target because she knows I understand.' He turned to face me. 'Don't try to talk to her about it, Nancy – you'll make it worse. She's likely to say some hurtful things – to lash out.'

He turned away again, hands stuffed into his trouser pockets, to gaze out of the window. The conversation was clearly over, but I didn't need to ask him what Lola was angry about. She was angry with *me*. I was the reason Mum was dead.

'I'm sorry, Dad,' I whispered, wondering if they would ever forgive me; if I would ever forgive myself.

I wanted him to turn to me and say he understood why I'd taken a sleeping tablet the night Mum died; that he knew I was exhausted, and it wasn't my fault I didn't hear her call me to help her from the bed; that I wasn't to blame for her fall. But he didn't move, didn't speak.

I dropped my head, devastated by my sister's condemnation and Dad's silence.

I couldn't help remembering that before Mum became ill, Dad and I used to be close. I loved helping him on the farm – especially with the animals. He called me *kochanie* – a word he'd picked up working as a steward on cruise ships, a job I couldn't imagine him ever doing. It meant sweetheart in Polish, and I'd asked him once why he called me *kochanie* and not Lola.

'Lola is very different to you. You help me with the pigs – you *love* the pigs. You don't mind getting your hands dirty. Lola thinks she's a princess. She likes to be the centre of attention, and she manages to get away with not lifting a finger by being charming and cute. You think about others – even if the pigs are your favourites.' He'd laughed and reached out to give me a hug.

That conversation seemed a long time ago, and as we stood in Aunt Helen's kitchen, Dad with his back to me, I finally understood how Lola must have felt when I was the favoured one. I wish now that I'd had a chance to tell her that.

FIVE

Detective Sergeant Stephanie King hadn't had the best of days. There had been a spate of burglaries in recent weeks, and although the CID team, of which she was a part, suspected the same gang had carried out every one of them, they were struggling to find any compelling evidence.

She was also suffering from a lack of sleep. Her partner, Gus, otherwise known as Detective Chief Inspector Angus Brodie, had been home last night for the first time in ten days. They'd had a lot of catching up to do, and the memory brought a smile to her face.

Stephanie had been convinced that when Gus was promoted to DCI he would have had to move to the opposite end of the territory covered by Devon and Cornwall Police, and she had been dreading the thought of him being so far away. To her relief he had been offered a new job in Newquay, and while that wasn't entirely handy for their home in Penzance, it was less than an hour's drive on a good day. Not that he was able to get home every night. He'd recently been working on a particularly unpleasant murder in Padstow and had to base himself close to the incident room, but now he was home, taking a couple of days off, lounging around. Meanwhile, she was at work, wishing she was there with him.

Her mind flicked back to that morning. Gus had been as affectionate as always and she'd struggled to leave him, but as she headed to the door, he'd reached out and pulled her close. 'When you get back tonight, I need to talk to you about something. Any chance you can get away on time?'

Stephanie hated conversations like this. If he wanted to tell her something, then he should either spit it out, or he shouldn't have mentioned it. Now all she was going to do was worry. But when she'd pushed him, he wasn't to be budged.

'I shouldn't have said anything.' He was right about that. 'It'll keep.'

In the end, she'd glowered at him, but she didn't have time to argue. She was already running late.

The ringing of her phone brought her back to the present, and she prayed it wouldn't be a report of yet another burglary.

'DS King,' she said.

'DI Harris-Cooke.' Stephanie almost groaned at the high-pitched staccato voice of the new local detective inspector – her boss. She wished Stuart Wilcox had never retired. At least he was a local who was happy to go to the pub with his team. DI Harris-Cooke was a career police officer who believed in a strict hierarchy and boundaries.

'Yes, ma'am. What can I do for you?'

'We've got a body – a skeleton, to be precise – and I need you to go and check it out. Unfortunately it's in a cave, and the bones are high up on a rock shelf. It can only be reached by boat at high tide, and even then with some difficulty. It's too late to set it up today, so it will have to be tomorrow morning, first thing. I realise I would normally attend the scene, but I have an important meeting, so you'll have to stand in for me.'

Stephanie bit her lip. Of *course* the DI had found something more important to do than go out at the crack of dawn in a small boat – especially as rain was forecast.

'Has the pathologist been informed, ma'am?'

'Yes, and she's contacting a forensic anthropologist who'll need to conduct the recovery. The pathologist is Molly Tread-well, whom I believe you know, and the anthropologist is –' there was a pause and a rustling of paper '– a Dr Carla Davies. We're liaising with the coastguard and the marine unit. They'll pick you up at the harbour in Newlyn at seven fifteen tomorrow morning. Take a couple of uniforms to help with the retrieval, and a crime scene manager.'

'Okay. Do we know anything else?'

'No. It's a remote spot. Some stupid boy was trying to scale the cliff and fell off into the sea. He swam into the cave and scrambled out of the water and onto a ledge. The RNLI got him out – at significant risk to their own safety, I gather – but he was a gibbering wreck because he'd seen what looked like a foot on a higher ledge. He'd thought the tide would come in before he was rescued, and he'd have to clamber up there and keep company with the dead. One of the lifeboat men had a look and discovered that it is, in fact, a complete skeleton.'

'Oh Lord, I think that would freak me out too.'

'The boy and his brother have been interviewed, but they had nothing useful to say.'

'Okay, I'm on it, and I'll check who's available to come with me. I'll get back to you when we have something to report.'

Stephanie hung up the phone.

A skeleton. She'd seen her share of dead bodies in the time she'd been in the police, but this would be the first time she'd had to deal with just the bones. She wasn't sure if that would be better or worse.

SIX

The door to the cottage sticks, as I knew it would. I give it a hard shove and hear the wood scrape on the stone floor. I step inside and take a sharp breath. Nothing has changed. It's as if I've just been for a walk and come back to make lunch. The only difference is there's no Dad. No Lola. The room is silent.

I shake myself and look around.

An image of Dad bursts into my mind. He's leaning against the sink unit, arms folded, cheeks flushed, shouting at Lola as she walks towards the front door.

'You're not going out in that skirt, Lola. Everyone will see your knickers!'

'They won't, because I'm not wearing any,' she yells back, cheekily flicking up the back of her skirt to reveal her skimpy bikini bottoms. Picking up her emerald-green backpack, she heads for the door.

'That doesn't make any difference!' he calls after her. But he is talking to thin air. She's gone.

It wasn't their first argument. Nor was it their last.

I'd ignored them, because by then – the second week of our holiday – I was wrapped up in my own thoughts and had gone up to my room to dream of a man, a beach and sand in my own knickers. I push that thought away. I don't want to go there, to relive my first love and its disastrous ending. At least not yet.

Vivid images of Lola dance across my eyes – fifteen years old, and obstreperous in a way I had never witnessed before. Am I going to go through the next few days seeing her everywhere I look? I slowly release the breath I didn't know I was holding. I've hoped and prayed for eleven years that she would get in touch, but I need to face reality. She doesn't want to know me, so I must get on with my life and put aside any hope that one day she will come looking for me.

I sniff the air. I was expecting to be greeted by the stale smell of an unused house, but it smells of polish and something warm and spicy that I can't quite grasp. It feels surprisingly welcoming, and I'm pleased I've managed to get through the first stages of my return. Now it's time for the next: *stage three – going into the room where Lola and I slept, the room I ran from that night, the room where I spoke to Lola for the last time.* I straighten my back, feeling a tingle down my spine. I can't stand here all day, so I pick up my case and make my way slowly upstairs to the bedrooms and tiny bathroom.

Lola's defiant attitude on the day of our arrival and her insistence that we share a room had briefly felt positive. She'd even given me a shaky smile, as if she wasn't sure what I was expecting from her, and I realised then how far apart we had grown in the previous two years.

I had imagined us whispering in the dark after Dad was in bed, getting to know each other again, because our lives had been so different. Caring for Mum had been the right thing – the *only* thing – for me to do, but I had missed out on school, friends, parties, and at almost nineteen I wanted to gossip with Lola about people I used to know who were still part of her world.

It soon became apparent that wasn't to be. Despite her insistence that we share a room, we quickly went our separate ways, and when I tried to talk to her, she didn't want to know. She trusted me enough to sleep next to me, but that was as far as it went.

I retreated into another world, one in which my past wasn't relevant, and meanwhile Lola took partying to heart, sneaking home late every night. I knew she was drinking. Dad was beside himself at her defiant attitude, although I'd tried to reassure him that it was only a phase and we'd be going home soon.

'Can't be soon enough,' he'd said, his face almost grey with concern. 'We should never have come.'

I couldn't help believing this was my fault too. I was the one who Aunt Helen had offered the cottage to. Did Dad think I should have said no? He didn't have to come, but he said he couldn't contemplate the idea of us coming on our own.

I'd given up trying to understand what he was thinking. After Mum became ill we'd turned into a family of two halves. I ate with Mum, watched television with her, slept in her room. Dad and Lola muddled along together, eating their share of the food I'd prepared during the day while Mum was sleeping, but I'd felt so separate from them. A few weeks after I moved into Mum's bedroom, I heard them laughing together downstairs. Mum was asleep and I'd been planning to join them. But I'd been uncertain of my welcome, convinced I would be an intruder, and after that it never felt like the right time, so I stayed upstairs with Mum. It set a pattern for the next two years.

Any hopes I had of the holiday uniting us as a family were dashed within days, and there was only one time in the entire fortnight when Lola tried to talk to me. I was lying huddled on the bed, curled into a tight ball, crying as if the world had ended – which to me it had – when I heard her come into our bedroom. 'What's up, Nancy? Tell me.' She sat next to me on the bed, stinking of booze, and reached out a hand to touch my shoulder. But I brushed it away.

'Go away. Leave me alone.'

'I saw you from the beach. You were running. What's upset you?' she asked, and then – more hesitantly – she said, 'And there's something I need to tell you too.'

But she hadn't wanted to talk to me before when I'd tried my best, and I couldn't bear to admit to her how foolish I had been, so I'd leaped up from the bed, shouting at her, and stormed out of the room.

I ran downstairs towards the front door. 'Not everything's about you, Lola,' I yelled over my shoulder. 'Just get lost.'

And that's exactly what she did. They were the last words I spoke to her. By the next day she'd gone.

SEVEN

I've just dumped my case on the bed, ready to unpack, when I hear a staccato triple knock, followed by a scraping sound as the front door is pushed open.

'*Shit!*' someone mutters.

I rush onto the landing, my heart pounding. *Who the hell is this?*

Standing at the foot of the stairs, looking up at me, is a young woman with wild black curls and bright red lips bearing a wide smile.

'Hi! You must be Nancy,' she says without a hint of an apology for just walking in. 'Sorry about the noise. Someone should have fixed that bloody door! I'm Effie. Good journey?'

To the best of my knowledge, I don't know an Effie, but she doesn't look particularly threatening, so I make my way slowly downstairs towards her.

'Hi,' I say tentatively. 'The journey was fine.'

As I reach the bottom step I get a better look at my visitor. She has the kind of luscious figure that I've always wanted. I hate being skinny, which I know is most women's dream but not mine. Effie is nicely rounded, and in her royal-blue baggy T-shirt and white jeans there's something instantly comforting about her. She doesn't feel like an intruder, although I've no idea who she is, or why she's here.

'I'm sorry, but should I know you?'

Effie laughs. 'What are you sorry about? Course you shouldn't. My mum keeps this place clean – Angie Dawson. She met you when you were here last time, but I guess with everything else you've probably forgotten. My nan knew your aunt Helen. They were great friends. But Nan's in hospital recovering from a hip replacement, bless her, and Mum's working, so I offered to be the welcome party – and here I am!' She throws her arms wide.

I'm slightly nonplussed by all of this, but I can't resist Effie's smile.

'It's good to meet you, and I must thank your mum. The house felt very welcoming, not at all the musty damp place I had imagined.'

Effie frowns slightly and looks away. I'm not sure what I'm supposed to do now. I'd offer her a cup of tea, but I haven't been shopping yet, so I stand looking a bit lost. Then I notice a large canvas bag by her feet. Her eyes follow my gaze, and she reaches down to grab it.

'Ah yes – I nearly forgot. Essential provisions!' she says. 'Got milk, tea, coffee, sugar – although you don't look as if sugar ever passes your lips – biscuits, sliced bread, butter, marmalade – you know, the usual stuff. But I also brought this.' And like a conjuror she fishes a bottle of white wine out of the bag, with a 'Ta-dah!'

She's making me smile already, and the feeling of unease that hit me when I walked through the door is fading fast.

'I don't think we should drink this now, though. It's not cold. I'll just put everything away, shall I?'

It's not really a question, and she starts opening cupboards and shoving things slightly randomly on shelves.

'Now, I've been given a list of things to talk to you about. Let's see if I can remember them.'

She has her back to me, lifting a jar of coffee to put into the cupboard, and she stops, her hand suspended in mid-air.

'Ah yes. First thing, I need to show you where the fuse box is. There's a faulty switch somewhere and sometimes the lights go out. I've brought you a torch, just in case.' She plonks the coffee in the cupboard and turns round. 'Mum also said she thinks it would be a good idea to get another key cut. No idea what happened to the one you had when you were last here. It seems to have gone AWOL.'

She puts the rest of the shopping in the cupboard and I should probably be helping, but I'm feeling a bit dazzled. I'm about to tell her that I won't need another key because I'm not staying any longer than I need to when she carries on.

'Third, I need to show you where the stop tap is. Not that we're expecting any plumbing issues, but always good to know.' She slams the door shut. 'Now, I bet you're starving. Shall we go and eat? Town's not so busy now the school holidays are over, and it's less crowded now the emmets have left.'

'Emmets?'

'Holidaymakers. Means ants, I think. The ones that swarm everywhere. Anyhow, the posh lookalike mums with their swinging blonde hair and whiny kids have gone, and we're left with the more sedate older visitors. Much better.'

'Don't you like kids?' I can't help asking, a bit surprised given her apparent warm nature.

'Love 'em, in general. But the lot we get in the summer with all the second-home owners – well, it's not their fault, poor little buggers. They're just whingey because no one ever has any fun with them. They're given a bucket and spade and told to amuse themselves where Mummy can see them – but not get down on her hands and knees and bloody play with them. The only rules they're given are not to disturb Mummy when she's drinking gin and talking to her friends about her latest find on Net-a-Porter.'

I can feel my eyebrows rising as she talks. Clearly a bone of contention.

She sees my expression and laughs. 'You'll get it if you come to live here – which I hope you do because it's a great place. The locals are totally fab – quite whacky, a lot of them – but kind and fun. I have to deal with the other lot because I work for the company that looks after all their properties when they're away. Maintenance, cleaning, letting them out, that sort of thing. Bloody nightmare, but interesting. Anyway, you up for a bit of food, then?'

I feel strangely invigorated just talking to her.

'I need to get changed. I'm a bit scruffy,' I say, looking down at my jeans and loose cotton shirt.

'Nonsense! You look fine. Just give your hair a bit of a shake – looks like you've been attacked on one side by a grizzly or something. Slap on a bit of lippy, and we're done.'

I glance towards a mirror and she's right about my hair. It's the result of opening the taxi window, and my hair doesn't like to be tamed.

'Oh gosh,' I mutter. 'I hadn't realised I looked such a mess.'

She chuckles. 'You sort your hair and I'll put the wine in the fridge for later. Then we're off. You'll like where we're going. The food's delicious!'

I feel a rush of optimism. The last few hours have been a rollercoaster. I was dreading coming here, but now, for the first time in as long as I can remember, I'm excited to be going out with a new friend.

EIGHT

Effie talks non-stop all the way into town. She's driving, but as we pass through the village she slows down, pointing out the landmarks.

'I love Trevyan. So quiet; everything seems to run at a slower pace than in town, even though it's just down the road. There's not much to the village, but the shop here is a local legend. Do you remember it?'

'Vaguely. It's small, isn't it?'

'Very. The aisles are too narrow for a trolley, so it's a faff if you've got a lot to buy – but Noreen, the owner, will get in anything you ask for and always buys in bulk, even though no bugger else might want white miso or whatever for the next millennium, so it's always worth checking out when you're looking to cook something exotic.'

I smile at the thought, embarrassed to admit that having spent two years as chief cook and bottle washer for my family, I now live on frozen meals and takeaways.

'Are you going to hire a car, while you're here?' Effie asks.

'I don't drive – not much point, living in London.' I don't

add that when your dad kills himself by driving his car into a reservoir, it's something of a deterrent.

'If you need to go to the supermarket or anything, just let me know. I'll take you.' She turns and beams at me, and I feel a rush of gratitude to her for turning up at my door. I had been expecting to spend the evening sitting alone in a dark cottage in sombre reflection. Instead, I am heading out in the evening sunshine with a woman who oozes joy.

As we get closer to town my moment of optimism collapses as I realise I must now face up to what I see as the final menacing moment from the past: *stage four – visit the beach where Lola used to hang out.*

I came with her the first few days, or to be more precise I followed her, hoping I might meet people of my own age. But I didn't know how to introduce myself, to break into their circle, so I hung back on my own, watching them. My confidence had waned over the previous two years, and I didn't think I spoke their language.

Lola had no such fears, and I watched with envy as she waltzed right down onto the beach to say hello, appearing self-assured and friendly, unrecognisable as the stroppy, belligerent girl Dad and I had to deal with. Not that we saw much of her. She didn't turn up for meals, and never lifted a finger – although that wasn't anything new. When had she become this person?

I'd had little to do with her while I looked after Mum, but it wasn't out of choice. She was at school during the day, and I was with Mum in the evenings. On the odd occasion when I'd asked Dad if she was doing okay, he told me not to worry. She was doing fine at school, and he was looking out for her. I was jealous, and ashamed of it. I'd always thought I'd had a special bond with Dad, and that Lola and I were good sisters to each other, but while I was nursing Mum, Dad and Lola had become a team from which I was excluded. To the sixteen-year-old I was then, it seemed dreadfully unfair that I was so isolated, and I resented the fact that Lola hardly ever visited Mum.

The Lola I remembered had always hankered after attention, wanting to be praised, but the Lola I saw that fortnight was wild. She didn't care a jot what Dad or I felt, and I didn't understand it. Why was she behaving that way? Dad said it was because of Mum's death, but I found it hard to believe as I watched her flirting with the boys, laughing too loud, swigging beer from a can when she thought no one could see her. I'd even heard her tell Dad that he had no right to tell her what to do, and I couldn't believe she would be so rude. If I spoke to her, she looked away and didn't bother to answer. I didn't know how to deal with her, or how to cope with Dad's despair, so I escaped to walk the coastal path. And that was the start of my pleasure, and my pain.

I have no more time to dwell on the past as Effie pulls into the car park and we both set off to walk the last few hundred metres to the main street. I had forgotten how lovely the town is, with its row of shops, restaurants and bars – many with outside seating – facing the wide sandy bay, and although it's mid-September it is still warm, and people are relaxing in the evening sunshine. I can hear the chinking of glasses, the soft buzz of conversation, and I take in a breath of sea air. If it wasn't for the memories, maybe I *could* live here.

I'm pleased that the wine bar Effie has chosen is not one I remember. It has a great view of the sea, and although it's busy, we're able to get a table outside. I choose to sit with my back to the beach, knowing that otherwise I would be unconsciously scouring the sands for Lola, seeing her face, hearing her laughter.

'I hope this isn't rude, but do you mind me asking where the name Effie comes from?' I ask, in an attempt to distract myself.

'It's not rude at all. I'm called Josephine, but it doesn't suit me – never did. Sounds far too proper. One of my kid brothers couldn't say my name so called me Effie, and it stuck.'

'I like it.'

'Thank you. So do I. Nancy's a nice name too,' Effie says.

I shrug. I never think about it much. For some reason, my apparent indifference makes her laugh.

A waiter appears with a menu. 'Hi, Effie. How are you doing?'

'Hi, Raff. I'm good, thanks. This is Nancy.' We exchange smiles, and Effie carries on talking. 'Listen, I've been meaning to ask...'

She starts a conversation with Raff, and I tune out and consult the menu. I don't know where to start. I don't eat out often, and there are so many things on here that I've never tried before.

In spite of not looking at the beach, my thoughts turn to Lola. She would have loved this wine bar, and if things had turned out differently, I might have been sitting here with her now, and perhaps Dad too. I ask myself for the thousandth time – if I hadn't been sleeping, would Mum still be alive? Maybe Lola wouldn't have run away, and Dad wouldn't have died. One mistake, *my* mistake, and no one to blame but me.

'What do you think, Nancy?' Effie says, and I look up, realising that Raff has gone and I've been ignoring her. I shake myself back from the hole I was about to fall into.

'Sorry? About what?'

'The *food*! Fab, isn't it? What do you fancy? Oh, thanks, Raff! That was quick.'

The waiter delivers a bottle of cold white wine and two glasses.

'Thought you might like to be getting on with this while you choose your food,' he says, winking at Effie as he fills our glasses.

I glance from one to the other and give her an enquiring look. Effie chuckles.

'Raff's a friend. Not my type, I'm afraid. Not into men. You?'

I feel a bit nonplussed by the direct question, but it seems it's Effie's style.

'I suppose I am,' I say without much enthusiasm. I don't really want to dwell on the subject of my non-existent sex life. I stare at the menu, but the choices seem endless.

'You know what?' Effie says. 'We'll ask Raff what we should have, shall we? He knows what's good – and we can have loads of tapas, lots of bits and pieces of deliciousness.' She almost shudders with pleasure at the thought.

I close the menu and smile. 'That sounds like a plan.'

'To new friends!' Effie says. She raises her glass to mine, and we both take a sip. Effie waves her free arm in the direction of the view behind me. 'Does everywhere seem familiar to you or is it so long ago that you've forgotten all about our lovely town?'

I lower my glass to the table, staring at the liquid, not sure how to answer. I don't want her sympathy, but I can't pretend that coming back here has been easy, or that the memories aren't haunting me.

Her hand reaches across to touch mine. 'Oh bugger – me and my mouth. Sorry, Nancy. Of *course* you haven't forgotten. How could you? Tell me about something else – about your job, whatever you want.'

I look up, relieved at the change of subject. 'I work in a care home. It's a cheerful place – very welcoming – and the people I look after are wonderful. They feel like my family now, and I love organising activities for them to keep them engaged. I've even set up a little choir. We sing songs like "Rhythm of Life" and "Happy", and those who are able stand up and jig around, laughing. They are truly delightful. I suppose I feel that I can do for them, with love, what I should have done for my mum – if only she'd let me.'

Effie nodded slowly. 'I remember you came here last time

because your mum had died. I can't imagine how that felt. I have no idea what I would do without mine. She's the best.'

I envy her that. I loved my mum, but she had seemed so unhappy, as if life had let her down somehow, but that's not a memory I want to share.

'She was ill for a couple of years. I took care of her.'

'Were you still at school? That must have been hard.'

'No, she needed full-time care, so I left after my GCSEs. You could still leave full-time education at sixteen then.'

I don't want to talk about this, to tell her I had thought I would only be caring for Mum for a few months after my exams before returning to school to study for my A levels, and I'm worried she's going to talk about *how* Mum died – a box I don't want to open. Or maybe she'll ask about her illness. I'm saved by Raff returning to the table to take our order. Effie gets involved in a detailed discussion about the options, and I zone out. I've tried to forget the day Mum collapsed, the day life changed forever, but now the memories come rushing back.

NINE

THIRTEEN YEARS AGO

I was in the kitchen with Mum, peeling potatoes, when it happened. She was standing by the old Rayburn stove that looked as if it has been in the house since it was built ninety years before. She had barely spoken to me since she came down from her room, and I knew something was wrong. When she finally tried to speak, the words were jumbled and her face looked strange – almost contorted. Then she stumbled and grabbed hold of the stainless steel rail on the stove.

'Mum?' I said. She didn't answer, but there was a look of fear in her eyes. '*Mum!*'

Lola looked up from her maths homework, first at me, then at Mum.

'Go and get Dad, Lola!' I yelled at her, and for a moment she didn't move, but then she was on her feet and running for the back door.

Mum was slowly crumpling to the ground and I dropped the potato in the sink and rushed towards her, breaking her fall. I wanted to wait for Dad, but I could tell it was serious so I ran into the hall, picked up the phone and dialled.

A calm voice asked me what the emergency was and, trying to be as coherent as possible, I listed the symptoms.

'An ambulance is on its way, love. Can you get her to lie down?'

'She's already lying on the floor – she was falling so I helped her down. Was that the wrong thing to do?' I felt the panic wash over me.

'No, that's fine. Put something under her head to raise it a little but don't move her. Don't let her stand up, and if she's wearing anything tight, undo some buttons. Can you do that, do you think?'

I heard a shout behind me. 'Nancy – why's Mum on the floor?' It was Dad.

'Don't move her, Dad!' I yelled.

I dropped the phone and could hear the tinny voice of the operator as I ran back to the kitchen.

'The ambulance is on its way! We need to talk to her, keep her awake. But we can't move her!' I shouted the last words as Dad put his arm under her. I was sure he was going to try to sit her up.

'Calm down, Nancy. I'll just put this under her head.' He bunched up a towel. 'Go back and talk to the operator – find out how long the ambulance will be. It's okay, *kochanie*.'

I glanced towards Lola, standing open-mouthed at the door, not having a clue what to do, and then ran back to the phone.

'Sorry,' I said. 'Is the ambulance coming?'

'It is. Is your mum conscious?' she asked.

'She's trying to speak, but she can't.'

'That's okay. Let me know if she becomes unconscious.'

The next minutes seemed like hours, but I later learned that the ambulance had taken just sixteen minutes to get to us, and they immediately started to treat Mum.

'Well done,' one of the paramedics said to me. 'You acted quickly, and that's the most important thing with a stroke.'

A stroke. I didn't believe it. I thought they had to be mistaken. Mum was so young.

Dad tried to give us a reassuring smile as he climbed into the back of the ambulance. 'I'll be back soon – once she's settled.'

The door closed, and Lola and I stood on the step, watching it drive away, blue light flashing, siren blaring. Lola moved towards me, and I lifted my arm and wrapped it around her.

'That was horrible,' she whispered.

She was right, and I gave her a squeeze. 'I know, but I'm sure she'll be fine. And Dad's with her. Come on. Let's go and have a mug of cocoa.' It seemed the most comforting thing I could think of.

Mum was in hospital for a week, and on the day of her return, Dad's car pulled up outside the front door. He got out but didn't come straight into the house. Instead, he stood looking towards the gate, and a few minutes later an ambulance drew up. Mum was home.

'She'll look a bit different, and she'll be in bed for a while,' Dad had warned us. 'She's finding it difficult to speak, but with time the doctor thinks that will improve.'

As Mum was lifted out of the ambulance, another car drew up and a woman I didn't recognise got out. I watched as she looked towards Dad, and even from where I was standing I sensed a degree of hostility. Then she marched towards the house.

'I'm your mum's Aunt Helen,' she said. 'Nancy, you might remember me from when you were very small, but Lola was just a baby last time I was here. I'm going to make sure Janice gets the care she needs.'

There was something fearsomely efficient about Aunt Helen. From her short pixie-cut grey hair to her perfectly tailored black trousers, she looked like a woman who wouldn't be messed with, and I felt myself stand straighter as she looked at me. Even Dad seemed to quail at a glance from her.

'When your mum's settled, I'll need some time with her to understand how she wants to be cared for.'

No one argued, despite the fact that we hadn't clapped eyes on this aunt for about twelve years.

Lola and I hovered at the bottom of the stairs while Dad went to check on the animals. We could hear nothing other than the murmur of Aunt Helen's voice through the closed door, but finally she came down and asked me to go and find Dad. She summoned him to the kitchen and another door was closed.

Lola wasn't interested and switched on the television. I couldn't hear what was being said, but voices were raised – Aunt Helen's crisp and cutting while Dad sounded angry. I caught a snippet when there was a lull in the programme captivating Lola.

Dad's voice was raised, but I couldn't make out the words. Aunt Helen seemed to lose patience with him. There was something about their tone that made me anxious, and I cuddled up to Lola. She looked at me in surprise, but rested her head on my shoulder.

'I can't come here again. You *know* why!' Aunt Helen proclaimed.

That was the last thing I heard before the kitchen door opened and the two of them came into the sitting room.

'Turn the telly off, Lola,' Dad said.

She looked a bit aggrieved but took one look at Dad's flushed cheeks and Aunt Helen's tightly drawn lips and did as she was told.

Aunt Helen perched herself on the arm of the sofa as if to appear relaxed, but her body was taut and I could see she was hating this.

'Girls, you already know your mum is quite poorly, but she wants to be here at home with you. She's finding it difficult to speak, but I've managed to work out what she was trying to tell me – at least, I hope so.' For a moment there was a flash of doubt in her eyes, but she shook it away and carried on. 'She'll need a lot of care – including at night – and given the unusual layout of the upstairs rooms, Nancy's bed will have to be moved into her bedroom.' She fixed her eyes on mine. 'You can sleep there so you're available if needed.'

Mum's room was down a separate corridor on the other side of the stairwell, so I understood why I would have to sleep in her room, but I was confused, scared. I had no idea if I would be up to the job. What would be expected of me? I'd just finished my GCSEs and would be at home every day for the next couple of months, so although I'd planned to help Dad and maybe get a part-time job at a café in town, there was no question that if Mum needed me I would do whatever was necessary. The problem was, I didn't know what that meant. Would I just have to care for her at night, and someone with experience would come in during the day? I looked at Dad, but he was staring at the carpet. I could feel Aunt Helen's eyes on me and knew what I had to say. This was my mum.

'Just tell me what I need to do.'

Aunt Helen glanced at Dad as if willing him to speak. But he just put his hands in his pockets and dropped his head even further. She tutted and turned back to me.

'There's not enough money to pay for a nurse, so you'll have to step up to the plate. You'll be your mum's full-time carer and it's a twenty-four-hour-a-day job, I'm afraid.'

I nodded silently, trying not to panic. What if I got it all wrong and she had another stroke? What if I made her worse, not better? I clutched at the straw Dad had offered – that the doctors said she would improve – and convinced myself that by the time the new term started she would be well again. I could return to school, to sixth form, and hopefully go on to art college.

I decided to make it my mission to do everything I could to make her well. I would feed her healthy food to build her energy, research exercises to make her stronger, read to her – books that would lighten her spirits. I was terrified of getting everything wrong, but I had to try for Mum's sake – for all our sakes.

When I look back at my life in the two years that I cared for her, it seems out of focus, devoid of any distinct feelings of either joy or despair. School became a distant memory, and my days followed the monotonous pattern of preparing food, changing beds, washing, cleaning, and doing everything I could to make her as comfortable as possible. But her health slowly deteriorated, and I didn't know what I was doing wrong. Why wasn't she getting better?

In all that time, no one told me it was natural for someone like me to feel stressed and alone, that it was normal to feel resentment for all that I was missing – friends, parties, boyfriends. Nor did they tell me that the guilt at my selfish thoughts would be so crippling. I felt isolated, cut off from the world – even from the rest of my family.

For every day of those two years, I prayed she would get better, devastated that despite my best efforts, nothing I tried seemed to work, and she faded before my eyes.

TEN

The sound of Effie's laughter brings me back to the present.

'I hope you like the choices, Nancy. Raff assures me they're perfect.'

I force a smile, and decide the best way of avoiding talk about my family is to talk about hers.

'Tell me about your nan. How's she doing after her operation?'

'I saw her earlier today. She's doing great – determined to be back on her feet in days!'

'You said she and Mum's aunt Helen were great friends.'

Effie nods. 'They were indeed. Even after Helen buggered off to Scotland, they wrote to each other regularly – actual pen on paper. My nan's fingers have become arthritic, and her eyes aren't great, so I used to write them for her, and read out the ones from Helen. Fascinating, and Helen was very kind to me.'

A sudden thought occurs to me.

'Do you know why she left me the cottage? Because I haven't a clue. I barely knew her.'

'Ahh.' She's unusually quiet for a moment, as if she's choosing the right words. 'From what I've read in her letters, I know she was uncomfortable with the distance between you, but I think she had her reasons.' Before I can ask what she means, Effie chuckles. 'She was a bit of a character, your aunt. She was the headmistress of the local private school; strict, almost fierce in some ways. But the person underneath was kind and generous. A bit of an enigma, really, and it's a pity you didn't know her better.'

I want to say that wasn't entirely my fault, but I don't want to deflect Effie from her explanation, and she carries on talking as I take another sip of my wine.

'Malcolm, her husband, is loaded, but she'd never been married or lived with anyone, and she was sixty-five when he proposed and whisked her off to Scotland. We couldn't believe it when she went through with it! She wouldn't sell the cottage, though, because she said she needed an escape route in case it was all a horrible mistake. That's why it's been standing empty for all these years.'

'Yes, but why leave it to me, and not to her husband?'

Effie waves a hand in the air. 'Oh, he didn't need the money. And more to the point, his two sons had been pretty horrible to Helen because they thought their dad would die first and she'd get all his money. So she decided – with Malcolm's agreement – that she'd leave the cottage to whoever she wanted. If it went to him, the shitty sons would end up with it, and she hated that idea. That's why she left it to you!'

I'm not quite sure what to think about this. Was her gift to me merely a poke in the eye to her stepsons, or had she *wanted* to leave it to me? Does it even matter?

'Do you think it would be possible for me to meet your nan? I adore her generation. They seem at peace, as if they've come to terms with life, and perhaps she could tell me a bit about Aunt Helen.'

'She'd be delighted – and I know what you mean about people of her age. My nan's the wisest, kindest person I know.

As soon as she's out of hospital, I'll set it up. She can tell you all your family secrets!'

I smile, but inside I'm thinking that the one secret I would love to have an answer to is one I doubt she can help with. *Where is Lola?*

For a while, as we wait for the food, we chat about Effie's family and her life growing up in Cornwall. Then the food arrives, and it's every bit as delicious as she and Raff had promised.

We're just testing out some tiny Thai fishcakes when Effie looks over my shoulder towards the beach.

'Ooh! Seems you have an admirer!'

'What? Who?'

'Don't turn round – he's staring straight at you.'

'He can only see the back of my head – he can't possibly know me.'

Effie laughs. 'You have the most amazing, glorious hair I've ever seen, Nancy. No one else has hair the colour of burnished copper. Anyway, he can probably see your face reflected in the window of the restaurant.'

Which means, of course, that I can see his.

I lift my eyes to the window, but a woman at the next table chooses that moment to stand up, and she blocks my view.

'What does he look like?'

Effie wiggles her eyebrows. 'Pretty hot, if you like that kind of thing. Dark curly hair swept back from his forehead, shoulder length, and perfect designer stubble.'

The woman at the next table sits down and I see a reflection in the window: eyes intent, staring.

'Hang on, I know him!' Effie whispers, leaning across the table towards me. 'God, he's changed a bit.' Before she can say more, Raff approaches the table, and the view is lost.

'How's the food?' he asks with a smile.

I rudely ignore him and swivel round in my seat, but the man has gone.

It doesn't matter. I would recognise those eyes anywhere – eyes capable of both a cajoling warmth and a blank stare of indifference; eyes that can darken to an intense black in the heat of anger.

I want to slither down in my seat so he can't see me, but it's too late for that, and I don't need Effie to tell me who he was. He's the man who broke my heart; the man I became so obsessed with that I didn't notice my little sister's unhappiness.

Liam Riordan.

ELEVEN

Stephanie arrived early at Newlyn Harbour. She'd told Gus that she had to be there for 6.45, but that wasn't true. She wanted some thinking space, without Gus trying to interpret her mood. Certain that no one else would turn up for at least half an hour, she hoicked herself up onto the wall at the entrance to the harbour so she would see Molly Treadwell as she arrived.

When Gus told her yesterday that he had something he wanted to discuss with her, he was rather downplaying its significance, and he knew it. She had known the minute she walked through the front door that Gus was trying to please her. Chicken was marinating in yoghurt and spices on the kitchen worktop, and she could see through the French window that the barbecue was lit. Gus wasn't a particularly enthusiastic cook, so he'd gone to some considerable effort. But why?

He greeted her with a kiss and a glass of ice-cold Sancerre – not the supermarket plonk they usually drank during the week – and led her out into the garden.

'Are we celebrating something?' she asked.

Gus gave her a sheepish smile. 'That might depend on your point of view.'

She hadn't liked the sound of that and had set her glass on the table to stand facing him, hands on hips.

'Come on, Gus. Spit it out, for God's sake.'

'Sit down, Steph. I need to tell you something.'

That was more than apparent, and yet uncharacteristically Gus seemed to be struggling to find the right words. Stephanie felt her internal defences spring into action.

'I'm okay standing, thanks,' she replied, not taking her eyes from his face.

Gus sighed. 'Stephie, you must know I would never do anything to hurt you intentionally, but I need to take you back in time a bit, to when we weren't together.'

'Before we met, do you mean?'

Gus shook his head. 'No, after you threw me out, and when I'd given up trying to persuade you to forgive me. I'd been on my own for a few months with no hope of us getting back together, so I decided to get on with life.'

Stephanie knew what he meant – other women – but as she had been the one to end their relationship, she could hardly blame him.

It had all been so stupid, in retrospect. She had overreacted when Gus hadn't responded in the way she wanted to the news that she was pregnant with their child. She thought he seemed horrified, but Gus claimed it wasn't horror – it was shock because the baby wasn't planned. It didn't mean he wasn't thrilled, but, ever the pragmatist, he had focused on the practicalities of two police officers whose time together was limited due to the nature and location of their jobs. Of course, she hadn't waited for an explanation of his reaction. Prickly and defensive as ever, she had told him to go, and hadn't told him until months later – when they had worked on the Evie Clarke case together – that she had lost their baby boy. It still hurt.

'The thing is, while we were apart I didn't necessarily make the most sensible choices,' Gus said.

'Of course you didn't,' Stephanie said, wondering why she needed to know this.

'I made the mistake of sleeping with another officer when we were on a residential course.'

'Slept with?' Stephanie asked. She considered it the most bizarre euphemism, given that she doubted any sleeping took place.

'Okay, I know you hate that phrase. Had sex with – is that better?'

'Infinitely. So what's the deal – is she blackmailing you, or asking you to get her a better job? Or is she joining your team, and you thought you'd better let me know?'

'Jesus, Steph, will you put a cap on your imagination and listen?'

'Fine. Go on then.' She wasn't enjoying this. Gus wouldn't be making such a meal of it if there wasn't something in this story she wouldn't like.

'I want you to know that from the minute I met you again at the beginning of the Evie Clarke case, there hasn't been anyone, even during the long months before you let me back into your life. You know that, don't you?'

'If you say so, then I believe you.' She had often wondered, but had never asked.

He shook his head slightly, as if he could read between the lines. But he let it go.

'The woman concerned has been in touch. Darling, I know this will be difficult for you.' Gus took a deep breath. 'Apparently she had a child. My child.'

Stephanie felt a stab to her heart and closed her eyes as a wave of sorrow for the child she had lost washed over her. Gus was expecting her to comment, but she said nothing.

'I don't know what to say to you, Steph. I know how this must make you feel.'

She had no idea how she felt, or even how she *should* feel.

'More to the point, how do you feel?' she asked, giving herself time to breathe.

Gus didn't take his eyes from hers. 'I've had more time to get used to the idea, so I can't deny a feeling of excitement, along with a sense of trepidation – because I know this isn't going to be easy on anyone.'

Stephanie gazed silently round the garden. She didn't want to look at Gus, to witness his anxiety as he waited for her reaction. She wanted to scream at the unfairness of it all; that a one-night stand could result in a child when her own had been lost.

'How old is the child?' she finally asked.

'She's two – nearly two and a half.'

Stephanie did the calculation in her head. That meant Gus must have been with this woman about four months after they had split. Their own child would have been nearly three by now.

'And you've only just found out?'

'Yes. Earlier this week. I wanted to wait until I was with you to tell you. Paula – the child's mother – hadn't thought of ever telling me. She's married, and it would have confused things.'

Stephanie sat down heavily on the garden bench, and Gus lowered himself next to her, resting his arm along the back. 'Does her husband think the child is his? God, how awful for him if he's only found out now.'

'No, it's not like that. Paula told him straight away that she'd been unfaithful, and when she discovered she was pregnant he said he didn't want to know who the father was. It could have been him, and he wanted to bring the child up as his own. But now she knows, and so does he.'

Stephanie dropped her gaze as she thought about the husband.

However difficult she was finding this, it was nothing to what he had been through. It couldn't have been an easy decision to accept the child – but why upset the apple cart now by involving Gus?

'How come he suddenly knows?'

'Because the child is ill. She may need a stem cell transplant.'

Stephanie turned her eyes to Gus. 'Oh God – the poor kid – and her parents.'

'I know. I can't imagine how they must feel. Devastated doesn't even cover it, and even though I've never met the child – Daisy, she's called – I can't stop thinking about what she must be going through. I want to do anything I can to help, and there's a chance that I might be able to. Normally they'd look to a sibling as a donor but she doesn't have any, so they check other family members first before looking elsewhere. Paula isn't a match, and her husband's test confirmed he isn't her father. That must have been a difficult moment for him, even though he knew it was a possibility.' Gus was quiet for a moment, and Stephanie leaned lightly against him. 'They want to know if I'd be prepared to be tested, although there's only a slim chance that I'll be suitable.'

'I presume you said yes. It's a no-brainer, Gus.' She meant that with her whole heart, any bitterness melting away at the thought of a sick child.

He smiled gently and stroked the back of her neck with his thumb. 'I knew you'd say that, but I had to talk to you first. This will inevitably stir up all kinds of emotions in both of us, but we have to tell each other how we feel, be honest with each other, no matter how difficult that might be.'

Stephanie knew that harboured resentments were toxic to a relationship. She had allowed them to fester before, and she couldn't let that happen again. But how could she tell Gus that the existence of a child who was part of him but not part of her filled her with a wholly inappropriate envy? She didn't know what to say, so she said nothing.

Gus reached for the bottle of wine to top up her already half-empty glass.

'The thing is, now that I know about Daisy, Paula thought I might want to meet her, but I didn't want to agree to anything without talking to you. How would you feel about that?'

She wanted to scream '*No!*' She wanted to pretend none of this was happening, that this child – a part of Gus that wasn't part of her – had no place in their lives. But she could see the hope in his eyes, and she could do nothing to quash it. The timing couldn't have been worse. Gus had tentatively mentioned several times that maybe they should try for another child, but having lost one baby Stephanie hadn't been sure she could handle the inevitable anxiety. Recently, though, she had decided it was no way to live and had planned to tell him this week that she was ready.

It no longer felt like the right time to raise the subject. She swallowed the pain in her throat and blinked away tears before Gus saw them, knowing her own dreams had to be forgotten for now.

'She's the only thing that matters, Gus, and of course I understand why you want to meet her. The one thing I would question is whether it's the best thing for her right now, when she's ill. The family must be out of their minds, and I suppose I worry that this might be an added stress – particularly for Daisy's dad.'

Gus dropped his gaze, and she felt as though she had burst his balloon. The worst of it was, she couldn't decide whether her motives were as honourable as she had made them sound.

Stephanie lifted her face to the warm morning sun, the cool air from the sea brushing the back of her neck. There was no sign of the promised rain, and she breathed in deeply, loving the briny ocean smell mingling with the scent of the night's catch, wafting across from the bustling fish market. It seemed fitting to be in this place, somewhere she had visited often at 4 a.m. on the many sleepless nights after she had lost both Gus and their baby boy. There was something reassuring about the level of activity, the shouts and laughter of those going about their jobs, sorting and preparing the fish for auction while the rest of the world around them slept.

Now, as she perched on the wall waiting for the team to arrive, she thought back over her responses to Gus the evening before, still concerned that her thoughts and words had reflected her jealousy of the fact that another woman had borne his child. Much as she wanted to howl with despair, she had to find a way to drive emotion from the situation, to view the options logically and think only of Daisy, although she had to admit she had selfishly been relieved to find that Paula lived in Norfolk with little chance of coming into regular contact with Gus. Irrational as that concern was, given he swore that until this week he'd had no contact with her since their night together, it was one less thing to worry about.

Her thoughts were interrupted by the sudden banging of a car door.

Her time for thinking was over. Not only had the pathologist, Molly Treadwell, arrived, together with a tall woman with a long sharp nose who Stephanie assumed was the forensic anthropologist, but a police car had also drawn up. Two uniformed officers got out and Stephanie groaned. She'd asked for the two brightest, but they'd sent Jason, a young officer who had first worked with her as a probationer. She'd been getting on with him better since she'd been in CID, but he wasn't the sharpest knife in the box and suffered from a complete lack of any sense of tact or diplomacy.

Molly was marching towards her, and even from fifty metres away Stephanie could see she was breathing heavily.

Not surprising either, given that she was wearing a heavy-duty red cagoule over her inevitable black trouser suit. Even in the mild morning air, she must have been roasting.

'Sergeant King, what a delight,' she wheezed. 'Exciting too. Some bones, I understand. Didn't you manage to persuade that handsome DCI of yours to come along for the ride? Shame – it's a while since I've seen young Angus.'

Gus had always been a favourite of Molly's and she never tried to hide it. She waved her hand vaguely in the direction of the woman who was with her.

'This is Carla Davies. She's our bones expert. Come on then – what are we waiting for?'

Molly strode off in the direction of the RIB, and with a smile at Carla, whose thin lips didn't so much as twitch, Stephanie followed in her wake.

TWELVE

I wake up late, feeling a little ashamed of how last night ended. I remember coming home from the restaurant, slamming the front door, locking it tightly and switching on every light. I flung myself onto the sofa, leaned back and closed my eyes, suddenly tired after a day of travelling, worrying, trying to be positive, and doing my best not to think of Liam Riordan. When I'd finally forced myself to go upstairs to bed, I left the lights on all night, not sure if I would be able to sleep, and not wanting to come downstairs into a cold, dark room.

I've chosen to use the double room – the one Dad had – because it seemed less painful than sleeping in the room I shared with Lola. There are no memories for me here, but despite that I tossed and turned all night, wishing – despite Effie's friendliness – that I had never come.

I drank far too much. Effie was driving so only had one glass, and I think I drank the rest of the bottle. That's a lot for me, and don't I know it this morning. Goodness knows what she must have thought as she dropped me off at the door.

'See you tomorrow,' she called with a cheery wave, and I remember that we've agreed to meet for an early lunch. She promised to show me the town this afternoon, to extol its delights, she said, in the hope that I would decide to make it my home. I said nothing, not wanting to break the mood with my determination to get out of here as quickly as possible.

The restaurant last night was excellent, but knowing Liam had been there watching me had ruined my appetite – for food, if not for wine. He rarely came into town when I knew him, and I'd prayed I could escape back to London before he found out I was here. The sight of those eyes that I once thought mesmerising hadn't helped to curb my drinking, and realising that Effie knew him made things worse.

'How do you know Liam Riordan?' she asked when she had remembered who he was. She didn't give me time to answer before she carried on talking. 'I haven't seen him in years. He keeps to himself these days – not like he used to.' She pulled a face, and I wanted to ask what she meant but I was hoping we could move on to another subject. No such luck. 'Liam's one of those guys that the older generation somehow believe is charming. My nan calls him a young rogue. Why do older people seem to think it's vaguely endearing when good-looking men – and even I can see that he falls into that category – play the love 'em and leave 'em game with women?'

'Does he?' I muttered.

'Not now, as far as I know, but it started when he was about sixteen. He had endless flings with girls who were here on holiday. Ended up marrying one of them when he was really young – early twenties. Monique, she's called. She left after a couple of years and he returned to his old ways, but then she came back and as far as I know he's calmed down. He used to call the girls his fortnighters, because that's how long they were usually here for, so two weeks was the sum total of his commitment. That was before the word was adopted by players of the online game of the same name, of course.'

I didn't want to hear this – about his wife, the girls he'd

unscrupulously picked up just because they were going home soon, or the fact that it was all a game to him.

I took a huge gulp of wine. 'Why don't you tell me more about what it's like to live here?'

She didn't comment on the totally random question, but she narrowed her eyes. I could see she was wondering if maybe I had been one of Liam's fortnighters, but she never asked the question.

The knowledge that I had been one of many to be seduced by his charms sickened me and I'd done my best to drown my dismay in wine, because despite all evidence to the contrary, until that moment I'd still harboured the absurd belief that I had been special to Liam.

THIRTEEN

'Bit of a storm out at sea overnight,' the ruddy-faced crewman sitting next to Stephanie shouted. 'Sea's a bit choppy. You going to be okay?'

She nodded, the roar of the wind making conversation difficult. Stephanie glanced behind her. Molly looked as if she was having the time of her life. Squeezed into an orange life jacket over the top of her thick cagoule, she had turned her face into the breeze and was smiling happily as she chatted to Tai, the crime scene manager who had only just made it in time for the boat's departure. Carla Davies looked rather bored by the whole situation, but the same couldn't be said of Jason, who had a tendency to feel queasy even on dry land. Stephanie put it down to the fact that he usually had a hangover, but she felt sorry for him.

The cool sea air felt good on her cheeks as they raced along, hugging the coast on their right-hand side. She used to love sailing, but in recent years had barely had an opportunity to get out on the water, and it was a while since she had seen the breathtaking sight of her home county from the sea. She gazed at the cliffs rising majestically out of the water, the waves crashing against them, throwing their white foam into the air. It was at moments like this that she appreciated how trivial her problems were. The world suddenly seemed such a beautiful place, and despite the grim purpose of their trip, she vowed to keep her own life and troubles in perspective.

'Nearly there,' said the chirpy crewman, and she heard the engine note drop back a little.

The cliff face appeared solid with no sign of a cave, but the skipper seemed to know where he was going, and the boat bobbed up and down as the engine was cut to little more than a gentle purr.

'How does he know where the cave is?' Stephanie asked quietly.

'He was one of the team that helped with the filming here about twelve years ago. Do you remember? There was a television series about smugglers, and they used this cave as one of their locations. It was nearly a disaster movie, because it's a bastard to get into and out of except around high tide, and they kept overrunning on the shooting schedule. Almost got marooned here themselves more than once.'

Stephanie cast a quick glance at her watch. She'd checked the tide times, and guessed they had at most a couple of hours to retrieve the skeleton.

The crewman pointed to a narrow black slit in the cliff, which looked no more than a foot or so across. The skipper steered the boat to the left of the opening and the wide entrance to the cave, almost invisible from the sea, was revealed.

Slowly, carefully, he nudged the RIB forward until they were inside, and turned on the searchlights.

Stephanie gasped. The cave was much deeper than she had imagined, going back about thirty metres into the cliff face. The lights illuminated the area immediately ahead, glinting off the wet rock, but the rest of the cave was thrust into black shadow. Out of the sun, she shivered.

'You okay?' asked the crewman.

'Fine. It's cold in here, though.'

'Yeah. Pretty much the same temperature all year round at a guess – only a few degrees in it. I'm sure that might tell your experts something about the body.'

He was probably right, but for the moment she had no idea where the body was. As she glanced around, her eye was caught by Jason, huddled into his life jacket, looking as if the end of the world had come. She shook her head at him, and he looked away.

Although the cave was deep, it was narrow.

The skipper was pointing to a ledge on their left. 'That's where the boy dragged himself to when he got washed in here. The skeleton's on the other side, a little higher up. Look – you can see what he saw.'

Stephanie followed his pointing finger, and he was right. The remains of what was clearly a foot were just visible, and she imagined the horror the boy must have felt when he saw them. The officer who interviewed him said the kid was still shaking an hour later – and not just through cold.

'There's a narrow stretch of rock where you can get out of the RIB. Then you'll have to scramble up to the level where the skeleton is.' He pointed to the crewman sitting next to Stephanie. 'Ben will go up and secure a line for those who need to see the scene. How do you want to play this?'

Stephanie turned to Tai.

'I need to go first,' he said. 'I'll give you a shout when you can follow.'

That said, he stepped out of the boat and climbed, unaided, to the ledge.

Molly raised her hand. 'I'll need photos of the body, so I should go next.'

Stephanie looked at her with concern. She wasn't dressed for the job, and she was hardly fit and young.

'Don't look like that, young Stephanie,' Molly said. 'I can manage.'

Ben glanced at Stephanie and raised his eyebrows, but she shrugged. What could she do?

The forensic anthropologist spoke up. 'I need to see the bones and take control of retrieving them. These two officers can help me bag and label them so we can reconstruct the skeleton back at the mortuary.'

That was everyone taken care of except Stephanie. 'I'll go up with Molly, if there's room up there,' she said. 'I need to see the scene for myself.'

'We need to work quickly,' the skipper said. 'We'll have to leave in a couple of hours, or we'll all be here all night.'

Stephanie wasn't looking forward to this, but she couldn't let Molly go up there while she stayed in the boat, and the pathologist was already being secured with ropes. At a call from Tai, Ben started climbing, making it look easy.

'The ledge up here is quite wide,' he called. 'It's an easy climb, and once we get you up, you'll be fine. Who's first?'

Molly stepped forward.

'No, Molly,' Stephanie said. 'I'll go first. I need to get a feel for the scene before there are too many people.'

Molly gave her a look. She didn't believe her, and she was right to be sceptical, but Stephanie wanted to be sure for herself it was safe. Ben had fixed a line, and she took a deep breath and stepped off the boat.

Ben had been right about the climb. It wasn't difficult, although the rocks were cold and slippery and there had been a couple of dodgy moments. She had made it to the top, as had Molly – although the pathologist had to have some help.

'Don't be so limp,' she'd shouted at Jason. 'Put your hands under my bottom and *push*!'

Jason had looked faintly horrified at the thought, but had complied, and Molly landed safely on the wide ledge, a little out of breath but no worse for wear.

The bones lay intact, and Stephanie could see immediately that he or she had a broken leg. A pair of red shorts, relatively undamaged, lay loosely over the hip bones, and the remnants of a white T-shirt were draped over the rib cage, suggesting the shorts were made of a synthetic fibre while the shirt was cotton. There were no shoes, and Stephanie couldn't decide if this was relevant.

The skeleton lay flat on its back and there were no obvious signs that a struggle had taken place – no weapons or even loose rocks. The scraps of clothing clinging to the bones might give them a clue if anyone dressed in a similar outfit had been reported missing.

'What do you think, Molly?'

Molly was struggling to stand on one leg while pulling a protective cover over her other foot. 'I don't know. You've probably observed that the left leg is badly broken, so how did he or she get up here? The skull looks intact, but I can't see the back of the head and I don't want to move anything until we're sure there's no evidence close to the body. Are you going to get forensics out here, Tai?'

The crime scene manager scratched his head. 'I wasn't sure we'd need to, but I can't tell if our victim is a product of an unfortunate accident or something more sinister, so yes – we should. It means we can't let anyone else near the body for now, but it's been here a while so another few hours won't make any difference.'

Stephanie wasn't sure how Carla Davies was going to feel about this. They couldn't retrieve the bones until all bases had been covered, which meant the anthropologist would have to come back later with the forensics team, and she wasn't looking forward to telling her.

'What happened to the poor beggar? That's what I want to know,' Molly muttered.

The goosebumps on Stephanie's arms were itching, and she didn't know if it was the cold, dank atmosphere of the cave or the thought that someone had slowly died on this rock.

She shook herself. That was an assumption. Despite a lack of clear evidence to suggest foul play, this could be a murder victim.

FOURTEEN

Despite my intention to start emptying cupboards today, a plan designed to distract me from drowning in memories, I'm still lying in bed, listening to the hypnotic ebb and flow of the waves washing over the pebble beach. It's soothing; so soothing, in fact, that I realise time is running away with me and if I don't get up now, I will be late for Effie. I leap out of bed, pull the duvet back to air the sheets and head for the shower.

The walk to town takes about twenty-five minutes, and although I had planned to check out the local estate agents, I barely have time to do anything other than locate a couple that seem to be advertising similar properties, take quick photos on my phone to look up online later, and hurry to find the café that Effie suggested last night.

I take a seat where I have a good view of the door, and at 12.30 precisely the door opens. I look up expectantly. It's not Effie. It's a man in his early thirties, small, wiry with close-cropped hair and a thin face. He sees me looking at him, smiles and nods, as if he knows me. I look away, confused, and then realise that in this small town people are probably a good deal friendlier than they are in London.

I wait another hour, but there is no sign of Effie. I check my phone, and although we swapped numbers last night, she hasn't left me a message. The café has almost emptied by the time I give up on her. I haven't eaten because it would have seemed rude if she'd turned up when I was in the middle of a meal, but I can't sit staring at my empty coffee cup any longer.

I don't like the idea of sending her a 'Where were you?' message. Perhaps she only said she would *try* to make it. Or perhaps the drink really got to me, and it was for an entirely different day. I toy with texting her to say 'Thanks for last night and sorry you couldn't make lunch' but she might think the last bit is sarcasm. In the end I do nothing. I pay for my third cup of coffee and head home.

As I walk back towards Trevyan, I feel a little despondent about Effie's failure to show up. I know I drank too much last night, and maybe she thinks I'm not the kind of person she wants to know. It didn't feel like it at the time, but maybe that's what I wanted to believe.

As I turn through my gate, head down, I hear a voice shouting behind me.

'*Killer! Killer! Killer!*'

I spin round, heart thumping. My eyes are drawn to two kids, playing on the pebble beach.

'I didn't see it!' the accused child shouts. 'It was only a crab, anyway.'

The 'killer' chant starts again as I walk into the cottage. I close the door behind me to block the sound, throw my bag on the kitchen table and slump into a chair. The silence and loneliness press down on me, and I groan softly to break the stillness.

Why did I come here? Although life in London may have been predictable, it felt safe, and despite the distraction of a pleasant evening with Effie, I feel unsettled. Only the memories seem real.

I know my life has become too narrow. I rarely see anyone other than those I care for, and I excuse myself on the grounds that I spend all day talking to people so it's lovely to go home, put my feet up and read a good book. I convince myself that I'm content with my life, but in truth I lost everyone I cared about in the space of a few weeks, and I never want to experience pain like that again. Far safer to be alone.

Whichever way I look at it, my mum died when I was supposed to be looking after her, my sister ran away, and I ignored her when she needed me. Maybe Dad decided that without them life wasn't worth living. I wasn't enough.

My family fell apart, and now I don't know if it was ever whole. Perhaps the flaws were always there, even before Mum became ill, but I was too young to recognise them.

The memories rush at me, bombarding me from all sides, as if somehow by remembering I can change the outcome. But of course I never can.

I lower my head onto folded arms, the childish shouts of 'killer' echoing in my head.

FIFTEEN

FOURTEEN YEARS AGO

I was laughing as I walked into the kitchen, Dad close behind, tugging gently on my ponytail as I reminded him to take his boots off. Mum went mental when he trod muck into the house. Lola was at the table doing her homework and Mum was standing by the sink staring out at the garden beyond. She looked over her shoulder and her lips tightened.

'There you are, Nancy. You should have done your homework before gallivanting off.'

'I'd hardly call mucking out the pigs gallivanting, Mum. But don't worry – I'll do it after we've eaten.'

I never objected to doing my homework. I loved school, especially art lessons, and I was determined to work hard enough to go to college.

'I'll just have a shower. I'm a bit pongy.'

'Me too, *kochanie*,' Dad said. 'I'll race you to the bathroom.'

'You'll do no such thing, young lady. Ray, you go and take a shower. Nancy, you wash your hands and face in the outhouse and have a shower before bed.'

Lola watched from the table. She hated it when Dad called me *kochanie*, and I felt a pang of guilt.

'Okay.' I agreed without argument.

I could see from Mum's hunched shoulders that she was tired, and she was far too thin. I don't know when that had happened, but it struck me for the first time that she didn't look well.

'Dad, can you help me with my homework?' Lola called.

'Not now,' he said without turning towards her. 'Maybe when I've had a shower.'

'What's the subject? Perhaps I can help,' I said.

'It's maths, Nancy, and you're rubbish at maths,' Lola grumbled.

'This is true, but I've had three years more than you at being rubbish, so you never know. Give me a minute.'

I had a quick wash in the icy outhouse and went back to the kitchen. Mum was leaning over the sink, her head bowed.

'Mum, why don't you sit down and I'll make you a cup of tea?' I said.

'I thought you were going to help me,' Lola moaned.

'I will, in a minute. Mum – are you going to sit?'

She turned, and I looked at her narrow face with deep grooves running either side of her mouth. She wasn't even forty years old, but she looked worn out as she trudged over and slumped into a chair at the table. I put the kettle on the old Rayburn.

'Here you go,' I said a few minutes later, placing a mug of tea in front of her, giving her shoulder a squeeze.

She lifted her hand and placed it over mine. 'Thanks, Nancy. You're a good girl.'

Lola looked up with a scowl. 'You never say that to me.'

'Lola,' Mum said, her voice sharp. 'You have to stop telling people to love you. Love isn't something that you can demand as your right.'

I winced at her words, which seemed unnecessarily harsh, but recently Mum's behaviour had ricocheted between bleak silence and brittle antagonism, aimed at whoever had irritated her the most. I had learned to say as little as possible, but Lola hadn't yet grasped the benefits of holding her tongue.

From across the hall I heard the sound of the evening news. Dad had come down from his shower and gone straight into the front room to watch television. Lola's brows knitted together as she realised he wasn't coming to help her, and Mum shoved back her chair, pushing herself to her feet.

'Dinner's not going to make itself,' she muttered, taking her cup of tea with her to the sink. 'It's time you did more to help me in the house, Nancy, instead of messing around with the pigs all the time.'

I wanted to argue that I wasn't messing around – I was helping Dad and it was one of the highlights of my day, especially when the piglets ran to me as I called their names – but I didn't want a row with Mum. Last time that happened, she dropped the pan she was holding into the sink and walked out of the room. We didn't see her again all day.

'It's time you took responsibility for cooking our evening meal, then perhaps I too can go and watch the news occasionally.'

I wasn't sure if she was having a dig at me or Dad, who had taken to eating his evening meal in front of the television while the three of us ate in the kitchen.

I sighed, and her shoulders stiffened as she heard me. I was sure she was going to turn round and give me hell, but she stood for just a moment, then her head dropped back down to focus on the vegetables, and I moved quietly to sit by Lola, rolling my eyes at my sister, who grinned as we shared a moment of solidarity. Mum was clearly having one of her bad days.

There was a shout from the living room. '*Kochanie*, come here! There's something on the news about some pigs escaping onto the motorway!'

Before I had time to respond, Mum chucked the knife onto

the chopping board, ran her wet hands down the front of her apron, and stormed out of the room, banging the door behind her. Lola and I looked at each other but didn't speak. We tried to hear what Mum was saying, but her voice was little more than an angry hiss. Dad, however, was less able to disguise his irritation.

'Give it a rest, Janice. You're stuck with me, like it or not. You need me, and you know it.'

The door was flung open again, and Mum stomped back in while Lola and I both pretended to study her maths problems.

She threw the potatoes into a pan and slammed it down on the Rayburn. It suddenly felt as if it was only Mum's anger that was keeping her going.

My natural inclination was to stay quiet until things had calmed down, but Lola had different ideas.

'Are you getting a divorce, then? Kirsty at school says her parents are splitting up because her dad hits her mum.'

I stared at Lola, willing her to be quiet, but Mum turned round from the stove and gripped the rail behind her.

'We're not getting a divorce, and I don't think your friend Kirsty should be sharing the details of her parents' relationship with you or anyone else. I've told you this before. What goes on in this house, in this *family*, is private.'

'I was just saying, that's all. You don't seem very happy, though.'

I cringed at her words, even though they were true.

'Lola, you will soon come to realise that for the vast majority of people happiness is an illusion. Life is about getting through each day as best you can, living with the decisions you've made – whether good or bad. Nothing more, nothing less.'

I stared at her, horrified that this was her take on life, and her gaze moved from Lola to me.

'And don't you look so shocked, missy. You'll learn. And

from now on, you're not working on the farm. You're helping me. End of story.'

My eyes filled with tears. Only minutes before she'd said I was a good girl, and I loved looking after the animals. Lola thought they were nasty smelly beasts.

I was surprised to feel Lola's hand reaching for mine below the table, giving it a quick squeeze. She might have been jealous of the attention I got from Dad, but she was still my sister.

We both sat, heads bowed, wanting to avoid any further upset. But there was no need because Mum reached behind her back to untie her apron, dropped it onto the draining board, and without another word trudged wearily towards the door. We heard her footsteps dragging slowly upstairs, and a door closed softly.

And that became the pattern. It was the beginning of all that was to come.

SIXTEEN

Remembering Mum and how she was in the last few months before her stroke always hurts, because I constantly think I should have noticed how bad things were getting a long time before that evening in the kitchen. The nights when she disappeared upstairs had become increasingly frequent, and there was a heavy air of defeat about her, but I was happy with my life, my friends, and I realise now that I didn't pay enough attention to how she was feeling. When I had asked Dad if there was a problem, he told me not to worry. 'She's just hit a rough patch, *kochanie*,' he said, shaking his head sadly as he pulled me into a hug.

I wanted to believe him. It was easier to look away than to admit that my mum wasn't happy.

She and Dad hadn't shared a bed for as long as I could remember, and when she headed upstairs in the evenings to shut herself in her room, alone with her thoughts, she made it clear she didn't want to be disturbed – an easy wish to fulfil in our house due to its strange layout. The staircase – narrow and steep with solid walls on both sides – led to a dark and dismal landing with no natural light. On one side there were three small bedrooms, one each for Dad, me and Lola, and a tiny shower room. On the other side was a fire door which accessed a wider corridor with a window at each end. This was Mum's domain – 'the master suite' as Dad called it. Not that there was anything grand about it. The bedroom was larger and there was a bathroom with a bath, but it was as run-down as every other part of the house, with peeling wallpaper and a few cotton rugs over bare floorboards.

Mum's withdrawal behind that closed fire door became almost the norm, and before her stroke there were days when we didn't see her at all. It was only later, much, much later, that I understood why.

I lift my head and lean back from the table. This is achieving nothing. Strong as the temptation is to scurry back to London to my safe, if somewhat narrow, life, I still need to go through the contents of the house, and the best way for me to avoid wallowing in self-pity is to do something. So I push myself to my feet and decide to make a start in the sitting room.

There is only the sideboard to empty, and the first drawer reveals nothing more than some neatly ironed napkins and tablecloths that we never used during our stay.

I open the other drawer and pause, staring at a pale blue folder that I instantly recognise. I know what's inside. Even though Lola was considered a runaway, there was some local press interest in her disappearance, and the police put out a low-key plea for information. Inside this folder are the press cuttings. The journalist had to work hard to get Dad to agree to have his picture taken with me, but we hoped Lola might see the coverage and realise how concerned we were; how much we missed her. We hoped it would persuade her to come home.

I think about opening the folder, but I can't face it. Not today. I slam the drawer shut.

The cupboard at the bottom reveals little at first – some candles, a long-forgotten bottle of sweet sherry, a few ornaments of no interest to me, and one rather lovely, decorated jug I think I might keep.

I open the second door and give a small gasp. *My camera.*

With everything that had happened, I had forgotten all about it. After Lola disappeared I had no desire to take photographs, preferring to pace the streets in the hope that I might find her, although I was certain she'd gone. Then we decided that if Lola had gone to London, as the police suspected, she was more likely to return to Shropshire, so we'd hastily packed and left. It was weeks before I remembered shoving my camera in the cupboard. I was glad I'd left it behind; it held too many memories.

I take it out now and hold it, feel its weight in my hands, remembering how excited I felt when I took my first photograph. We'd been in Cornwall for three days, and nothing had turned out the way I'd expected. Lola pranced off each morning, her emerald-green backpack slung over her shoulder, not even bothering to say goodbye. Dad was losing his patience with her and she seemed intent on winding him up. She wouldn't listen to me. She couldn't even look me in the eye.

I'd hoped to make a few friends on the beach, just as Lola had, but I felt so out of touch. I didn't feel part of their world, with talk of university, gap years and the like, so I kept out of everyone's way and mooched around the town, checking out the shops because, to my surprise, I had some money of my own to spend.

Unbeknown to any of us, Mum had set up bank accounts for Lola and me when we were children, and while Lola had already made a sizeable dent in her funds, I hadn't spent any of mine. I had no idea what clothes suited me, and I couldn't think what else to spend it on. I was meandering around, staring blankly into shop windows, when I came across a camera shop. I still had ambitions to go to art college, and I thought learning about photography might be a good start.

The man in the shop talked me through the options until finally I decided on a second-hand Nikon. It didn't have all the features, but it had a great zoom lens. He showed me the basics of how to use it, and I left the shop feeling a little lighter in spirit. I didn't need to hang around the beach like a spare part any longer – I could take myself for walks along the coastal path, snapping photos of the gannets as they soared above the waves, and I couldn't wait to start.

Perhaps, if I'd realised the problems it would cause, I would never have set foot inside that shop.

SEVENTEEN

The camera gave me a purpose each day, a reason to get out of bed and somewhere to go to escape the pressure of my family. I'd tried to talk to Lola about helping to make the holiday a success, but she had given me a black look and told me I didn't understand, and anyway I was as much a part of the problem as she was. So I slung my camera round my neck each day and took myself off with a backpack and some food, my thoughts on nothing but the sea, the birds and the flowers.

I walked for miles, following the coastal path as it hugged the edge of the cliff, smiling hello at other walkers, the numbers thinning as I moved further from the popular areas. Gradually, I became more daring, straying from the path where it moved inland to draw walkers away from the sheer drops into the sea. I felt brave, ignoring the rules and the warning notices, crawling on hands and knees to the very edge of the cliffs, where I could look down onto the rocks, deserted apart from the occasional oystercatcher sounding its shrill, piping call as it searched for food, prising open shells with its powerful bright orange bill.

It was almost the end of our first week when everything changed. It was raining, but that wasn't going to stop me. I had taken a groundsheet so I could lie on the grass right at the edge of the cliff where I'd spotted some huge rocks. To one side of the outcrop was a tapering inlet, and at high tide the waves crashed spectacularly onto the cliff face, throwing their white crests high into the air. I wanted to capture the moment on camera.

As I lay there, waiting for the next big wave to strike, over the hypnotic sounds of the ocean I heard the throb of an engine, and swivelled round to look out to sea on the other side of the promontory. A boat, not big or fancy enough to be called a motor yacht, but something I had heard Dad refer to as a cabin cruiser, was sailing towards the shore towing a small RIB. I gave up on the waves and shuffled across the bracken, flattening it as I went. It was hard to see what was below, and only by crawling to the very edge could I see a sliver of beach and, nestled halfway down the hillside and hidden from the coastal path, a single-storey white-painted cottage.

The engine died, leaving no sound but the gulls and the waves. After a moment or two, someone appeared on the deck and I grabbed my camera and zoomed in to get the best view. It was a man – young, probably mid-twenties – dressed in bright blue swimming shorts and a white T-shirt, showing no regard for the thin drizzle. I snapped not once, but at least three times.

He moored the boat to a buoy a hundred metres from shore, then disappeared from view. A few minutes later I heard the putt-putt of an engine as the RIB appeared from behind the cruiser and headed for the shore. I could see the man more clearly now – dark hair cut short, clean shaven. Another snap of the camera. As soon as the RIB touched the sand, he jumped out and began to pull it out of the water, and I lifted my camera, zooming in again through the telephoto lens. I panned up from his calves, past the powerful muscles in his thighs to his flat stomach, where his wet T-shirt was clinging to his skin, and finally up to his broad shoulders as he tugged the RIB onto the strip of beach. Another click, maybe more.

Then he stopped. I lowered the camera as he turned slowly and raised his eyes to where I was lying, peering over the edge of the cliff. I was too far away to read the expression in his eyes, but they seemed to bore into me. I was transfixed.

It felt like minutes, but it could only have been a few seconds before I shuffled back, out of sight. I felt breathless and suddenly scared that he would come racing up to the top of the cliffs to berate me for spying on him.

I pushed my camera back into my bag as I struggled to my feet, half wanting him to appear over the headland, half terrified for no reason that I could explain.

Keeping my head low, I started to run – back along the coastal path, back to the safety of Aunt Helen's cottage.

But I knew I would be back.

EIGHTEEN

The day after I saw the man in the cove – the man I came to know as Liam – I went back to take another look. The thought of seeing him again thrilled me, so once again I turned off the path and squeezed through the gap I'd found in the hawthorn the day before. Keeping low, I shuffled to the edge of the headland and lay down to peer over, hoping he would be there. The shore was empty. The boat was there, though, so I was sure he had to be somewhere around and I waited, watching, hoping I would see him. The sun was warm on my back and I felt myself getting drowsy. I could smell the earth, still damp from the previous day's rain, and could hear the gulls calling, the waves lapping onto the sand. I drifted off into a dreamless sleep.

I woke, suddenly cold, as if the sun had disappeared behind a cloud, and I shivered. Before I could move, I heard the crunch of bracken trodden underfoot. I lay still for a second, holding my breath, the shadow chilling my back. I was a long way from the path. No one could see me. And yet I knew someone was behind me.

Finally, I turned my head. It was him.

'Looking for someone?' he asked. He wasn't smiling. With the sun behind him, his face was shaded, his eyes dark hollows.

I felt my face flush with embarrassment and more than a little fear. He'd caught me, and I was sure he knew I had come there for him. I glanced beyond him, but there wasn't a single walker in sight – no one to come to my rescue if he wanted to hurt me.

'I saw you yesterday,' he said, 'peering over the headland.'

My voice was little more than a squeak. 'I didn't think you'd notice me.'

He smiled, but I couldn't see him well enough to decide if it was a friendly smile or a sneer. 'Who could miss that hair?'

I lifted my hand self-consciously. I had always hated my red hair and vowed to dye it black as soon as I got home. I never did, though.

'As you're so interested in my tiny patch of beach, would you like to get a little closer? I don't encourage visitors, but I might make an exception for you.'

I wanted to tell him I was sorry if he thought I was spying on him – I'd leave and never come back – but as I stuttered out my apology, he held out his hand.

'No need for that. No harm done – but don't tell anyone I've invited you because it's strictly off limits. Can you promise me that? If not, I might have to kill you.' He laughed at my terrified face. 'I'm teasing. Are you always so gullible?'

I was, of course, but I didn't want to admit it.

'Why is it off limits?' I asked, scared I might be breaking the law if I went with him.

'Because it's a little slice of heaven, and if it was discovered by tourists it would quickly turn into Benidorm.'

I didn't take his hand, and he dropped it and shrugged. 'Please yourself. You'll never find the way down on your own, though. This is your last chance.'

As he turned away, I made a decision. It was time to come

out of my shell, to take some risks, and as he turned to the side and the sun caught his profile I could see he was even more attractive than I had thought, with thick dark brows over intense brown eyes and a strong, determined chin.

I scrambled to my feet and picked up my bag, relieved that my camera was hidden inside and he hadn't seen me taking photos of him. Somehow I felt certain he wouldn't like that.

'I'm coming, if that's okay.' My words tumbled over each other, and I felt gauche and cross with myself for my lack of confidence. He smiled as if he had never doubted my acceptance. From that moment onwards I don't believe I was capable of refusing him anything.

The path to the cove was concealed amid hawthorn and gorse, and it fell steeply, snaking one way and then the other. I stumbled a couple of times over the rough ground and prayed I wouldn't make a fool of myself by falling flat on my face.

We passed the white-painted cottage, which I later came to understand was Liam's home, although I was never invited inside, and finally stepped over the last of the pebbles and onto a tiny sandy beach with high cliffs standing tall on each side.

'Do you own this beach?' I whispered, awestruck by its beauty.

'Technically, no. But I own the land that people have to walk through to get here, so unless they come by boat – and it's quite tricky to navigate the rocks – no one ever finds me here. Do you like it?'

No words would have described how I felt about it. To me it was paradise, and Liam was the master of it all.

'Fancy a swim?' he said, ripping off his T-shirt.

I looked away, embarrassed by the proximity of his naked chest.

'I didn't bring a swimsuit,' I said.

I thought for a moment he was going to be predictable and suggest I didn't need one, but 'Next time' was all he said.

I wasn't sure I would want to reveal my pale body, but the idea of 'Next time' thrilled me.

Liam sat down beside me. For a while we said nothing and stared out to sea. I was desperate to find something to say, so I asked him if he had a job. It sounded so crass and dull, but he didn't blink. He said he fished for a living – that was what the boat was for.

I told him how beautiful I thought the cove was, and he turned his head to look at me.

'It is, but you can only come here with me, never on your own.'

I stuttered out a promise, excited at the idea of coming again but terrified he might change his mind if I said or did the wrong thing.

Liam talked to me about the sea, about how treacherous it was to be mid-ocean when a sudden storm struck, fighting to keep the boat on track, praying you wouldn't lose the battle as waves crashed over the bow. He made it sound dramatic, exciting, as if the fear aroused a powerful thrill in him.

'And then,' he said, 'there are moments like this: when the surf gently laps the shore, the sun beating down, and it's impossible to believe in the fury of that same ocean.'

He lay on his back, hands behind his head, and closed his eyes. It gave me a chance to look at him properly, to explore his body. Now that I'm older and maybe a little wiser, I suspect that was his intention. Without him touching me, I was already smitten. To me, he was as wild and dangerous as the ocean.

That was the first time I went to the beach, but it wasn't the last. As I left that day, Liam put out his hand and touched me lightly on my lower back as he walked me up the slope to the coastal path. I felt my body jolt at his touch. He must have felt it too.

'Come back tomorrow, if you fancy it,' he said. 'And if you do, bring a swimsuit.'

As I walked away, I didn't know if I would be back. I didn't know if I could trust myself.

But of course I returned. And that second day he kissed me for the first time.

With each touch I felt increasingly dizzy – it was all so new. I was nearly nineteen and a virgin. I'd only had one boyfriend, when I was fifteen – a bit of a disaster, as most first boyfriends are – and for the previous two years I had barely left the house. Liam was older – twenty-five, he told me, and he must have realised how innocent I was. Had he rushed me, I would have bolted. Now the cynic in me realises he knew exactly what he was doing as his fingers brushed the tender skin of my inner thigh.

It was my first experience of desire. I wanted this man, and he knew it.

On the third day I took a picnic, hoping that would be okay. He didn't smile, and I thought I might have overplayed my hand. He narrowed his eyes, then without a word he disappeared back to his cottage and came back with two cold cans of beer. I didn't think I'd be able to eat, but I picked at a few morsels, and he thrust one of the cans into my hands.

'Drink,' he said. And of course I did.

Why did I not realise he was playing me? Why did it not occur to me to ask if he lived alone?

He spread a rug under the shelter of the overhanging cliff to provide some shade from the scorching sun and told me to lie back, his voice mesmerising in its softness.

Gently, he eased the straps of my swimsuit off my shoulders, and I was lost.

NINETEEN

I'm sitting cross-legged on the floor, clutching the camera, when my stomach starts to rumble and I realise that I haven't eaten anything at all since I got up. If I'm going to eat this evening, I need to go to the local shop.

I pull the camera charger from the cupboard and plug in the battery, which as I expected is as flat as a pancake. I'm not sure I'm ready to look at photos just yet, but I may feel differently in a day or two.

Picking up my purse from the kitchen table, I head to the door. The tide is going out, exposing the rocks, protruding sharp and black from the ebbing water. There is no one around, no traffic on the road, and the little car park is deserted. For an area generally swarming with tourists, I can understand why my aunt chose to live in this secluded spot.

I pull the door closed behind me but don't lock it. We never used to bother during the day, and it was only at night that Dad used to hide the key so whoever got home first could let themselves in.

As I walk towards the shop, I try to convince myself to be more positive. After last night, Effie seems to have decided I'm not worth the bother, but I've no intention of staying here so I don't need to make friends. I just need to sell the cottage and think about how I will spend the money.

Before I left London my work colleagues were full of ideas.

'Think of all the clothes you could buy,' said one of them. 'I could come shopping with you – we could make a day of it.'

'Travel the world,' said another. 'And I would *definitely* come with you.'

'Don't go for long, Nancy,' muttered Doreen as I massaged her arthritic fingers with hand cream. 'We'd miss you.'

And I would miss them. They're my family now, but maybe I could take a trip to Florence and spend a day in the Uffizi, a gallery I have only seen in pictures.

I'm so deep in thought that I step off the pavement, almost into the path of a grey van that swerves past and pulls into the car park past the cottage. I'm half expecting the driver to jump out and berate me, but nothing happens, and I return to my daydreams.

Feeling a little better than I have for most of the day, I push open the door to the shop. It seems even stranger than I remembered, like something out of a time warp. A wooden-topped counter sits at one end, with a wall of shelves behind. A woman stands next to a till, and I guess this must be Noreen. She's talking to someone who has her back to me, so I give her a smile and pick up a basket. I've no idea what I'm going to buy, and it's not the kind of place to have a big freezer stuffed with ready meals. As I walk up and down the narrow aisles, hoping for inspiration and grabbing nothing more exciting than some antibacterial kitchen spray, the old-fashioned bell over the door tinkles as customers come and go, but still I can't seem to decide.

As I turn down the next aisle, I notice a man reading the back of a packet of instant mash. He looks at me, opens his eyes wide in recognition, and smiles. It's the man who came into the café at lunchtime.

'Hello again,' he says, putting the packet back on the shelf.

He squeezes past me, holding his hands high in an unnecessary demonstration that he wasn't trying to touch me, and grins. I'm too flustered to respond, and a moment later I hear the bell. He's gone.

Grabbing a packet of pasta and a jar of tomato sauce to add to my basket, I head towards the till. I notice Noreen look at the woman – still standing talking to her – and she tilts her head as if to let the woman know that I'm behind her. I place my basket on the counter, and the woman turns towards me.

I have a strange feeling that I know her, but I'm not at all sure who she is. She gives me a tight smile and picks up her bag of shopping from the counter.

'See you soon, Noreen,' she says.

Noreen starts to remove the items from my basket to scan them through the till, but I sense that the woman is still there, standing behind me. I turn my head. Her mouth is set in a tight line, as if there's something she wants to say but is trying not to. Eventually, the impulse to speak appears to win.

'Nancy.' She must see the look of surprise on my face. 'Yes, I know who you are. I'm Angie Dawson. We met a couple of times all those years ago, but I appreciate you had other things on your mind back then.'

'Oh! I'm sorry I didn't recognise you, but thanks so much for looking after the cottage.'

She looks a bit startled at my friendly tone, but then she frowns.

'Listen, it's none of my business and you must do whatever you want. But my Effie was only trying to be friendly, you know. Maybe you don't want to stay here. Perhaps you don't *want* any new friends. But you've hurt her feelings, and I don't think she deserved that.'

I open my mouth to ask what on earth she's talking about.

'That's twelve pounds ninety-three,' Noreen says.

I glance back towards the counter, groping in my purse for a twenty-pound note to hand over, and before I can stop her, Angie Dawson walks out of the door. I'm about to run after her to ask what she thinks I've done, when Noreen speaks as she slowly counts out my change.

'They're a good family, you know. Good friends to have in these parts, and Effie's one of the best.'

I stare at her, shocked at what has just happened. I want to ask what she means – what Effie's mum meant – but my throat feels tight, my eyes burning.

By the time I've blinked away the tears that threatened, Noreen has disappeared into a back room, so I grab my bag and head quickly for the door, hoping I can catch Angie. But there's no sign of her. I stand dumbly staring up and down the street, the ball of anxiety growing once again in my chest. Did I say something dreadful to Effie last night – something I've forgotten? Is that why she didn't turn up?

I have no answers, so I draw in a deep breath and, head down, walk slowly home, trying and failing to block out the question I have asked myself for years: *Why does every relationship in my life go wrong?* Right now, all I want to do is get into bed, curl up in a tight ball and hope that tomorrow will be better.

There is still no one about, and I've no idea how Angie managed to disappear so quickly.

The thought of eating no longer has any appeal, and as I push open the gate, trying to convince myself that a plate of spaghetti will make me feel better, I look at my front door.

I closed it. I know I did.

But now it's standing ajar.

TWENTY

I'm not sure if I should go into the house or call for help. What if there's someone in there? I spin round, hoping to see a friendly face who can help me. But there's no one there. Even the grey van has gone, so I'm on my own.

I lower my shopping bag onto the rickety table in the front garden and tentatively ease the door open. It catches on the floor, but I push harder, jumping as it bangs off the wall.

'Hello! Who's there?' My voice sounds weak, feeble, and I am greeted by silence.

Should I head for the kitchen? There's a knife in the top drawer, but I couldn't stab anyone. Then I remember there's a poker next to the wood burner – a better choice.

I take a step inside.

'Who's there?' I repeat, my voice quivering.

The kitchen is empty. The sitting room – at least the part I can see – appears empty too, but I can't see the whole room. If I want the poker, I'm going to have to risk it.

Leaving the front door wide open for a rapid escape, I peer cautiously round the wall into the sitting room. There is no one there, and I allow myself to breathe.

Standing perfectly still, I listen. If I hear a sound upstairs, I have time to rush across the room to pick up my weapon, but there is only silence. Although anyone hiding in the house already knows I'm here, for some reason I tiptoe across the room to grab the poker, glancing out of the window, hoping again to see someone I can call on for help. The street remains stubbornly deserted.

I shout out again, this time with an effort to sound more confident, but the words come tumbling out as little more than a squeak. 'I'll let you go. I don't want anyone to get hurt. Please come down now.'

Nothing. I have to go up. My heart is thumping, my mouth dry, as I slowly take each step, the poker clenched in my right hand, my left grasping the banister tightly.

I reach the top. All the doors are closed. Did I leave them that way? I don't remember. What I *do* remember, though, is that some of the floorboards on this landing creak. Lola knew where they all were and managed to avoid them when she came home late, but I don't, and as I move along the landing I am giving fair warning of exactly where I am.

I approach the first door, reach out with my left hand to turn the old-fashioned china knob, and kick the door open with my foot. It bangs into the shower cubicle, but the bathroom is empty.

The next room is the twin that Lola and I shared. I press down the handle and push. The door crashes against the wall. I can see under the beds. There's no one there, so unless someone is in the wardrobe, this room is empty too.

The floorboards groan as I creep along the corridor towards the front bedroom. This has to be where they are hiding, and when I push open the door, I need to be ready.

'You can come out!' I call bravely, although I can hear the tremor in my voice. 'The door is open. Please just *leave!*'

I end almost on a scream, but there is no answer.

And for the final time I press down the handle and push open the door.

Suddenly there is a clatter of feet on the stairs and I spin round, flattening myself against the wall.

TWENTY-ONE

'*Jesus!*' Effie calls as she sees me brandishing the poker. 'What the fuck's going on, Nancy? I heard you yelling from outside.'

'Effie?' I say, wilting against the wall. 'What are you doing here?'

'I think that's the least important question right now. Why have you got that bloody great poker in your hand?' Standing with her hands on her hips, for once she's not smiling.

'I got back from the shops and the front door was open. I thought someone must be in the house.'

'But there's no one here?'

'I don't think so, but I've not looked in either of the wardrobes.'

'Right,' she says, dropping her arms and marching across the room. 'Come out, you little fucker!' She flings open the wardrobe. It's empty.

'Next door?' she asks me, and I nod, speechless as she disappears out of the door.

'Okay,' she shouts. 'All clear. Probably someone came calling and opened the door to give you a shout then didn't close it properly.'

She strides back into my bedroom and shrugs, as if this is perfectly normal behaviour, and perhaps it is here. I can't imagine anyone in London just opening the door, but it's exactly what Effie did yesterday. So now on top of everything else, I feel a fool.

'Weren't you frightened?' I ask, stunned at the way she had yanked open the doors.

'Course not. If there was someone here, it had to be a kid. Anyone who meant serious harm wouldn't have hidden from a skinny woman with a poker, would they? No offence.'

I shake my head at her optimism. I had, of course, assumed the worst.

'Come on,' she says, heading back out of the door. 'I'll put the kettle on. I guess it's a bit early for wine!'

I'm about to follow her when I pause and stare at the bed. The pillows are plumped, the thin duvet lying at a slight angle across the mattress, as if pulled up in haste.

When did I make it? I turned the covers back to air the sheets, but now it's made. Did I do this? Are stress and lack of sleep getting to me so much that I can't remember?

I back slowly out of the door as Effie skips down the stairs. She comes to a halt halfway down, and turns back towards me.

'I know you don't want me bothering you. You've made that clear. I just came to say I'm fine with that, and to let you know that I'll still be here if you change your mind.'

Before I can answer, she has turned back and reached the bottom of the stairs.

'Tea?' she asks, heading to the kettle.

'Please,' I answer weakly, but her words are spinning in my head. 'What do you mean that I don't want you bothering me? I just met your mum, and she said something about me being unkind to you. Why would either of you think that?'

Effie turns to me, a baffled look on her face. 'Because you emailed me telling me you'd decided you don't need any friends as you won't be staying. You asked me not to bother you again.' She shrugs and looks slightly sheepish. 'And yet here I am! I thought I should come to say that I understand. I know things must be difficult, but even though you don't think so now, you might decide you need a friend – or at least, someone to turn to.'

I can feel my brow furrowing, and she sees it too.

'What?' she asks.

'I don't know what you're talking about, Effie. I went to the café at lunchtime and waited ages. I thought you'd decided I wasn't worth the effort, and I don't know your email address.'

She frowns. 'I guessed you'd got it from the company website. Are you saying you *didn't* email me?'

'Of *course* I didn't! I was delighted to have found you – or rather you found me.' I drag out a chair and flop down into it. 'What email address was it from?'

She pulls out her phone and shows me.

'That's not my email address,' I say. 'Oh God. What the hell is going on here? Why would someone do this?'

Effie puts two mugs of tea on the table and sits down facing me. 'There's certainly something odd about someone trying to drive a wedge between us. Do you have any idea who might be behind it?'

I shake my head slowly. 'I don't *know* anyone here. Some-one's set up a fake email address, but *why*?' I can sense the panic in my voice and take a deep breath.

She leans forward and places her hand gently on my arm. 'We'll get to the bottom of it. Don't worry.'

If someone was in my house then I consider that dangerous, but Effie seems confident it was a random visitor who left the door open, and I can't prove otherwise. I want to share my suspicions about my bed, but it hits me how strange it would sound. Why would anyone break in to make my bed? Effie might wonder if I am the source of the problem – that I make things up to get attention. Or that I am losing my mind.

'Listen,' she says. 'Rather than sitting here worrying, let's do something practical. You told me last night that you plan to clear the cupboards of stuff to take to the charity shop. Why don't I give you a hand?'

I look at her kind face, for once not laughing but smiling sympathetically, and I feel a moment of anger. I nearly lost Effie as a friend, and suddenly that feels like a tragedy.

'If you're sure,' I say, draining the last of my tea. 'These kitchen cupboards have years of accumulated pots and pans that I don't want to keep. If you're happy to help, that would be brilliant.'

'Excellent!' she says, jumping up. 'I love a good clear-out. Have you got any boxes?'

I groan. I meant to ask at the shop, but the conversation with Angie threw me, although I can't really use that as an excuse to Effie.

'No, but maybe there are some in the garden shed. I've avoided going in there, because there might be rats, and I hate them.'

Effie laughs. 'I thought you were brought up on a farm?'

'A smallholding – nothing as grand as a farm. And I still hate the things.'

'Well, fortunately for you, I'm fine with rats. My brother used to keep one.'

I shudder at the thought.

TWENTY-TWO

Five minutes later, we're standing outside the shed. I'm staring at the door, and Effie gives me an enquiring glance. 'Have you never been in?'

'Briefly, when Lola disappeared. One of the police officers poked his nose in, but I stood well back. Worried as I was about my sister, I wasn't prepared to brave the rats.'

'What was he looking for?'

'Lola, I guess. Not sure whether he expected to find her hiding behind the lawnmower.' I force a smile, although I'm no more amused now than I was then. 'I suppose he had to check everywhere, but he just opened the door, glanced inside, said "Looks like she's not here, then!" with a stupid smirk on his face, and that was it. Talk about stating the bleeding obvious.'

Effie looks at me with raised eyebrows but doesn't comment on my bitter tone.

'From what I remember, Lola just disappeared one day, didn't she? Have you never seen or heard from her since?'

I shake my head, unable to speak for the moment. Effie looks at me and nods her head, instinctively knowing that I'm drifting off into the past again, as I seem to have done repeatedly since I came here. She goes to the shed and opens the door, while I stand well back and watch.

I don't tell her that I searched relentlessly for Lola after I moved to London. No one knows about the hours I spent combing the streets, visiting the hostels, the refuges, anywhere I could think of where Lola might have gone. I'd even risked visiting some of the dodgy areas at night where people were sleeping rough. After two years, I'd found nothing. Even now if I see someone whose hair looks like Lola's I run after them down the street. But it's never her, just some poor shocked woman, wondering why I'm chasing her.

I feel an ache at the memory of my part in Lola's disappearance. I can't forgive myself for ignoring her when she wanted to talk, for shouting at her as I ran out of the cottage to get as far away from everyone as I could. It's no excuse that I was too unhappy to listen. Liam, the man I thought I was in love with, had broken my heart, but my grief wasn't only about him. It was an accumulation of everything that had happened – losing Mum, the way everyone blamed me, the fact that I blamed myself.

I had wanted to die that night, and had cried until my body couldn't take any more. There seemed to be nothing worth living for. Everyone hated me, and for a moment I wondered how they would feel if I threw myself off a cliff. Then I thought about Lola. 'What's up?' she'd asked when she had seen me crying. 'What's upset you?' She was trying to show that she cared about me, and all she'd got in return was abuse. In the end, it was the memory of her concern that made me pick myself up from the damp grass and trudge back to the cottage.

I'd hoped she'd still be there, waiting for me. But she wasn't. I thought she must have gone back to the beach, so I climbed into bed and pulled the covers over my head, willing myself to stay awake until she was home. I didn't care that Dad had told me not to talk to her about Mum. I would beg Lola to listen while I explained what had happened and why. I would ask for her forgiveness and her understanding. And I would ask her what she had wanted to tell me. This time I would listen.

It was only when I woke, bleary-eyed, the next morning, that I realised Lola's bed hadn't been slept in.

Eleven years ago

My eyes felt as if they were glued together by tears. I rested my fingers on them, and slowly opened them to bright sunlight flooding the room. I could hear movement downstairs, and glanced over at Lola's bed.

She always left the covers in a messy heap when she got up, and usually I made her bed when I made my own. But the thin duvet was straightened, the pillows plumped, just as I'd left them the day before. Although she had been coming in late, she'd never stayed out all night before, and I groaned at my failure to stay awake. If I'd known sooner that she wasn't back, I could have gone to find her before Dad woke up. He was going to be furious.

Pushing myself wearily out of bed to go and look for her, I plodded over to the wardrobe to find a clean T-shirt and pulled open the door. For a second I stood and stared, bemused. There were some things of mine hanging on the left-hand side, but Lola's side was almost empty. Grabbing the bag we had been using for our dirty clothes, I upended it on the rug, separating my things from Lola's. Between what remained in the wardrobe and what was in the dirty washing, I could see that most of Lola's clothes were missing.

Her bright green backpack, which sat in the corner of the room when she was in, was gone – but I would expect that if she was out. She took it with her everywhere. I jumped up from my hands and knees and rushed to her bedside table, where she kept her money. Even Lola wasn't daft enough to take it with her to the beach. The envelope that she had been keeping it in had gone. She'd withdrawn the full £2,000 from the account that Mum had set up, saying she wanted to see the money, to touch it. Dad had been livid. He said Mum should have ensured Lola couldn't get her hands on it until she was twenty-one, but it was too late by then. I knew she'd spent some of it, but there had been at least £1,500 left in the envelope.

'Dad! Have you seen Lola?' I called from the landing, leaning over the banister.

'Isn't she in bed?'

'No, it doesn't look as if she slept here.' I ran downstairs. This wasn't something to shout to him. 'I might be overreacting but, Dad, her money's gone, and some of her clothes.'

Dad dropped his cereal spoon with a clatter. 'What?'

Without waiting for me to reply, he raced upstairs. I could hear him pulling out drawers, banging the wardrobe door.

'*Fuck!* What have you done, Lola?' I heard him cry.

I rushed up the stairs. 'We need to call the police, Dad.'

He spun round. 'Don't be ridiculous, Nancy. She's just gone a bit too far. She'll be back later – you wait and see.'

I didn't believe him. Or at least I hoped he was right, but I wasn't prepared to sit there and do nothing.

'I'm going to look for her. Are you coming?'

He looked away. 'No, I'll wait here in case she comes back. She and I have some talking to do, and the kids on the beach are more likely to talk to you than to me. You go, Nancy.' I was hurrying towards the door when he spoke again. 'Why didn't you realise there was something the matter? You're her *sister!*'

Tears stung my eyes because he was right, and if I hadn't fallen asleep I would have realised sooner that she wasn't back. But I didn't have time to try to make excuses. All I wanted to do was find Lola.

I ran all the way to the beach, but it was early and there weren't many people there. I recognised a girl who was already spreading her towel to catch the morning rays of the sun. To my shame, I'd watched my sister with her friends many times – or at least I had until I met Liam – and I'd seen this girl talking to Lola.

I raced down the beach towards her. She was a surly-looking girl with unnaturally dark hair that fell straight to a razor-sharp edge halfway down her back.

'Have you seen Lola?' I shouted as I ran, panic clear in my voice.

She looked shocked at my expression, but then her eyes slid away from mine.

'No, sorry.'

'When did you last see her?'

She shook her head, again avoiding my eyes.

'What aren't you telling me? I'm going to call the police if I don't find her soon, so you can tell me, or you can tell them.'

She looked scared then. 'Lola isn't my responsibility.'

'No, but she's mine. So where is she? What's happened?'

She dropped to her knees to straighten her towel, and I knew this was so she didn't have to look at me.

'She's not at home, then?'

I tutted loudly. 'If she was at home, I wouldn't be asking, would I? Her bed's not been slept in, and some of her stuff's gone. What do you know?'

She sighed. 'Oh fuck. She did it, then?'

'Did *what*?' I practically screamed the words at her.

'She's been planning to do a runner for a few days. Her and Quinn.'

'Who the hell is Quinn?'

She gave me a scowl. 'Everyone knows Quinn! You can't miss her – thinks she's bloody Marilyn Monroe.'

I knew who she meant. I'd seen her on the beach. She stood out because she was so different from the other girls with their identikit long hair, constantly being flicked back over their shoulders, and their skimpy bikinis. Quinn's hair was a mad mass of white curls – obviously dyed as her eyebrows were jet black. With her bright red lipstick and fifties-style all-in-one swimming costume, she certainly stood out from the crowd, which I presume was her intention.

'So Quinn was running away too?'

'Yeah. Her mum's always accusing her of stealing money, but it's her mum's boyfriend who's doing it. Quinn can't prove it, but she can't take it any longer. She's had it planned for days, and Lola asked if she could go with her. They were heading for London. That's all I know.'

For a moment I couldn't speak, and the girl started to unload things from her bag – anything to avoid my gaze.

'Did Lola say why she wanted to run?' I asked, my voice shaking.

'Not to me. I think she told Quinn – to make sure she'd take her, I suppose. But I don't have a clue.' Finally, she looked at me. 'I'm sorry – really – but that's all I know, and it's exactly what I'll tell the police, if I'm asked.'

I demanded that she gave me her name and turned to trudge back up the beach.

Lola had gone.

TWENTY-THREE

I tell Effie the basics of what happened, and how I finally
managed to persuade Dad that we had to call the police, saying
that if he didn't, I would. He wasn't happy.

'He was sure it was just a stunt, designed to get our attention. He thought she'd be back in twenty-four hours, and things
weren't helped by the police, who were prepared to dismiss the
whole thing because Lola had left with someone older – technically an adult. She'd gone with a girl called Quinn – a bit
different from the other kids.'

'I know who you mean. That'll be Quinn Asher – and
you're right, she was certainly different. Still is, but not quite so
extreme. She's come back to the area since her mum moved
away.'

I lean towards her, biting my lip. 'Are you serious? Do you
know where I can find her? She could tell me where Lola went.'

'I don't know where she lives, but I can ask around if you
like.' I feel a brief wave of optimism, but Effie is frowning.
'Nancy, there's no saying they stuck together after they left, you
know – it was eleven years ago – but I promise to find out what I
can. Didn't the police track Quinn down at the time?'

'They were useless. I got a load of bullshit about the fact that Lola had gone voluntarily with Quinn, who was eighteen – and that they didn't class Lola as vulnerable. But they could have done more to try to find her. They *should have* done more. She was just a kid.'

I remember the police interviews. They asked if we knew of any reason Lola might have felt she had to get away, and I told them about Mum dying. I even admitted that I thought Lola blamed me for it because she could barely bring herself to look at me. I didn't mention that she had been a bit wayward since we'd arrived in Cornwall, or about the arguments with Dad, convincing myself it was nothing more than normal teenage rebellion.

'They went through the motions,' I tell Effie as she starts to drag boxes from the shed. 'They tried to track Lola's phone, but it was switched off. They accessed her call history, and the last call she received was from Quinn's phone, which they said had been disconnected. They promised to continue to monitor both phones, but they didn't seem too hopeful. If neither of them wanted to be found they'd have both ditched their SIMs, if not their phones. The CCTV at the bus and train stations was checked, but I knew it wouldn't help. According to the other kids, Quinn had done a deal with a couple of guys who were driving to London. They were giving Quinn and Lola a lift, but no one had the first idea who they were. The police asked Quinn's family to get in touch if they heard from her, but the mother said if she knew where her daughter was she'd have her arrested for nicking her money, so she wasn't expecting to see her again.'

'Nice,' Effie said, her eyes wide at the thought of such maternal malice.

I remember the two police officers. One of them, a young woman with dark hair, neatly tied back in a bun, was sympathetic even though she didn't achieve much. She asked her colleague to check the house and the outhouses while she talked to Dad about the steps they would go through and I was charged with giving him the tour. Not that he was particularly interested. He wasn't much older than me, and I remember he had a long face and a spotty chin.

'I'll poke my nose in all the obvious places, in case she's hiding or you've bumped her off and hidden her somewhere,' he said with a grin that suggested I was supposed to find his words either amusing or engaging. They were clearly neither, and were in such poor taste that I was tempted to report him. But compared to my worries about Lola, it was nothing.

After the police left, Dad and I sat at the kitchen table, clutching cups of tea as if our lives depended on it.

'Why's she done this?' he muttered. His face looked haggard, and it struck me that this had hit him much harder than Mum dying. I'm sure he felt he should have protected his daughter better. 'She'll ruin us all, you know.'

I had no idea what he meant, but I felt sure that if I asked he would get angry with me. Despite my silence, it didn't stop him from throwing some of the blame my way.

'You should have kept a better eye on her, Nancy. You're her big sister, but you've hardly been here for the last week. Where the hell have you been, and why in God's name didn't you know there was something wrong with her?'

The guilt settled like a weight on my chest and it's still with me every day. Maybe Dad was right. I know I'd stopped worrying about Lola, thinking it was Dad's job to deal with her excesses, and he'd told me not to push her. But I should have paid more attention. If only I had, maybe she would never have left. And Dad was right. I'd hardly been at the cottage.

I'd been with Liam.

. . .

Effie is pulling things out of the shed, and I stand behind her, keeping my distance.

'There are no rats.' She laughs. 'Or if there are, we're making so much noise that they'll have scurried away. You can come a bit closer, you know.'

I edge warily towards the door. From my vague recollection of coming this far with the police officer, nothing seems to have changed. There's an old bike propped up against the back, plus an orange hover mower that appears to have never been used – and looking at the state of the grass in the back garden, I would guess that's true. A few tools are hanging from nails, and along one side are a series of plastic boxes, stuffed with goodness knows what.

'Hey, these are a bit of a find. They'll be great for trans-porting stuff to the charity shop. And they're sealed – so no rats in here!' Effie says, clearly delighted with her discovery. 'I wonder what's squirrelled away in them.'

'No idea. The police officer didn't open them as they're not big enough to have been hiding Lola,' I say with a sour note in my voice.

Effie pulls the first one towards her and prises off the lid. I can't see what's in there from my position by the door.

'Just bags of fertiliser. Here you go,' she says, hefting another box from the shed. 'I'll pass them all out, and you can check them.'

She passes me the next box. No animals, it's true. But lots of packets of seeds, some opened and looking slightly mouldy, others untouched.

'This one's a bit heavier,' Effie says, as she passes me a pink plastic box.

I dump it on the ground and lift the lid. There are some bits of scrunched-up newspaper on top, but I catch a glimpse of something underneath – a colour that I recognise.

I freeze, not wanting to believe what I'm seeing. In spite of the blistering sun on my back, I shiver. Then suddenly I'm scrabbling frantically at the paper, tearing it away to reveal what's underneath.

'What's up?' Effie asks, and a shadow falls across me as she moves towards me and blocks out the heat of the sun. 'Nancy, what is it?'

I don't answer.

'You're as white as a sheet.'

I still don't answer. I can't. Lying there, stuffed so full that clothes overflow from the top, is an emerald-green backpack. I picture it being lifted off the kitchen table each morning during that summer, being casually flung over one shoulder, holding nothing but a bikini and a towel.

It's Lola's.

TWENTY-FOUR

The green backpack is sitting between us on the kitchen table. I know I should look inside, but I can't. The minute I do, I will be forced to acknowledge the dreadful thoughts spinning through my mind.

Effie is making me yet another cup of tea. She has no idea what to say to me, so she's trying to keep busy. Finally she sits down and places a mug in front of me.

'Is there anything I can do? Would you like me to look inside?'

I shake my head, and without making a conscious decision jump to my feet and upend the backpack on the table, shaking it to dislodge the items rammed into the corners. It's not the biggest bag in the world, but Lola seems to have squeezed almost her entire summer wardrobe in there.

Effie is sitting across from me, silently watching. I'm glad she's not trying to come up with some inane explanation.

I flop back down in the chair again, and then I remember the pockets on the front. My shaking hands struggle to unbuckle them. One holds nothing more than odd bits of make-up, but stuffed well down into the other is an envelope. I know what it is. Lola's money.

I start to count, licking my fingers as I separate the notes. With a groan, I throw the money back on the table. It's all here – every penny. Fifteen hundred and twenty pounds.

Finally, Effie speaks. 'What are you thinking, Nancy?'

I don't want to think. It's too painful. She left. She ran away with Quinn. We know this. The police interviewed the kids she'd hung out with, and everyone agreed that was what happened.

I can almost convince myself that she might have left without her clothes – beach clothes. But I find it impossible to believe that she left without her money.

My mind is flooded with shocking, horrifying images of someone hurting Lola, dragging her, kicking and screaming, into the back of a van or the boot of a car to be taken God knows where for purposes that don't bear contemplating. I shake my head as if it will clear the thoughts and stop worse ideas from taking root.

I want to scream, *What happened to my sister? Where are you, Lola?*

Effie's voice is quiet. 'I hate to say this, Nancy, but you need to call the police.'

I groan and point at the backpack. 'They should have found this eleven years ago, but they didn't try hard enough, did they? What are they going to find out after all this time? They'll just tell me she's twenty-six now, no longer a vulnerable fifteen-year-old. If they weren't interested then, do you really think they will be now?'

'I do, yes. Call the police, Nancy.'

Effie leaves the room and takes herself off to sit on one of the old chairs in the cobbled front yard. I'm grateful; glad she's close by and that I'm not alone. With shaking fingers, I make the call, but at the last minute I decide I'm not going to tell them anything on the phone. I want to see the expression on their faces – to see if this is every bit as serious as I think it is. I don't want them to have any chance to dismiss me, and anyway, I'm not certain I can say the words out loud.

A few moments later, Effie cautiously pokes her head around the door.

'Have you finished?'

I nod and do my best to smile at her.

'How did it go?'

I sigh. 'It didn't, really. I mentioned there was a female officer who dealt with the case initially, and I wondered if she was available. She was at least sympathetic, and I thought it would be better to talk to someone who was familiar with the case. Apparently she's a detective sergeant now. She's out right now, but they said if I don't need someone to come urgently, they'll speak to her when she gets back.'

'Do you remember her name?'

'She was PC King, now DS King, apparently.'

Effie's lips form a perfect O shape.

'What?' I ask.

'I know her. Stephanie King. Look, I realise you don't think much of how the police handled Lola's disappearance, but Steph's okay, you know.'

I make a scoffing sound. 'Really?'

'Yes. She'd have been very junior back then, but she's smart. She was at school with my sister. I used to trail round after them both, thinking they were the bee's knees, but she had a tricky time of it herself, if I remember. Her dad was a bit of a prick. Left his family for his wife's best friend, and then wasn't in touch with his kids for years. Steph's anger showed through for a while and she was well known for being stroppy, but her brother suffered the most – ended up depressed. I think he still lives with his mum, although he's my age.' She chuckles. 'What am I talking about? I still live with *my* mum! All I'm saying is that I think you can trust Stephanie. You need to trust *someone* and, stroppy or not, she has a good heart.'

I am only half listening. I can't take my eyes off the money, and although I try to tell myself there is a logical explanation and Lola will be somewhere in London with a job, a home, a partner, I know that's wishful thinking. There are other explanations that are far more plausible, and infinitely more disturbing. I try to swallow, but my throat feels too tight.

'What do you want to do now?' Effie asks. 'I guess you don't want to carry on sorting out the house?'

I shake my head. I can't even think about china, embroidered doilies and the like.

'I need to walk, to get out of here for a while. Do you mind?'

'Course not. If you want company, I'm happy to walk by your side and speak as much or as little as you like.'

'I think I need to be alone for a while. Is that okay?'

She gives me a gentle smile and nods. 'Course it is.' Effie stands up and leans down to give me a peck on the cheek. 'Call me, any time you like.'

I look at her, tears burning my eyes, unable to speak. But I can see she understands, and she closes the door softly behind her as she leaves.

After a few minutes I stick my phone in the back pocket of my jeans and follow her out of the door. I don't need to think about where I'm going. I yearn for the sound of the ocean pounding against the rocks, the cries of the gulls, the wind whipping my hair around my face, every sense stirred. It will calm me and bring some perspective. At least, that's what I'm hoping.

TWENTY-FIVE

'DI Harris-Cooke, DS King here.' Stephanie hated the formality, but the new DI insisted on it, except with those she considered her peers or superiors, to whom she was HC. Unbeknown to her, that was also the name used by everyone else out of her hearing.

'I presume you're calling to tell me your mission to retrieve the skeleton was a success?'

'Yes and no, ma'am. We located the skeleton and Molly – Dr Treadwell, that is – climbed up with me to look at it in *situ*. All we know for sure is that our victim had a broken leg, and they weren't wearing shoes – which may suggest they were swimming, or they fell from a boat. But we don't know if they got *themselves* onto that ledge, or if they were helped, pushed, or carried by someone else, so the crime scene manager decided forensics should have a look before we remove the bones.'

'And does Dr Treadwell concur?'

'She does. Dr Davies, the forensic anthropologist, agreed to return later today, when the tide allows. We'll take a couple of CSIs to gather any evidence, then Dr Davies will collect the bones.'

'Do we know any more about the body – male, female, age?'

'Dr Davies hasn't seen the remains yet, and Molly didn't express an opinion because some of the clothing was still in place. She doesn't want to remove it until the skeleton has been taken to the mortuary. A few of the bones have been dislodged, probably by scavengers – bats or possibly swifts – so Dr Davies wants to put the whole thing together to get measurements and conduct a full examination. The body could have been lying there for up to twelve years, but no longer because the cave was used in a scene in a BBC drama, if you remember.'

'I don't watch drama – especially when it involves crime.'

Stephanie had an image of the DI sitting there with a notebook jotting down all the inevitable inaccuracies in police procedure. When she and Gus watched, they yelled at the screen. That would be far too undignified for HC.

'Let me know when you have more details,' she said. 'In the meantime, you have other cases that need your attention, including the burglaries.'

'I do, but something came up while I was out. A teenage girl – Lola Holland, a holidaymaker – went missing from Trevyan eleven years ago. I was the first responder, and we did all the usual checks, but several people knew she'd been planning to run away, and we couldn't find any evidence of a crime. Now her sister, Nancy, is back in Cornwall – her first time since it happened – and she's left a message to say she's discovered something new.'

'Did she say what?'

'No. She wants to talk to me.'

'Send a uniform to take the details.'

'She asked for me specifically, so I'd like to follow it up. It was a dreadful time for the family. The mother had just died, then Lola went missing, and a few weeks later the dad died too.'

'And nobody thought it odd that a girl – Nancy, you said –

had lost her mum, her sister and her dad in the space of a few weeks? Was there a lot of money involved?'

Stephanie blew out a long breath. She knew how it sounded, and she should have expressed it better.

'Sorry, ma'am. I see this as more of a tragedy for a young girl. I never felt a moment's suspicion.'

'Some of the world's most prolific killers have been apparently above suspicion, Sergeant King. Go and see her, but when you do, think about what I've just said.'

'I'll bear that in mind. In any case, it will have to be tomorrow. I'm back out in the boat in a couple of hours, so I'll ask her if I can pop round in the morning, before my shift, so it doesn't interfere with my other cases.'

There was a weighty silence from the other end of the phone, and Stephanie knew that the DI had more to say.

'It must be clear to Nancy Holland that the chances of discovering the whereabouts of her sister after all this time are remote. If one assumes she has evidence suggesting something else happened – something we hadn't considered – we have to ask ourselves why, after all this time, she's bringing it to us now. Is there something else in play here? Is she attention-seeking, perhaps? Or is there something she's known all along but has been holding back? Keep your mind open to all possibilities.'

Stephanie ended the call and sat back in her chair. Could HC be serious? Maybe it was just her way of telling Stephanie not to make assumptions.

She looked at her watch. She hadn't eaten anything for hours, but it was nearly time to set off for the second boat trip of the day and she wanted to refresh her memory of Nancy and her family. She had requested the files on the deaths of both Janice and Ray Holland years ago, so turning to her computer, she pulled up the notes she'd taken, together with Lola's file. With one hand she started to scroll through the documents.

With the other she opened her desk drawer and grabbed three chocolate biscuits from her emergency stash.

She didn't need the notes to remind her that Nancy had been the one to discover her mother's body, but she struggled to square what she remembered of the girl with the suspicions HC had put into her mind. As far as she could see there was no way Nancy could have been implicated in her father's death. He died in a fatal car accident an hour away from their home and Nancy couldn't drive – although for a girl brought up on a farm, Stephanie had to concede that the lack of a licence wasn't necessarily conclusive evidence.

Closing the file, she leaned back in her chair and nibbled at a biscuit. As Gus often told her, people are not always who we think they are. Maybe her younger self was too ready to accept Nancy's apparent grief at face value.

TWENTY-SIX

As I trudge along the coastal path, I stare out to sea, waiting for it to work its magic, but it's not happening. I can think of nothing but the backpack. The thought that something happened to Lola, that I didn't look hard enough, makes me dizzy.

I argue to myself that she was impetuous, and something must have made her change her plans. Maybe Quinn had plenty of money and had offered to help Lola out. Maybe the boys who were driving her to London had moved their plans forward and Lola didn't want to miss her chance by coming for her backpack. I can only guess that she hid it in the shed so she could collect it when Dad and I were asleep. The only thing that makes any sense is that the timings changed. At least, that's what I try to convince myself.

I'm so lost in thought that it takes a few seconds for me to realise that my mobile is ringing, and it's a number I don't recognise.

'Hello?'

'Good afternoon. This is Detective Sergeant Stephanie

King, Devon and Cornwall Police. Am I speaking to Nancy Holland?'

'Yes, that's right.'

'Hello, Nancy. I believe we met when you reported your sister Lola missing. I was a uniformed constable then.'

'I remember you.'

'It was a tough time for you. How are you doing?'

I can hear the sympathy in the other woman's voice, and suddenly I feel like crying. I want to shout that she didn't do enough eleven years ago, and I don't know why I should trust her now. In fact, I *don't* trust her – or any of them. We're just statistics, and one missing fifteen-year-old is worth nothing. They put up a few photos around town, asked a few questions, but it wasn't enough. She was my sister!

I don't say any of that, of course.

'I'm okay,' I manage, swallowing the lump in my throat.

'I understand you've come across some new information about Lola's disappearance. Do you want to tell me about it?'

I pause, but not for long.

'I'd rather show you, if that's okay?'

'I'm sorry, Nancy, but there's somewhere I need to be right now. Can I call round to see you tomorrow? It will be about eight in the morning.'

'That's fine. She's been gone for eleven years, so another few hours won't make much difference.'

I don't try to hide the sour note in my voice, or tell her that her response just reinforces my belief in their lack of interest.

'If you think it's urgent, I can send someone else now, if you prefer?'

'I'd rather talk to you.'

'Right. Well, I'll see you in the morning, then. If you change your mind, phone the station and we'll get someone out to you.'

We say our goodbyes and hang up. At least she hasn't dismissed it out of hand, but I'm frustrated it will have to wait until tomorrow. On the one hand, I want her to take it seriously; on the other, I want her to say that it's nothing – it's not important.

But I don't think that's what she will say.

I suppose it was inevitable that I would end up here, only a few hundred metres from the route down to Liam's cove and cottage. My feet have followed their well-trodden path, and subconsciously I was probably planning this all along, but now that I'm here I feel a strange pang of fear. What if he comes up the path and sees me?

I feel drawn to the cliff edge. I want to see the cove – to decide if I imagined feelings far more powerful than they were – and it will distract me from dark thoughts about Lola.

If I stand on tiptoe to peer over the tall hedge I can just make out the clifftop, but the hawthorn seems thicker since my last visit, its slender branches intertwined like fingers holding tightly to each other. It's hard to find a way through. I trudge up and down, peering at the thorny shrubs, looking for a weak spot. Then I see a gap, barely noticeable beneath the ivy, and, casting a furtive look over my shoulder, I tear the leaves and creeping stems away and scramble through without too many scratches.

I'm not sure what I'm doing or what I hope to achieve. Maybe I need to exorcise Liam's ghost, to laugh at the child that I was.

After those first couple of days, I ran happily to the cove each morning. He never let me go down alone and always came up to guide me, saying the path was too steep, tricky in places. I didn't mind, because he told me to hang on to him – to grab the waistband of his shorts and follow his footsteps. Sliding my fingers under the fabric against the bare flesh of his lower back felt both daring and erotic to me, and by the time we reached the beach I couldn't wait for him to turn and kiss me.

For that short period of time, I could think of nothing but Liam. He was the focus of my every waking moment, and he invaded my dreams. His laughter, his teasing, the shape of his shoulders as we swam together in the cove, every stroke strong, forceful. He would roll onto his back in the water and laugh at my prim breaststroke, my chin resting on the surface, terrified of taking a mouthful of the salty brine.

As we lay on the sand, he would draw the back of his finger up my leg and tell me how he loved my pure white skin, and for the first time in my life I felt sexy and desirable. It was all part of his game plan. He must have realised how desperate I was to feel loved.

I didn't want anyone to know about him – not Dad, not Lola. He was mine, and mine alone. I made excuses to be out for lunch, saying I was taking photos, and Lola was rarely home during the day. I always returned to the cottage in the evening. I didn't think it was fair to leave Dad alone, although he was quiet and withdrawn. Liam fished at night, so the days were his and the evenings belonged to my family. Not that Lola ever came back to eat with us, and most nights Dad went to one of the bars in town as soon as we'd eaten.

Lola knew something was going on with me, though.

'Who is he?' she asked one night on one of the rare occasions when we were both in our bedroom and awake at the same time.

'I don't know what you're talking about,' I said, and she glared at me with an intensity that I didn't understand.

'Good for you, Nancy.' It wasn't said with any conviction, and I didn't know why it should annoy her if I'd met someone. She almost sounded sarcastic.

I'd debated telling her about Liam, but there was something off in her response, and anyway I wanted to keep him close. It was as if I was wrapping my love for him tightly, hugging it to myself. I wasn't ready to open the parcel for anyone else to see.

It felt like an opportunity for me to try to talk to Lola, though. Perhaps I could find out why she was being so difficult.

'Tell me about your friends,' I'd said. 'The people you hang out with at the beach.'

'Nothing to tell. They're okay. Good fun.' She was a bit dismissive, so I tried another tack. I needed her to know that I was there, if she needed me.

'How are you feeling, now that Mum's gone? Please tell me you don't blame me, like Dad does.'

She just looked at me. She said nothing for a few moments, then: 'I don't know where to start, Nancy, so let's not go there.'

With that, she grabbed a towel from the bed and marched off to the bathroom.

I was desperate to know that at least someone in my family believed me about Mum, but I'd refused to tell Lola about Liam so I couldn't criticise her for not wanting to talk. I'd have to tell her and Dad soon, though, because I was in love and, child that I was, I believed he was my future.

That bubble burst the very next day.

We'd had a wonderful day at the cove. The weather was perfect and we'd made love twice under the shelter of the over-hanging cliff where we couldn't be seen – even by walkers as nosy as I'd been.

I was lying on my towel, stroking his back as he sat hunched, facing out to sea.

'I can't see you again, Nancy,' he said.

My hand stopped moving. 'What?' I was sure I must have misheard.

'I'm sailing across to France tonight. I'm picking up my wife. She's been there visiting her family. We'll be home tomorrow, so obviously you can't come here again.'

His wife?

He still wasn't looking at me, so I scrambled onto my knees and crawled round to kneel in front of him.

'Say that again.' I heard my voice crack as I stared at him, expecting his mouth to lift at the corners, to hear him say it was some sort of sick joke. But he didn't.

'My wife. I should have told you about her before now, but you looked as if you needed someone to pay you some attention, even if it could only be for a while.'

Could this be true? Could he really be married? Had I been lying naked next to someone else's husband? What did that make me? And he didn't even look sorry.

Sobbing, I leaped to my feet, grabbing my clothes and pulling them on.

'You *bastard*. How *could* you, Liam? I thought you *loved* me.'

How childish those words seem to me now.

The eyes he turned on me were cold.

'Well, you thought wrong,' he said. His lip curled in a half-smile. 'It was fun, though.'

I didn't wait to hear any more. I ran back up the steep slope and raced along the coastal path, but I didn't return to our cottage. I couldn't face Dad or Lola, so I found a bench and sat facing the sea, arms wrapped tightly around myself, sobbing, my heart breaking.

I had never thought for a moment that Liam might be married; he was only twenty-five. Was he telling the truth, or was it simply a cruel, wicked way to get rid of me? Had he realised I was hoping for more?

The sun was hot on my bent head, and I could feel it burning my tender scalp. People passed by, one kind lady asking if I was okay, but I shook my head, unable to speak, and waved away her concern.

Finally the sobs subsided, my tears dried, and I was about to wend my way wearily back to the cottage when I was hit by an extraordinary thought. What if Liam had made up the story because my holiday was coming to an end? Was that possible?

I lifted my face to the sun, wild hope stirring in my heart. Maybe he believed telling me he was married was the kindest thing to do – the cleanest break; that it would be easier for me to return home and put my love for him behind me forever.

The wife was a lie – she had to be.

I don't know how – the optimism of youth, I suspect – but I was confident I was right, and by the time I returned to the cottage my tears had dried. No one knew – not Dad, not Lola – that only an hour earlier I had been grief-stricken, all hopes of a future with Liam shattered.

I could hardly wait for the next day. I knew what I was going to do. I would go back and tell Liam I understood what he had done and why, but he was wasting his time. I was going nowhere.

TWENTY-SEVEN

Once again, Stephanie was sitting on the harbour wall, ready for another trip to the cave. She wasn't looking forward to it. There was something ominous about that dark, dank space.

This time, only the forensic anthropologist was needed, accompanied by the crime scene manager and a couple of CSIs, who would gather any evidence from the scene then help Carla Davies retrieve the bones.

Stephanie's phone pinged with a message: *Shall I light the barbecue again?*

She knew Gus was worried – concerned at her reaction to the news of Daisy, the daughter he had fathered but never met. He had to be if he was cooking for her two nights in a row.

Stephanie's eyes started to burn with tears.

'Oh, for God's sake,' she muttered to herself, angrily brushing the tears away. 'Get a grip, woman!'

This was no time to be irrational. She had to put her own emotions aside and focus on the poor child who was lying sick in hospital.

Her phone pinged again. *I thought I could do some fish? Spice it up a bit. Is that okay?*

There was only one answer she could give. *That would be perfect. I'll be late though – another boat trip. I'll let you know when I'm on my way back. xx*

She stared at the screen for a few seconds longer. She hated to feel vulnerable and didn't want to be like her mother, who still mourned the man who had cheated on her and left her over twenty years ago. But now wasn't the time to bolster her own emotional defences. Daisy wasn't a threat to her unless she made her one.

Her thoughts were interrupted by the sound of voices. Carla Davies had arrived, and Stephanie was pleased to see that the same crew would take them back to the cave. They exuded an aura of calm efficiency that neutralised the eeriness of the cave.

Unsurprisingly, Carla didn't seem inclined to talk as the boat pulled out of the harbour, and that suited Stephanie. It gave her a chance to think about Lola Holland. She had taken the initial missing-from-home report with an officer called Drew, who had a weird surname she couldn't remember. What she *could* remember, though, was that Drew was an idiot, and it had irritated her that she'd had to drag him along with her. She had sent him off to search the house under the watchful eye of Nancy while she spoke to the dad.

She hadn't known what to make of Ray Holland. He seemed anxious, but angry with Lola for running away.

'What will happen if she's found?' he asked.

'I'm sorry, I don't entirely understand the question?'

'Will she be in trouble? Will you have to question her or anything? Does she get a record?'

'All we're concerned about is your daughter's welfare, Mr Holland. I'll take your initial statement, and we'll be talking to the people she knew to try to understand where she may have gone, but the majority of teenagers who run away from home turn up after a day or two realising it was a daft thing to do, and she won't be in any trouble from us. There'll be what we call a return-home interview in the interests of finding out where she went and why she left. And of course we'll want to make sure she's okay and that no harm came to her while she was away.'

Mr Holland had run his fingers through his fine, fair hair. His eyes looked unfocused, and he had bitten his bottom lip so hard a spot of blood had sprung up.

'It's obvious why she's gone. Her mum just died. She's upset, not herself. She's probably confused, doesn't know what she's doing.'

'Is there anything else you can think of? Anything happening back at home that might make her not want to return? Is she bullied at school? Does she have a boyfriend? Maybe there's someone she doesn't want to see.'

Mr Holland's eyes had opened wide, and he stared at Stephanie without speaking. 'That makes sense, doesn't it? I don't know if she has a boyfriend, but I bet that's it. Maybe he dumped her. She'd never admit it, though. She keeps things to herself, does Lola. I wish she'd told me what was bothering her.'

Stephanie thought Lola's father seemed relieved to have an explanation, something rational to cling to; something that didn't feel like a rejection of him and Nancy.

Before they left, Stephanie managed to speak to Nancy on her own.

'Can you show me her bedroom, Nancy?'

'I've already looked,' Drew said. 'Nothing to see.'

Stephanie glared at him. 'Nevertheless...'

Nancy seemed distraught and Stephanie didn't want to prolong her pain, but the girl turned and walked up the stairs and Stephanie followed.

'Sometimes it's easier to talk one to one, and I wondered if there's anything you've noticed about Lola recently – anything out of the ordinary in her behaviour. How have you all been getting on?'

Nancy had hung her head. 'It's my fault. I've been seeing someone and not paying Lola enough attention. Dad says if I'd kept an eye on her this wouldn't have happened.'

'You can't know that for sure, Nancy – and from what I can gather, she was having a good time with friends on the beach. She's nearly sixteen and you couldn't be expected to monitor her movements. What were things like at home? Was she finding it tough since your mum died?'

Nancy had made a *pfff* sound, so Stephanie waited.

'Look, it's hard to describe how things were at home. Mum had been ill for over two years, and I looked after her. Lola kept out of the way. It bugged me, to be honest, because as she got older she could have done more – even reading to Mum or something would have been good, maybe giving me the occasional night off. But she was at school all day, then said she had homework to do. She did her washing and Dad's, some housework and stuff, but she hardly ever visited Mum's room. I tried not to resent it, and I was hoping we'd get closer over this holiday, you know? That I'd understand her a bit better.' The pain in Nancy's eyes was so devastating that Stephanie had to look away.

'And it didn't work?'

'No. She made it clear that I was of little or no importance, and I felt I didn't know her at all. Perhaps it was my fault. I don't know. I just feel I've messed everything up.'

At that Nancy had dropped her head and started to weep silent tears – always the worst kind in Stephanie's mind. They spoke far more strongly of despair than noisy sobs.

She had seen Nancy a few more times after that, but the girl appeared to have withdrawn into herself.

Stephanie sighed at the memory. Whatever Nancy had found now, she hoped it was something positive that might free her of the guilt she undoubtedly felt.

'Steph?' The voice of one of the CSIs interrupted her thoughts. 'We're there. You ready?'

She looked towards the shore as the engine note of the boat changed. They had arrived at the cave.

She pulled her jacket closer across her chest. She was already shivering, and they hadn't yet left the early evening sunshine.

TWENTY-EIGHT

I'm getting close to the edge of the cliff, and I suddenly feel dizzy as the memories come flooding back. I can picture every detail of the first time I came here. I should have run then, but instead I followed Liam to the beach and was quickly consumed by an intense but fatal passion.

I remember my racing heart, my dry mouth, the promise of what was to come, but the memory that lingers longest and hits hardest is of the last time I came, the day *after* Liam told me he was married. I can't stop myself from looking over my shoulder now, as if the thought of him may have summoned his presence. But there's no one there.

It's hard for me to accept how foolish I was, but despite Liam having told me it was over I made the mistake of going back. I didn't go down to the cove. I wanted to watch from the clifftop, to see him arrive back from France, to prove there was no wife, convinced I was right.

I lay on the edge of the cliff all day, waiting for him to sail into the bay, but time passed and there was no sign of his boat.

I remember the midday sun beating down, scorching me through my thin T-shirt. And still he wasn't back. It was early evening before I heard the chug of the engine and watched as his boat edged its way into the bay.

My heart was thudding as I pulled the camera from my backpack, adjusting the zoom lens to maximum amplification, the first doubts hitting me. What if I was wrong?

Liam came out onto the deck to drop the anchor. He was alone. I felt a stab of pure joy. I had been right. There was no one with him.

Then he leaned towards the cabin. He looked as if he might be speaking and I began to feel slightly sick. I couldn't hear his words from so far away. Who was he talking to?

I pointed the lens at the wide oblong windows of the cabin. Was that movement I could see inside? It was, but before I could make out a face, Liam was moving again, climbing into the dinghy. Whoever was on the boat seemed to be staying there. He was coming ashore alone.

As the dinghy chugged towards the beach, I kept watch on the boat. There was still no one on deck, but someone moved the thin curtain at a window and I took a photo. I couldn't see who it was.

As Liam reached the shore and pulled the boat onto the sand, I took some quick shots of him and lowered my camera. Then, like the first time, I saw his head lift and his eyes swing towards mine. I felt a shock run through me. Whatever he was feeling for me at that moment, it had nothing to do with desire.

He dropped the rope he was holding and set off – racing across the sand towards the path.

I pushed the camera into my bag, slung it over my shoulder and scrambled to my feet, heading as fast as I could for the gap in the hedge. I didn't know if I could outrun him; I didn't know why I thought I needed to. This was Liam – my lover, the man I dreamed of night after night.

But this was a man incensed by my actions, and he was coming for me.

I ran, but I'd only just got through the hedge when he was on me. He grabbed me by the shoulder, spun me round and pushed me back through the hawthorn, away from prying eyes. I struggled to free myself, but he was too strong.

His face was white. 'What the fuck are you doing here, Nancy? I told you to stay away. I told you I didn't want to see you again – that my wife was coming home. What part of that was hard to understand?'

His hands were gripping my upper arms tight, and he shook me.

'You're hurting me, Liam,' I cried.

'This isn't hurting you,' he said. 'You don't know what the word means.'

He shook me again and lowered his head so his face was level with mine.

'Go, Nancy. You were a bit of fun, an easy target. But my wife's back now, and she can't know about you. Not *ever*. *Stay away!* Do you understand?'

His eyes were black, his lips a tight line. For a moment I thought he looked scared, but of what? Not of me. It had to be fear that his wife would find out, and in that moment I understood my dreams were just that – illusions, fantasies, the ridiculous hopes of a lonely girl.

He pushed me towards the hedge. 'You have no idea what I'm capable of, but if I ever see you here again, you'll find out.'

A touch of bravado made me splutter, 'You wouldn't hurt me.'

'You think? If I see you here again, I'll take you to a place where no one will ever find you, where the sea you love so much will rise up and swallow you in its depths. *Do you understand?*'

I stumbled away, scared to turn my back on him. I groped along the hedge behind me, sharp thorns scratching my hands until I felt the gap, and with a gasp of relief crouched low and squeezed through, looking at Liam one last time before I turned and ran.

I hadn't stopped at a bench this time. There was no point searching for excuses for his words – his threats. He meant every word, and all I wanted was to get back to the cottage, to throw myself face down on my bed and hide from the world.

I was still running fifteen minutes later as I passed the town beach. My little sister saw me and followed me to find out why I was crying.

And I told her to get lost.

I'd pushed those memories of Liam so far back, but it is thoughts of Lola, of the last time I saw her, that have brought me here today. If I hadn't been so devastated by the way Liam had treated me, it wouldn't have ended the way it did.

I'd been waiting nearly two weeks to talk to my sister, but I threw the opportunity away. I've tried to block the memory from my mind, choosing only to remember that I told her to get lost. Those words might be forgivable. But I can't fool myself any longer. It's time I faced up to the rest of what I said during my vicious, destructive outburst.

'Not everything's about you, Lola.' There was more. 'When have you ever shown a moment's concern for anyone else? Not for me, not for Mum. You couldn't even bring yourself to visit her room, so don't think you can start being the caring sister now. Just get lost.'

I'm so ashamed. I'm the reason she left. That's what I've always believed, and why I have never stopped looking for her. I thought she had a new life in London, and maybe she does. But since we've found her backpack it's harder to convince myself, and I feel sick with worry about what it might mean.

I'm angry – with myself for my verbal attack on Lola and with Liam for his careless disregard for my feelings – but despite my bitterness, I shiver as a moment of cold fear spirals through me. What if he sees me here again? What would he do to me now? Eleven years have passed, but if his wife discovers our affair I'm sure she will be just as devastated now as she would have been then. Maybe more so, if she thinks she's been living a lie all these years.

If he sees me, will he threaten me again? I feel my jaw clench. I'm not a frightened kid any longer.

I drop to my hands and knees and crawl towards the edge of the cliff, quickly untying my black hoodie from round my waist and putting it on. I pull up the hood to tuck my hair inside.

I lie flat on my belly, wishing I had my camera with me. I want to see how much he has changed, and I could zoom in with the powerful lens, but the beach is deserted. A boat is moored in the bay – a bigger one, so I guess fishing must be bringing in more money than before.

A shout startles me, but it's not a man's voice. It's a child's.

I look towards the cottage. The door is standing open, and a boy with sun-bleached hair runs out of the house and down onto the sand. He looks about ten or eleven, and he's quickly followed by two little girls, much younger and both with dark curls like Liam's. They look like twins. The children are laughing, the girls chasing the boy.

I hear someone call from the cottage. I can't hear what he says, but I don't need to. I'd know that voice anywhere.

The boy replies, and he's right below me so I hear his words. 'It's okay, Dad. I'll watch them – we won't go near the sea.' He turns and runs to the far side of the beach.

The twins are giggling as they chase their brother, but suddenly there is a wail as one of them trips and falls. The boy spins on his heel and hurries back towards her. He bends down and gently picks her up off the sand, rubbing her knee while she wraps her arms round his neck.

I rest my forehead on my folded arms. These lovely chil-

dren are his, and if the son wasn't already born when I met
Liam, it couldn't have been long afterwards. Maybe his wife –
Monique, according to Effie – was already pregnant. I groan at
the thought, and despite how I felt at the time, I pray she never
found out about me.

TWENTY-NINE

Returning to Liam's cove was madness. I thought it would be another ghost I could lay to rest, but the sight of his children has unnerved me. Liam was cruel to me, cruel to his wife, and yet his children appear delightful. Maybe he's a changed man.

Confused by the events of the day – Lola's backpack, Liam's family – I trudge home, determined never to go near his cove again, glad to be able to close the front door behind me and shut out the world.

I've just managed to persuade myself that it's not too early to open the bottle of wine that Effie brought last night when there's a knock at the door and I nearly jump out of my skin. It's early evening and still daylight, but I open the door just a crack and peer round.

'Hello, love. I've come to say I'm sorry.' I pull the door wider as I recognise Effie's mum, Angie. 'Effie's told me what happened, and I feel awful for giving you a hard time. Are you okay?'

'I'm fine, Mrs Dawson. Would you like to come in?'

'If you can spare five minutes – and please call me Angie.'

'Would you like a cup of tea?'

She sees the bottle of wine on the table.

'If that wine's open, I wouldn't mind a quick one,' she says with a grin. 'If that's okay?'

'Of course.'

I grab another glass and pour.

'It sounds like you've had a rough day, and I'm sorry about that. Have you decided what you want to do with the cottage, because despite how you might feel now, this town really is a great place to live?'

I don't know how to answer that. Finding Lola's backpack has changed everything. My plans to run back to London are forgotten, and I'm going nowhere until I know what happened to my sister.

Angie takes a sip of her wine, but like her daughter she doesn't wait for an answer. 'If you decide to sell, you'll have people biting your hand off. It's difficult for people with a small budget to find property here – especially youngsters like my Effie – so don't be surprised if you find someone knocking on your door asking if you're putting the cottage on the market.'

'Do you think people know that I own it now?'

Angie rolls her eyes. 'Of course! Helen was well known here, and everyone knows she's died. And they knew about you from your last visit. The older ones all wanted to have a nosy back then to see if you look like your mum.'

Angie carries on talking, but I'm not really listening. I'm trying to absorb what she just said.

'Sorry to interrupt, Angie, but how would they know what my mum looked like?'

Her head tilts to one side. 'Because they remember her – even though by the time you and Lola came here it was twenty years since they'd last seen her.'

'I didn't know she'd ever been here. She never mentioned it.'

Angie's eyebrows shoot up. 'How very strange. She came here all the time when she was a child, to stay with Helen during the school holidays. And when those useless parents of hers – sorry to speak ill of your grandparents – cleared off to Canada, she lived here for a year or so until she fell head over heels for your dad.'

Angie must see the look of bewilderment on my face. Why hadn't I known this? Why, if Mum was so close to Helen, had they lost touch all those years ago?

'Do you know anything about your grandparents on your mum's side?'

I shake my head. I thought both sets of grandparents had died long before I was born.

'Your grandma was Helen's sister. She and your granddad never wanted children, but then along popped Janice. They were determined she wasn't going to slow them down, so they did exactly what they wanted, packing her off here, expecting Helen to fill in the missing maternal bits. As soon as Janice was eighteen, they cleared off to their new life without a backward glance. Helen did her best to give your mum a home, but she was restless and Helen decided it would do them both good to go on a Mediterranean cruise – let her see a bit of the world. She wasn't expecting her to fall for the steward – your dad.'

That was one part of the story that I *did* know – that they had met on board the ship.

'What was she like – my mum?'

Angie is quiet for a moment, her head to one side.

'Truthful answer? I would say she found life quite a challenge. Despite everything Helen tried to do, she must have felt unloved, given that she was effectively abandoned by her parents time after time. I don't think she had much of a sense of self-worth, and I got that. Piss-poor parenting, if you'll excuse the phrase. Then she met your dad, and it was a real love match. She adored him, and I'm sure he gave her all the self-esteem she'd lacked.'

I find myself lost for words. However Mum and Dad must

have felt about each other all those years ago, I can't remember seeing anything of the adoration that Angie recalls.

Angie takes a last gulp of her wine. 'Anyway, love, I won't keep you. You should meet my mum some time. She can tell you far more about your aunt Helen and Janice than I can.'

She stands up and I follow her to the door. She stops and turns towards me, her face serious.

'There's one other thing, Nancy. I wasn't sure whether to mention it or not, but I'd rather you heard this from me than from anyone else.'

I swallow. There's only so much I can take right now.

'A teenage boy had a fall from a cliff and swam into a cave yesterday. They sent the lifeboat for him, but while he was waiting he saw something. I don't want you to panic, but they've discovered some bones – a skeleton.' I take a gulp of air and Angie hears me. 'I'm sorry, love, and I'm sure it's got nothing to do with your sister, but I wanted you to know what's being said. They know there was nothing in that cave twelve years ago, so it's more recent.'

She sees the expression on my face and reaches for me to pull me into a hug.

'Don't think the worst, Nancy. It could be anyone. But the whole town's talking about it, so I thought I should be the one to tell you.' She leans back, still holding my shoulders, and looks at me. 'Do you want me to stay?'

I shake my head and try to smile. 'No. It's kind of you, but I'm fine.'

I close the door behind her and lean against it. My legs give way beneath me, and with a low moan I sink to the floor.

THIRTY

Stephanie had found the second trip to the cave more gruelling than the first, mainly because she'd spent most of the time in the boat. The CSIs had examined the scene and helped a rather monosyllabic Carla Davies remove the skeleton, bone by bone, while Stephanie sat shivering in the cold, dank atmosphere.

'Why would smugglers use this cave?' she asked one of the crew. 'There's nowhere to go – no passage through the cliff, is there?'

'No, but it's well hidden and it's not accessible from the shore even at low tide. So they'd have holed up here with their stash of contraband until after dark.'

It was weird to imagine those men, sitting huddled in their small boats, waiting to bring ashore their smuggled stash of French brandy, or even tea – if Stephanie remembered her history lessons correctly.

She was brought back to the present by Tai, who plonked himself next to her in the boat, pulling off his white coverall as the engine rumbled back to life for their return journey to the harbour.

'Can't see any evidence of foul play in the cave, Steph, and apart from his broken leg, there was no obvious injury.'

'You said "his", so has sex been established?'

Tai shook his head. 'No, sorry. Easier than constantly saying "him or her". Dr Davies flatly refuses to speculate. She wants to get the skeleton back to reconstruct it. It's more difficult to tell the sex if the bones are those of a young person.'

'And are they?'

'That's what she intimated, but she's not the most forth-coming of people.'

Stephanie smiled. His thoughts mirrored hers exactly. 'Thanks, Tai. Let me know when you have your report, even if there's nothing much to say.'

'We've swept up everything that was on the ledge with him – but it was hard to see if there were any small artefacts that might give us a clue. We'll have a better look when we're back in the lab, although there was nothing obvious. Sorry, Steph.'

They travelled the rest of the way back in silence, and had just pulled into Newlyn Harbour when Stephanie's phone rang. 'Sarge, it's me.'

Stephanie closed her eyes and counted to three. 'Hello, me. How can I help?'

'Sorry, Sarge. I mean it's Jason... erm, PC Graves.'

'Yes, I know who me is. What's up?'

'We've had a call from Nancy Holland. She said she spoke to you earlier, and now she needs to speak to you urgently. Do you still have her number?'

Stephanie felt a tingle of alarm. Initially, Nancy had suggested she had found something that might be relevant to the case. She had sounded upset and worried, but this sounded much more concerning.

'I've got it, Jason. I'll call her now. Thanks.'

Stephanie ended the call as she stepped out of the boat. The transport was waiting for the skeleton, but she needed to speak to Nancy so signalled them to hang on for a moment.

Her call was answered immediately.

'Nancy? Stephanie King. I understand you want to speak to me?'

Stephanie listened as Nancy spoke, her voice high-pitched with a note of panic. Her words were lost as a ship sounded its horn close by.

'Slow down, Nancy. You'll have to repeat that – I'm sorry.'

'The skeleton – I heard about it. Do you think it's Lola?'

Stephanie would find it hard to deny that the thought had crossed her mind. They knew the body had to have been there for some time to become skeletonised, and they also knew that the timing fitted, but that didn't mean it was Lola.

'We don't know anything yet, Nancy, and whoever it is, we don't know how they got there. I read the reports of Lola's disappearance this afternoon to refresh my memory, and no one talked about your sister going sailing. For now we're assuming that whoever we've found in the cave must have fallen into the sea – probably from a boat, although possibly from the cliff. Your sister was due to meet the other girl – Quinn Asher – by the beach, and that's a long way from where the body was found. We'll know more tomorrow.'

Stephanie heard what sounded like a smothered sob, and she wished she had more to tell her.

'I can't come to see you right this minute.' She didn't want to mention accompanying the skeleton to the mortuary. 'But if you don't think it will wait until the morning to talk, I could call round to see you this evening.'

There was a juddering intake of breath. 'No. It's okay. I'm probably being ridiculous. After what we found this morning—'

'You haven't told me what that was,' Stephanie interrupted.

There was a pause before Nancy spoke. 'Tomorrow's fine.

As I said before, another few hours won't make any difference, will it?'

Nancy ended the call. She had sounded rattled, and Stephanie hoped and prayed that the remains she was about to accompany to the mortuary weren't those of her sister.

THIRTY-ONE

I shouldn't have panicked about the skeleton. Why on earth did I jump to the conclusion it was Lola? I'm rather ashamed of myself, but I still think it was the right decision not to tell the sergeant about the backpack. If she's going to dismiss it as unimportant, I'd rather she told me to my face. She won't, though, and I know I'm trying to delay the moment when I'm forced to accept that it's every bit as significant as I think it is.

And what was Angie saying about Mum and Dad? It's hard to imagine them being so much in love, but at least they stayed together – an increasingly rare phenomenon – and most failed marriages probably start with love.

My phone rings, and for a moment I am convinced it's going to be the police telling me the body is Lola's. But it's Effie.

She launches into her speech before I get a chance to say hello.

'I know you're probably sick of the sight of me and my family, but I was supposed to be going out with my girlfriend, Patsy, tonight to a very nice restaurant that it's taken us *weeks* to get into. And now she has to work. Could you put up with me again – dinner instead of the promised lunch that we missed?'

I'm silent for a moment, trying to work out what to say.

'I don't think it's a good idea,' I say finally. 'Not because I'm sick of the sight of you, but because I'm feeling a bit morose.'

'Exactly! Of *course* you are! Which is precisely why you should go out. I *know* how dreadful this must be for you, so don't try to be jolly. If you want to scream, shout, rant at the world or cry, it's all fine by me.'

I pull a face. 'I'm not given to making a spectacle of myself in public.'

'Who cares? You don't know anyone here, at least not yet, so I can't see why it matters. And anyway, what an introduction to the neighbourhood that would be!'

I have to laugh at her. She's so kind, and maybe it's what I need. If I sit here, all I'll do is think, worry and remember.

'Okay, if you really don't mind. But tonight is my treat. Please, Effie. It's the only way it's going to happen.'

She gives a theatrical sigh then tells me she'll organise a cab to pick us both up because if all else fails we can knock back a few tequila slammers.

Feeling slightly less gloomy, I take a long shower, letting the scalding water beat down on my back. There is something very comforting about the hot pinprick of each droplet.

Finally, wrapped in a towel, I wander towards the bedroom. A floorboard on the landing creaks and I shiver. I know my tread caused the sound, and I am sure no one crept in while I was in the bathroom, but as if to prove it to myself I walk slowly back, retracing my steps. The board creaks again, and I breathe out.

There is no one here. I am sensing danger where there is none, but nevertheless, as I comb out my long hair I decide to let it dry naturally in waves. I can't bring myself to switch on the hairdryer, uncertain of whether it would mask other sounds in my house.

· · ·

The restaurant is packed, and there's a background buzz of people chatting, laughing, the clatter of cutlery on crockery, the pop of a cork being pulled from a bottle. A happy noise and far preferable to sitting in the silence of my cottage.

The menu once again offers a safe topic of conversation, but as soon as we have placed our order, Effie wants to know who the cook in our house was. I'm about to tell her when her phone rings.

'Oh, Jesus. Sorry, Nancy. I know this is really rude, but it's Patsy and as this was supposed to be a special night for us, the least I can do is give her five minutes. Do you mind?'

I shake my head and smile so she knows I'm not offended. She's already explained that Patsy is a junior doctor. She had to do an extra shift and cancel their night out. Her loss, I must admit, is my gain.

I ponder on Effie's previous question about the cook in our house. Growing up, it had been Mum, and our food was always plain – stewed meat, potatoes, whatever vegetables we had to hand. In the months before her stroke I had tried to help more, but cooking didn't come naturally to me. Despite that, when Mum was ill, preparing her meals became the best part of the day. I would make sure she was watching a programme she liked on the television we'd installed in her room, and then I would head to the kitchen while Lola was at school and Dad was working, and try to come up with something that might tempt her to eat. She was wasting away, although her stomach was swelling alarmingly.

She was still suffering from some paralysis after the stroke, so I helped feed her, and the recollection of those times brings a lump to my throat. The menu here with its extensive choice of fish dishes reminds me that cod was one of the things she found easiest to eat, and I have a sudden memory of an evening not long before she died. I'd cooked fish pie with a soft mashed potato topping, but as I tried to feed her she'd pushed my hand away – a sign she'd had enough although she'd barely eaten anything. I looked at her for confirmation, and saw her eyes were filled with tears.

'What is it, Mum?'

She hadn't fully regained her speech, but after two years I understood most of what she said, even though she didn't use complete sentences.

'Sorry, Nancy.'

'It's okay. It's only fish pie. It doesn't matter.'

'Not that. He's right. Not fit to be mother.'

Tears were running down her cheeks now, and it wasn't like her. She didn't cry. She just withdrew into herself and didn't speak, sometimes for days.

'That's nonsense, Mum. Course you are.'

She shook her head. 'No. Tried... made mistakes. Wanted you safe. Liar. Weak. Scared for you.'

I was about to try to find out what she meant when we heard a tread on the stairs and with a trembling hand she pointed to a tissue on the bedside table. Dad was on his way, and she didn't want him to know she'd been crying.

I never did find out what she meant, because when Dad paid his nightly visit I was shooed from the room and always took the opportunity to have a soak in the bath. He only stayed for half an hour, but it seemed to wear Mum out. When I returned to the bedroom she was on the point of nodding off and I knew I wouldn't get anything else out of her that night. Somehow, the right moment never came again.

I am dragged back to the present by Effie returning to the table as the waiter delivers our food.

'Everything okay?' I ask as I tuck into my sea bass.

'Fine. Patsy's not like me – she's the sensible one. Works hard, but looks after herself. She tries to look after me, but she's fighting a losing battle. Drinks too much cinnamon tea and not enough wine, in my opinion, but she's the best.'

I chuckle at the thought of Effie being with someone health conscious. She strikes me as a woman who lives for the here and now, and I can only imagine that Patsy is a stabilising influence.

I'm about to ask how long they've been together when there's a burst of laughter over by the door of the restaurant.

My eyes are drawn to the girl who laughed. She's about to leave, and turns to smile at the man she's with.

She's barely changed. I know who this is. Quinn Asher.

THIRTY-TWO

The woman is pulling open the restaurant door. She's leaving. I have to speak to her.

I push my chair back, never taking my eyes off her.

'What is it?' Effie asks.

'Quinn. It's Quinn.'

I glance briefly at Effie. Her eyes have opened wide at my agitated tone of voice, but I don't have time to explain. I practically run between the tables, a waiter dodging swiftly out of my way. I wonder for a moment if I'm seeing Quinn because she's been on my mind, but I'm sure I'm right. She still has curly white hair and she's wearing a bright red fifties-style swing dress.

I fling open the door. I can see her heading towards the passenger door of a sleek black car. A man is with her, about to get in on the driver's side, and he's laughing at something she is saying.

'Quinn!' I shout as loud as I can, and she glances over her shoulder.

I can see she has a vague idea that she knows me, although

she looks puzzled, as if she can't quite place me. But at least she pauses and waits for me to reach her.

'Sorry,' she says. 'There's something familiar about you, but I can't think what.' She gives a hesitant smile, as if she should feel guilty about this.

'I'm Nancy – Nancy Holland. Lola's sister. Do you remember Lola from eleven years ago?'

Her face clears, and she gives me a genuine smile this time. 'Of course! How *is* Lola?'

I am suddenly lost for words. Where do I start? In the end I blurt out, 'I haven't seen her for eleven years, since the night she ran away. With *you!*'

Quinn's brow creases in a puzzled frown, and she shakes her head. 'No, Nancy, she didn't run away with me. She was going to – that was the plan. But she never turned up that night. The boys wouldn't wait. I tried to call her, but I got her voicemail. I was about to leave a message, but then I thought someone else might pick it up, so I hung up.'

The second part of her explanation floats in one ear and out the other. I am fixated on the words 'she never turned up'.

Quinn touches my arm. 'Are you okay?'

I shake my head. I don't know what to say, but Quinn fills the silence.

'I heard when I came back here that Lola had left the same night, but I didn't think much about it. I just assumed she'd made other plans, or she'd decided to stay.'

I try to stutter out an explanation. 'I've never seen her since that night. The police investigated, but everyone said she'd gone with you, and because you were older they hoped she was safe. She never came home.'

She stares at me as if lost for words, then sucks in a short breath. 'Shit, I'm so sorry, Nancy. I was having a tough time myself with my mum's bloke, and when Lola shared her problems with me, I wanted to help. I would have taken care of her, but I honestly thought she'd changed her mind.'

'What problems?' I ask, my voice rising. 'Do you mean Mum dying? How could Lola think her running away would make things any better?'

She gives me a quizzical look. 'No, not your mum. She was sad, from what I can remember, but said she hadn't seen much of her in the last couple of years.'

I try to stop the surge of resentment at the reminder. None of that matters now.

'Quinn, will you tell me why she left? I have spent the last eleven years worrying about her.' I reach out a hand, but don't quite touch her.

For a moment her face grows harder. 'Maybe you should have thought of that and helped her when you could.'

'What do you mean?'

The man with the car keys is rattling them in his hand and pointing to the car door. 'Quinn, we need to go. I'll miss my train.' Quinn raises her arm in acknowledgement but doesn't take her eyes off me.

'Surely you knew what was bothering her? She was certain you did, but you weren't prepared to do anything. She thought you were punishing her for not helping with your mum.'

The fish I've just eaten churns in my stomach. I have absolutely no idea what she's talking about.

Quinn opens the car door and gets into the passenger seat. The engine is already running.

'Please,' I beg. 'Tell me what you mean.'

She shakes her head. 'It's not for me to tell you. Ask your dad. He knows.'

With that, she slams the car door and the driver doesn't pause. He pulls out into the road and I watch as they drive away.

Confused and shocked by her words, I wait until the car has

disappeared from view, hoping it will turn back and Quinn will tell me what she knows. But she's gone.

I turn slowly, knowing I should go back into the restaurant but wishing I'd never come. As I trudge back towards the door, my eyes are drawn to the harbour opposite, where a low metal railing separates the pavement from the sea. A man is leaning against it, legs crossed at the ankles, smoking a cigarette. I recognise his wiry frame and thin face. *What is he doing here?*

As I stare at him, he lifts his hand and gives me a finger-wiggle wave. I don't know how to respond, so I turn and hurry back into the restaurant.

THIRTY-THREE

Gus had been as good as his word and had lit the barbecue again. The wine was cooling, the glasses were ready. He turned as Stephanie walked onto the terrace, and she could detect a slight edge to his smile, as if he wasn't sure what she might say.

She walked across and put her arms round him. 'I love you, Angus Brodie,' she said. 'That's all that matters.'

Gus held her close. 'And I love you. I don't want any of this to hurt you, but I understand why it might.'

She hugged him tighter but could feel the tension in her body. So could Gus.

He leaned back slightly and gently lifted her chin with his finger.

'Hey, I can practically feel those walls of yours building, brick by brick. None of this is meant to hurt you, Stephie, so tell me how it's making you feel.'

She wanted to say she was scared that this child – a child who wasn't hers – would be enough for him, or that the nightmare of having a sick child would deter him from having other children – their children. Although she had hesitated about committing to another pregnancy, she had always known it was only a matter of time. But now wasn't the moment to share these feelings.

'It's not about me and what I feel, is it? It's about Daisy.'

Gus let go of Stephanie and handed her a glass as they sat down together on the garden bench. 'Okay, let's have your thoughts – and don't hold back. We have to get this right.'

Stephanie took a big glug of her wine, swallowed, and allowed herself to breathe for a moment.

'You're thrilled that you have a child, and I understand that.' Gus looked about to interrupt, but Stephanie lifted a hand. 'I don't resent it, Gus – honestly I don't. How could I resent a poorly little girl? If you can help Daisy, I'll support you all the way.'

Gus's face wore a troubled frown. 'Steph, I know you too well. What's worrying you, really?'

She didn't like exposing her innermost fears, even to Gus, but although she couldn't tell him everything, there were things she could say.

'I know that if you meet Daisy, you'll love her. I don't think there's any doubt. But she lives in Norfolk, and I'm worried that you might want to move there. I'm worried that even if you don't, she'll be a part of your life that doesn't involve me, and the time we have together will be even less than now. I *know* this is selfish and you must do whatever you think is right, but then I keep thinking that if *I'm* scared like this, what must her dad be feeling? He must want you to be a match for Daisy's sake, but it's all going to rock the boat, isn't it?'

The lines between his brows deepened. 'I'm not going to make any decisions without your input, and if Daisy becomes part of my life, she becomes part of yours too – if that's what you want. Did you really think I'd go off and see her without you?'

She had, but his words lightened the weight that had settled on her a little.

'As for her dad,' Gus continued, 'I assume he must be okay with it, or why would they have told me?'

Stephanie just managed to stop herself from tutting. Gus had an uncanny ability to identify evil beneath a veneer of innocence, but wasn't quite so good at seeing vulnerability below a carefully constructed façade of composure.

'Their child is very sick. They would do anything in the world to save her. But it's not only about now, the next days or weeks, is it? It's about forever. If they agree to you seeing her, then you have to think about offering financial support, and work out some form of ongoing access.'

'They can't actually stop me from seeing her if she's mine,' he said quietly.

'*Gus!* Is that going to be the line you take?'

He lifted a hand to rub the back of his neck. 'No, of course not. Sorry, I didn't mean it to come out like that. But what if they decide not to tell her and we agree I'll never meet her, then she finds out when she's older? Not only would she discover that her dad isn't her father, but she would also find out that I knew she was my daughter and did nothing about it.'

He had a point. The truth was, Stephanie didn't know what was best for Daisy, other than to do everything they could to make sure she got better.

'You need to talk to Paula and her husband. You can't make any decisions or decide anything until you know how they feel. And you'll have to tell them to be completely honest with you, because, Gus, if they agree to one thing now and change their minds when she gets better, which I hope and pray she will, it's going to be hell. Any commitment they or you make, it's for life.'

Stephanie saw the journey ahead as a tightrope. Emotions would be running at fever pitch and decisions might be taken, promises made, that – when life returned to normal – suddenly seemed irrational. Gus would fall in love with Daisy, without a doubt. But Paula and her husband might decide to move to the other side of the world, or Daisy – when she was old enough – might refuse to see Gus. And it was a tightrope that would have to be trodden carefully, because one wobble and they would all fall off.

As if by tacit agreement, they didn't talk about Daisy or Paula again. Instead, as they ate, Stephanie brought Gus up to date on her day – the trips to the cave and the retrieval of the bones.

'Did it freak you out?' he asked. 'I remember my first skeleton and it wasn't a great experience.'

'This one wasn't so bad in one way, because it wasn't buried. It was lying on a shelf in a cave. Or most of it was. We've no idea how it got there, and there's nothing to give any clue as to who he or she is.'

'What does the forensic anthropologist have to say?'

'Nothing yet. She hardly bothers with conversation – I guess she prefers bones to people. Anyway, she'll examine the remains in the morning.'

Gus gave Stephanie a wide beam. 'I might join you!'

Stephanie glared at him. 'It's my case, Gus, not yours. And it gets me away from dealing with all those bloody burglaries. They've been driving me insane!'

'Whether it's your case or not depends on how your victim died. If there's anything suspicious, I think you'll find it could well be *mine*.' He gave her a cheeky smirk. Every time a case became interesting, it was transferred to Gus's team. He teased her about it, but he knew when to stop. 'Has Missing Persons turned up any matches?'

'We haven't got enough to go on. The anthropologist won't confirm the sex yet, let alone age. After tomorrow, we'll have a better idea where to focus. But there's one case that's worrying me a bit.'

'Go on,' Gus said.

'A fifteen-year-old holidaymaker went missing from home eleven years ago, and she's still missing. It was a sad case. I did the initial interviews, and life was a bit shit for her sister, Nancy. She's back here now and wants to see me.'

'Why was it shit – apart from worrying about her sister, of course?'

'Lola went missing a few weeks after their mother died. I reread my notes, and they reminded me that Nancy was her mum's carer – slept in her room too. The doctor had prescribed a mild sleeping tablet for Nancy because she was exhausted, and her mum somehow managed to get out of bed. She fell and died where she lay. Nancy blamed herself, and when the family came here to try to recuperate, Lola did a runner. Their dad died a few weeks later.'

'Fuck! That was a lot for her to deal with.'

'It was, and now she's heard about the skeleton we found, it's freaking her out in case it's Lola.'

'And you're thinking she might be right?'

Stephanie blew out a long, slow breath. 'It's not so much that I think it's her. It's more that I hope it's not. The clothes don't match what she was wearing, but that doesn't mean anything. There's no saying she died on the day she went missing, but if it *is* Lola, it's down to us that we didn't solve it back then.'

Gus put down his fork and reached across the table to rest his hand on Stephanie's.

'I know you feel bad about every case that goes unsolved, but you shouldn't. We both know how many kids go AWOL every single day, and we can't find them all. I'm sure you did everything you could.'

Stephanie squeezed his hand, and they went back to eating.

'The thing about Nancy that really got to me was that she kept saying she should have listened to Lola, as if it was all her fault. She seemed to be burdened with guilt about everything, including her mother's death.'

'Poor kid. That's a lot of tragedy in a very short time.'

'I know, and I never felt entirely comfortable with how Lola's case was left. I went to see Nancy before they returned to Shropshire. Her eyes had that bruised look – you know? As if she hadn't slept and had cried all night. She looked at me as if she thought we'd done a hopeless job, and it didn't help that the officer I was with was bloody useless.'

'It wasn't Jason, was it?' Gus chuckled.

'Hardly – he would have been about ten at the time – and to be fair to Jason, he had a tough start in life and he's genuinely trying to improve. No, this guy really fancied himself for reasons that escape me. He was so unprofessional that I was embarrassed to be with him. He's left now, thank God.'

Gus raised his eyebrows. 'What did he do?'

'From the minute Nancy opened the door, he behaved as if he was on the pull. *Totally* inappropriate. There was a sense of wounded vulnerability about the girl, which seemed to come from more than just the shock of her sister's disappearance, and he tried to flirt with her. I was mortified. I think he thought he was Dennis Waterman in *The Sweeney* or something.'

Gus threw his head back and hooted at the idea. *The Sweeney* was well before their time, but one of Gus and Stephanie's favourite winter pastimes was to sit on the sofa in front of the fire, sharing a pizza and a bottle of beer, watching old cop shows, screaming at the television every time someone behaved inappropriately or trampled all over a crime scene.

'When are you seeing Nancy?'

'First thing tomorrow. I just hope that whatever she's found is good news for the girl, but somehow I doubt it.'

THIRTY-FOUR

Stephanie parked her car in the small car park just up the road from Nancy Holland's cottage, thinking what a great place to live this must be. Much as she loved Cornwall and never wanted to leave, sometimes she got sick of the holidaymakers. The crime figures rose by over thirty per cent during the tourist season, which kept her busy, but here in this sleepy little village it didn't feel as if there were either tourists or crime.

She raised her hand to knock on the door, but before she could connect, the door swung open.

'Sergeant King?'

Stephanie would have recognised Nancy Holland by the colour of her hair alone, but today she was looking frazzled, her skin blotchy as if she'd been crying. Whatever had happened, whatever she'd discovered, it was clearly tormenting her.

'That's right, and you're Nancy Holland. I remember you – you have very memorable hair.' Stephanie smiled to try to ease the tension.

Nancy touched her hair, as if trying to remember if she had brushed it.

'What can I help you with?' Stephanie asked. 'You said

something had come to light regarding your sister's disappearance.'

Nancy pulled the door wide to let Stephanie in and pointed to a chair at the kitchen table, which Stephanie took as an invitation to sit. Walking over to the worktop, Nancy grabbed a bright green backpack, then turned and dumped it in the centre of the table. She stood back, wrapped her arms around her waist and stared at Stephanie.

'It's Lola's. We found it in the shed – in a box. It's got her clothes in – the ones I said had gone from our room – and all her money.' Nancy swallowed with apparent difficulty. 'It's hard to believe she'd have left without it – in fact, left without anything at all. Where did she go?'

Stephanie felt a beat of apprehension and cursed the young PC who had been so busy trying to impress Nancy with his wit that he had obviously not bothered to search the shed properly. 'Did she have any other source of money – maybe a prepaid debit card your parents gave her for small items?'

'No!' She pointed at the backpack. 'This is it – every penny she possessed. How could she have left without clothes, without money? Why didn't we find her backpack at the time? I never thought to look. I thought that's what *you* were for.'

Nancy's voice had grown thick and unsteady, and she raised a hand to brush her hair from her face.

'We shouldn't have missed it. I'm sorry.'

Nancy appeared to wobble slightly. Stephanie could see she was only just holding on and could understand why. If these really were all of Lola's possessions, it was difficult to think of a single positive explanation.

'Why don't you sit down, Nancy?'

Nancy frowned, as if for a moment she didn't know what Stephanie was talking about. But then she collapsed into a chair and leaned towards Stephanie across the table.

'There's something else,' she said. 'I don't know if you

remember, but when Lola left, you thought she was with a girl called Quinn – a few years older than Lola.'

Stephanie nodded. 'Quinn Asher. I remember.'

'I saw her last night. I asked her about Lola, but she said my sister never turned up that night. They left without her.'

Stephanie struggled to keep her face impassive. She couldn't let Nancy see how concerned she was.

'Where *is* she, Sergeant King? Where is my sister? What happened to her? Is she the skeleton you've found?'

'There's absolutely no reason to suspect it's Lola. We don't even know yet if it's the body of a young girl, but I'll have an answer to that in the next hour or two and I promise to let you know as soon as I have any further information.'

Nancy slouched back on the chair, an air of defeat about her. She needed answers, and Stephanie didn't have any.

'What happens now? Can I trust the police to investigate properly this time?'

Stephanie tried hard not to cringe at the words. 'We'll take this very seriously, I can assure you. There's every chance that Lola decided to go her own way rather than with Quinn—'

'Without any money? Without any clothes? You *know* that doesn't make any sense!'

'I promise you we'll explore all possibilities, but for now will you excuse me just for a moment? I need to pop outside and bring my boss up to date.'

A bewildered Nancy nodded, but Stephanie was as sure as she could be that this was about to become far more uncomfortable for the woman.

Stephanie sat on the wall at the front of the cottage and called DI Harris-Cooke, filling her in on everything Nancy had told her.

'We both know what this suggests, but maybe let's keep our

thoughts to ourselves for now. Do we know how to get hold of Quinn Asher?' the DI asked.

'No. She lived with her mum, but when we did a routine follow-up on Lola's case, we found out Quinn's mum had moved. The phone number Quinn had eleven years ago has been out of action since the day she left. We'll find her, though, if she's living round here again.'

'Right. Get on to that as soon as you're back. It may have been eleven years ago, but I think this needs to be a priority.'

'I have to go to the forensic examination of the skeleton first, ma'am.'

There was a tut of frustration from the other end of the phone. 'Fine. I suppose you'll have to do that. At least if Nancy Holland reported this, it seems that, contrary to my previous comments, it's unlikely she was involved. She'd hardly raise doubts about Lola's disappearance, unless of course it's to gain attention. But that theory doesn't entirely stand up now, does it?'

Stephanie didn't know how to answer. She had never thought it stood up in the first place.

'In any case, tell her we don't want her leaving Cornwall until further notice.'

'I don't think she's planning to. What's going to happen next?'

There was silence for a moment or two. 'In view of the backpack and the money, we have to treat this as a serious issue. I'll have to consult with the Major Crimes team. Is DCI Brodie staying with you at the moment?'

Stephanie didn't understand why her boss always talked as if Gus was an occasional visitor – much as it sometimes seemed that way to her. This was his home.

'He is, yes, but he'll be heading back to Newquay in the morning.'

'Hmm. Maybe they'll make him SIO on this case. I'll let you

know when it's confirmed. For now, you need to warn Nancy Holland what's about to happen. Whether or not the skeleton is her sister, any SIO – Brodie or otherwise – will insist on re-examining every inch of the previous investigation.'

She was right, and Stephanie wasn't looking forward to the next part of her conversation with Nancy.

Walking across to her car, she opened the boot, got out the equipment she needed and made her way back into the house. Nancy hadn't moved from the kitchen table, her eyes following Stephanie as she walked over and pulled out a chair.

'Nancy, it's going to be difficult for you to have to go through everything again, but in view of the circumstances – the backpack and Quinn's assertion that Lola didn't leave with her – we have to make some further enquiries.'

The strain was clear in Nancy's voice. 'That's fine. Just find her this time. That's all I ask. I always thought she would come back some day, even if only to tell me why she left. I looked for her, you know. Everywhere I could think of.'

'I know you must be finding it hard to believe in the police, to trust us, but there are a couple of things I need to tell you. An SIO – that's a senior investigating officer – will be appointed; someone who has experience in dealing with cases like your sister's. We can no longer assume she ran away, although in every likelihood that's exactly what she did.'

Nancy's mouth had settled into a thin line, and Stephanie could feel the woman's distrust. 'What will they do to try to find her? It's so long ago, surely any trail that might have been followed will have gone cold by now?'

Stephanie tried not to wince at her words. 'There was no evidence of a crime at the time, but the circumstances are now a little more suspicious, so the team will review the original missing-from-home case notes and I'll have to take the backpack, with its contents, for forensic examination. Are you okay if I do that now?'

Nancy nodded, her eyes fixed on the emerald-green backpack.

Stephanie pulled on the gloves she had brought from the car and opened a large forensic bag. Picking up the backpack, she pushed it inside, sealed and labelled it.

'What will you do with it?' Nancy asked.

'I'll get an exhibits officer to separate it all out. We'll then decide what kind of forensic testing we think is appropriate.'

No one said it, but Stephanie could sense the word 'blood' in the air, so to defuse the situation, she carried on speaking. 'We'll go back over the phone records to see if we missed anything, and we'll track down the people she was friendly with to see if they can cast any further light on the situation. I'm sure we'll discover that some other friends were heading north – to London or another city – and that's all there is to it.'

She didn't believe it, but until they knew more, she couldn't let Nancy suffer any more than she already was.

Nancy cleared her throat and blew her nose. 'And the skeleton?'

'I'm on my way there now and I'll be in touch as soon as I know anything. But I promise we'll investigate Lola's disappearance thoroughly. We'll leave no stone unturned.'

Stephanie watched Nancy's face, hoping the woman had read the subtext. Did Lola leave of her own volition? Was she forced? Or was it something worse?

THIRTY-FIVE

Stephanie glanced at Gus as they walked towards the door to the mortuary.

'You don't have to be here, you know,' she said.

'I know, but HC has phoned my DCS, and I'm hoping he'll ask me to take on the Lola Holland case. So until we know who your skeleton is...' Gus was watching her face, and he leaned closer to her ear. 'Consider this a bonus. It means I might get to stay home for a bit longer.'

She gave him a look, but there was no more time for chat. As she pushed open the door to the examination room, she could see the skeleton had been reassembled on the stainless-steel table. A figure in scrubs was leaning over the bones, apparently taking measurements.

'Dr Carla Davies, this is DCI Angus Brodie,' Stephanie said. 'He's here to observe only, unless this becomes a murder case.'

Carla Davies raised her eyes and gave Gus a brief nod. Stephanie had already told him that the forensic anthropologist was a woman of few words, but she was glad of the silence. She stared at the arrangement of bones on the table, mentally adding organs, muscles, skin, hair. This had been a living, breathing person, and she couldn't imagine how he or she could have ended up on that ledge in the cave, or how they might have died there.

'It's not my place to say if it's murder,' Carla responded. 'But Molly will be back in a second.'

'We have a girl who went missing about a year after the film crew was in the cave, and if it turns out the body is hers, it may become my case,' Gus said.

'If that's what you're thinking, I can tell you now this isn't the body you're looking for. The deceased is a young male—'

'Are you sure?' Stephanie interrupted rudely.

Carla lifted her head. 'Yes, Sergeant. I'm quite sure.'

Stephanie felt mildly chastised by her tone, but she didn't care. 'I'm sorry, but if that's the case, can I make a quick call? There's someone for whom this will be good news.'

She walked away from the examination table and pulled her phone from her pocket.

'Nancy, it's Stephanie King. I have some news. The skeleton we found is male. The forensic anthropologist is certain of it. It's not Lola.'

Stephanie heard a sharp intake of breath.

'Are you okay, Nancy?'

'I think so. Thanks for letting me know.'

With that, she hung up.

'Sorry about that,' Stephanie said, pushing her mobile back into her pocket and returning to the table. 'Can we start again, please?'

Carla nodded, apparently unperturbed by the interruption.

'As I said, it's the body of a young male, sub-adult.'

'How can you tell the gender?' Gus asked.

Carla frowned at him over her glasses. 'We refer to it as the sex – the biological aspect of an individual. Gender refers to the social expression of a person's identity, often self-defined.'

Gus looked contrite. 'My mistake. So how do you know this?'

'The pelvis is the primary indicator once a person has reached adolescence or adulthood. Before that, the difference is slight. A woman's pelvis is designed to give birth, but also the skull of a male has several characteristics that differ from a female's.'

'What's sub-adult, then?' Gus asked, and Stephanie gave him a frustrated glare. Until instructed otherwise this was still her case, not his – especially as it wasn't Lola Holland.

'It refers to a person below adulthood. This boy is border-line, but not a fully grown adult. If you look at the ends of these bones –' Carla pointed to the end of the femur '– you can see the epiphyseal plate – this glassy cartilage area. It's where growth takes place. In a full-grown adult this is replaced by what's known as the epiphyseal line.'

Stephanie looked at the skeleton again. 'We noted when we extracted the bones that the left shin bone had been broken. Is there anything you can tell us about that?'

'The tibia – yes. Badly broken.' Carla tapped an iPad next to her and pulled up a photo of the skeleton in situ in the cave. 'It's a spiral fracture, and looking at the position of the bones when the remains were found, I would say it almost definitely penetrated the skin.'

'It wouldn't have killed him, though.'

'Not directly, no. But it may have been the injury that prevented him from swimming out of the cave. There is some evidence of healing having started, and if I can see that macro-scopically, I would estimate that he must have been alive for at least seven days after the injury. You would need to confirm this with the pathologist, but she indicated that in all probability he died of dehydration.'

There was a sound of a door slamming and feet trudging across the floor towards them.

'DCI Brodie! Delightful as it always is to see you, what brings you here? I haven't said the boy was murdered – at least not yet.'

'Molly!' Gus beamed at the pathologist. 'I'm here for a couple of days, and I was intrigued, so Steph's allowed me to tag along on condition I keep quiet.'

Molly chortled at the notion. Carla Davies lifted her head slightly to look at Stephanie and raised her eyebrows. She'd clearly got Gus's measure.

'We've also got a case that might be coming my way,' Gus continued. 'A girl who went missing eleven years ago. We thought this might be her, but clearly not.'

Molly walked around to the other side of the table. 'Nope. Definitely male. Anyway, I believe I interrupted Carla telling you that I suspect our victim died of dehydration. In fact, I'm certain that's the case. It must be hell to be dying of thirst when you're surrounded by water, but even if he attempted to drink seawater, he would still have died from dehydration. The kidneys can't cope with the salt, and he'd have ended up urinating more liquid than he was taking in.'

What a death, Stephanie thought. His leg must have been agony, and he would have been getting more and more thirsty with every passing hour.

'Poor kid,' she muttered. 'Carla, do you have any idea how long the body had been lying there?'

Carla shook her head. 'That's more difficult. There are so many factors to consider. The cave never receives sunlight, but neither does it freeze. The temperature variations won't have been significant, and the body won't have been subjected to any large scavenging animals. Normally in a climate like Cornwall's I would say he has to have been dead for at least six months, but given the atmosphere in the cave I would say it's more likely to have been a minimum of a year.'

'We're fairly certain the body wasn't there twelve years ago,'

Stephanie said. 'You'd think the BBC film crew would have spotted it, if it was lurking on that ledge.'

'Which means the body's been there some time between one and twelve years,' Gus added. 'That's helpful. We can begin by checking the Missing Persons register. Are you able to tell us anything about his ethnicity?'

'There are some features of his skull, such as the orbit shape, the degree of prognathism—'

'Sorry. The *what*?' Gus asked.

'It's the anterior projection of the mid-face. There's also the shape of the nasal arch and the palate. All these features lead me to suggest his ancestry is Asian. I'll put the full details in my report. There was some hair found by the body too, but hair morphology isn't my specialism. We could send a sample for testing if you think that's necessary – but again it would be a broad categorisation that may only confirm the Asian hypothesis.'

'Okay, we'll maybe think about that,' Gus said, and Stephanie rolled her eyes. 'In the meantime, is there any evidence on the bones – apart from the break – of any trauma? Maybe knife wound, bullet?'

Carla shook her head. 'Nothing that I can see, but I'm still measuring and compiling my notes, so if I find anything I'll let you know.'

'Looks like it's definitely not your case, Gus. Are we all agreed?' Stephanie asked.

'Not our call,' Molly said. 'But neither of us has any reason to suspect foul play. He broke his leg, climbed out of the sea and died where he lay.'

Gus shook his head. 'The big question is, though, how did he get there in the first place?'

THIRTY-SIX

I've not been able to do anything in the house since Sergeant King called. I've been sitting at the kitchen table drinking cup of coffee after cup of coffee. It's now two hours since she broke the news that the skeleton isn't Lola and I feel weak with relief.

I don't know what to do with myself. I probably shouldn't carry on sorting through the cupboards in case I disturb something that relates to Lola's disappearance. Maybe they'll want to search the house again, because they certainly didn't look very hard last time – or at least that spotty PC didn't. To him, Lola was simply another runaway kid, heading for the bright lights of London. The only thing I know for certain is that she *wanted* to leave – in fact *intended* to leave. Quinn thought I should have known why, and she said that Dad knew. Could that be true? Why didn't he tell me?

There is no point in me trying to work out why she ran away. I've thought of, and discounted, everything. I wondered if she'd become involved in drugs and owed money, but she had the money that Mum left her, and I'd have gladly given her what was left of mine if she'd needed it. Perhaps that's what Dad meant about ruining us. Maybe he thought he'd have to bail her out, although after he died it turned out that there was no money; he'd been borrowing against the farm for years.

I am startled back into the here and now by a sharp rap on the door.

As I open the door, Sergeant King gives me a sympathetic smile. I'd been too stressed to notice when she came earlier, but I realise now that she hasn't changed much in the last eleven years, still the same slim face and generous mouth. Only her hair is different, hanging in dark waves to her shoulders instead of tied back in a neat bun. A broad-shouldered man with a closely trimmed beard stands next to her.

'Nancy,' Sergeant King says, 'this is Detective Chief Inspector Angus Brodie. He's been asked to reopen the Missing Persons enquiry into your sister.'

I wish none of this was happening; that I had never returned to Cornwall; that I still believed Lola left with Quinn and is living happily somewhere, waiting for the right moment to pluck up the courage to come and find me, to tell me why she left.

'Hello, Miss Holland,' says the chief inspector, a slight Scottish burr in his voice. 'I understand this must be very distressing for you.'

'Please call me Nancy,' I say, rather inanely.

I stand back so they can go into the kitchen, and the chief inspector gives me a kind smile.

'Do you mind if we sit down?' he asks, and I wave vaguely towards the chairs. 'Nancy, I think Sergeant King told you we'll be re-examining the evidence we collected at the time of your sister's disappearance, and we'll also be interviewing everyone who knew her. But I need to ask you if, during the years since she left, you have discovered why Lola decided she wanted to leave home so abruptly. Did she talk to you about it at all?'

Memories of that night come back to me again, and I feel my face flush with shame at the words I had spoken to my sister.

But they don't need to know about that. 'Lola said she had something she wanted to tell me, but I was upset. Not with Lola – it was a personal issue – and I'm afraid I ignored her.'

Sergeant King rests her arms on the table. 'Nancy, you shouldn't beat yourself up about that. You had no reason to believe she wouldn't be there the next morning when you might have felt more inclined to listen. We're not always in the right frame of mind when we need to be.'

I lower my head. She's being kind – but I shouldn't have yelled at Lola. I should have listened. I shouldn't have fallen asleep. I should have known sooner that she hadn't come home.

'When I saw Quinn last night, she couldn't believe I didn't know why Lola wanted to leave. She said my dad knew, but if he had, he'd have told me.'

'I'm sure he would,' DCI Brodie says, his expression understanding. 'We'll be looking at every aspect of the case, I can assure you, but for now I need to ask if you have anywhere nearby where you can stay.'

I feel my body tense. 'What do you mean? Why can't I stay here?'

'Because I'm afraid we are going to have to treat the cottage as a crime scene. It's the last place Lola was seen. We have to find out if something happened to her here.'

THIRTY-SEVEN

'Poor woman,' Stephanie said as she got into the passenger seat of Gus's car. 'She only came back here because she inherited the cottage, and I bet she wishes she'd stayed at home, safe in the belief that her sister had simply packed her stuff and run away. No one's said it yet, but she's not stupid. She must be thinking the worst.'

'If she doesn't now, she will when she realises what we're going to have to do.' Gus started the car but didn't move.

'What exactly *are* you going to do?' Stephanie asked.

'It's going to be difficult after so long. Any signs of a struggle would be almost impossible to identify, so I guess we'll have to focus on blood. We'll go through all the initial reports from the missing-from-home enquiry, check up on all the people she knew down here and perhaps back home – Shropshire, did you say?'

'Yes, but their home was repossessed, and after her dad died Nancy moved to London.'

'Lola took her phone when she ran away, didn't she?' Gus asked.

'Yep, but it was switched off. Last communication was a call from Quinn Asher, but it lasted less than a minute and neither her phone nor Quinn's have been switched on since. I asked if they used any family tracking apps, but they weren't a big thing back then. Nancy didn't have a mobile and her dad had never thought of tracking Lola's. He said she wouldn't have allowed it.'

Gus raised his eyebrows. 'I think if I had a fifteen-year-old daughter I might track her phone, whatever she thought about it.'

Stephanie didn't remind him that he *would* have a fifteen-year-old daughter in a little over twelve years' time. It was best left unsaid.

'Why didn't Nancy have a mobile? A bit odd for a kid of nearly nineteen, isn't it?'

'It's eleven years ago, Gus. Not everyone had a mobile. I asked her about it, and she told me the family couldn't afford to pay for two. As she never went anywhere she didn't need a phone, but Lola did. I suspect Nancy didn't have many friends either, since she was always at home with her mum. This was unusual, but we didn't think it particularly strange under the circumstances.'

'Maybe not, but it sounds like a sad life for a young girl, and now she's got a tricky few days ahead. Could you prepare her for the fact that I'll want to take a look at the back garden, Steph? I'll need to brief the forensics team about the search, but when I've got everything set up could you have a word and tell her we'll have to cut back some of those weeds?'

With that, Gus put the car into gear and reversed out of the parking space.

Stephanie said nothing. She knew without asking what Gus was planning and wondered how Nancy would cope with the news.

.   .   .

They drove in silence for a while, each locked in their own thoughts, and it was only as they approached police headquarters that Gus spoke.

'You'll be working on this case with me – you okay with that?'

'Of course,' Stephanie said. 'The skeleton's mine, though. We know it's not Lola, and there's no evidence of murder, so I'll have to pursue that at the same time.'

'There's a limit to what you'll be able to do. It's going to be a nightmare to find out whose body it is.'

'I know. We don't know how long he'd been there, and we don't have any MFH cases that fit the bill, so I'll circulate the details to all forces and ask them to review their cases against the very limited criteria.'

'Hmm. Good luck with that. Thousands of Asian males go missing each year, especially in that age range, and you've got a wide time period to cover.'

Stephanie sighed. 'I'm not holding out much hope. I'll do some digging, visit the Islamic Centre and ask them to speak to their community. But it won't stop me from working on Lola's case, so don't worry.'

'I'm not. I realise it matters to you.'

Stephanie leaned back against the headrest. 'I can tell Nancy thinks we did a crap job first time round, and she's probably right – although it didn't seem as if Lola had been coerced into anything. You know as well as I do that a child is reported missing every five minutes in the UK, so we have to prioritise. The vast majority return, and even in sleepy Cornwall we don't have the manpower to follow them all up.'

Gus turned his head towards her and raised his eyebrows before returning his eyes to the road.

'Okay. You're right. It sounds like an excuse,' Stephanie said. 'I wish we could find every one of the poor souls and take them to a place of safety. But we can't.'

'No one's going to blame you for this, you know – except perhaps yourself.'

'And Nancy,' Stephanie muttered. 'Although she largely blames herself. She thought she'd taken her eye off the ball with Lola because she was seeing some man, and I gather it turned out he wasn't as keen as she'd hoped. She seems to have been let down everywhere she turned. Then her dad died.'

'Yeah, you mentioned that. How did he die?'

'He drove his car into a reservoir.'

Stephanie tried to imagine what Nancy's life must have been like at that moment, but couldn't.

'Accident?'

'There were skid marks on the road, as if he'd tried to avoid another car, although no one else came forward. There was one witness who saw the car go into the water and called it in.'

'Maybe he had a heart attack. What did the post-mortem say?'

'Nothing. The police were on the scene quickly, but they were unable to recover his body. They got the car out, but a window was open so he must have managed to escape. Unfortunately the car went in close to the dam, and the currents under the surface there are really strong. Something to do with the pumping station, as I understand it.'

'What was the conclusion?'

'Open verdict. Given that he'd lost his wife and one daughter, and was about to be made homeless due to debt, there was a query that it might have started as a suicide attempt; that maybe he changed his mind at the last minute, tried to escape and got dragged under. An accident is the more likely explanation, though. The guy on the other side of the lake who reported it had his binoculars trained on the water the whole time. He saw some bubbles to start with, but then nothing.'

'Christ. Disaster certainly appears to follow the girl around. Let's hope we don't discover her sister's been dead for eleven years too. To lose all three members of your family in the space of a few weeks seems rather more than unfortunate.'

'The next few days are going to be shit for her, whatever we find,' Stephanie said, ignoring the innuendo in Gus's words.

THIRTY-EIGHT

I've finished packing and take a moment to sit on the bed to look out of the window. I knew coming back here would be difficult. I thought it would just be the memories I'd find hard to deal with, but it's become much more painful, and while I long for my predictable life in London, I'm going nowhere until I know what happened to Lola. I'm trying to stay positive, although it's impossible not to believe the worst.

I push myself up from the bed and pick up my case to take to the B&B a couple of doors away where I'm staying until the police have finished whatever they need to do. Effie offered to take me to stay at her mum's, but I want to be close by. And I need to be on my own right now.

The landlady of the B&B, Mrs Roskilly, could see that there were police at my cottage, and when I knocked at the door to ask if a bedroom might be a possibility, she craned her neck out of the doorway.

'What's going on, then?'

I did my best to explain to her in simple terms with as few details as possible, but she wanted more.

'You mean you don't know where your sister is? Even now,

after all these years? Do they think something's happened to her? Is that why there's that crime scene tape outside?'

It was obvious that she remembered Lola's disappearance and I didn't want to answer her questions, but if I wanted to stay in her home I didn't have much choice. I offered the bare minimum.

'You'd best get your stuff, then,' she said. 'I wasn't planning on letting any rooms this late in the season –' she gave a little sniff as if to indicate how much I was putting her out '– but I can see you need somewhere so I'll take you. You can tell me all about your sister when you're settled.'

There was a glint in her pale blue eyes, and I'm sure she was on the phone to her friends as soon as I left to pick up my bag.

It's time I stopped procrastinating, so I make my way downstairs. As I pick up my laptop, I see my camera sitting on the coffee table and it reminds me of Lola's comment when I bought it.

'Typical of you,' she'd said dismissively. 'Why can't you be normal and buy clothes like anyone else?'

What had I done to make her dislike me so much? Would I ever find out now?

I sling the camera round my neck, put the charger in my laptop bag and, dragging my case behind me, I head to the door.

As I pull the door of the cottage closed, I wonder if I will ever sleep within these walls again. Maybe I should put it on the market and return to my safe life with my lovely oldies, as I call them. I'd tried to think of another term, such as seniors or golden agers, but they had laughed at me.

'We're old, lovey. It's just a word; a fact, not an insult. We don't need fancy euphemisms. We were all born before political correctness became a thing.'

So oldies they became. And I miss them.

I feel a strange sadness. Even though I never wanted to come back, it feels weird to be leaving the cottage, as if I'm saying goodbye to my past. I shake my head in irritation. I'm being too fanciful.

As I reach the road I notice a grey van in the tiny car park, and I'm certain it's the same one I nearly walked into yesterday. There's no one on the pebble beach – there rarely is when there are such glorious sandy beaches so close by – and yet I'm sure there's someone in the van, in the driver's seat. I can just make out a face behind a pair of sunglasses. The driver appears to be watching me in the wing mirror.

I don't want to stare, but I can feel eyes on me.

The van is facing the sunlight, which is shining straight into my eyes, blinding me. If this is the van that was here yesterday the driver may have seen who went into my house when I was in the shop, and I'm just debating whether to dump my case and walk over to ask when the engine fires up and the van reverses out, driving quickly up the hill away from me.

Maybe it's just rubberneckers. I've no doubt the crime scene tape will be attracting attention, and the revitalised investigation will be all over the local news later, but for some reason the van has given me an icy chill.

What if someone took Lola, and they're here to check what the police discover? What if they're watching me?

The van disappears from view, and I shake my head again. I'm seeing shadows where there are none, and I know it's fear for Lola that's thrown me.

THIRTY-NINE

Much as Stephanie wanted to be with Gus as he organised the search of Nancy's cottage, first she had to trawl through the Missing Persons register to see if she could identify their skeleton. Her team had decided to call him Lek, rather than 'the skeleton' or 'the body'. Apparently it was a Buddhist name meaning 'small built person' and that seemed about right.

She and Gus had discussed it on the drive back.

'What are the options as you see them, Steph?'

She had given him a look. 'Is this some kind of initiative test-cum-training programme, DCI Brodie?'

Gus chuckled. 'No, but you always say I take over, so I'm giving you an opportunity to speak before I inevitably butt in with some ideas of my own.'

'I've told you – I'll raise an action asking the HOLMES manager in each force area to run an enquiry into their current and cold cases. We have nothing on file that matches, except a boy from Bangladesh who was picked up as part of a raid on illegal workers and housed by the local council while his immigration was processed. He did a runner. Unfortunately, our victim is a couple of inches shorter than him.'

'You've kind of voiced one of my concerns – that this boy isn't on any register at all, which is why no one has reported him missing.'

'I know. Since that case a couple of years ago when all those people were smuggled into Newlyn Harbour, we've been on constant alert for similar operations.'

Gus shook his head. 'How they thought they could sail into the harbour and walk twenty-nine people to a waiting van without being spotted is a mystery to me.'

'Well, fortunately they were nicked. The judge said the victims were "carted around like freight" and we know they're not the only ones. Other smugglers will have been more shrewd, so we need to ask around some of the hotels where they've used illegal workers in the past. I guess if Lek was under the radar, it won't be easy.'

'There's another thing to consider.'

Stephanie resisted the temptation to groan. Gus always had 'another thing', and it was usually something she wished she'd already thought of. 'Go on. Share your wisdom.'

'We may not know who he is yet, but if we can work out how he came to be in that cave, we might have a clue where to start looking. Did you ask the crew about the tides?'

Stephanie gave him a smug smile. 'I did indeed. I've asked one of the team to talk to the coastguard about where Lek might have gone into the water. He could have fallen in from the cliff, like young Ollie did – he's the boy who found the body – but that seems unlikely. Ollie didn't fall from the top. If he had, he would have crashed into the cliff halfway down, and would have suffered far more than a bust leg.'

Gus pulled the car into the police car park and reached over to give Stephanie's hand a quick squeeze. 'I'll leave it with you, then. See you later, DS King.'

'You certainly will, sir.'

She wanted to lean across and give him a kiss, but they'd

agreed long ago that even though everyone knew they were a couple, public displays of affection weren't very professional, and as soon as they entered the building, he was her boss once again.

As she walked to her desk to make sure every action was in hand to try to trace Lek, her thoughts returned to Lola. What could have happened to her? She could just about convince herself that Lola had left without her backpack, but without any money? However hard she tried, Stephanie couldn't think of a single explanation that would result in a good outcome.

FORTY

It feels odd to be waking up at the B&B, two doors from my own cottage in a room that feels claustrophobic with too much furniture. I had to force open the window last night to rid the room of its stale musty smell – the remnants of too many people sleeping in this bed, I suspect, their dirty clothes piled in the corner waiting to be taken home and washed. My stomach is already churning with stress, and I wish I could go back to sleep and wake up in my own bed, the investigation over. I never thought I would miss the cottage, but I do.

My room at the B&B is at the back of the house, and as I try to raise the energy to get up and face the day, the peace is disturbed by what sounds like a garden strimmer. The sweet smell of cut grass wafts through the open window and I push myself up from the bed to look out. I can see into the back garden of my cottage, and it looks as if the ground has been marked into a grid. A man in a white coverall is working through each section with the strimmer, cutting back the tall grass and weeds, but he only appears to be cutting the tops – this summer's growth. Two other people similarly dressed – a man and a woman – drop to their knees behind him and crawl through the shortened grass, feeling the ground in front of them.

I swallow a lump in my throat. *What are they looking for?*

Another woman emerges from the cottage with a metal detector. I hear it squeal, and the sound makes me jump.

What has she found?

Everyone stops and turns to look at her. She bends and picks something up. I can't see what it is, but she shakes her head and everyone gets back to work. She bags it, though, in case – I suppose – it proves more useful than she first thinks.

I watch and wait. The strimming is finished – it's not a big garden – and the two people searching by fingertip stand up. I don't get the impression they've found anything useful. Apart from the odd screech from the metal detector, which finds a few objects although nothing that raises a cry of excitement, it seems as if they have been wasting their time.

I don't know how long I've been standing here, but suddenly I realise I can smell coffee. There's a knock on the door.

'Come in,' I call, unwilling to leave the window.

'I brought you some coffee and toast, Nancy.'

I turn and see Mrs Roskilly carrying a tray which she puts on the chest of drawers. With a strange sideways move, she shuffles towards where I'm standing.

'Quite a bit of activity in your back garden, I gather,' she says. 'I can't see properly from downstairs.'

She tries to peer round me, and I can't help myself. I move to block her way.

'I appreciate the breakfast, Mrs Roskilly, but as you can see I'm not dressed yet. Thank you so much, and I'll bring the tray down when I'm finished.'

Her lips tighten. 'Fine. I was just trying to be helpful.'

Even then she can't help herself from rising on tiptoe to look over my shoulder. I don't move, and with an audible tut she turns to leave. If she was expecting me to be excited that the police are searching my garden, she must be very disappointed.

I plonk myself down heavily on the end of the bed, and thoughts of Lola come hurtling at me.

The memories are always the same: Lola, the cute little girl with the chubby cheeks who loved her big sister; the little princess she became when she was about nine; the sullen teenager who couldn't bring herself to spend any time with her seriously ill mother.

She wasn't perfect, but which of us is? She was still my sister and I mourn the fact that we drifted so far apart in the last two years she was with us.

I walk across to the chest of drawers where Mrs Roskilly left the toast and coffee, take a bite and a big gulp. Despite the woman's ulterior motives, I am grateful for this, but I feel drawn back to the window. I need to know what's going on.

In the space of the few moments that I was away from my lookout, things have changed. Someone has come into the garden with what looks like an electric lawnmower. I put my coffee cup on the window ledge and lean closer to the window as a tall thin man starts to push the yellow contraption over the long grass, but there is no trail of cuttings.

What is he doing?

I grab my phone, open Google, tap the lens icon and point the camera through the window. With fingers that suddenly feel fat and rubbery I click to take a photo and select search. The picture is taken from an angle looking down on the machine so the suggestions are varied, but one appears to be a perfect match.

'Oh my God,' I mutter, horrified at what this is telling me.

I click on the image, and the description suggests all kinds of uses for the machine – archaeology, the study of bedrock – but that's not what this is.

I click on the link to *uses in police investigation*.

I know what I am about to read, but I have to be sure. *The use of ground-penetrating radar in detecting buried remains.*

They are looking for Lola's body.

FORTY-ONE

Nancy was speaking quickly, almost breathlessly, down the phone, and Stephanie closed her eyes as regret washed over her.

'I'm so sorry, Nancy,' she said for the second time. 'This is my fault.'

'Well, it's definitely *somebody's*! Why did no one tell me you were going to be checking out the back garden? That you were looking for Lola's *body*?'

'I hadn't realised you'd be able to see into the garden, and it seemed kinder to only let you know if we find it necessary to explore further.'

'By that, I assume you mean dig the garden up?'

'I do, yes.'

'You think she's dead, don't you? Tell me! I need to know.'

Stephanie could hear the rising tension in Nancy's voice and kicked herself for not handling this better.

'We have to consider every option, I'm afraid. Right now the team is checking for all types of evidence – anything discarded that may have been hidden in the grass or buried in shallow soil.'

'Why would you think her body might be in the back

garden? Do you think *I* killed her? Or Dad? Or maybe you think we did it together!'

'Nancy, I can only imagine how difficult this must be for you, and I feel for your distress, but it's our job to look at everything. I know you think we got it wrong last time, so this time we're making sure we cover every angle. I'll check with DCI Brodie and see what – if anything – they've found. If it's significant, I'll phone you immediately. Is that okay?'

'I suppose it will have to be.'

Nancy's voice had lowered, and Stephanie hoped she had calmed her a little.

'I'd like to pop out to see you later, to run through the steps we're taking to find Lola and perhaps explain everything a little better. What do you think?'

She heard a deep sigh.

'Thank you. I'd appreciate that. You've got my number, in case I go for a walk. I won't stray far.' She paused. 'Sorry for losing it.'

'You've nothing to apologise for. I'll see you later then, and Nancy? I'm so sorry you had such a shock.'

Stephanie hung up the phone and cursed. She should have warned her, but Gus had said they wouldn't be able to get the GPR equipment until the next day, and she hadn't thought it was worth worrying her until they were about to start.

She picked up the phone.

'Brodie,' came the response. A man of few words, as usual.

'Why didn't you let me know the GPR kit had turned up? I've had Nancy on the phone – she's seen it from her window.'

'*Bollocks!* I suppose you didn't have a chance to warn her. Sorry, Steph. I was just keen to get going.'

Stephanie's irritation abated. Typically, Gus hadn't tried to pass the blame on to her, which he would have been within his rights to do. He'd asked her to explain what they were going to do, and he wasn't the one who set the timescales.

'It's not your fault. I'm cross with myself, not you. Did you find anything?'

'Not yet, but it's early days. I need to ask – do you think Nancy could be involved in her sister's disappearance?'

'HC asked the same question, but I doubt it. Although if we'd found the backpack at the time Lola went missing, she'd have been a suspect for sure, as would her dad.'

'Agreed, and if we'd found anything today, he'd be top of my list. Until we know more, I guess he still is – especially as there is more than a suspicion that his death could have been suicide. Guilt, maybe?'

'I'm trying not to make any assumptions until we know what happened. The good news is that one of the admin staff here at the station remembers Lola from that summer, and she's on her way to talk to me. Let's hope she's got something to tell us.'

'Sounds promising. Someone out there knows what happened to her, Steph. And we're going to find them.'

FORTY-TWO

I want to go back to bed, bury my head under the pillow and pretend none of this is happening.

Where are you, Lola?

I bite back a sob. Is she dead? Why didn't I try harder to find her? Dad was so adamant that she would come back in her own time and was best left to her own devices, so perhaps Quinn was right. Maybe Dad did know something. But he never said.

I try to think of anyone Dad might have confided in if he knew something was troubling Lola, but he was a bit of a recluse. We never had visitors, and when Mum was ill, the only people who came were the part-time carer – Mandy – and Dr Phelps. He had always been so supportive, and yet we ended up not being able to look each other in the eye after Mum died because we blamed each other.

I've only realised how odd this lack of social contact was since I've been working at the care home. Some of my oldies have visitors all the time, and others appear to have no one. My parents would have fallen into the latter category.

It's strange to look back on my childhood. Like all kids, I

accepted everything for what it was. We didn't have any money, but I never felt conscious of being poor. Friends weren't welcomed into our home at a time when other kids at school were having regular sleepovers, and although I was envious, I accepted what I was told – that life on a smallholding was busy and it would have been difficult. But surely not *too* difficult? Is that why Lola was so keen to make friends on the beach – to compensate for what had been missing at home?

My eyes settle on my camera. When she disappeared, the police wanted photos of Lola for the local news and for the 'missing' posters that appeared around town. I chose ones that showed Lola smiling. For some reason, it felt important to show her as a happy girl, rather than a troubled one. I thought it might make people more inclined to help.

Are there other photos that might show a different Lola?

I'm slightly embarrassed when I think of the number of pictures I took of my sister in the first couple of days after I bought the camera. It was before I met Liam, and I was envious of the friends she'd made, so I followed her to the beach and used my telephoto lens to capture her laughing, lying in the sun, fooling around in the sea.

I grab the camera. Maybe my pictures could help the police find the people she spent time with.

The battery is now fully charged and I scroll through the images. It's an old camera with a small LCD display, so I put my camera and laptop on the chest of drawers and attach the cable to transfer the photos. The pictures flash across the screen – too fast for me to make out details – but I'm amazed at the colours as I catch glimpses of the beach, the sea from a cliff, a soaring gull.

I feel a sob building in my chest. The photos are bound to bring back all sorts of memories, and I'm not entirely sure I can face them.

. . .

I force myself to take a quick shower while the photos are downloading, and fling on the first clothes I can find. Tying my wet hair in a ponytail and feeling the water trickle down my back, I pluck the laptop from the chest of drawers. With shaking fingers, I open the images folder.

The first pictures are of the front of the cottage, and I can tell by the light that it was the end of the day. I remember that I couldn't wait to get home from the shop to charge the battery and start using my camera, but Dad sent me off to look for Lola, and then I had to cook dinner. By the time the green light was flashing on the charger, the food was ready. Lola wasn't there – but that was nothing new – and as soon as we'd eaten, I was impatient to take my first photo.

I asked Dad to bring his beer outside and sit at the table, but not to look at me.

'Look past me, at the sea, as if your mind is somewhere else entirely,' I said.

'No, Nancy. I'm not photogenic at all. I don't want any pictures of me.'

I recall feeling cross with him, because I wanted to try out my skills.

'You don't have to pose. Those are the worst kinds of photos. I want natural pictures – you won't even know I'm taking them.'

'I said no!' He was irritated with me, but then I guess he was stressed by Lola, and it didn't take much to set him off. I grabbed a few of him over the next few days, when he wasn't looking, but I never showed him.

That first evening I'd gone outside to explore some of the camera's features and now I flick through far too many similar shots – a few of the cottage, and others of a calm sea, a silvery grey colour that merges into the evening sky.

The colours come alive in the next set of images. It's a sunny day, the sea an intense cyan colour close to shore, a vibrant royal blue further out in the bay. My first shot is wide, taking in the full glory of the town beach swarming with people. I can see striped beach umbrellas thrust into the sand, leaning at strange angles as if they are about to topple over. Bright towels in bold reds and greens are spread out, and the contents of picnic bags are tumbled onto groundsheets. Children are playing with plastic buckets, building sandcastles, but despite all the colour, my eye is drawn to the centre of the image – the focus of my photo.

Lola.

She's standing still in a blue striped bikini, hands on hips, staring out to sea. Her long straight hair, a lighter red than mine, is blown back from her face. I've captured her from the side, and while in my memory she's always been a child, I can see she was anything but. I have always considered myself to have little or no shape, but that wasn't true of Lola. She was shorter than me, with more curves than I remember.

I flick to the next image. Very little has moved or changed since the previous shot, except in this version a boy is talking to Lola. She has her head thrown back as if she's laughing at something he's saying. In the next shot, she's running towards the sea, holding his hand.

I have no idea who this boy is. I zoom in and I see he's blond, possibly a few years older than Lola.

I feel my pulse quicken. Is this a lead? Did she run away with this boy instead of Quinn? Perhaps all the searching of the cottage is irrelevant. I feel a jolt of excitement.

I carry on scrolling, enlarging each image to search for clues, feeling slightly ashamed of how obsessed I seem to have been with the fun Lola was having while I hung around on the edge of all the action.

Then the photos change again. The lively beach scenes are replaced by pictures taken from cliffs, of waves crashing onto rocks, of seabirds, and finally of Liam's cove; a tiny, deserted bay of sand, with not a towel, umbrella or sunbather in sight.

The last photos are of Liam, alone in the slice of paradise he fought so hard to protect from intruders.

I don't want to look at him. This is about Lola, so I reach out to switch the computer off. Maybe the boy she was with on the beach will provide the police with a lead, but I'm probably clutching at straws.

FORTY-THREE

Stephanie was getting frustrated. She was making little progress with Lek and nothing had turned up yet from any other police force. He hadn't been reported missing in Cornwall, and every apparent lead turned out to be a dead end. Why had no one missed a boy so young?

The ringing of her phone interrupted her thoughts.

'Steph, it's Tai.'

Steph sat up straight. If the crime scene manager was phoning her, surely it was because he had something to tell her.

'Yes, Tai. Tell me you've found something. *Please!* I'm desperate for a lead on our skeleton.'

'I do have something to tell you, but I'm not sure how much it will help. Do you remember we swept the flat surfaces around the body, and the level below in case there was anything of interest?' Tai didn't wait for a response. 'We found a small wooden bead – two, actually. They have holes through them, so we think they might be part of a *mala* bracelet or necklace. We didn't find any more, but I suspect originally there *were* more.'

'Please tell me they mean something to you.'

'They do, although I don't know how much it will help. The beads are made of agar wood.'

'What's that? Never heard of it.'

'It's formed in large evergreens called Aquilaria trees when they're infected with a type of mould.'

'Yuk. Why the hell would you wear something made of mould?'

Tai laughed. 'Because it results in a dense, dark resin that's very aromatic. In some cultures, they believe an agar wood *mala* can bring luck to health and life.'

'Which cultures? Will it tell us where he was from?'

Stephanie heard a sigh from the other end of the phone. 'Not that simple, I'm afraid. Agar wood is revered in several religions, and because it's said to lower blood pressure and even help cancer patients – which you can believe or not, as you see fit – *malas* are worn by people everywhere.'

Stephanie felt her momentary excitement drain away.

'Bugger.'

'Quite. Agar wood is grown all over South East Asia, but Vietnamese agar wood is particularly popular, and it's closely tied to rituals in Vietnam. I don't know how much that helps.'

As she ended the call, thanking Tai for keeping her informed, she tutted with frustration. They already knew Lek was probably Asian, based on the forensic anthropologist's findings, so the bracelet could mean nothing at all. Then again, maybe the religious angle might be something she could pursue. At least it was somewhere to start.

Stephanie looked up from her desk to see an anxious-looking young woman with short auburn hair standing in front of her.

'Can I help you?' she asked.

'You wanted to see me – to talk to me about Lola Holland?'

'Of course. Sorry,' Stephanie said. 'You must be Chrissie

from the admin team. Take a seat, and don't look so worried. I just need to ask you some questions about Lola. You said you knew her eleven years ago.'

Chrissie nodded, not looking even slightly relieved. 'I met her, but it was for such a brief time. I'd have forgotten her name and everything about her if we hadn't all been questioned at the time.'

She dropped her head and twisted a slim engagement ring round on her finger.

'Yes, you gave your statement then. I have it in front of me.' Stephanie patted the file on her desk. 'You knew she was due to leave with Quinn Asher – it's what everyone believed. We now know that Quinn left, but as far as we can tell Lola didn't go with her.'

Chrissie's head jerked up. 'You're joking! It was all planned, down to the last detail. I sat with them as they worked out the timings.'

'I understand Quinn's back in the area. I've been trying to track her down, but I've not managed to catch up with her yet. Have you seen her?'

Chrissie shook her head. 'We weren't close, although I'd heard that she's back. I can ask around and get an address, if you like.'

Stephanie made a note. 'That's helpful, but I'd rather no one knows we're looking for her right now.' She spotted a look of alarm on Chrissie's face. 'Not because we suspect her of anything. We just need to keep this close until we have a better idea of what happened to Lola. What we *don't* want is specula-tion and people inventing memories in place of real ones.'

Stephanie had visions of old friends gathering, each remem-bering snippets and then together building their own interpreta-tion of events.

'Do you know why she wanted to leave?'

Chrissie shrugged. 'I know she didn't want to go back to

Shropshire. I seem to remember hearing her say to Quinn, "I can't go back. It will all start again, and I can't deal with it." Something along those lines. I asked Quinn later what she was talking about, and she shut me down. As I said, we weren't close.'

Stephanie said nothing for a moment. Lola went missing a couple of days before the family was due to return home. What was it that she couldn't face? What if whatever it was had caught up with her here in Cornwall?

'Apart from Quinn, was Lola particularly friendly with anyone else? Were there any boys involved? I'm wondering if she went off with someone else, maybe.'

Chrissie thought for a moment. 'It's quite a while ago, but there was one guy who was keen on her. She seemed interested to start with, then she cut him dead. I got the feeling he wanted more than she was prepared to give.' Chrissie's face scrunched into a frown. 'Look, I don't like to say this, but as she's missing I think I need to. She flirted like crazy with the boys – liked them flocking round her – and some of the girls were getting pretty pissed off with her. The thing is, as soon as any of the guys wanted to get close, to go off on their own with her or even snog her on the beach, she laughed and pulled back.'

'Any boy in particular?'

'The one I was thinking of was here on holiday, but I can't remember his name.'

'If it comes to you, perhaps you could let me know.'

Chrissie nodded, but Stephanie felt it was without much conviction.

'You said Lola was reluctant to return home. Do you remember anyone turning up that you didn't know – maybe someone she knew before she came here?'

Chrissie was quiet for a moment. 'It's difficult to say. There was always a core of local kids, and we hung around together at the beach every summer, until we were old enough to get jobs.

People – visitors – came and went. There were kids who'd been coming here for years on holiday, and then there were randoms – like Lola. She turned up one day, said she was here on her own and could she join us. There were probably others. I don't remember.'

Stephanie couldn't help thinking that it must have taken some guts for a fifteen-year-old to approach a group of kids she didn't know, and she said as much to Chrissie.

'You know, Sarge, there was a defiance about Lola – almost as if she was acting a part for someone else's benefit. We were a friendly bunch, and we accepted her straight away. Now that I think about it, though, there were moments when she was particularly flirtatious, but it never seemed genuine. It seemed more like a performance.'

'And who did you think she was performing for?'

'I don't know for sure, although I vaguely remember Lola finding it amusing that her sister was hanging about taking photos of her for a day or so. She went into overdrive with the flirty stuff, and it seemed an odd way to behave – as if she was trying to prove something.' She shrugged. 'I can't see how that might help.'

Neither did Stephanie. But as Chrissie closed the door behind her, she had to wonder if there had been signs of sibling rivalry that she had missed.

FORTY-FOUR

It's late afternoon before I hear any more from the police. I've spent the day glued to the window, scared of what I might see, and equally terrified of what I might miss if I leave my post. They erected a tent at one end of the garden, and I can't decide if it's to stop me seeing what they're doing or to keep the sun off them.

Whichever way you look at it, they are searching for my sister's body.

I saw the chief inspector arrive a couple of hours ago. He glanced up at my window and gave me an apologetic smile, so I know Sergeant King has told him I'm watching. At one point there was a shout from under the tent and he scurried across the newly cut lawn. I was practically hanging out of the window. After a few minutes he came out again and looked up to give me a small shake of the head, and I wasn't sure if I was relieved or sorry that nothing had been found. He seems to have gone now, so perhaps they're giving up the search.

There's a knock on the door and a disgruntled voice shouts, 'You're needed downstairs. Police.'

It seems Mrs Roskilly hasn't forgiven me for earlier.

I grab my laptop from where I left it on the bed and make my way downstairs. Sergeant King and DCI Brodie are here, standing in the dark hallway of the B&B.

'Can we have a word, Nancy?'

Mrs Roskilly appears from where she has obviously been listening through the open door to the kitchen.

'You can use the guest lounge, if you want,' she says, pointing to the first door on the left.

'Thank you,' I say, leading the way into another room that holds too much furniture, upholstered in shiny brown fake leather that looks as if you would slide around on it. It doesn't matter. I have no urge to sit down, so I stand, arms tightly clasping the laptop to my chest. 'Have you found anything?' I blurt out the words before they are through the door.

'We found no evidence that anything happened to your sister either inside or outside the house, Nancy,' the chief inspector says. 'I'm sure that's a relief to you, and I'm sorry you had to see what we were doing from the window.'

'Did you honestly think she might be buried in the garden?'

'We were hoping there'd be nothing to find – but since according to Quinn Asher she didn't leave with her that night, we had to check.'

'We need to speak to Quinn ourselves,' DS King says. 'She may have been lying to you for reasons of her own.'

'Haven't you spoken to her yet?'

She shakes her head. 'She's not at her original address, but we'll find her.'

I feel a sense of frustration. Why hadn't I asked her where she lived? I could have gone to talk to her about Lola myself.

'I've been talking to a young woman who works with me,' DS King says. 'She knew your sister – she met her that summer. Of course it's a while ago and she wasn't close to her, but she seemed to think there were a few boys keen on Lola. Did she ever mention any names to you?'

'No. I took some photos of her on the beach, though, and I just downloaded them from my camera. There's one boy she seemed interested in.'

I prop my laptop on a bulky sideboard and lift the lid while the sergeant carries on speaking.

'Chrissie – my colleague – thinks you might have quite a few photos of your sister. In fact, she thought Lola might have done a bit of posing for the camera – you know the kind of thing. Acting up. Showing off, maybe.'

I can tell that the sergeant is thinking through her words before she says them. I get the feeling there's something she's trying *not* to say.

'She was showing off all holiday, Sergeant. Dad and I didn't know what had got into her.'

I find the images I'm looking for and turn the computer towards the police officers. 'This is the boy I was talking about.'

Sergeant King leans in closely, with the chief inspector hovering over her shoulder.

'Is it okay if I enlarge this?' she asks.

'Sure. I can send you a copy, if you like.'

'That would be great, but this is fine for now.' She enlarges the face – not Lola's, but the boy's.

There is a stillness about her as she stares at the screen.

'You know him, don't you?' I ask.

'I do, yes.'

'Does that mean you know where to find him? Maybe he knows something about Lola?'

'I do know where to find him, and I will be speaking to him as soon as I can arrange it.'

'Who is he? What aren't you telling me?' I know there's something, and I can tell that the chief inspector wants to know too. He's looking at her with a puzzled frown.

'I wouldn't normally share this with you, Nancy, but if you show this photo to anyone else round here – which I'm sure you will if I don't give you the facts – someone will tell you. His name is Toby Makeland. He's well known in the area – and I know where he is because he's in prison.'

I hold my breath for a moment. 'What for?' I finally ask.

'He's a convicted rapist.'

FORTY-FIVE

I've been allowed to move back into the cottage. Sergeant King – Stephanie as she says I must call her – left with DCI Brodie, but she's coming back soon to ask me more about Lola. I could see she was worried about my reaction to what she told me about Toby Makeland, although she tried to convince me that he hadn't always been in trouble.

'As far as we know it was a one-off. Previous girlfriends said he had never shown signs of violence, but on this occasion his girlfriend ended things after a row. Then he saw her with another man, and he lost it completely. We have no evidence that he'd ever assaulted anyone before.'

I know she thought those words would be a comfort, but maybe it's the first time he's been caught. Was Lola his first victim? I can see from the photos that she was flirting with him. Did she reject him and he couldn't deal with it?

Stephanie wanted to know if Lola had a boyfriend at home, and I'm ashamed to admit that I don't know the answer. I don't even know who her friends were during the two years that I was taking care of Mum. No one ever came to the house, but that was the norm for us, and as I wasn't at school I had no means of knowing who she hung out with.

I feel so useless.

They're going to use Lola's picture to search social media. It's hard to imagine someone of her age – twenty-six now – having no presence on any of the platforms if she's alive, so I've put all the images of her into a shared folder. I've also searched every single photo to see if there is anyone I recognise from Shropshire, but there's no one.

Until now I've ignored all the other photos, but now I flick through them, starting with Dad and the photos he didn't know I was taking. I don't know why he hated having his picture taken. I always thought he was quite a handsome dad with his grey eyes and wide smile. He's not smiling in the pictures. He looks worried, with two deep grooves between his eyebrows.

I remember he had just lost his wife and he blamed one daughter for her mother's death, while the other seemed to be waging a one-woman war against her family, so I guess he had plenty to worry about.

There are endless photos of the sea, the birds, close-ups of wild flowers. Some of them are beautiful. Perhaps I would have done well at art school, had I gone.

And then the photos change. I lost interest in the dazzling world around me, in my dad's changing moods and my sister's brash behaviour. There was only one thing of interest to me.

Liam.

The first photos are taken from the clifftop the day I saw him sail into the bay – the day it all began. I remember his blue shorts, his white T-shirt clinging to his body as the rain drenched him. There are pictures of the cove and his boat, and a few of Liam that I snapped before he saw me. The only close-ups I have of him are those I took later, when I was allowed onto the beach. He was sleeping, lying naked, face down on the sand.

He didn't know I had a camera and I didn't tell him, some instinct telling me he wouldn't be pleased.

The last photo is one that I haven't looked at since I took it on the day Liam sailed back from France. When he saw me spying on him from the clifftop, I'd hidden the camera in my bag before he reached me. He was so furious that day that I'm sure he would have thrown it into the sea, had he seen it.

I never looked at that final photo because Lola saw me run past the beach. She left her friends to follow me home, to ask if I was okay. She wanted to tell me something, but I was too distraught to listen to my little sister, and I blame Liam and his cruelty for that. I forgot about the camera after that night because Lola had gone, and nothing else mattered.

I do remember thinking that Liam hadn't been lying about his wife – I saw him talking to someone in the cabin; I saw the curtain move – but it seems strange now that he came ashore without her.

I peer at the picture I took of the boat's window. I can see the shape of a person, but not much more, so I zoom in.

It's not one person, it's two – maybe a third in the shadows behind. I can't see much detail, but there is enough to be certain that the two I can see are not his wife. They are both young men.

FORTY-SIX

I wish I hadn't looked at the photos. I thought they would divert me from thoughts of Lola, but I was wrong. They merely served to remind me that my obsession with Liam did nothing but damage. Whoever was on the boat with him, they are of no interest to me. I close my laptop and push it to the far side of the table.

Both Effie and her mum have called to see if I'm okay, and I've told them I'm fine. Effie wanted to know if I'd like to go out with her and Patsy tonight, but I made my excuses and I think she understands.

Stephanie warned me that she had a few more things to talk to me about, so when I hear a knock on the door, I am not surprised to see her standing there, a concerned look on her face. I show her into the sitting room and she takes a seat on the sofa.

'I'm sorry to bother you again. I had to go back to the station with DCI Brodie so we could clarify our next steps, but there's something I'd really like to talk to you about, and I'm afraid it's sensitive.'

I look at her and feel my stomach flip. I lower myself into the armchair and wait for her to continue.

'I'm trying to understand Lola's mindset at the time she disappeared. However much we investigate her relationships with people she met here, we feel there are two angles we need to look at. We have to consider if she never left the area, or maybe she didn't leave voluntarily.'

I know what she's saying, and as they've already checked the garden for her body it should come as no surprise that they think she may have been killed, but my skin tingles with an icy chill as she carries on speaking.

'We know that she was *planning* to run away – even if she never did – and she'd only been here for about ten days before she started making plans with Quinn. Because of that, we feel it's more likely the root cause of her decision is something closer to home.'

'I don't know much about her life at that time. I should, but I don't.'

'I know, and I understand why. We're making enquiries with the school and tracking down any friends that were close to her. But how did she seem at home?'

'Things were difficult for all of us, with Mum being ill,' I say.

'I can only imagine. I remember when I spoke to you at the time of her disappearance, you intimated that Lola blamed you for your mum's death. I read the reports, Nancy, including the post-mortem report. Do you want to tell me about it?'

I don't, but I don't imagine I have much choice.

'You know I was Mum's carer?'

The sergeant nods, and I look away, staring at my hands as I interlock my fingers.

'I tried so very hard to make her better, although nothing seemed to work. I'm ashamed to say that part of my dedication was selfish. I was desperate to get my life back, and I thought if she was well again, I could be a normal teenage girl, so I found exercises to strengthen her muscles and made sure she ate the right food. No one ever told me why she'd had the stroke in the first place, what her ongoing problems were, or why her health wasn't improving. Dad wouldn't let the doctor tell me, although I know he wanted to. The doctor seemed to blame me too, when she died, but for a while I blamed him.'

Stephanie says nothing. She waits, knowing there's more to tell.

How can I say that I was exhausted, that I rarely slept for more than a few hours because Mum's snoring had become deafening? It was the doctor who told me I was wearing myself out. He gave me some mild sleeping tablets and told me to wear earplugs. 'A good night's sleep will give you more strength to get through the days, Nancy.'

I remember the night she died as vividly as if it were yesterday. I'd woken feeling groggy from the tablet. It was the first time I'd taken one and, exhausted as I was, I had fallen instantly into a deep sleep. But something had disturbed me – some instinct, perhaps.

The earplugs blocked out external noise, amplifying the sounds of my breathing, of my heart beating faster as I rolled over to face Mum's bed. She wasn't there. I struggled to sit up, still woozy, and shook my head to try to clear it. I staggered from the bed. Panic and guilt hit me. I had been sleeping when she needed me. I groped for the light switch, and that's when I saw her, lying on the floor, her eyes open – staring at me, not seeing me. I remember how yellow her skin looked in the light from the bare bulb hanging above her. Blood had pooled by her head, but it was dry and I realised she had been there for a while. And I had been sleeping.

My screams must have woken Dad and Lola, who came running from their bedrooms. I couldn't hear what they were saying. I still had the earplugs in, and all I can remember is the sound of my own screams echoing in my head. Dad was shouting. I pulled out one of the plugs. 'How did this happen, Nancy?'

I realise that while I have been lost in my memories, Stephanie has been waiting, so I take a deep breath. 'Mum didn't often need me during the night. She was out like a light. On the night she died, she must have woken up and decided to go to the bathroom. She could just about make it – I'd been working with her to get her moving, and with the help of her walking frame she could manage it if she took it slowly. I can only think that the rug slipped and that's why she fell. By the time I woke up, it was too late to save her.'

'Why did anyone think it was your fault?'

My eyes sting with tears.

'I should have been awake when she needed me. That's what I was there for. And she should have got better. Why couldn't I make her better?' I hear the note of anguish in my voice and struggle to regain control.

I hear a trace of an inward breath of air. 'Nancy, did you ever see the post-mortem report?'

'No. Dad didn't want me to. He said it would distress me; I guess he thought it might highlight my shortcomings.'

Stephanie is shaking her head. 'I don't want to upset you – you've had so much to deal with – but did you know your mum was an alcoholic?'

I look away, finding it hard to admit how blind I had been. It's only since I started to work at the care home that I've realised Mum displayed all the signs of liver disease. Her distended stomach, jaundiced eyes and swollen ankles were clear indicators, but to me as a teenager, they meant nothing. Only that she was ill.

When I turn back, I see compassion in Stephanie's eyes, and I nod slowly. 'I do now, and I understand it's probably what caused her stroke. All those days when she left Lola and me in the kitchen and escaped to her room, I suppose it was to drink vodka. I didn't have a clue at the time and I never saw her drinking. I thought the liver could repair itself if she stopped drinking, but I guess in her case it didn't.'

'What makes you believe she stopped?'

I feel my cheeks flush with anger. 'Because I prepared all her meals, drinks, *everything*, and I wouldn't have given her alcohol, even if she'd asked me to get some for her. Which she never did!'

Stephanie looks down at her hands where they rest on the table. I can see she's thinking what to say.

'Nancy, I'm so very sorry that no one has told you this before, but I've seen the post-mortem results and the reason she fell over that night is because her blood alcohol levels were dangerously high. I'm sorry, but your mum was very drunk. And her liver was severely damaged, which suggests that she never stopped drinking, even after her stroke.'

I stare at her. What is she talking about?

'From the expression on your face, I am guessing you didn't know this?'

'She can't have been. How did she get the stuff?'

'Your dad? Lola?'

I shake my head furiously. Dad wouldn't have given it to her, and Lola hardly ever saw her.

'Did Dad think it was me? Is that why he blamed me, do you think?'

I can feel tears streaming down my cheeks, and I lift my hand to brush them away. The thought that Dad believed I would do such a thing is tearing me to shreds. Maybe it's what the doctor thought too, and that's why he glared at me.

'Was there anyone else who saw her?' Stephanie asks, her voice gentle.

'Apart from family and the doctor, there was just a carer – Mandy – who came in a couple of times a week to help me get

Mum in the bath, among other things. But she wouldn't have bought Mum vodka with her own money.'

I close my eyes and think. It's a long time ago, but I remember there was always money missing from the house-keeping tin. I had assumed it was Lola, treating herself, so I'd decided to say nothing, if I could manage with what was left. How did I not see what was happening?

Since Stephanie left I've been sitting curled up in the armchair with a single lamp casting its yellow glow around the room. It's late and I should go to bed, but I seem to have lost the will to move. Everything I have believed to be true for eleven years is a lie.

I remember Aunt Helen's words at the funeral: 'You mustn't blame yourself for your mother's death. Whatever anyone tells you, it's not your fault.'

I didn't believe her then, but I do now. Mum's failure to get better wasn't my fault and I should be relieved, but I'm too confused for that. Surely the doctor knew she was still drinking? He told me I had to watch what she drank, but I thought he meant she needed more water. Why wasn't he more specific? Would that have been contrary to patient confidentiality rules? Couldn't he even tell Dad?

When Mum died, Dad would have seen the post-mortem results. Is that why he blamed me – not because I was sleeping, but because he thought I'd somehow been supplying her with vodka? It had to be vodka – I would have smelled anything else.

Had he told Lola?

I'd asked my sister if she thought Mum's death was my fault, but she'd glared at me. 'Why do you think everything's about you, Nancy?' she said and walked away.

Stephanie's words ring in my ears: 'your mum was very drunk'. She hadn't said much more before she left, but I could see what she was thinking – that Lola wanted to leave home because she couldn't bear to come back with me and Dad, him blaming me for something I hadn't done, while I was constantly begging for forgiveness.

She gave me a small box before she left. 'These are a few things the search team found under furniture and in places you might have missed. They may be yours or your aunt's, but I thought we should keep them for you.'

Apart from a few coins that I guess they found down the back of the sofa, there are only a couple of items of interest: a lottery ticket, which is dated earlier this year – long after my aunt was last here – and a gold stud earring in the shape of a delicate flower, missing its butterfly. It's not mine, and I can't imagine it belonged to my severe aunt Helen either.

Right now, I don't care. I feel in a strange limbo, lost with nowhere for my thoughts to settle because there is no longer anyone left to ask for the truth. Should I have seen what was happening to Mum? Should I have *known*? Is Lola dead?

I feel broken. I missed the signs with Mum, and with Lola. And to this day I don't know if my dad died in an accident, or if he took his own life because he had lost everything. Everything but me.

FORTY-SEVEN

To Stephanie, it didn't feel much like a Sunday. It was just another working day, and with two big cases to focus on, she was up bright and early to crack on with the tasks she had earmarked for the morning.

First, she would call HMP Dartmoor, where Toby Makeland was serving a seven-year sentence. Gus had said she didn't have to trek all the way there to see him. He would get one of his Newquay team to do the interview if she could set it up.

That was the straightforward part of the day. More tricky was the pursuit of the identification of Lek. Stephanie had done some reading since the beads were found and had discovered that agar wood bracelets were likely to be worn by people of the Buddhist or Hindu religions. They already knew Lek was Asian, so that wasn't a particularly stunning revelation, and she couldn't afford to be distracted by a single piece of evidence, but it suggested that she needed to visit the local Hindu and Buddhist communities, as well as the Islamic Centre.

As she didn't want Lek to slip down the priority list, Stephanie had decided to send someone else to interview the different groups. She hated doing this, always feeling there may be some nugget that might be missed if she wasn't there in person, but needs must.

'Arrogant bugger,' she muttered to herself as the thought struck her.

'Talking to yourself, Sarge?' The voice came from the door, and she didn't need to look up to see who it was.

'What do you want, Jason?'

'I'm told you need to brief me on the questions to ask the various religious groups.'

Stephanie groaned inwardly. Not Jason. Intuition wasn't his strong point.

'You'd better sit down, then.'

Jason obligingly took a seat. 'Thing is, Sarge, I'm not sure I'm the right man for this job.'

That makes two of us, Stephanie thought, and wondered for a moment if she'd said it out loud. But Jason carried on talking.

'I don't get all this religious mumbo jumbo. Do they all believe in the same god, but it's packaged differently – you know, like Kellogg's cornflakes versus those in Asda that are the same but in a different box?'

Stephanie shook her head. *What the hell was he talking about?*

'I don't get it, you see. I don't get *God*, so should I be the one asking the questions?'

Probably not, Stephanie thought. At a guess, there was no one else available.

'You don't have to believe in their religion – and Buddha wasn't a god.'

'Really?'

'Never mind. You don't need to understand who, why or how they worship. You simply need to talk to them about Lek: what we've discovered, his age, his Asian ethnicity, when we think he might have disappeared – although that's quite a wide timescale. Push them on anyone who was part of their community and then suddenly wasn't. Dig deep, Jason.'

Jason shrugged. 'Sounds straightforward enough. No need to talk about God, anyway. I'm on it!'

He got up from his chair, and Stephanie couldn't help wondering if she was doing the wrong thing, letting him loose like this, but at that moment there was a shout from across the room.

'Sarge, we've tracked down Quinn Asher. I've got her address.'

'Contact her and ask if she can come in, please? Today, if she can.'

She sat back in her chair. Even if Quinn didn't know where Lola was, she might well know why Lola had felt she needed to go.

Stephanie pulled up the photos of the beach scenes that Nancy had forwarded and stared at them on her computer screen. Although they had already identified a few people, including Toby Makeland, there were other kids there too, some of whom may well still live in the area.

'Someone has to know what happened to Lola,' she muttered. Those kids may have known more than they were prepared to admit to back then. They needed to jog some memories, so she chose a selection of the images and forwarded them to the admin team for local circulation, asking for anyone in the pictures to come forward.

One of the photos was of Lola, walking out of the front door towards the gate with a scowl on her face. Behind her in the open doorway stood Ray Holland, arms folded, his mouth a hard line. Stephanie remembered him. His fair hair was long on top and brushed back from a wide forehead, his prominent nose giving him a slightly hawkish appearance. It was a regular enough face, although neither Nancy nor Lola seemed to have inherited his grey eyes or the colour of his hair. Both girls had red hair – Lola's lighter than Nancy's – and green eyes.

She thought back to her interview with Ray Holland. It was so long ago that it was a blur, but she remembered one question she had put to him.

'Do you have other family in England – or anywhere in the UK – that Lola may have gone to?'

'Only Janice's aunt Helen, and she would tell us if Lola turned up there. She lives in the back of beyond in Scotland, so it's unlikely. Lola barely knows her.'

'And there's no one else in the UK? What about overseas? I notice you have a slight accent.'

He had looked shocked and shaken his head. But he *did* have an accent, detectable by the way each word ending in a consonant was sounded separately, rather than run together, which most English people did. And there was a hint of a rolled 'r' in the middle of a word. It was subtle but there nevertheless.

'I was brought up in the south of England, near Portsmouth. I travelled a lot as a steward on cruise ships. Most of the people I worked with were foreign – I guess it must have rubbed off.'

There was nothing to indicate that Ray Holland was involved in his daughter's disappearance, but Stephanie decided to do a bit of digging. They had his details on file, and it didn't take long to establish that Raymond Holland was indeed born in Hampshire, so despite the trace of an accent, he was telling the truth. Nancy had said that, as far as she knew, he had no living family, but Stephanie made a note to look into that too.

His date of birth was interesting. He must have been twenty-seven when Nancy was born, which put him in his mid-forties in these photos. He looked older. She stared for another minute or two, then shrugged. He worked outdoors and his wife had just died. She could hardly expect him to be looking his sparkling best.

Even so, there was something about him that Stephanie found uncomfortable. She didn't have a clue how it related to Lola's disappearance, but she was going to keep digging.

FORTY-EIGHT

I hardly slept again last night. I don't know how to fill the long hours of each day as I pray the police will discover what happened to Lola, but I force myself to get out of bed, have a shower and make a piece of toast. It sticks to the roof of my mouth and I push the rest of it away.

As I sit at the table, head in hands, my phone pings. It's a notification that someone wants to be my friend on Facebook, and I stare at the screen, the thought of social media adding to my queasiness. I have kept well away from it, unwilling to look in case I see posts about the crime scene – my cottage – but the friend request is from Effie. I accept, certain she won't have posted about Lola, and I take a peek at her girlfriend, Patsy. She has such a happy face – just what I would expect of someone with Effie – with long blonde hair, tucked prettily behind one ear.

I pull my phone closer to my face, tap the screen and expand the visible ear. She's wearing an earring – a delicate flower, in gold.

I sit back and place my phone on the table. I'm sure lots of people have gold flower-shaped studs, but I reach for the box with the odds and ends found by the police and pull out the earring. It looks like a perfect match. And then there was the lottery ticket, from earlier this year.

Something else suddenly occurs to me. When I first arrived, I thought the house had the smell of polish, but there was a warm, spicy fragrance too. I breathe again. The scent has gone now, but I can remember it and I'm sure I know what it was.

Cinnamon.

Hadn't Effie said that Patsy drank too much cinnamon tea?

Effie knew her way around the house perfectly. She knew which cupboards to open to store the food, which door led to the bedroom and not the bathroom. Angie told me Effie and Patsy can't afford a place of their own and this house had been standing empty for years. It must have seemed like a gift to Effie and Patsy. Angie had the key, and it gave them somewhere to be – somewhere they could pretend was their own.

Was her friendship genuine? Was the bogus email intended to unsettle me? Is she only staying close so she will be the first to know if I want to sell the cottage?

I've found it hard to trust people for the whole of my adult life, and now – when I thought I had met someone I could count on – I have to accept that I may have been fooling myself.

'*Arghh!*' I shout. 'Get a bloody grip, Nancy!'

If I start to suspect Effie of trying to drive me away, our budding friendship will be tainted, and whatever the reason for Patsy's earring being in my house, I won't solve the mystery by sitting here. I should go for a walk; wear myself out. Maybe tomorrow will be a better day.

The weather is a little overcast, so I grab my jacket, sling my camera round my neck and slam the door behind me. I set off at a march down the road towards town and, beyond that, to the coastal path.

I stomp along the track, pulling out my camera now and

then to grab something vaguely interesting, but my heart isn't in it. I'm too wound up.

I know this route will inevitably take me past Liam's cove, but I've no intention of looking down on his beach again. I'll stick to the path.

As I get closer though, I glance towards the headland – my snooping spot. There's a man standing there, and for a moment my heart thuds. Is it Liam? I don't think so, but I can't see properly from where I am. He's on the other side of the hedge, right on the edge of the cliff. Strangely, though, he's not looking out towards the sea – he's staring inland.

He's watching me, and as I get closer he lifts a pair of binoculars to his eyes. He's not moving, and I try to walk normally, casting a furtive glance at him every few seconds. He's following me with his binoculars. *What is he doing?*

This man is too broad across the shoulders to be Liam, and as the sun breaks through, I can see glints of fair hair. He lifts something to his ear – a mobile phone or a walkie-talkie. His binoculars are still following me, but he doesn't move.

I walk head down, focusing on the path ahead. The snaking path down to Liam's beach is just ahead, and as I glance towards it, I see a tall wrought-iron gate set between two stone pillars guarding the entrance. It wasn't there before.

As I draw close, through the bars of the gate I catch a glimpse of a second man – this time too thin to be Liam. He has a phone pinned to his ear too, and he stops when he sees me and watches as I walk by.

I know this man!

It's the wiry man with the thin face who came into the café when I was waiting for Effie; the one who pushed past me in the village shop. He was outside the restaurant when I went to talk to Quinn too – and now he's here. Does he know Liam? Has Liam asked him to follow me? Maybe he thinks I'm going to stalk him, or try to speak to his wife and let her know what a bastard her husband is; tell her what we used to get up to while she was in France and very possibly pregnant with his child – all to get back at him for hurting me so much.

What kind of a sad person does he think I am?

The wiry man is standing on the other side of the gate, watching. The fair-haired man on the cliff is following me with his binoculars. I try to act unconcerned and glance out to sea. A boat is moving away from the land – the one I saw in the bay the other day – Liam's, I'm sure.

Without looking at either man again, I stride past, my head high. I no longer feel safe continuing along the coastal path so far from town, from other people, but I don't want them to feel my discomfort. I turn towards a track that I think leads to the main road. I can't resist twisting round to see if the man is still standing by Liam's gate. He is, but he's not looking at me. He's unlocking a fat padlock. I take a quick snap. He starts to look up, so I spin away from him and hurry along the track heading inland. This may have been a mistake. There's not a soul around, but there is a building ahead. Perhaps there will be people there.

I keep walking as fast as I can without breaking into a run, but when I reach the building, it's a barn, not a house, and it's deserted. One of the doors is hanging from its hinges and I can see inside clearly as light floods in through a vast hole in the roof.

I stop dead. There's a van inside. A grey van. I've seen it before. I nearly walked into it; then it was parked near the cottage. Is it Liam's?

Has he been following me?

FORTY-NINE

Stephanie had had a frustrating morning. Progress on all fronts seemed to be slow, so while she waited for Quinn Asher to arrive, she decided to put together a plan to look into Lola's life in Shropshire in more detail. Had someone followed her here to Cornwall – a boyfriend, perhaps? It seemed clear there was something they hadn't been told at the time of her disappearance, so she picked up her phone.

Her call to Nancy was answered quickly, but the woman seemed out of breath.

'It's Stephanie King. Are you okay, Nancy?' she asked.

'Yes, I'm fine,' Nancy gasped.

'Sorry if I've disturbed you. Are you out for a run?'

There was a squeak of a laugh down the phone. 'No, that's not my thing. I'm just walking quickly.'

She sounded nervous. 'Is everything all right?' Stephanie asked.

There was a momentary pause. 'Yes – it's fine. Have you discovered anything about Lola?'

Whatever was bothering Nancy at that moment, she didn't

seem inclined to say, so Stephanie ploughed ahead with the questions.

'I'm going to speak to the school tomorrow, and I wondered if she used to belong to any clubs – a church, a sports club – anything outside of school.'

Nancy was still panting as if she was rushing, and perhaps this wasn't the best time for the conversation.

'Would it be easier if I came out to see you later, Nancy? You seem in a hurry and it's not urgent.'

'No, it's fine. There isn't anything that I know of.'

There was a pause, and Stephanie waited to hear if she said more. All she heard was a gasp, and a muttered '*Shit!* Sorry, I've got to go.'

The line went dead. Stephanie stared at the silent phone. Something was clearly wrong. She decided to send a text. *Nancy – I'm worried about you. You sounded stressed. Do you need some help? Please let me know you're okay.*

She pressed send and waited. Nothing. No response.

Her desk phone rang, and she reached for it without taking her eyes off her mobile.

'Sarge, Quinn Asher's here. Shall I put her in an interview room?' There was a pause. 'Sarge?'

'Sorry! Yes, I'll be down in a couple of minutes.'

There was nothing more she could do for Nancy right now, but Stephanie hoped she would respond soon.

FIFTY

The man I saw coming along the path from Liam's cove is following me. I'm sure of it. Stephanie's call threw me. It stopped me in my tracks, and when I glanced over my shoulder I could see he was right behind me – heading towards me along the track, and I don't know how far it is to the road.

Am I being paranoid? This man could be anyone, and totally harmless. Perhaps he was visiting Liam's family. A brother, maybe. He's just a man, walking to town. The van might not even be the same one.

Somehow these explanations don't seem right to me. It was the way he looked at me, as if he was expecting me. And the fair-haired man on the headland – not staring out to sea, as a sightseer might do, but looking inland, his gaze raking the path as if he was on guard duty.

There's no doubt now that the man behind me is walking quickly, drawing closer, and I'm not sure if I should run. He'll catch up with me soon unless I do something.

My camera is hanging heavily round my neck, the lens fully extended. It bangs on my chest as I start to jog, so I lift an arm to hold it steady. I stumble, letting go for a moment, and it swings towards my lowered head, almost hitting me full on the nose. I manage to right myself and slow to a fast walk, glancing over my shoulder as I do.

The man is no closer, but he's no further away either. Surely any normal person would have called out to ask if I was okay? But he just walks, hands in pockets, his thin face expressionless. He is less than forty metres behind me, and if he's nothing other than an innocent walker, why doesn't he speak? Why does he watch me?

I turn back to the track and lift my phone to my ear. Should I phone Stephanie back?

I think of what she might ask me. Has the man tried to get close to you? Has he called out to you? Has he said anything offensive? Why do you think he's a threat?

My answers would be no, no, no, and I think he's a threat because I've seen him three times since I've been here. And there's a van that looks like one that was parked near my cottage. It might be his.

I almost laugh at the thought. The police did nothing when Lola disappeared because she wasn't considered vulnerable. And here I am, in broad daylight, panicking about a guy I don't like the look of.

I could pretend to make a call. He won't know I'm not connected, so I press my screen and bring the phone to my ear, speaking loudly enough for the man to hear as if it's a bad line.

'Is that Detective Sergeant King? Hi, it's Nancy. Sorry we got cut off earlier. I was on the coastal path, but I've just turned inland.'

I pause.

'Oh, that's great! I'll ping you my location. Hang on...'

I fiddle a bit on the screen of my phone as if I'm accessing Google Maps, then lift the phone back to my ear.

'You got it? Excellent. It looks like I'm a few minutes' walk from the main road, so I'll see you there.'

For a moment, I wonder if this was a stupid idea. My fake call may have put him under pressure, and he could decide to act now, before I reach the road.

My breathing is coming fast and furious, and it's not through exertion. Whatever I said in my fake phone call, I have no idea how long it will take me to get to the road.

To my relief, a few minutes later I hear traffic, and as I turn the corner I see cars passing the end of the lane. I hurry towards what feels like safety and turn right onto the road. Gasping for breath, I rest against a stone wall a few metres from the end of the track, as if I'm waiting for someone.

The man follows me to the road. He stops, and as he looks my way, his mouth turns up at the corners. He nods his head towards me, turns left and saunters away.

I feel a fool. Once again, I am seeing shadows where there are none.

FIFTY-ONE

Quinn Asher was standing by the window, staring at something on her phone, when Stephanie entered the interview room. She looked up as the door opened and smiled.

'Hi, I'm Quinn,' she said, walking towards Stephanie and holding out her hand to shake.

Quinn certainly lived up to her reputation for style, wearing a blue polka dot dress, cinched in at the waist with a full skirt that swung as she stepped forward. She looked fabulous with her white hair and bold red lipstick, although Stephanie was certain that if she wore anything like that, she would look as if she was on her way to a fancy dress ball. Quinn carried it off with pizazz.

'I'm Detective Sergeant King, Miss Asher. Please take a seat.'

'Call me Quinn. Everyone does.' She smiled again, seeming unfazed at being in a police interview room. 'I'm assuming this is something to do with Lola? I saw her sister the other night. She seemed shocked that Lola didn't leave with me, as planned.' She pressed her lips together and gave a small shake of the head.

Stephanie was tempted to jump right in and ask why Lola

was running away in the first place, but despite Quinn's smiles, she had a feeling this woman would not be a pushover.

'It's been difficult for Nancy. She's spent eleven years believing her sister ran away with you, an older girl who may have looked out for her, only to discover that she didn't. And she has no idea where she is.'

Quinn gave a small shrug, as if to say, *What can I do about that?*

'Can you talk me through the plan, so we might have a better idea about timings?'

'I'll do my best, but it's so long ago and life's been up and down since then. If I'm honest, I'd completely forgotten about Lola. She was in my life for less than two weeks, at a time when, frankly, everything was shit.'

Stephanie nodded. 'I understand, but anything you can tell us might help. Do you remember what the plan was that night?'

'There were two guys down here on holiday. Thought they were surfer dudes.' She chuckled and shook her head. 'We got chatting, and they mentioned they were driving back up to London on the Thursday night, late, and I asked if I could bum a lift.'

'Where did Lola fit in?'

'She told me she had no intention of going back to Shropshire and had been planning to take a bus to Bristol, and then to Manchester. She had some money – so I said why not keep hold of the money and come with us to London. The boys were more than happy – thought with two of us, it might be fun.'

There was a dry tone to her voice, and the slight curl of her lip told Stephanie exactly what Quinn believed the boys were thinking.

'Did Lola understand what the plan was?' Stephanie asked.

'Absolutely. I told her the lads were probably expecting some sort of payment in kind, and I remember the look of horror on her face. I made it clear that nothing was going to happen. They could dream on.'

'You arranged a time and place to meet?'

'We did. We always hung out on the beach until it got late, or sometimes until we crashed out from too much drink. The plan was that Lola would stay until her dad had gone to bed, then she'd sneak back for her stuff. She'd hidden it outside and said she'd be able to get it without going back into the house – but it all went tits up, I'm afraid.'

'What do you mean?'

Quinn gave a dramatic sigh. 'Lola pretended she didn't give a damn about her sister – there were all kinds of issues there – but we were hanging out, waiting for the boys to turn up, when we saw Nancy run along the promenade. She was coming from the coastal path, and she was obviously crying. Lola didn't say a word, but she jumped up and ran after Nancy. That was the last I saw of her. The boys came, I tried to phone her but got no answer, and they weren't prepared to wait. I thought maybe she'd gone to find out what was wrong with Nancy and had changed her mind about leaving. That was all I could think. When I returned to Cornwall someone told me there had been a low-level investigation into her disappearance, but I just assumed she'd gone to Manchester, as originally planned.'

'You didn't think to let us know that she didn't go with you?'

'What, after eleven years? I didn't persuade her to leave, you know. She was going anyway, and I just offered an alternative option. When I heard she'd left that night, I didn't think anything other than she'd decided to do her own thing after all.'

Stephanie was about to tell Quinn that Lola's backpack had been found, but for now it suited her for Quinn to know as little as possible. She decided to save it for later to shock some additional information from her.

'I've heard from another source that Lola flirted with quite a few of the lads. Can you tell me anything more about that?'

Stephanie had been interviewing people for years, and she recognised this as the moment Quinn clammed up. There was no outer sign, but she could feel the woman withdraw.

'Not really,' she said, with a look of indifference. 'She was fifteen. She wanted to be liked. I think it was all part of her defence mechanism.'

'What do you mean?'

Again, Quinn pulled back. 'Oh, you know how it is when you're a teenager. You want to be fancied, but you don't necessarily want to deal with the consequences. I don't think she liked any of the boys much, but she enjoyed the attention.'

'What about Toby Makeland?'

Quinn's eyes flashed with surprise. 'Toby? Why are you asking about him?'

'I have a photo of Lola with him.'

Quinn shook her head. 'He was just another boy on the beach back then. Look, I know about Toby. His behaviour towards Caz was a fucking disgrace, and he deserves his punishment. Thank God she's okay.'

Stephanie knew Caz was the girlfriend that Toby had raped and beaten, and was about to ask her more about him and Lola, but Quinn hadn't finished.

'No one can excuse what he did, but I've known Toby all my life and I honestly never saw that side of him. I guess his feelings for Caz released the animal that must have always been lurking within him, but Lola was at most a passing fancy, and it's hard to imagine she would have roused such feelings of anger in him. Obviously I can't say for sure, but I never saw any sign of it.'

It was clear that Quinn had no more to add, so Stephanie changed the subject. 'You mentioned issues between Nancy and Lola. Can you be more specific?'

This time Quinn's reaction was visible. Her body stiffened, and her mouth grew tight.

'Not sure. Nancy was the one who cared for her mum. Maybe Lola thought she was the favourite or something. Perhaps she felt excluded.'

'I don't think you believe that, Quinn. I think you know more than you're saying. Do you know why Lola wanted to run away?'

Quinn looked Stephanie in the eye, but her expression was blank. 'I guess that's something you might want to ask Lola, when you find her. Or ask her dad.'

Stephanie waited for a beat. 'I would, but he's dead. Only Nancy is left.'

For a second Quinn looked as if she was about to say something, but instead she took a deep breath.

'In that case, I think it's probably best to let sleeping dogs lie.'

'*Shit*,' Stephanie muttered, slamming her papers on the desk and collapsing into her chair. She hadn't been able to get anything else out of Quinn and had to let her go, but she should have done better. Quinn was their best lead, and Stephanie was frustrated, regretting her decision to go ahead without Gus. What had she missed?

In an effort to break through the barrier Quinn had erected, Stephanie had decided to tell her about the discovery of the backpack, and she could see from the woman's shocked expression that she understood the inference. She also told her they had searched the house and the grounds for evidence of any harm that may have happened to Lola on the premises.

'And did you find anything?' Quinn had asked, an expression of concentration on her face that Stephanie had found hard to interpret.

Stephanie had been forced to admit that they had found nothing. They still had no idea what had happened to the girl, and she had tried to appeal to Quinn's conscience, imploring her to share anything she knew. But all she would say was that Lola had always believed Nancy knew what her problems were. It seemed she was wrong.

And that was it. Quinn was gone. What was she hiding?

Stephanie's musings were interrupted by the ringing of her phone, and she could see it was Gus.

'Hi,' he said. It was his short sharp voice, and she knew he meant business. 'I'm calling to give you the feedback from the prison. Wally – the officer we sent to interview Toby Makeland, who incidentally is a much better police officer than his name might suggest – doesn't believe Makeland had anything to do with Lola. He said the guy's broken, deeply ashamed and knows he deserves his punishment.'

'That's all fine with hindsight, but he's obviously capable of violence, so I'm not sure we should automatically write him off as a suspect simply because he's developed a conscience.'

Gus chuckled. 'Ever the compassionate one, eh, Steph? I agree with you, though. Wally says Makeland looked puzzled by the mention of Lola. He claimed he didn't remember her until Wally showed him the picture. Apparently his eyebrows shot up, and he's either been studying for a role in a blockbuster movie while he's been locked away, or he'd genuinely forgotten all about her until he saw her picture – which is unlikely if he'd been involved in her disappearance.'

'Did he have anything of any use to say?'

'I'm not sure it's helpful, but once he remembered her he said she was more than a bit screwed up. Wally tried to get him to be more specific, but all he said was he thought she was hot to start with, but then he decided she was weird. I'm not prepared to rule him out, though. How did you get on with Quinn Asher?'

Stephanie didn't feel now was the time to criticise her own performance. 'Nothing that's much help. I'll fill you in later, but it's clear that plans were in place for their escape and Lola didn't turn up. She left the beach to run after Nancy, who seemed to be upset. That was the last she saw of her.'

Gus gave a tut of frustration. 'Do we know what had upset Nancy?'

'No. But I'll see what I can find out. I'd prefer to do that face to face. I spoke to her earlier, and she seemed very stressed, so I'll either call on her tonight or first thing in the morning.'

'Right. See you later then,' Gus said, and before she could answer, the line went dead.

She tutted into the silent phone. Honestly, there was being professional and there was being downright rude.

FIFTY-TWO

To make Stephanie's day complete, Jason had phoned to say he was on his way back and did Stephanie have five minutes to go through his findings?

It was hard to switch from Lola to Lek. Both were important, but one was a long time dead and the other was missing – with still a slim chance of being found. She knew where she wanted to put her efforts, but both deserved her attention.

As Jason swaggered through the door, Stephanie could tell he was pleased with himself. She pointed to the seat, and he straightened his trousers as he sat down, as if pulling them into non-existent perfect creases.

'Went well, then?' she said, raising her eyebrows.

'I think so, yes. I might have a lead.'

'Excellent.' She waited, and Jason sat looking at her expectantly. 'And are you planning on telling me?'

He shuffled in his seat and looked a bit irritated, as if he was expecting more enthusiasm from her, and with a look that said, *If that's the way you want to play it*, he pulled out his notebook.

'First, I went to the Hindu temple. Interesting one, that. Did you know they think cows are sacred?'

'I did. They also believe in karma – in other words, you get what's coming to you, whether in this life or the next. Carry on.'

Jason looked slightly bewildered by this comment, but shook his head as if she was talking gibberish. 'They said they would put the word out. They didn't know of anyone missing, but family ties are very strong in their culture, so they'd be aware if anyone was concerned about their son.'

'Okay. That makes sense. Anything else?'

'I went to the mosque and same story, I'm afraid. It's a bigger community so there's more chance that someone has fallen through the cracks, but I spoke to a man who's a part-time imam and volunteer, and he said he'd ask around and get back to me if he has anything to tell me.'

Stephanie felt her initial optimism start to fade. These were the two tight-knit communities that she thought held the most hope for identifying Lek.

'However,' Jason said, with a self-satisfied smile, 'then I went to the Buddhist place, and I think there might be something. It took a while to find it because I was expecting some kind of temple covered in gold, like the movies. I must have gone past it about three times. Turns out it's a Buddhist sanctuary where people come to find peace rather than a temple. It was... I don't know, soothing, I suppose.'

Jason seemed to have had something of an epiphany and for a moment Stephanie felt for him. She knew he'd been brought up in difficult circumstances, and any sort of belief was outside his comprehension. She should be kinder to him.

'Given that you came in here looking as if you had something to report, I guess the person you spoke to was helpful?'

'Sort of, yes. She said she'd had a visit from two boys a couple of years ago – maybe a bit longer. They spoke little English, but she'd travelled around Asia studying Buddhism, and she thought they were speaking Vietnamese to each other. But when she asked if that's where they were from they said no. The thing is, they seemed scared and were looking over their shoulders the whole time, so she asked if they lived locally. They wouldn't answer her, but she got the idea that they were trying to find someone. She understood the word for "brother", so she got her phone and used Google Translate. They were very cagey, because obviously the app picked up that they *were* speaking Vietnamese. Anyway, it turned out that their brother was lost, but they wouldn't give any more details. They thought he might have come in search of somewhere to worship as he was very...' Jason paused and looked at his notebook '...spiritual – that was the word she used.'

'Well done, Jason. This sounds positive. Does she know where we can find the boys?'

'That's the thing. She asked where they were living so she could contact them if the brother turned up, but they didn't want to say. They argued with each other, but they were whispering and the only word she recognised means "farm". That sounded alarm bells for her, so she used the translator again to tell them she could help them. She thought they were afraid because they were probably being controlled by someone, and they shouldn't have been out and about. But when she pushed them for more, they glanced at each other and turned and ran. She's never seen them since.'

'*Bugger*. It's not as if there's a shortage of farms in Cornwall for us to look into, is it?'

Jason gave her a puzzled frown. 'No, but if they're illegal, surely there are only a few places that would consider taking them on?'

'Possibly – but which? And "farm" could mean anything – it could be a sheep farm, or a cannabis farm in someone's 1960s semi.'

'I did ask her how she thought the boys got to her, because she's a bit remote.'

Stephanie gave Jason a nod of approval. 'Good thinking. And?'

'She said they were on foot when they arrived. No sign of bikes or a vehicle, but her place is on a bus route.'

That wasn't good news. They could have come from anywhere.

'I know it sounds like we've got nothing, but Sarge, if they are illegals or modern slaves or anything like that, they're not likely to have money for long journeys, not to mention they'd be missed if they were away for too long – and more to the point, the only way they might have heard of this Buddhist place is if they're local. I somehow doubt they would have had ready access to Google.'

'I'm not sure you're right about that. We know illegal immigrants bring phones. Remember those tragic calls from the back of that lorry a few years ago? But it's a good starting point. Well done.'

She meant it. He may have gone round the houses three times to get to the relevant point, but he had given them somewhere to start looking. Her only worry was that if this was indeed a cannabis farm rather than a sheep farm, organised crime might be involved. And that was one area of policing that she hated with a passion. It was the province of people without conscience, morals or scruples, but nevertheless, it meant she had a call to make.

FIFTY-THREE

It felt like weeks since Stephanie and Gus had been at the mortuary with Carla Davies and Molly Treadwell, but it had only been a couple of days, and now the pathologist's and forensic anthropologist's reports on Lek were in.

There were no surprises, unfortunately. Molly's report was purely factual – as it had to be – but Stephanie knew her well. The pathologist was good at making assumptions she wouldn't commit to on paper, and perhaps she had some glimmer of an idea that Stephanie could follow up. Although it was Sunday, she was sure Molly would be at her desk.

'Molly, it's Stephanie King. Sorry to bother you at the weekend.'

She heard a soft chuckle. 'Nothing special about weekends – just days, like any other. What can I do for you?'

'I've read the reports, but I wonder if you have any theories that you don't want to commit to in writing?'

Molly sighed. 'I hate cases like this. Give me a good murder, where I can tell you about the weapon, its size, shape, which hand they used it in, how tall the assailant might have been.

That's when I'm at my best! But this... well, it disappoints me to say I can only hazard guesses.'

'Yes, but yours are much better than most, and I don't have a bloody clue. So fire away!'

'Okay, but I can't prove any of this. You understand that, don't you?'

'Of course. I just need *something*.'

'Well, we know your Lek had a broken tibia. As documented, it's a spiral fracture – the kind of injury you might get snow-boarding or skiing where your leg gets caught and then you twist – that kind of thing. Not much of a demand for that in Cornwall! I guess he could have been waterskiing, but that's an expensive hobby and his clothes were cheap as chips. If he'd fallen from the cliff and hit a rock, I wouldn't have expected this injury. It's more likely that he slipped clambering over rocks to get out of the sea, catching his foot and twisting as he fell. Or maybe he fell from a boat and got his leg caught in something – a rope, perhaps. This is all quite hypothetical, but I doubt it was a fall from the cliff.'

'I doubt that too,' said Stephanie. 'It's not the kind of cliff you would climb barefoot.'

'Quite. But the barefoot thing is interesting. I would say he's spent a fair bit of his life barefoot.'

'Really?'

'Yes, and if you have children of your own, you should make sure they go barefoot as much as possible. It's much better for the development of their feet, you know.'

Stephanie felt a jolt as she always did when people spoke to her about having children, although of course Molly didn't know about her miscarriage. No one did.

'Why do you think he didn't wear shoes?'

'By the shape of his toes – they're straight and well spaced. Then there's the arch, the width of the foot; they suggest that he at least grew up for several years without shoes. We're all so keen to shove children's feet into their first pair of shoes. Bloody silly. No wonder we've all got bunions and corns.'

Stephanie tried not to laugh. She would make a point of studying Molly's footwear the next time she saw her.

'And does that suggest anything to you?'

'Sensible parents?' Molly chortled again. 'Just joking. I think he grew up somewhere where shoes weren't worn much – at least in the home – or he was poor. Having said that, there was no evidence of stunted growth or lack of bone density, so I wouldn't say he was malnourished. Is any of this helping?'

'It is. You've given me something to think about. Thanks, Molly.'

'Pleasure! Say hello to young Angus from me!'

Stephanie grinned as she ended the call. Gus would love it that Molly still considered him to be young.

As she'd hoped, Molly's insights had been helpful. She needed to do some research, but Jason's Buddhist contact had said the two young men who came looking for their friend were Vietnamese, which tied in – somewhat loosely – with the *mala*, and she was pretty sure that in Vietnam it was polite to remove your shoes before going into a house, and even into some offices.

The nature of the break to the tibia, though, painted a different picture. If Lek didn't fall into the sea from a cliff, but was somehow scrambling over the rocks, how did he get there? There was no way onto those rocks, except from the sea, so he must have either swum there, or got there by boat. There was no record of an abandoned boat being found, although it could have sunk, but if he was swimming, where the hell had he gone into the water? There was no accessible beach nearby. It didn't make any sense.

Stephanie's phone rang.

'Is that DS King?' The voice had a lilting Welsh accent.

'This is Dave Trebbith from the South West Regional Organised Crime Unit. We haven't met – I'm new here – but I understand you left a message. What can I do for you?'

'Thanks for calling back. You may have heard that we've got
a skeleton, found in a cave. We don't know much about him,
other than he probably died between one and twelve years ago,
and he's of Asian descent. We've been checking if anyone who
fits the description has been reported missing, but nothing has
come up. Some young guys – probably Vietnamese – were
asking at a Buddhist centre about their brother who'd disappeared. The woman who runs the place said they were nervous,
checking over their shoulders, and they did a runner when she
asked too many questions.'

'Ah,' Dave muttered. 'You think they were working under
some form of duress?'

'It's a thought, yes. They mentioned a farm, but whether it's
a normal farm or perhaps a cannabis farm, I have no idea.
Before I go blundering in and scupper an investigation into an
organised crime group, I thought I'd better check with you
guys.'

'I'm glad you did. There's a particularly vicious OCG oper-
ating out of Bristol, and they're monopolising the south-west
region right now. We've got multiple surveillance operations in
place, mainly in Somerset. But we're aware that their tentacles
stretch into Devon and Cornwall. They're into everything,
including modern slavery, so it's not impossible that it's related.'

Although it sounded as if this organisation fitted the bill,
Stephanie knew that the owner of the 'farm' could just as easily
be an enterprising local scumbag working alone who had
recruited some illegal immigrants newly arrived in the back of a
lorry from France.

'Okay. I can't sit on this, though.'

'I understand, but tread carefully. If this farm is in any way
connected to the OCG, they're extremely dangerous. They

have no respect for human life, and although we don't have any bodies, we know of at least three people connected to them who are missing. In the meantime, I'll put out the word across all local teams to see if there's anything you should know.'

As Stephanie thanked Dave and hung up, she shivered. Much as she hated having anything to do with organised crime, it seemed to be everywhere. Their unscrupulous pursuit of money spread its tentacles far and wide, from the distribution of drugs to the supply of firearms, from fraud to money laundering, child sexual exploitation and human trafficking. They thought nothing of using violence and intimidation against anyone from small shopkeepers to vulnerable children.

Stephanie now had a sickening feeling that she wasn't going to be able to avoid coming face to face with some of its gruesome manifestations if she was going to discover what had happened to Lek, and, on that cheerful thought, she switched off her computer and picked up her bag.

FIFTY-FOUR

I'm pouring myself a glass of cool white wine when there's a knock on the door. I'm so jumpy, I spill most of it.

'*Bugger!*' I mutter, mopping up the mess quickly.

I glance through the kitchen window and see it's Stephanie, and she's on her own.

I pull the door open and start to speak before she has the chance to say hello.

'Have you got news? Do you want to come in? I was having a glass of wine. Are you still on duty, or would you like one?'

I'm in danger of gabbling, and I force myself to stop.

'No, I'm good, thanks, Nancy. Sorry to call round unannounced, but feel free to drink that wine before it gets warm.'

'Okay. Would you like a tea or coffee? Or a soft drink, if you prefer.'

She shakes her head, a slightly puzzled expression on her face. I'm gabbling again, so without meeting her eyes, I pick my wine up from the worktop and sit down.

'Any news?' I ask again, thinking that can be the only reason she's here.

'Nothing concrete yet, I'm afraid. But we're getting lots of responses to the photos we've posted, and we're following up on everything. I wanted to check if you're okay. When I spoke to you on the phone, you seemed a bit stressed.'

I remember that I had muttered '*Shit!*' when I saw the man following me, and that she'd sent me a text that I never answered.

'I'm sorry. I should have got back to you.'

Stephanie looks at me and says nothing, clearly waiting for more from me.

'I went for a walk. I thought I was lost, but I wasn't. There was a man on the path behind me, so I decided to walk a bit faster, to put some distance between us, and then I nearly fell over. That's why I swore.'

'Were you worried about him?'

I shrug. 'I'm worried about everything right now. I'm seeing demons in the shadows, to be honest. He never caught up with me, didn't even speak to me. He was just some bloke out for a walk – same as me.'

She looks as if she doesn't quite believe me, but I need her to focus on Lola.

'As long as you're sure you're okay.' Stephanie pauses, waiting to see if I will fill the silence, but I don't, and she carries on speaking. 'So – to bring you up to speed – I've spoken to Quinn Asher, and she raised a few points. She says the last time she saw Lola was on the evening she and your sister were planning to leave, but Lola saw you run past the beach, and it seemed you were upset. Is that right?'

I don't particularly want to get into this. 'What, that I was upset, or that I ran past?'

'That Lola followed you.'

'I suppose so. I got back here and ran straight up to the bedroom. She appeared minutes later, asking what was wrong.'

Stephanie is clearly waiting for me to say more.

'It was just boy trouble. Lola knew nothing about him, and I didn't want to tell her. You need to understand that she was incredibly self-absorbed on that holiday. I'm amazed she was concerned enough to follow me when she saw me crying. I'm afraid I told her to mind her own business.'

I'm ashamed all over again and feel my cheeks burning. I risk a look at Stephanie, and she gives me a gentle smile.

'Quinn seems to think there was something troubling Lola, something she thought you knew about but were ignoring. Your dad knew, apparently, and I don't think she was lying. Do you have any idea at all what it could be?'

I stare at the detective. Lola had been acting up all holiday, so was it there in front of my eyes all the time, and I just didn't see it? I feel my throat contract and a burning sensation behind my eyes. I don't want to cry.

'We were like two separate families inhabiting the same house when Mum was ill. I can see why she would have told Dad, and I should have listened when she wanted to tell me, but I was tired of the Lola show, to my immense regret. It sounds mean now, but she behaved as if she despised me, as if I was the reason Mum was dead.'

'Okay, I understand, Nancy. I'm sorry if I've upset you. Just a couple more questions, and then we're done for now. As you ran past the beach, did you know Lola was there?'

I close my eyes and try to think back. 'I vaguely remember, yes, because I didn't want her to know I was crying. She seemed to think I was pathetic anyway, so I didn't want to give her something else to ridicule me for.'

'And did you see anyone else – anyone she was with who might have followed too?'

'No. Only Dad. He was sitting in a beach café having a drink. I don't think he noticed me. He was watching Lola.'

FIFTY-FIVE

It's the silence that wakes me – that quality of stillness that tells me there is something or someone in the room absorbing the sound; something that wasn't there before.

The air feels denser, flatter, as if a body is blocking the gentle breeze coming through the open window. The soft murmur of the waves as they hit the pebble beach seems duller, the edges of the sound smothered by another presence.

I know without a doubt that I'm not alone, yet instinct tells me not to move a muscle.

Who are you? Why are you here?

Every inch of my skin prickles with fear. If I open my eyes, he'll see, but if he thinks I'm sleeping, maybe he'll fade back into the night as smoothly and silently as he came.

I hear nothing. No sounds of breathing or movement, but there's someone here. I'm sure of it. The air is still, heavy, hot. The urge to scream is overwhelming, but I must control my breathing, give no sign that I'm awake, alert, my body primed for fight or flight.

There's a whisper of sound, fabric stroking fabric. He is standing by the bed, his clothes brushing the thin duvet, hanging over the edge where I threw it earlier as the sticky heat got the better of me. He's so close I could touch him, and it's all I can do not to reach out to check he's really there. My mouth is dry, yet I mustn't swallow.

I imagine I can feel his breath, grazing my skin, and in that moment I realise I am uncovered. My vest top has rolled up. The loose legs of my pyjama shorts weren't designed for modesty and my limbs are spread wide in search of a cool spot in the bed. It takes every ounce of my willpower to resist the temptation to tug my top down and pull something over my legs.

Go! Just go! What do you want? Leave me alone.

I feel a faint stirring of air. He's moving. Is he coming towards me or walking away? I am certain he will notice I'm trembling, hear my heart beating. The fast hammering is throbbing in my ears.

If he touches me, I'll scream. I won't be able to help myself.

But as the thought strikes me, there's a change in the room. The air seems lighter and there's a sudden draught.

I hold my breath, tensing every muscle so I can hear. If he's still here, he'll know now that I'm awake, so I force myself to relax my breathing again.

I wait, expecting to hear the floorboards creak on the landing. But there's nothing. All is silent. Has he gone?

Slowly I open my eyes a little – the smallest slits – knowing that if he's here, watching, he will see the whites of my eyes. A thin beam of moonlight casts shadows around the room, but none appear to be human.

Did I imagine it?

No. My bedroom door was shut. Now it stands ajar, as if he didn't want to risk the sound of it closing.

I don't know if he's still in the house. I don't know if he will be back.

I lie there, my body shaking, bathed in sweat, until the

moonlight fades and the first glow of dawn reaches into the room. Only then do I move.

Slowly, I swing my legs out of bed. I can't be sure he's gone, but if he wanted to harm me, he had every chance. I tiptoe to the door and ease it open gently, silently, and edge along the landing. The bathroom door is open, but he could be on the other side.

There's a creak as I tread on the loose board and I gasp, freezing against the wall. But I hear nothing. Plucking up courage, I race to the head of the stairs and thunder down, desperate to get outside.

I reach the bottom step and stop.

The key isn't in the front door. I'm sure I left it in the lock when I went to bed. And then I realise the door isn't quite closed.

He's still here.

FIFTY-SIX

Gus had called his usual morning meeting in the hastily set up incident room. Concern that they had overlooked something significant in Lola's disappearance all those years ago was ramping up, and Stephanie was feeling the pressure. She may have been a junior officer back then, but it didn't take away her guilt at the thought that she had missed a vital clue.

'I'd like to recap where we are with Lola Holland's disappearance,' Gus said, facing the group in the room. Behind him, Nancy's photos of Lola were pinned to the board, along with pictures of Ray Holland, Toby Makeland, Quinn Asher and Nancy herself. 'We know she was planning to leave with Quinn Asher, but as of yesterday afternoon, I think we're inclined to believe Asher's assertion that she never turned up.' Gus turned towards one of the team. 'Bernie, I need you to follow up on the boys who took Asher to London. She gave their first names to Steph, and she knows where they were staying, so we need their confirmation that Lola never left Cornwall with them.'

Bernie nodded and made a note.

'There are several scenarios we need to consider, based on what we know. The first is that Lola found some other means of leaving – but that's unlikely without any money. We also need to consider that she *did* meet Quinn and the boys, but maybe she came to some harm when she was with them and one of them subsequently put her backpack in the shed to throw us off the scent. We need to speak to them separately and get them to explain what happened that evening without giving them the heads-up that we believe Lola never left.'

Gus looked around the room to ensure everyone was paying heed to what he was saying, but to Stephanie that wasn't in doubt. He had a charisma that never failed to demand attention.

'We should also consider that she could have been abducted, maybe trafficked, either somewhere in the country or overseas. Let's face it, there are plenty of boats and no end of opportunity. Or – and I know it's what we've all been thinking – she's been killed. Either by accident or deliberately – but either way, her body disposed of. There's no trace of her in the garden or the cottage where they were staying, so if she's dead she probably wasn't killed there.'

'Unless she was strangled,' came a shout from the back of the room.

'Indeed. We need to look at the timeline to see if that was possible, presuming Nancy wasn't involved – which may, of course, be a false assumption. The last time Nancy saw her was at around 19.30 on the 23rd of July. According to the original interview notes, the father claimed he came back from having a beer in town and heard Lola talking to Nancy in their room. Steph, can you please repeat what he told you at the time?'

Stephanie glanced at her notes. 'He and Lola had had a few disagreements that week – just teenage girl stuff – and he didn't want to get into another argument with her, so he went to his room to read. He fell asleep, and presumed when he went back downstairs at about midnight that both girls had gone to bed.' She put her notes down. 'It's not for me to say, but if I had a slightly wayward fifteen-year-old girl, I think I would want to *check* that she was in bed, but he claims he didn't.'

'Do we know anything else about their relationship – how they were getting on?'

'There were issues. Lola was being difficult, but what fifteen-year-old hasn't been from time to time? Nancy felt that both Lola and her dad blamed her for Janice Holland's death – although that seems completely unreasonable from what we know. There was, without a doubt, a lot of tension.'

Gus nodded. 'I don't like the thought that a girl disappears and then the dad dies in an accident that has a whiff of suicide. Did he kill her, and then the guilt got to him? If he did, we need to think where that might have happened, and how he disposed of her body. Nancy ran out of the cottage after Lola spoke to her, and returned about an hour and a half later. Lola wasn't there, but we need to remember it was July and still broad daylight at that time. It would have been difficult to get a body out of the house. Of course she could have been hidden in the back garden, or even his bedroom, until it was dark enough to move her. No one remembers Lola returning to the beach that evening, although some of them were still partying there. So where did she go? You will all have heard that Lola knew Toby Makeland, and on the board is a photo of her taken by Nancy Holland in which she's holding hands with him. We can't, and mustn't, rule him out. There's no evidence of him hurting anyone before his girlfriend, but that level of violence is unlikely to have come from nowhere. What are we doing to check on him that night?'

A young detective at the back of the room raised her hand. 'It's hard because it was eleven years ago, but it's stuck in people's minds because they were interviewed at the time. Makeland's a significant part of every conversation and it seems clear he was there earlier, before Lola ran after Nancy, but no one saw Lola after that, and they can't remember if Toby stayed late.'

'Okay. Keep on it,' Gus said. 'We need to learn everything we can about Lola Holland – not only what happened when she was here, but before she came to Cornwall. We've got her phone log from that time, so every friend and contact needs to be spoken to. Let's understand what made the girl tick, and see if anyone – from here or Shropshire – can tell us what was troubling her. And Steph, we need to push Quinn Asher again on why Lola wanted to run away. She doesn't think it's relevant, but it's not her bloody call.'

'I'm going to talk to the school as well,' Stephanie said. 'They were spoken to at the time, but the notes are sketchy. They refer to the fact that there were difficulties at home – with the mother, I presume that means – and that Lola kept pretty much to herself. But I'll dig deeper.'

'Thanks,' Gus said. 'We're getting the impression that she wasn't a happy, well-balanced girl – but that's not helping us to find her. Is there anyone else we might talk to?'

Stephanie raised her hand again. 'The original team tried to contact Nancy and Lola's aunt Helen, but it was Helen's husband, Malcolm, who they spoke to. I'll read you the file note: "Spoke to Malcolm McEwan, husband of Helen McEwan, Lola's great-aunt on her mother's side. He said his wife was unwell and couldn't get to the phone, but he would check if she'd heard from Lola. He reported back that she'd heard nothing, and was unlikely to. Apparently Lola 'clearly doesn't even know their address as she has never once sent a thank you note following a birthday or Christmas present'. In the highly improbable event that she got in touch, he said they would phone the police in Cornwall immediately." That was the sum total of the response, and nothing was heard from them again.'

'I need you to follow up on that, Steph, and see if he has anything more to say now the situation has changed. Of course, his wife died recently, but she left her cottage to Nancy so she must have felt some attachment to the family. Then can you go and talk to Nancy again? See if she'll tell you more about what upset her so much that day. Might be irrelevant, but we can't decide without more information.'

'She said it was just boy trouble and Lola knew nothing about it, but I'll push her.'

'Good. Anything on social media?' Gus asked.

'Nothing yet,' Bernie said. 'Obviously we've also checked all the standard sources – DVLA, National Insurance, bank accounts – but nothing.'

A PC who had been answering incoming calls at the back of the room called out: 'Boss, got a man on the phone who's seen the info in the local paper and reckons he saw Lola that night. Says he's happy to come in to talk to you.'

'Good. Take his details and ask him when he can get here.'

Gus turned back to the team. 'Goodness knows where this guy's been for the last eleven years, but no doubt we'll find out. Whatever's happened to Lola Holland, we need answers.'

Stephanie had been a police officer long enough to know what everyone was thinking. She never left Cornwall, and there was no trace of her anywhere. It all pointed to the fact that Lola Holland was very probably dead.

FIFTY-SEVEN

As soon as she was back at her desk, Stephanie decided to give Nancy a call to ask if there was a particular teacher at the school with whom Lola had had a good relationship – someone who might have known what was going on in the girl's head.

Nancy's mobile just rang out. Stephanie grunted with frustration and left a brief message asking her to call back.

Hoping she would have better luck with her next call, she dialled the number for Helen McEwan's husband.

'Rothmore House.'

'Hello, could I speak to Mr McEwan, please? This is Detective Sergeant Stephanie King of the Devon and Cornwall Police.'

'This is he.' He didn't give Stephanie a chance to ask a question. 'Given where you're calling from, I suspect it's about the cottage, and if that's the case, Helen left that to her great-niece. You need to talk to her.'

The Scottish accent was very strong, and the voice clipped. She had the impression that if she didn't speak soon, he'd hang up.

'Thank you, Mr McEwan. We know about the cottage, and

we've met Nancy. It's about the disappearance of her sister, Lola. It was a while ago – eleven years – but some new evidence has come to light, and we're trying to find out more about the girl, and what might have made her want to run away.'

'What new evidence?'

Stephanie wasn't sure whether to answer this, but she probably wouldn't get any more out of this man without giving him something in return.

'Some of her personal belongings – items her sister thought she would definitely have taken with her – have been found at the cottage.'

'You know Helen never went back there, don't you? She left before the girls went there on holiday, so she won't have known anything about things that were left behind.'

'I understand, Mr McEwan, but we're trying to get a full picture and fill in any gaps.'

'Fine, but I never met Lola, and Helen certainly never heard from her again after her mother died. Nancy was in touch occasionally, and Helen contacted her after Ray, or whatever he was called, died. But that's all.'

The man's voice was brusque, impatient, as if he wanted nothing to do with this family and their problems, but Stephanie persevered.

'I wondered if your wife ever spoke to you about problems in the family? Anything that might have upset Lola?'

There was a loud bark of laughter down the phone. 'Problems? That family was *rife* with problems. Look, Helen worried about them endlessly, and it didn't do much for her health, I'm sure of that. She never approved of the decisions her niece took – Janice, she was called. Helen thought she'd made some grave mistakes, but Janice wouldn't be told. In the end, Helen had to pull away from her. I told her – let it go, now. You've done what you can.'

Stephanie hoped there was more, but McEwan was silent.

'Can you help me unpick that a little, Mr McEwan? You say there were problems, and that Janice had made some mistakes, but what exactly do you mean?'

There was a prolonged sigh. 'That man she hooked up with. I'm sorry, Sergeant, but I don't know the facts. It all happened before I met Helen and she said it was better for me not to know. That's all she would say, but I'm sure she wouldn't want it all dragged out into the open now – for Nancy's sake. She's the only one left, so she's the one who matters.'

'We're still hoping Lola's alive too, sir.'

'For what it's worth, I don't think Helen believed that. She never said it in so many words, but she left the cottage to Nancy when she could have left it to both of them. She thought that if Lola was alive, she'd have gone back home when that man – Ray, or whatever he was called – died. But look, I've said enough. I'm sorry – anything I say is purely speculation.'

The line went dead, and Stephanie found herself staring at the phone in her hand. Why did Helen have to pull away from the family, and what did she know about them that she wasn't prepared to share with her husband?

FIFTY-EIGHT

The day had been less successful than Stephanie had hoped, and Nancy had never called back even though she had left a second message. Added to that, the conversation with the school had been disappointing, although the headteacher agreed to ask those staff who knew Lola and said she would get in touch in a day or so.

The one thing they had managed to prove was that Quinn Asher had told the truth. Lola Holland hadn't travelled to London with the two guys. They'd tracked them down easily as one of them was the son of a second-home owner with a holiday cottage close to the town.

'We barely knew Lola,' one had said. 'We knew Quinn – everyone knew Quinn. When she asked if we would take her and Lola back to London with us, we were happy to get a bit of help with the petrol money, but when Lola didn't turn up, it was no big deal.'

There was no hint of them hoping for something more in the way of thanks from the girls, but anything that might have been said in that regard even as recently as eleven years ago would be met with disgust now, thank God.

With a soft groan at the lack of progress, Stephanie was about to leave for the day when her phone rang. Tempting as it was to ignore it, she never found that possible.

'Stephanie King,' she said, trying to keep the sigh out of her voice.

'Sergeant King, it's Malcolm McEwan, Helen McEwan's husband. We spoke earlier.'

Stephanie sat down again. The man hadn't seemed particularly keen to talk, but perhaps he'd thought of something. 'How can I help you, Mr McEwan?'

'First of all, I owe you an apology. I was a bit frosty when we spoke, but you see, it's Helen's birthday today – my first without her – and you chose a bad time.'

'I'm sorry, sir. That must have been difficult for you, particularly when I wanted to talk to you about your wife. But you didn't need to call to apologise.'

'No, but I've been thinking through everything that Helen told me about Janice and wondering if there's anything I can tell you that might help. I'm not sure, because I don't know it all, but I thought you might be able to piece it together. I'm just worried about Helen's name getting dragged through the mud in all this.'

'I'm sure that won't happen, Mr McEwan, but perhaps you could give me some idea of your concerns, or Helen's?'

Stephanie could hear the man sigh, as if he didn't want to tell the story but knew he must.

'Here's what I know, and it isn't much. This all happened before Helen and I were married, and I never met any of them, so I only know what Helen allowed me to know.'

Stephanie thought that was an odd choice of words, but gave the man space to continue.

'Let's start with the farm – their home. You know they had a smallholding, don't you? In Shropshire?'

'Yes, it was sold after Ray Holland died.'

'He won it in a poker game, of all things. I gather he liked a flutter, and on this occasion he was lucky, although on many others he was anything but. He worked on cruise ships – a real charmer, or so I'm told. Janice didn't have an easy time of it. She was effectively a single parent because he was away at sea for weeks on end, and Helen told me she wasn't particularly emotionally robust due to her own upbringing. My wife supported the family financially for a while after Ray won the smallholding. He'd packed Janice off to Shropshire, thinking it would be a better life for them, but the place was in a terrible state, and initially Janice had to run it on her own.'

'But she managed to get Ray to take responsibility for his family, in the end?'

'Ah,' Malcolm McEwan said. 'That's where it all gets rather complicated.'

'How do you mean, sir?'

'This is where the story ended with Helen. I don't know what changed, but Helen said that Janice was stuck with *that man* whether she liked it or not, because they'd committed a crime – a serious one. If discovered, they'd go to prison and the girls would end up in care. Helen hated the fact that Janice told her what they'd done, because it made her an accessory. My wife found lying abhorrent, so she had to walk away. Then Janice became ill. Helen wanted to pay for a nurse – but if she had, it would have been impossible to claim ignorance of her niece's wrongdoing, should it have come out.'

'Did your wife ever consider reporting this crime?'

'She debated long and hard whether to inform the police, but worried about the impact on the girls, so she said nothing.'

'Did she keep in touch with Nancy and Lola?'

'Not while their parents were alive, and it was difficult after Janice died because Helen was torn. Of course, Lola disappeared soon after. I know Helen worried about Nancy but didn't want to lie to the girl about her parents, and it wasn't her place to tell her the truth either. She felt she should leave any good memories that Nancy had intact.'

'And you've no idea what Janice and Ray Holland's crime was?'

'No, only that Helen said nothing good could come from it being discovered. She wouldn't tell me because it would make me culpable too, but she wanted me to know this was hanging over her before we got married. Helen went back to Shropshire briefly when Janice had a stroke, and she was shocked at how things had deteriorated. She felt Janice was trapped and her crimes were catching up with her. She'd found solace in the bottom of a bottle. That's really all I know.'

'Well, it's very helpful, Mr McEwan. Thank you. Just one thing, though. A couple of times you referred to Ray Holland as "that man" – which suggests that your wife didn't have a very high opinion of him. Was that because of the crime he and Janice committed together, or was there another reason?'

'I'm not sure. It's just what she always called him.'

With no more questions to ask, Stephanie was about to hang up when McEwan spoke again.

'There was another thing. In the last few weeks before she died, she sometimes became quite delirious. She kept talking about someone called Carl and became quite distressed. She said she should have had more courage and perhaps she could have saved them. I have no idea what she meant.'

Gus was in deep discussion with another member of the team when Stephanie arrived in the incident room. He looked up and signalled her to come over.

'What is it, Steph?'

'I don't know if it means anything, but I was about to leave for the day when Malcolm McEwan called me back, and I'm not sure what to think.'

She repeated the conversation about the crime that had been committed and why he wasn't able to say what it was.

Gus gave her a puzzled frown. 'How do you think that helps us?'

'He gave me the impression that Nancy didn't know about it, and her aunt didn't want her to find out, but I wondered if somehow Lola had discovered her dad's secret? Nancy said she was a bit off with him when they were here on holiday, but she thought it was because her dad was trying to curb her wild behaviour. What if she'd found out what he'd done?'

Gus nodded. 'And you think that might have been a motive for murder?'

Stephanie shrugged. 'If it meant he would go to prison, people have killed for less. And for all we know, the crime they were covering up could have been murder.'

'True,' Gus said. 'If Ray Holland did kill Lola, I think our chances of finding her are remote. If you were a killer in Cornwall, would you dig a grave or throw someone off a cliff?'

Stephanie pulled a face. 'You know the answer to that.'

'Did McEwan have anything else to say?'

'Only that his wife kept talking about someone called Carl. It was always in relation to Janice. I'll do a search on Ray Holland and the name Carl and see whether it throws anything up. Maybe he was involved in the crime they committed. And I'll ask Nancy if she remembers a man called Carl. I was planning to see her tonight, but it's a bit late so I'll go first thing.'

'Sounds good. I'm still not convinced of Toby Makeland's innocence, despite what Wally said. You don't make a guy a monster in five minutes.'

'What are you going to do about it?' Steph asked.

'I might just take the time to talk to him myself. Fancy a trip to a prison?'

Stephanie would have loved to go, even if only to spend a chunk of the day with Gus. But they both knew this wasn't realistic and they shared a smile that said more than words.

FIFTY-NINE

It was all Stephanie could do to keep her eyes open as she got in the car to drive home. She wished she had slept well the night before, but she hadn't. Gus had received the DNA results confirming he was Daisy's father and he couldn't hide his joy at the news. Next step was a blood test, and he'd told Stephanie that whether or not Lola's case was solved, he would make himself available to the doctors whenever he was needed.

It was good news for Daisy and her family, but unfortunately when Gus phoned Paula to tell her, he had ended up having a tricky conversation with her husband, who was worried that Gus would want Daisy's birth certificate changed, now they knew for certain he was the child's father. Gus had done his best to reassure him, but emotions were running high, and Gus had tossed and turned all night.

Today had been a long day, and now there was a storm brewing. The air felt heavy. The clouds over the sea were black, with flashes of distant lightning brightening the sky every few seconds. She wouldn't want to be out in a boat right now.

The sound of her phone broke into her thoughts.

'Stephanie King.'

'Sarge, it's me.' There was a pause. 'Jason. PC Graves.'

'Yes, Jason. You on nights, then?'

'Just filling in. Couple of guys have got a bug, so I volunteered.'

'What can I do for you?'

'We've had a call from an Effie Dawson. Says she's a friend of Nancy Holland, and she knows you.'

She remembered Effie, the garrulous younger sister of Tessa, one of Stephanie's friends from school whom she still saw occasionally. When they were teenagers, nine-year-old Effie used to chatter through every film they tried to watch.

'Did she say what she wanted?'

'No, said she'd rather talk to you. Shall I'll ping you her number?'

'Okay. Thanks, Jason. I'll call her now.'

Stephanie ended the call and within seconds Effie's number appeared on her screen.

'Effie? Hi. Steph here. How are you doing? Not seen you for ages, but I had a drink with Tessa last week.'

'I heard. Sounds like it was a good night.'

Stephanie chuckled at the memory. 'It was. But I'm sure that's not why you're ringing. What can I do for you?'

'I've been spending a bit of time with Nancy Holland – my nan was a friend of her aunt Helen, and Mum's been looking after the cottage. I was there when she found the backpack.'

'Oh God, it must have been awful for her. I think she mentioned you, but I hadn't joined the dots.'

'I phoned her yesterday to make sure she was okay. She didn't want company, which is fair enough, but I've been calling her today and she's not picking up. So I popped round. She's not at home.'

Stephanie felt a moment of alarm. Nancy hadn't returned her calls either, but she didn't want to alert Effie to her concerns.

'And you're worried because…'

'Yeah, I know it sounds a bit extreme. She's a thirty-year-old woman, for God's sake. But I thought I should flag it with you, in case you knew where she might be. I offered to go to the supermarket in town for her – get her some frozen meals so she doesn't have to think about feeding herself. We agreed I'd drop them off this evening, which is why I was calling her – to confirm the time. It's odd that she's not there. With the fake email and everything, I'm a bit concerned. I'm sure it's nothing, but still…'

'What fake email, Effie? She told me today that she thought a man was following her, but decided she was just being jittery.'

She heard a tut down the phone. 'I'm not surprised she's jittery. Not only is she having to face the fact that something terrible might have happened to her sister, but someone sent me a bogus email pretending to be her, basically telling me to keep away. And she thought someone had been in her house when she was out. Didn't she tell you?'

'No, but I wish she had.'

There was a brief silence. 'I guess she wanted you to concentrate on finding out what had happened to Lola.'

That silence had spoken volumes. Nancy hadn't told her because she didn't trust her to take it seriously.

'Christ, poor woman. I'll call by her place now – check she's there and have a chat. There's something I need to ask her anyway.'

'Would you mind letting me know if she's okay? I sensed something was a bit off last time I spoke to her, and I'm happy to keep her company if it's all getting too much.'

As soon as they hung up, Stephanie called Nancy, but the call rang out.

Swinging the car round in a neat U-turn, Stephanie headed towards Trevyan.

. . .

Despite it only being eight o'clock, the evening was dark with heavy black clouds growing ever closer, and as Stephanie pulled up outside Nancy's cottage, she was surprised there were no lights shining through the windows.

It was possible that Nancy had gone out for something to eat, and maybe Stephanie was overreacting, but she banged on the door and opened the letter box to peer inside. There were no signs of life.

'Where are you, Nancy?' she muttered.

At that moment, her phone rang again. Gus.

'Hey, Steph. I thought you were heading home, but I've beaten you to it. Everything okay?'

'I've called to see Nancy. There's no one here, and the cottage is in darkness.'

'She's probably gone out for dinner – why so worried?'

Stephanie repeated what Effie had told her, and about the man she thought was following her. 'She's not what I would class as a vulnerable adult, but still, why would someone try to drive a wedge between her and Effie? It's as if someone doesn't want her to get too comfortable here, and I can't help wondering if it's related to Lola's disappearance. Perhaps things are starting to come back to Nancy – things that were buried deep at the time. If someone abducted Lola, they might think Nancy knows too much. I don't know, but I don't like the feel of it.'

Gus didn't question her thinking or tell her she was being too dramatic.

'What's your plan?' he said.

'I'll get a torch from the car and shine it through the window. She might be sitting in the dark, looking out at the approaching storm and ignoring the rest of the world. Hang on.'

Stephanie hurried back to her car, opened the boot and pulled a powerful torch from the bag of tricks she kept there.

'Okay,' she muttered into the phone. 'Give me a moment.'

She walked up to the sitting-room window and shone the

torch through the glass. The room was empty. A laptop sat on the coffee table – open, but the screen was blank.

'No one in the sitting-room,' she told Gus as she moved across to the other window.

'I can see into the kitchen. There's no one there either,' she said.

For all she knew, Nancy could be fast asleep upstairs, but as she moved the torch its glare fell onto the kitchen table.

'Gus, her mobile and purse are both on the table. If she's gone out it must be for a walk – and would she seriously go out with this storm on the horizon?'

'You know her better than I do.'

Stephanie wished that were true. Nancy still hadn't really changed her view of the police, as far as she could tell.

'I guess none of this means anything's happened to her, does it?'

'Probably not, but you're worried, aren't you?'

'I don't like it. She sounded really rattled yesterday, despite saying she was getting things out of proportion. Until we know for sure what happened to Lola, I don't like taking a chance. Someone may think we're getting too close.'

'Okay. I'm on my way. At the very least I can keep you company if we decide to wait and see if she comes back.'

The call ended, and Stephanie perched on one of the chairs in the front yard, hoping that at any minute Nancy would come strolling up the road.

SIXTY

The rumble of thunder was growing ever closer, the wind picking up, and Stephanie was just beginning to think she should wait in her car when Gus swerved into the parking space, skidding to a halt. She stood up to wait for him by the gate.

'You didn't need to come, you know,' she said. 'I can cope with going into an empty house on my own, if that's what we decide to do.'

'I know,' he said, grinning. 'Scared of nothing, are you, my love?'

He knew that wasn't true, but strangely Stephanie's fears were never of people jumping out of dark alleyways or waiting behind closed doors. Her fears were not so much about protecting her body as protecting her heart.

She merely grunted, and Gus laughed.

'What do you want to do? Do you want to sit and wait, or do you want to get inside and check she's okay?'

Stephanie shook her head, unable to decide. It was a big decision to force entry into Nancy's home.

'Hey, come here,' he said, pulling her into a hug. 'I know

you feel bad about this whole situation, Steph, but the lack of follow-up on Lola's disappearance wasn't your fault. I've looked at your reports. They were thorough. The decision that she wasn't vulnerable and that she'd left of her own choice was taken at a much higher level, so stop beating yourself up.'

'I know, but I can't help thinking we missed something. Maybe it's got something to do with the crime committed by Nancy's parents.'

'They're both dead, so let's focus on Nancy for now. Are you concerned enough for me to kick the door in?'

She took a deep breath. 'Yes! I know she could have met some man, gone back to his place and forgotten all about her mobile, but that seems implausible, given how concerned she is about Lola. And Effie was buying food for her freezer; she wouldn't have forgotten that.'

'I agree,' Gus said. 'You ready?'

Stephanie nodded and Gus raised his right leg and kicked. The door gave immediately, but only opened a few inches.

'Not much of a bloody lock,' he muttered. 'I'll go first. And don't argue.'

He pushed against the door. For a moment it didn't move, and Stephanie wondered if someone was pressing against it from the other side. Gus put his shoulder to it.

'It's old. It's just got warped in the sun over the years. And my kick didn't help. Come on.'

Although they had no reason to suspect the house was a crime scene, they took the precaution of putting on gloves. Gus reached for the light switch.

'Nancy?' Stephanie called, wondering whether she was perhaps in bed. 'It's Stephanie King and DCI Brodie. Are you there?'

They both stood silently by the door and waited. Stephanie turned to Gus and shook her head.

'I'll double-check,' she said, heading for the stairs. 'Nancy, if you're there, I'm coming up. I hope that's okay, but shout if it's not.'

She walked slowly upstairs, giving the woman a chance to call out. But her shout was met with silence.

With the tips of her fingers, she pushed open the first door she came to. It was the bathroom. A shower curtain hung over the bath, and she reached out to push it back.

'Bathroom's clear,' she called.

The next room held twin beds, and both were made with no sign of use.

She walked to the last door along the corridor and gently eased it open. A double bed lay empty. It was unmade, as if Nancy had just got out of it. The window was ajar and rattling in the wind.

Stephanie moved to the wardrobe and opened the door. Her clothes were still there.

'Nothing up here, Gus,' she called.

She heard the back door open and realised he had gone to check the garden, so hurried downstairs to follow him.

'Anything?' she asked.

'No. You're right about the phone and the purse. There's money in the purse, but no debit or credit card. Doesn't mean much. She may not have had either.'

Stephanie gave him a quizzical look. 'Really? It's almost impossible to exist without one or the other, I'd have thought.'

'Me too, but I wouldn't want to make any assumptions. Her laptop's here. It's quite an old one, and it doesn't appear to be password protected.'

'Do you think we can justify taking a look?'

'Yep. No question. If someone took Lola all those years ago, they might think Nancy could point the finger at them. I'll check the laptop; you check her phone.'

Like her computer, Nancy's phone was an old one with neither facial nor fingerprint recognition.

'Clearly not a woman with secrets,' Stephanie said as she scrolled through the phone without having to enter a passcode. 'How are you getting on, Gus?'

He grunted and didn't respond for a moment. Stephanie turned towards him.

'What have you found?'

'I'm checking the activity logs for the computer. I'm not an expert at this stuff, but it looks to me as if someone has used this computer in the last three hours. I'm not sure what for – it's all a bit techie for me. But either she was here three hours ago and ignoring Effie's calls, or someone else was using her computer.'

Stephanie sat down heavily at the kitchen table and rested her chin on her fist.

'I know we can think of lots of rational reasons why she might not be here, how she might have gone out without her purse, without her phone, and ignored calls from her friend. But I don't believe any of them, Gus. Something's happened to her.'

SIXTY-ONE

I wake to the sound of my own moans of pain. My head aches with unbearable ferocity as I open my eyes, but everything is black.

I can't see. Am I blind?

My heart flutters in panic as I realise that apart from my own groans I can't hear a thing. There's a thick, dull silence.

Where am I?

I'm lying on what feels like an uneven stone floor, and I stretch my arms out, hoping to touch something that will tell me where I am. But there's nothing on either side of me within reach.

I try to sit up, and cry out in pain. There is no other sound and not a glimmer of light. The air feels dank; there's a musty, earthy smell, and I'm cold, shivering. My body aches almost as much as my head. My left knee is throbbing, the skin on my cheek burning.

'Help!' I scream. 'Is anyone there?' But the sound reverberates around the space, and I know I'm alone.

Why am I here?

Groaning in agony, I manoeuvre my trembling body very

slowly so I'm sitting up. Behind me there seems to be a rough wall, but it feels damp under my fingers. I sniff the air. It tells me nothing.

With a wail of anguish I grasp my head in my hands, trying to ease the pain. It doesn't work.

How did I get here?

Then it hits me. I know where I am. I know how I got here. Snatches of memory, images of faces, moments of pure terror come to me, and I know I'm a fool.

SIXTY-TWO

SIXTEEN HOURS EARLIER

The cottage is quiet. The front door stands slightly ajar, a crisp breeze chilling me in my pyjama shorts and vest top as I stand, frozen to the bottom stair.

Is he still here?

There was a man in my house, standing by the side of my bed, watching me, and I don't know if he's gone. I can hear myself breathing – panting almost – and a thin layer of sweat chills my body.

I cling to the banister for support, but I have to move. I can't see into the sitting room, but I propel myself from the bottom step and run. As I reach the front door I spin round with a gasp, certain he's behind me. The hall is deserted, the stairs looming up to the dark landing beyond.

My bare toe touches something cold and I glance at the floor. The key is lying on the stone flags. How did it get there?

I force myself to look to the left, into the sitting room. It's empty, as is the kitchen.

I pull the door wide open and rush out into the courtyard. It's early; there's no one around. I collapse onto one of the dilapidated chairs, trying to control my breathing, gulping in the cool morning air. He's not downstairs, but he could be hiding in the other bedroom or the bathroom.

I can't see any evidence that the lock has been forced. Was the key pushed through from the outside? Who would do this?

A sudden memory of Dad hits me. He's bending down to remove one of the loose stones in the wall – his hiding place for the key in case we came home at different times. The stone was a darker shade than the others and I'm staring straight at it. I leap up from my chair, run to the wall and scrabble to pull out the stone. It comes away easily in my hand, but the space behind is empty. I don't know what I expected. It's years since we hid a key there, and Effie told me there is no spare.

I return to my seat, knowing I should check the other rooms upstairs, not sure if I'm brave enough. Maybe I should call the police, but what would I say? There's no evidence anyone was in my house. Just an unlocked door. Did I forget to close and lock it? I don't think so, but they might.

To my relief, I hear a cough; it's coming from Mrs Roskilly's garden. If she hears me scream, I'm sure she will do something about it. I stand up so she can see me, knowing I must go back into the house. The thought makes my heart beat faster, but I can't sit outside in my nightclothes all day. I need to be certain he's gone, and this is probably my best chance.

I wish, like last time, Effie would come to the rescue, but I'm on my own, so, telling myself that if he wants to hurt me he had ample chance during the night, I run into the house and race up the stairs, flinging open the door to the bathroom, then the bedroom.

Both are empty. I lean against the wall to get my breath back. Then, realising I left the front door open so Mrs Roskilly would hear if I screamed, I tear back down the stairs, slam the door, pick up the key and turn it, leaning all my weight against it.

It doesn't feel like enough. I grab a kitchen chair and prop it behind the door. It might not stop anyone, but I'll hear if it falls over.

From where I'm standing, I can see into the living room. My laptop's there, sitting on the coffee table, exactly where I left it. I turn my head to the kitchen. My purse is on the table. Nothing appears to be disturbed. What did he want, if it wasn't to steal from me?

I scan the room. Something feels wrong. What's missing?

And then I realise. My camera has gone.

My legs are shaking, so I pull out a kitchen chair and flop onto it. Why take my camera and leave my purse and laptop? Neither has been touched.

I now have a legitimate reason to call the police, but will they believe me if everything else of value is still here? There's no evidence of a break-in, and I'm not sure they would even follow it up. I read somewhere that ninety-five per cent of burglaries go unsolved, so is it worth reporting?

Could the man who followed me have broken in? Was he behind it all? But why would he want my camera? Perhaps he saw me taking his picture at the gate, but that doesn't seem a good enough reason unless he's a wanted criminal.

The whole town must know about my photos by now. They've been in the local paper in a call for witnesses with an acknowledgement to me, as the photographer, under each image. Does someone believe I have a photo that would implicate them in Lola's disappearance? The police have all the photos of Lola, so taking my camera was a waste of time. There isn't a single image that hasn't been scrutinised.

I think of the other photos I took, mainly views, some of Dad, and a few of Liam. He may not have known I had a camera back then, but I'm certain he will do now.

I remember how he responded when he saw me on the

headland the day he sailed back from France, his fear that I would expose him to his wife, his fury, his threats. Has he guessed I have photos of him? Does he think I'll reveal our affair? It happened a long time ago, but if I discovered my husband had been having sex with another woman on *my* beach, outside *my* cottage, it would break my heart. It wouldn't matter that it was eleven years ago; it wouldn't matter if it was *twenty* years ago. It would still be devastating, and it could destroy his marriage.

I think of the early snaps I took of him from the cliff, and the sneaky shots I took when he was sleeping. Anyone who saw them would know what they meant. A picnic was spread around us, my clothes, my bag, Liam lying naked, face down on the sand, his face turned to the side, his eyes closed. I have never shown those photos to anyone, and never would – for his wife's sake, not his. But he doesn't know that, and a voice at the back of my head tells me that he might deserve it. If he hadn't been so cruel to me, I wouldn't have lashed out at Lola.

I drop my head onto my folded arms. I shouldn't have come back here.

7 hours earlier

I've spent the whole day doing nothing, sitting slumped in a chair, my mind spinning in circles.

I need to get bolts for the door so I'm safe at night, but I don't want to leave the cottage. I've called a locksmith to replace the lock with a stronger one, but he can't come until tomorrow, and I'm terrified of going out for fear of coming home to find someone in my house.

Liam is the only person I can think of who has any motive for taking my camera. I shudder at the memory of his anger, his threats on that last day. Why did I let him intimidate me?

Of course, I know the answer. I was immature, weakened by

the events of the previous two years spent caring for Mum, her death, and the role I believed I had played in it. Dad had said it was my fault. And I had believed him.

In the years since then I have tried to put the past behind me, but I've carried its weight on my shoulders for all to see. One of my sweet old ladies tried her best to help me put it in perspective.

'Nancy,' Hilda said in a determined tone that brooked no argument, 'I know you've had your share of problems, but they're not unique. People here rarely make a big deal of their sad histories, and I'm not much of a one for gossip, but I'm telling you this for your own good. There's one woman who discovered her husband was a murderer. Imagine that! He killed a boy and she didn't have a clue, but she still managed to bring up two girls – and they're lovely lasses. And there's a chap whose house went up in smoke while he was in the pub, celebrating a football victory. He lost his wife and three kiddies. Neither of them were responsible for the events that devastated their lives, just as none of the stuff with your family was your fault – whatever you think. You have to pick yourself up and get on with life. Use what happened to put fire in your soul. We love you, and we'll all be cheering you on from the sidelines.'

I had smiled and agreed, but deep inside I still knew I was the reason Mum was dead. And if she had lived, Lola wouldn't have run away, and Dad would still be alive.

Suddenly I sit up straight, remembering what Stephanie told me. Someone had been giving Mum vodka.

How could anyone have believed that was me? I was the one trying every single day to make Mum stronger! I wasn't the reason she didn't get better, and Dad never told me, even though he knew she'd been drinking. Perhaps it's finally time to stop blaming myself.

I realise now that I allowed myself to be persuaded that it was my fault, just as I allowed Liam to bully me. The memory of his final threat is the only thing preventing me from confronting him now.

I think of Hilda's words and I know it's time to take control and put that fire in my soul. Liam can't intimidate me any longer, and if he's taken my camera, he needs to know he's not going to get away with it.

I take a deep breath and pull my laptop towards me. I'm going to show him the photos and tell him that unless he leaves me alone, I'll post them on social media. I wouldn't be the first to exact revenge that way, and he doesn't know I wouldn't do that to his wife – an innocent victim.

Selecting a few photos, including the one of Liam arriving back from France, I email them to a print shop in town. Perhaps when he sees the pictures he'll realise that stealing my camera was a dirty trick but he's gained nothing. To be on the safe side, I upload all the images to a cloud service in case he comes back to steal my laptop too.

For a moment, I almost waver. It would be so much easier to forget this and return to London, where I'm safe and loved. But then I slam my palms on the table and push myself to my feet. If I don't do something, I'll end up scared of my own shadow.

I pull my debit card from my purse and stick it in the back pocket of my jeans, pick up my leather shoulder bag, drop my phone inside and leave – triple-checking that the door is locked before I set off.

SIXTY-THREE

FIVE HOURS EARLIER

My trip into town took longer than expected, but I managed to sort out some sturdy bolts for the doors – both front and back – because I can't sleep another night in the cottage without additional security. I thought I would only need the bolts and some screws, but after the man in the shop had given up trying to sell me an electric drill, he told me I'd need to make a pilot hole for the screws, and I'd need something called a bradawl, plus a hammer and a suitable screwdriver. Now I feel as if I've got the best part of a toolkit in my bag.

My photos took forever to be printed, but I'm determined to see Liam while the anger is still burning. If I don't go today, I'll lose my nerve.

I stomp onto the path, feeling conviction in every stride. I wish I hadn't left it so late in the day, but unless I want to spend the rest of my time in Cornwall looking over my shoulder and jumping at every sound in the house, I have to find out once and for all if Liam's behind this.

It's a miserable afternoon. Dark clouds are coming in from the sea, and I can hear thunder rumbling in the distance over the crash of the waves. The coastal path is deserted, everyone having the sense to stay off an exposed clifftop path in a storm.

I'm hoping Liam will be on the beach or working on his boat, but if he's not there, I'll wait and hope the weather hasn't forced him indoors. I push the creeping despondency aside as I approach the track that leads to his cottage.

I force my way through the hawthorn. I don't care if I leave broken branches, nor do I care if I get scratched, and I have no intention of crawling to the edge on hands and knees. I'm going to stand there and let him see me. If he's on the beach, I'm certain he'll come storming up to confront me, and that's what I want.

I walk as close to the edge of the cliff as I dare, and stare down.

The beach is deserted. The tide looks like it's on its way in, and there is no boat in the bay. The anger and determination seep away, leaving me deflated and strangely tearful.

He's not even here.

I pull up the collar of my jacket, tuck some of my hair in to prevent it from getting too wet in the damp air and shove my hands deep into my pockets. Is there any point in waiting? I don't suppose so, but if I leave now, I don't know if I'll be able to pluck up the courage again.

It's too wet to sit on the ground, so I stand, looking out to sea. The swell of grey, stormy water reflects my mood, and for a moment I wonder what my life might have been like if Liam had been as serious about me as I was about him. I realise now that what I felt was passion, desire, and for the first time in a very long while I had someone's sole attention. But I didn't know him. I remember the way he spoke to me on that last day. He was as cruel, harsh, and as frightening as the sea I am staring at.

This is useless. There's no point waiting here.

With a last look out to sea, I turn back to the path, and I freeze.

SIXTY-FOUR

I can't move. I'm glued to the spot, and even if I wanted to run, there's nowhere to go. There's only one way off the headland, and that route is now blocked.

Two men stand in front of me. One tall, fair-haired, with broad shoulders and a round, moonlike face; the other smaller, leaner, with hollow cheeks and a thin top lip. I recognise them both from yesterday, but it's the wiry one who is the more frightening. His thicker bottom lip lifts at the corners, like a cat smiling at a mouse.

'Hello again!' he says, his tone apparently friendly. The men look at each other and then back at me. The big guy smiles too, but I'm not fooled.

'What are you doing out in this weather? There's a storm coming, you know.' The thin man glances at the deserted path. 'It seems everyone else has the sense to stay indoors. Were you looking for someone?' He takes a step towards me. 'You're a bit close to that edge. I'd be careful if I was you. We don't want no one falling over.'

He's too close, and I want to step back, but I can't. Behind me is nothing but thin air. The big man stands behind him, not speaking. It's clear who is in charge.

My voice comes out as a hoarse whisper. 'I was about to leave.'

'Not found what you were looking for?' He turns to the big man and shrugs. 'What do you think, Dan?'

'Please, I didn't mean any harm.'

I can't get past them. I know that, and I wonder what the hell I thought I was doing. Why did I think it was time to be brave?

My words come out in a rush, panic audible in every syllable. 'I only wanted to speak to Liam.'

'About...?' Scary Man asks.

'I'm not here to make trouble.'

He takes another step towards me, and now he is almost touching me. His face is close to mine, and I can smell cigarettes on his breath.

'See, that's difficult to believe. What did you come back here for? Why come to this headland, to his cove, if you weren't planning on causing bother? Why are you spying on him?'

They know about me. Liam must have told them to warn me off. I'm sure of it now. I stutter out a response.

'I... I'm not spying on him. Why would you think that?'

He twists his neck slightly to speak over his shoulder to the man called Dan, but he never takes his eyes off me. 'She must think we're a bit thick down here in this part of the world, Dan. What do you reckon?' He turns back. 'We saw where you'd broken through the hedge. We saw the flattened bracken where you'd laid down to watch over the edge of the cliff. It's what you do, what you've always done – and if that's not spying, missy, I don't know what is. You came back yesterday, only Dan was keeping watch, weren't you, Dan?' Dan grunts a response. 'Put paid to your snooping, didn't he?'

'I just wanted...'

My speech tails off. I don't know *what* I wanted, really, or why I came here the other day. I suppose I wanted to see Liam's wife for myself; to spy on his life; to be certain that he dumped me because he had to and not simply because I was worth nothing to him.

'Look, I'm sorry. I don't want to cause trouble. I just wanted Liam to know he didn't need to take my camera. I won't use the photos. I'll wipe them off my laptop too – whatever he wants. Just let me go.'

The Thin Man turns to the one called Dan and frowns. Dan shrugs and Thin Man turns back.

'So what's on these photos, then? You took them when you were spying, did you?'

I thought they would know, that they'd have looked at them on the camera. But I need to get away from here, from them, so I don't ask questions. I scrabble around in my bag for the prints, and as my hand touches the hammer I wonder if I should take the initiative and attack them. Had it only been one man I might have considered it, but I wouldn't stand a chance, so instead I pull out the photos and hand them over. He sees my hand trembling, and smirks.

I try to swallow, but my mouth is too dry. 'I came here to show Liam the pictures. I want him to believe that no one will see them if he leaves me in peace.'

The man isn't listening to me. He's looking at the photos. He sees the ones I took of him by the gate and raises his eyebrows, but says nothing. He turns to the next one, smiles and passes the page to Dan, who sniggers like a child. It must be the one of Liam lying face down on the sand. When he gets to the last photo I see a change in his face, a change I don't like. He holds up the photo of Liam's boat.

'When did you take this?' he demands, his voice tighter, sharper than before.

'A long time ago. It's nothing – really. It was that night Liam brought his wife back from France. I... I only wanted to see what she looked like.'

I'm ashamed of how childish that sounds but I can't take my eyes off the man's face. Any trace of a smirk has gone.

He holds out his hand. 'Keys,' he demands.

'Why?' My voice cracks on the word.

'Dan is going to pay your cottage a visit. These pictures are on your laptop, you said?' He tuts and shakes his head. 'We'd best have your phone too.'

There's a sudden squall and a gust of wind rocks me, the rain soaking my back. Every inch of my skin prickles, and when I speak, my voice seems to echo in my head.

'Why do you want my phone?'

He shakes his head without answering and turns to Dan. 'Check if anyone's around, Dan. Let me know if I'm clear to move her. Then take her phone and follow the lane to the road. It's the way she went yesterday, so if it's tracked it will make sense. Wipe her photos on the laptop and leave the phone on the table. Best wipe any pics from that too. You got that?'

Dan nods. 'Yep, Cal. Will do.'

The man called Cal turns towards me. 'Keys. Phone.' He holds out his hand.

I look wildly towards the hedge, hoping someone will walk by so I can scream for help, but the weather's getting worse by the minute, and if I shout, he'll push me over the cliff. I'm only inches from the edge.

'Please, I don't know why you're doing this. I don't mean any harm – I've not done anything to hurt you, or Liam, and I'll say nothing to his wife – that's a promise. Please. I'd like to leave now.'

I fight the sob that's building in my chest as he ignores everything I've said and waves his outstretched hand for my keys and phone.

'If you fall over the edge, lady, no one will say you were

pushed, because you won't be. I'll just keep walking and you'll keep backing up. So give me your bag, there's a good girl.'

I don't want to give him the bag and I pull it tight to my chest. I know what's in it, but he doesn't. He reaches to grab it, so I quickly dig down into its depths and pull out my phone and my front door key.

'Passwords?'

I shake my head.

'You'd best not be lying. It'll make things much worse for you if you are.'

I shake my head again as Cal hands my keys and phone to Dan, who is about to turn away when he seems to think of something.

'Do you want help getting her into the cave?' he mumbles.

I swallow hard. *The cave?*

Cal sees my expression and gives me a look of mock horror. 'Oh dear – the cat's out of the bag.' He turns to Dan and shakes his head. 'No, she won't give me much of a bother. She's a scrawny bint.' He laughs nastily. 'Let me know when it's done.'

He turns back to me. 'Now. You coming quietly, or do I have to throw you over my shoulder? Or there's option three – you fall backwards off this cliff. All the same to me. What's it to be?'

SIXTY-FIVE

FOUR HOURS EARLIER

The path down to Liam's cove is steeper and more twisty than I remember. Every limb is shaking and my legs are barely holding me up.

I said I'd walk. I didn't want to be slung over his shoulder. I couldn't bear the thought of where his filthy hands might be. Surely Liam won't allow him to hurt me?

My feet slip on the loose stones, and the hawthorn and gorse on either side of the path seem closer, denser than last time I walked down here. They're blocking the view, and I can't see anything except what's immediately in front of me.

'Are we going to the cottage?' I ask. The words sound as if I'm being strangled.

'You heard where you're going.' He gives me a shove in the back. 'Hurry up. I want you off this path.'

Finally we turn a corner and hit the beach. I stumble over the pebbles and then my feet sink into the soft, damp sand beyond. He keeps pushing me forward, and when we're almost at the sea, we veer off to the right.

I want to ask where he's taking me, but I haven't forgotten what Dan said. *The cave*. Once again, I think about screaming, but even if someone was on the path they wouldn't be able to see the cove. Nor could they get to it.

The tide is out now, but from the marks on the rocks I can pinpoint the level the water reaches when it's in. It's way above head height. Will the cave flood when the tide comes in?

As I clamber over the low rocks and around the headland, Cal's hand pushing me if I slow down, I spot an opening in the sheer cliff face, visible only from the sea. I start to sob. I don't want to go into the cave. What else lives in there? And what will happen when the tide comes in?

'Please don't make me go in there,' I say, swivelling to face Cal, hoping that some part of him will soften. All I get is a delighted grin. He's thrilled by my fear.

'Shouldn't have stuck your nose in where it's not wanted, should you?'

'I haven't stuck my nose in! I don't know what you mean!'

In some small pathetic way, I was attempting to take control instead of always standing back, allowing things to happen to me. And look where it's got me.

I stand firm. My feet are refusing to step into the cave.

'You can't make me go in there.'

He laughs again. 'You walk in there, or I carry you. Same as before. Your choice.'

I try to swallow, but my throat is closed. Feeling I have no option, I gingerly step onto the sand in front of the cave. The ground is sodden, and my feet are sucked below the surface. Each step is an effort.

Cal gives me another quick shove in my back, and I move through the mouth of the cave. An impenetrable gloom faces me. Apart from the sound of the sea, all I can hear is the echo of a steady drip of water somewhere ahead.

'Wait,' he says.

Suddenly, there is light. I turn my head, and he's holding a lantern aloft, one of many hanging from the roof by the entrance.

Ahead of me the floor of the cave rises sharply, sand quickly giving way to solid rock with steps carved into its surface, leading steeply upwards. He pushes me towards them.

For a moment I consider pleading with him again, but I am certain it will do no good. If I'm going to get out of here, I need to pray that Liam will have some sympathy and will let me go.

I reach the top of the steps where a narrow passage turns to the left. Even with the lantern held high, I can barely see where I'm going, but as I round another corner the walls fall away, and the cave opens into a vast cavern.

'Home sweet home,' Cal says. He moves to my side, grabbing my hair in one hand as if he thinks I might bolt.

He's right. If I could run now, I would, because at that moment the light catches something metallic ahead of me. He swings the lantern slightly and I see strips of steel. My whole body turns icy cold.

The cavern is large, but I can go no further because in front of me thick metal bars have been drilled into the rocks, stretching from the uneven ground to the rough stone of the roof. A door stands open, and there's no disguising what it is.

It's a giant cage.

SIXTY-SIX

'In!' Cal grunts, giving me another shove in the back, hard enough to make me stumble but not to fall.

I spin towards him, my heart hammering. 'No way! It's a *cage*. You're not locking me in there.'

He pulls a face, which I know is supposed to replicate my look of horror, with wide-open eyes and mouth. Then he smiles.

'Deadly.' His smile widens at his choice of words.

My breath is coming in short bursts. I have to do something, no matter what the consequences, and I need to act quickly.

Without another moment's thought, I fly at him, my hands raking his face as I try to raise my knee to kick him in the groin. I miss, hitting the top of his thigh, and I stagger back.

With a roar, he transfers the lantern from right hand to left and I barely see his free arm flash across the shadow of his body. Only at the last moment, a second before it connects, do I know what's coming.

I scream as the back of his hand whips across my cheek. I feel my lip crack and I taste blood as I fall to the ground, my left knee smacking into the rocky floor of the cave. I cry out again.

'Do as you're fucking told!'

Any hope that he might see the error of his ways evaporates, and tears of pain and desolation stream from my eyes. I know I can't win, and I don't want to stand up to be knocked down again, so I crawl through the open doorway into the cage, each contact between knee and rock sending stabbing jolts of pain through the bone.

I stay crouched on the floor as the cage door slams shut.

'The lamp won't last long, and it gets *very* dark in here.' I hear him spit on the floor and I shudder, knowing he's enjoying my pain and humiliation. 'When the battery goes, you're fucked.'

I hear his footsteps moving away. I don't know where he's going or when he'll be back, but I'm not risking the question.

I lift my head. The lamp is outside the cage, beyond my reach, and it's flickering already. I wish I could turn it off so I could save the battery for when I might need it. But it's too far away. It provides enough faint light for me to see that the cage is huge.

What I can't understand is why it's here at all.

I don't know how long I've been here. I don't have a watch, and I always use my phone to tell the time. It feels like hours, but it probably isn't. The lantern is dim now; it won't last much longer.

After Cal had left without another word, I crawled to the side of the cage to sit with my back against the rough damp wall. What can they possibly plan to do with me? I don't see how they can let me go, but what have I done to make them treat me this way?

My mind is spinning. It's clear they thought I was spying on Liam. They knew I'd been there before. What did they think I was going to see?

It was the photo that seemed to concern Cal. I couldn't see

Liam's wife in the picture, so I hadn't been particularly inter-ested, but there were at least two men in the boat from what I remember. Young guys. Cal seemed keen to know when I'd taken the picture – but it was eleven years ago. Surely that can't be relevant now?

There is no explanation that makes sense.

I pull my jacket tight around me, raise my knees and wrap my arms around them. It's so cold in here.

My lip has stopped bleeding but my face feels swollen and sore from where he hit me. I reach into my bag, wondering if I have any painkillers. My hand settles around the handle of the screwdriver, and I pull it out, but it's no use to me. I heard Cal turn a key as he left, and I could tell it was no ordinary lock. Even if I knew how to pick it, there is a bigger problem. The door has additional security in the form of the fattest padlock I've ever seen.

Why do they need so much security for an empty cave? Is the cage used to store stolen property or maybe smuggled goods that need to be kept under lock and key to protect against thieves?

I drop my useless tools back in my bag, all hope of escape lost. I want to sink to the floor and wail at my stupidity, but I need to move around to keep warm. It's a deep cave, and I know hypothermia can strike at temperatures under ten degrees Celsius. It feels colder than that.

My eyes have become accustomed to the gloom, and although the lantern is fading, it's casting a pale, blue-white glow around the cave. I feel my way along the walls, trying to get my bearings before I lose the last of the light, and as I reach the back I see some strange marks on the rock face. I run my fingers over them, feeling the rough gouges, as if someone has scraped the surface with a smaller stone.

I peer closer and realise they are letters, etched into the surface.

HANH
MINH
BAO

I lean heavily against the cold, damp rock. *Names.* The locks on the cage aren't there to keep precious contraband safe. They are not intended to keep people out. They are designed to keep people in.

SIXTY-SEVEN

TWO HOURS EARLIER

I'm still leaning against the wall when the battery in the lantern finally flickers and dies. I gasp with shock at the total blackness but can't stop myself from reaching out to touch the scratched names – evidence that others have been here before me – wondering if they escaped alive.

I'm too lost in all this to even cry. My head feels as if it's about to explode with confusion, and my chest feels tight and heavy. I grope my way to the corner and huddle down, trying to conserve as much body heat as I can. There isn't a sound; not even the distant murmur of the ocean breaks the silence, and I'm in a darkness so absolute it feels as if the world has ceased to exist.

I drop my head onto my knees as a wave of hopelessness washes over me.

I don't know if it's minutes or hours later when I hear something. Footsteps, a heavy, ponderous tread, coming towards me. I raise my head. The walls are getting lighter.

Seconds later, Cal rounds the corner, his lantern below his thin face, shining up, throwing his eyes into shadow, high-lighting his sharp cheekbones.

I instinctively move away from the wall. I don't want him to know that I've seen the names.

'Change of plan.'

He unlocks the cage. I wish I'd known he was going to do that so I could have armed myself, but my bag is by the door and I can't reach it.

'Out!'

'Why are you keeping me here?' I'm certain he will enjoy hearing the tremor in my voice. 'Let me go. *Please!* I won't say a word to anyone about what's happened.'

'Shut the fuck up, woman. You're going nowhere. And if you've sent those photos to anyone, you're dead. Do you understand that?'

'I *haven't*! I promise you. I only downloaded them from my camera a couple of days ago.'

'I told you to shut it. The skipper will sort you.'

He must mean Liam, and I feel a rush of relief. I can't believe he'd let me suffer like this.

'Weather's causing a hold-up, and he wants you moved before the tide's in.'

Thank God.

Cal opens the door and stands back. I reach for my bag and step through, turning towards the mouth of the cave.

'Where do you think you're going?'

'You said I was being moved.'

He laughs nastily. 'Did you think you were going to sit by the fire to wait for him? Cute.' He points with his finger in the other direction – to a narrow passage that leads deeper into the cave. 'That way.'

My heart is pounding. *Where am I going?* My body is blocking the light from the lantern and I stumble, falling to the ground with a scream as my bad knee hits a rock.

'Get up!'

He grabs me by my hair again and yanks me to my feet,

keeping hold of me so I can't fall. Then, just ahead, I see there is another cage – smaller this time, but the walls are wet, as if water seeps into the cell-like space.

'In,' he says.

I try to resist. 'I'll die if you put me in there,' I say.

'That'd solve a problem or two, wouldn't it?' He gives me that cruel smile again. 'You're going to die anyway, so best to get it over with. Skipper wants to talk to you first, then I guess there'll be a boat trip.'

He seems to think this is funny, and I know I must do something. Once I'm locked in again, I can't escape. The only weapons are inside my bag, and if I put my hand in, he'll stop me. But my bag is heavy with the bolts and the tools – heavy enough to do him some damage, if I get it right.

I turn towards the cage, as if I'm going in, and lower my right hand so my bag is close to the ground. Before I reach the door, I take a step forward then, spinning on my good leg, I swing the bag up in an arc with every ounce of strength in my body, aiming for his head.

He yelps. '*Fuck!* You little bitch!'

He drops the lantern, and I know immediately that my attack wasn't enough. I didn't even knock him over.

I have no chance of getting past him to run back down through the cave. I wouldn't get far without the lantern, and it's rolling around by his feet. There's just enough light for him to see me and I know he's going to hit me, so I take the only option I can. I drop my bag, dive into the cage, push the door shut, and lean against it.

Before he has a chance to reach through and grab me with his bony hands, I hear the sound of footsteps echoing through the cave.

'*Shit!*' he mutters, reaching into his pocket and pulling out a key.

There's someone here!

'Stay there!' he shouts to whoever it is. 'I'm coming.'

'Help!' I scream at the top of my voice. 'I'm here! He's locked me in!'

'Shut your fucking mouth!'

I'm right by the gate, still forcing it closed with all my weight behind it. He reaches an arm through, grabs me around the neck and cracks my head against the bars.

'Keep it shut, or I *will* kill you. It doesn't matter to me one way or the other – do you hear me?'

I do, but I'm going to die anyway, so I have nothing to lose. I hear the footsteps drawing closer, and I can tell he doesn't want this person to see me, but they must have heard my scream.

'Stay there!' he repeats. 'I'm coming.'

'Let me out! Don't let him leave me here! My name is Nancy Holland. The police will be looking for me. Help!'

I'm risking everything, but it feels like the only choice I have.

He lifts his foot and kicks hard against the gate, forcing it open. He steps inside and swings the lantern. In that split second I see something. Another name scratched on the wall.

And then the lantern connects with my head.

SIXTY-EIGHT

NOW

I've remembered it all now – how I got here, what they did to me, how he hurt me. I don't know how long I've been uncon-scious, and I'm scared to touch my head where the lantern connected. It's pounding painfully, but at least I'm alive. Cal must have taken the lantern with him, or perhaps it went out when he hit me, because it's pitch black again. I know I'm deep in a cave, and it's not just my head that hurts – my knee and my face throb with pain.

What time is it? How long have I been here? Is anyone missing me? I have no answers, and I sink into a deep pit of despair.

At the back of my mind, though, there's something I need to remember. Something I saw as the lantern swung towards my face.

Before it comes back to me, I hear a voice. It's Cal. He's made it clear that he doesn't care if I live or die, and I start to shake. He's coming back for me, and there's someone with him.

'You shouldn't have come.' I hear Cal's voice echo around the cave. 'The tide's on its way in. I've got this, and the skipper will sort the woman out when he gets back. He'll know what to do.'

I can just see a glimmer of light, and I crawl towards the bars and grip them in my hands.

'Give me the water and blankets. They won't be back for a bit – too stormy. He's waiting till he can get in safely.'

I don't know who 'they' are, but I don't care. I had hoped the blankets and water were for me, but it seems I was wrong and I wrap my arms around my body again, unsure if I should risk another scream. It hardly seems worth it as it would probably incense Cal even more.

His voice is fading now as they move away. I hear him talking about getting the van ready, and something about tomorrow. Is the van for me? Are they taking me somewhere?

My bag with the tools inside is somewhere beyond the wall of bars, but now Cal has gone I can't see a thing, so I push my hand through the cold metal and grope around, hoping it's within reach. There's no padlock on this gate – only a lock – and if I can get my bag, I might be able to break out.

I work my way along, thrusting my arm between each set of bars until my shoulder feels bruised with the battering it's getting, but I find nothing.

I stand up. Holding my hands in front of me, palms flat so I can feel when I reach a wall, I turn and blindly stumble towards the back of the cage, to where I'm sure I saw something. I touch the stone, feel it with my fingers.

Nothing. The surface is uneven, cold and damp, and I have no way of identifying any scratches.

Whether or not I can see or feel the letters, though, I am certain that when Cal swung his lantern at me, I saw a name etched into the rock.

LOLA

SIXTY-NINE

Stephanie's phone said 2 a.m.

She groaned. It was at least the tenth time she had looked at the screen in the couple of hours since Gus had persuaded her to come to bed.

They had found nothing at Nancy's house to suggest anything had happened to her, and despite Gus repeating that she had probably met a man and gone back to his place, Stephanie knew he didn't believe it any more than she did.

They'd had to secure the cottage door before they left, and as Nancy wouldn't have been able to get in if she came home, an officer was parked outside with strict instructions to let Stephanie know – whatever the time – if Nancy turned up.

They had heard nothing. Not a peep.

Where are you, Nancy?

Realising that sleep wouldn't come while she just lay there, Stephanie swung her legs from the bed and took her phone into the bathroom to call the officer keeping watch.

No sign of Nancy, he confirmed.

There was something wrong. There had to be.

She crept back into the bedroom and lowered herself gently onto the bed.

'I heard you, Steph,' Gus muttered. 'You need to sleep. You're no bloody use to anyone when you're tired and ratty. Come here, darling.'

He lifted his arm so she could snuggle against him – usually all she needed to help her drift off. But not tonight. It made her hot and fidgety, so she wriggled away and turned over.

Not only was she worried about Nancy, she couldn't stop thinking about Lola, especially since Gus had interviewed the man who had come forward in response to their enquiries. He believed he had seen her the night she disappeared.

'I wish to God this man had got in touch eleven years ago,' Gus had told her. 'But it wasn't national news. He was here on holiday and left the day after she disappeared so knew nothing about our enquiries. The only reason he remembered the date and time so precisely was because it was the night before he left Cornwall.'

'Do you think he really did see her?'

Gus nodded. 'And you won't like what he told me. He said he'd been for a last walk along the coastal path and he was heading back to town. It was late – early evening – and he saw a girl marching towards him, half running away from town. As she passed, he asked if she was okay. "I'm fine," she'd snapped. But she didn't look fine. He thought she muttered something like "or I will be", but he wasn't sure.'

'Was she on her own?'

'Yes, but he got the impression she was running away from someone, or possibly running towards someone. When he saw the photos this week he realised who she was. He didn't think anyone was following her, although when he reached the end of the path he saw a man sitting on a wall. He wasn't doing anything – just gazing along the coastal path as if he was waiting for someone. I showed him the photos of Ray Holland

and Toby Makeland and asked if he recognised either of them. He said it was a man, not a kid – which rules out Toby, but he couldn't swear it wasn't Ray Holland. He said there was nothing particularly distinctive about the guy.'

Was it Lola's dad that he'd seen? If it was, then it seemed he wasn't chasing his daughter, although he might have been waiting for her to come back. But he said he'd been reading in his room. Did he follow her after the man passed him?

Stephanie reached for her phone again. She would set an alarm for 6 a.m. There was nothing she could do before then, but if two sisters had disappeared from the same place, it couldn't be a coincidence.

SEVENTY

The cave is no longer quiet. The silence was broken a while ago by the echo of water lapping against the rocks at the entrance. The noise built steadily until I could hear the roar of breakers, forcing their way through the narrow mouth, surging into the cave, and I could smell the sea. I didn't know if it would reach me, although it felt as if it was coming for me, but the sounds are fading now, the sea ebbing from the entrance, and I can breathe again.

Did I really see Lola's name, or was it my imagination playing tricks on me? I can't think of a single reason why she would have been here. She knew nothing about Liam – he was my wonderful secret – so why would she have been in this cave? I try to convince myself it was a different Lola, but it's hard to imagine that's true.

Maybe some of the local kids she hung out with brought her here. Liam always said he didn't own the beach, only the path to it, and it was freely accessible by sea. A few of the kids had kayaks and Lola would have been up for the adventure, but would they have stayed long enough for her to scratch her name on the wall?

A dreadful thought slams into my mind. What if they brought Lola here and the tide came in, trapping them inside? But that didn't make sense. As soon as the tide went out, they'd have been able to walk out onto the beach. Perhaps they locked her in as a joke, got scared of what they'd done and never came back. A prank gone wrong?

Ever since we found Lola's backpack I've been refusing to accept that she is dead, although I know it's what the police think, and it's the obvious explanation for why I've been unable to find her. Now, seeing her name etched into the wall and knowing what Cal says is planned for me, I am forced to admit the truth.

I huddle down again, forehead resting on raised knees, arms pulling my legs close. My face still hurts and I feel as if someone is trying to pierce my skull with a sharp knife. A howl breaks loose from where it's been building inside me for hours, and the floodgates open as sobs shake my body.

I must have passed out again, because when I come round, I can no longer hear the sea. The tide has retreated from the mouth of the cave, but it doesn't make me feel any safer. I take a long shuddering breath.

As I breathe out, a loose rock clatters across the floor of the cave somewhere outside my cage and I leap to my feet. Do rats live in caves? It sounded too big to have been dislodged by an animal. Is there someone here? Should I shout for help?

It is so silent I can hear my heart thumping.

Gradually I recognise the whisper of footsteps heading towards me. Certain that it's Cal returning to hit me again, I clasp my arms round myself. He's angry, and he wants me dead.

Too scared to breathe, I open my eyes and stare towards where I think the bars are. There's a glimmer of light. Someone is coming.

I don't move, waiting for whoever it is to turn the corner. It doesn't sound like Cal. The footsteps are light, tentative, as if whoever is coming is looking at the ground. A figure rounds the corner, head down, looking at their feet – a woman in jeans with a waterproof jacket, hood up. It must be Liam's wife.

'Oh, thank God,' I whisper, stumbling towards the bars.

She comes closer to the cage.

'Please, if you're Monique, will you help me?' My voice cracks with tension.

Lifting the light higher, she pushes back her hood.

'And why would I want to do that?' Her face is set as if some inner anger is about to explode.

I grasp the bars, not believing what I am seeing.

'*What? Why?* I don't understand,' I gasp.

'You don't need to. You shouldn't be here. You should have left, gone back to your own life. Now he'll have no choice. He'll have to kill you.'

I can't speak. I just stare.

Waves of shock roll over me as I realise this is not a sweet French woman called Monique.

It's Lola.

SEVENTY-ONE

'*Lola?*' I gasp, my voice little more than a broken whisper. Tears flood my eyes and I press my face against the bars, hands clutching the cold metal on either side. 'Oh God, Lola. It really is you. I thought you were *dead*! We found your backpack and your money – I thought something terrible had happened to you.' I'm choking on the words, on my tears.

Lola's face looks as if it's carved out of granite, but I thrust my arms through the bars, wanting to touch her, to check that she's real. She steps back, out of my reach.

'Something terrible did happen to me, and my name is Monique. Lola no longer exists.'

I'm shocked to silence by her tone. Her voice is flat, devoid of emotion, but her eyes tell a different story. They are dancing around, looking everywhere but at me.

'The storm's fading,' she says. 'Liam will be back soon, and he can't catch me talking to you. I only came to check it's really you.'

I don't understand why she won't touch me and, barely listening to what she's saying about Liam, I stretch my arms further towards her. She doesn't move.

'Lola, come here, *please*! Let me touch you. I've been so scared for you. I looked for you everywhere when I thought you'd gone to London. I even moved there, hoping I might one day see you in the street.' My voice breaks on a cross between a sob and a laugh at the notion. 'Why are you here? Is Liam forcing you to stay? Does he hurt you? Let me out and we'll get away from here together, before he's back.'

I'm talking too quickly, trying to find some words that will break through her icy indifference, but when she finally looks me in the eye, her gaze is resolute.

'I have three children, Nancy. *Three*. I'm not going anywhere.'

I am too stunned to speak. The children on the beach must be hers – Lola's and Liam's. How is that possible?

Before I can absorb what she has just told me, she speaks again.

'I can't save you, Nancy, even if I wanted to.'

It's like a punch to the chest. I was sure she was here to rescue me, but her voice is distant, as if she has rehearsed the words. I try again, desperate to get through to her.

'Tell me what happened, Lola. How did you end up here? Are you happy?'

I'm asking too many questions and for a moment I see a flash of emotion. But then she has it back under control.

'I'm here because eleven years ago I wanted to say goodbye to my sister.' One side of her mouth curls in a sneer. 'But I saw too much and was given a choice – lose my life and that of my unborn child, or stay and be whatever Liam wanted me to be. I'm here because of you, Nancy. You let me down and I despised you for it. But that night – the night I was planning to run away – you seemed so devastated, and I wondered if I'd been wrong. I tried to talk to you. But you didn't want to know, which only confirmed what I'd believed all along.' The acrimony in her voice is clear, but it's the only thing that is.

'How did I let you down? Do you mean Mum? Lola, you have to listen—'

'No! It wasn't that. We don't have time for this, Nancy. I knew something like this might happen when I heard you were back in Cornwall.'

'You *knew*? Why didn't you come and see me, let me know you were okay?'

She looks at me as if I am insane.

'How could I? No one knows I'm here. Even Cal and Dan believe I'm Monique, and I never leave the house or the beach.'

I don't know where to go with my questions. There are so many, and so little time.

'Just tell me how you found your way here, Lola, and why you're *still* here.'

She sighs and I reach through the bars again, but she stands her ground. 'You thought Liam was your secret, but I knew something was going on. It was right there, under our noses, every single day of that ghastly holiday. The meek nineteen-year-old girl who wouldn't say boo to a goose was suddenly swanning around with a ridiculous smile on her face all the time. We knew you were shagging someone. Dad knew too, not that he cared.' The bitterness drips off her tongue and my eyes don't leave her face. 'I was so bloody angry with you for turning your back on everything that was happening to me.'

I don't know what to say. There is so much in all of this that I simply don't understand, but she hasn't finished. She comes closer to the bars, and I can see tears glistening in her eyes, but her lips are clamped into a hard line.

'For days you'd been hanging around the edge of the beach, scared to join in with the rest of us, and then suddenly you weren't there – and you were happy. So I followed you down the path to this beach, but neither of you noticed me. You were too busy. I was jealous as hell that you could let some guy touch you like that and seem to enjoy it. I hated you for it. Then, that last night, I saw you crying and suddenly I had to tell you I was leaving, and why. I thought this was where you'd come when you ran out of the cottage, but when I got to the cove you weren't here. That's when I saw what Liam was up to, and I had to pay the price. I was locked in the cage for two months, all because in a moment of weakness I wanted to say goodbye.' One side of her mouth twists into a sour smile. 'Liam knew the police were looking for me, but they thought I'd run away and they had no reason to suspect him. He couldn't let me go, of course, so he had to keep me out of sight while he decided what to do with me.'

I want to rip my gaze from hers, to stare around the cave and imagine how it must have been to live here, but I'm scared that when I look back, she will have disappeared as if she was just a fantasy.

'What did you see?' It seems the least important question, but the easiest to ask.

'The same as you, according to Cal.'

Lola isn't making sense. I'm about to tell her to slow down and explain when we hear a sound.

'*Shit!*' Lola turns her head as if she's listening. 'The storm must have eased off quicker than I thought. Liam's back.' She swivels back towards me. 'I can't help you. My kids come first.'

'Monique!' I hear a voice echo around the cavernous space and, like the last time he spoke to me eleven years ago, I can feel the heat of his anger in that one word. My heart leaps, whether an instinctive reaction to the man I thought I loved or utter terror, I don't know. Part of me aches to see him, but mostly I want to cower out of sight.

I stare at Lola, whose eyes are wide with alarm. He must be well inside the cave, heading towards us, and without another sound she hurries away, taking the light with her, and my last hope. He must have been nearly on us because I can hear every word.

'What the fuck are you doing?' he snaps. 'You shouldn't be talking to her. You owe her nothing.'

'I know, Liam, but maybe it would be better for all of us if you let her go,' Lola says, her voice wavering. 'She won't say anything about me. She'll stay quiet for my sake, and she doesn't know anything else.'

He barks out a harsh laugh. 'She's been watching, spying, like I said she would. Cal should have kept a better eye on her. And her photos are evidence – you know that! Just remember – if the police come, you're as complicit in all of this as any of us. The kids will be taken into care, and you can't protect them from all the wicked men of the world when you're in prison, can you?' There is a derisive tone to his voice, as if he's mocking her. My hands grip the bars so tightly that my nails cut into my palms.

Lola's reply is so quiet I can barely hear her. 'I know the score. I won't help her if you don't think she can be trusted.'

'Forget her. There's too much to do. The boat has to be unloaded. Is everything ready?'

'Yes, of course.' Lola sounds relieved. I choke back an urge to scream at Liam for bullying her. I need to listen. 'Cal's checked the van, but I guess it will have to be tomorrow night now before we move them.'

'Fucking storm. It's too light to go now. You'll have to help. We don't want any clever bastards deciding to jump ship and go for a swim, do we?'

I hear footsteps, then quiet. They've gone.

I rest my forehead on the bars. There is so much in all of this that I don't understand, but I can't focus. All I can think about is that Lola is alive! My sister, who I've been desperate to find for all these years, has been here all this time.

Why does she hate me so much? What did I do? Did she mention an unborn child? Did Liam rape her? She was *fifteen*.

Still clinging to the bars, I slither down to the ground, my legs like jelly. My whole body is shaking, my heart thumping as I try to replay everything she said, fighting my way through a fog of confusion.

Only one thing seems clear: Lola isn't going to help me.

SEVENTY-TWO

No matter how many times I go over every word Lola said, I can't make any sense out of it. *Why does she think I let her down? Why was she running away? What does Liam think I saw? What does she mean about an unborn child?*

I shouldn't be wasting time trying to puzzle everything out. I should be concentrating on how I can get out of here, but I am so floored by everything she said that I can't focus.

I close my eyes and think about her face, or as much as I could see of it in the lamplight. It's the face of a young woman now, with all traces of the child gone and more worry lines than she should have. I wanted to touch her skin, feel its silkiness under my fingers, to know she was real and not a figment of my imagination. She always had such soft skin. But she wouldn't come close enough.

I think of the three children I saw on the beach and how I would love to meet them. Whatever her life is like here, I'm sure she takes good care of them. They seemed happy enough that day.

Although fear is fizzing through my veins, at my core there is a warm glow of relief that my sister is alive, and it fires up my determination. I'm not giving up. I'll fight to my last breath because I need to save Lola – and save myself.

My thoughts are interrupted by noises. I sit perfectly still and listen. A babble of voices echoes around the walls, high pitched, quivering. I can't make out what they're saying, and I clamber to my feet. A faint glow is heading towards me.

'Quiet!'

Liam's voice breaks through the hubbub. The chatter stops, leaving only the sound of soft whimpering.

The light is growing stronger as they progress further into the cave. A voice cries out, but I can't make out the words so I stumble across the rough ground to the corner where I have a slender view of the other cage.

A stream of people shuffle through the gate, their trousers rolled up from their bare feet to above their knees, wet as if they've had to wade through the sea. Some are holding back, weeping openly. They appear to be young men, but Liam shoves them until they're all inside.

I can't hold back a gasp of horror, but there is so much noise that he doesn't hear me. He must know what I've seen – that I know what he's doing. Any remote hope of him setting me free is now crushed.

I think of the scratches in the cave, HANH, MINH, BAO, and I wonder whether these men will add their names to the wall.

'You *bastard*, Liam,' I whisper to myself. 'You utter, utter *bastard*.'

It's the first chance I've had to see him, and even now it's only from the side. His hair is longer, swept back from his forehead, and dark stubble covers his cheeks and chin. My whole body shudders, and for a moment I think I will buckle, dizzy with weakness and nausea. Like before, it's as if he can feel me looking at him, and he turns his head. His eyes are hard, like black flint, and I don't see any hint of a memory of those days on the beach.

He turns back and the gate clangs shut.

'You've got blankets and water,' he says.

There's a shout from one of the men, his voice ragged with anguish. But the words mean nothing to me, and Liam seems unmoved by his distress.

He shouts over their noise. 'You'll stay here as long as I say. Do as I tell you. Mess with me, and you'll be taken out to sea and thrown overboard. Got it?'

There's more crying and shouting, but Liam doesn't respond. To my surprise, I see Lola beside him. She is staring into the cage, her expression blank, her eyes unfocused as if she's trying not to see what's in front of her. I hope she is faking her indifference to the plight of those poor souls.

SEVENTY-THREE

Stephanie had asked for an early meeting with DI Harris-Cooke, and Gus had suggested he join them, although he promised to let her do the talking. True to his word, he stood leaning against a low window ledge, hands thrust deep into the pockets of his black trousers, jacket off, looking totally relaxed. But Stephanie knew he wasn't. He'd half-heartedly tried to justify Nancy's absence the night before, suggesting she may have simply gone to stay at a hotel.

'Without her purse!? Without her phone!?' she'd ranted.

Gus was worried too – she could see it in his eyes – and every bone in Stephanie's body told her Nancy's absence had to be related to Lola's disappearance. They had to act now, rather than wait to see if she turned up.

The DI was seated behind her desk, and Stephanie refused the offered chair, preferring to stand – and occasionally pace – the office.

'Are you suggesting that we use precious, limited resources to look for a thirty-year-old woman who has been away from her home for a few hours?'

Stephanie had already provided her boss with every reason

she could think of to convince her that something had happened to Nancy, but HC looked sceptical.

'I am, ma'am, yes. In view of the ongoing investigation into her sister, I don't think we can ignore her absence. I've met her. I know her. I don't think there's an irresponsible bone in her body – and she's desperate to find out what happened to Lola.'

HC turned the pen she was holding over and over between her fingers, and Stephanie kept quiet, knowing she had said everything she could.

'And why are you here, DCI Brodie? Are you the support act, in case I say no?'

Gus pulled his hands out of his pockets and held them up, palms outward, as if in defence mode.

'Absolutely not. I think Steph's more than capable of making the case, and I wouldn't patronise her by sticking my oar in.'

Stephanie tried hard not to raise her eyebrows. Gus usually found it impossible not to stick his oar in.

'But you must have an opinion on Nancy Holland's disappearance?'

'It's a bit soon to call it a disappearance,' he said, 'and normally I would agree it should be low priority – but as I'm already heading up a team to investigate Lola's case, I think we could consider Nancy to be an extension of that investigation, particularly as it seems logical to assume the two are related.'

The DI looked at Stephanie. 'You remember I was concerned that Nancy Holland might have played a part in her sister's disappearance and maybe even in the deaths of her parents. Does the fact that she now appears to be missing herself make this hypothesis more or less likely, in your opinion?'

Stephanie wanted to say she had never thought much of the hypothesis to start with, but restrained herself to a single word: 'Less.'

'Hmm.' HC tapped the pen on the desk. 'You haven't considered that perhaps she thinks we're on to her, and she's done a runner?'

'Not for a single moment, ma'am.'

'And you, sir?' The DI never forgot that, as a DCI, Gus was her superior.

'I agree with Steph. Whether Lola Holland was abducted or murdered, I doubt Nancy was involved. But it's possible the perpetrator thinks she has information that might implicate them. As for the parents...' Gus recounted the conversation he and Stephanie had the evening before about the crime Ray and Janice Holland had apparently committed. 'It's probably entirely irrelevant, but we need to keep in mind that either one or both of the daughters may have discovered something.'

'But the parents are dead!'

'They are – although whatever they'd done, they may not have acted alone. McEwan mentioned someone called Carl, and we're trying to find a link, but in the meantime there are other areas of investigation we can pursue. Nancy's phone is at the cottage – we left it there in case we were overreacting and she returned home – but if you're happy for me to add Nancy into the mix I'll ask the officer who's parked outside to bring it in. We should look at her calls and at historical cell-siting to see where she's been. Anything else, Steph?'

Stephanie nodded. 'I was thinking about Nancy's camera. She told me she took photos of anything and everything that holiday. She downloaded them to show to us when she was at the B&B, but there are no photos on her laptop now. We checked last night, and the tech guys have confirmed that her computer was accessed *after* the time she apparently went missing – at least, the time according to Effie Dawson. They're trying to find out what, if anything, her computer was used for.'

'Did you find the camera at her cottage?' HC asked.

Stephanie looked at Gus and he shook his head. Neither of them could remember a camera.

'No, although I suppose she might have it with her,' Stephanie said. 'But if the photos are still on there and she hasn't wiped the card, I'm wondering whether there are any, other than those we already have, that might be of interest.'

'I think someone should go to the cottage,' Gus said. 'See if the camera's there. Her purse was on the table, but no debit or credit card. If she has either, she's taken it with her, so we'll request bank details.'

HC nodded. 'I'll leave it with you, then. I'd like to be kept in the loop, sir, if possible.'

'Of course,' Gus replied.

He pushed himself off the window ledge and opened the door for Stephanie.

'I think I should go back to the cottage myself,' Stephanie said, once the door was closed behind them. 'I know where we looked last time, so it'll be quicker for me to find the camera, if it's there. What do you think?'

Gus gave her a knowing smile. They could ask the officer tasked with picking up the phone to look for it, but he knew how concerned she was, and she would be looking for more than just a camera.

'Good idea. Let me know what you find.'

Stephanie grabbed her bag and hurried out of the door before he could change his mind.

SEVENTY-FOUR

Stephanie arrived at the cottage to find the locksmith hard at work replacing the temporary lock. She flashed her warrant card.

'I heard there was crime scene tape here a few days ago. What's been going on?' he asked.

Stephanie raised her eyebrows, which the locksmith correctly interpreted as *Mind your own business.*

'I'm going inside for a look round. Do you think you'll be long?' she asked.

He sighed theatrically at her lack of cooperation. 'Ten minutes, max. The door wasn't damaged. You didn't even split the wood – the lock just gave way. I need to screw a new strike plate in position and replace the lock itself, then I'm done.'

Stephanie thanked him and walked into the cottage, then slowly made her way round the kitchen. There was no camera on either the table or the worktop. The cupboards were almost empty too, although some bin liners and boxes were piled in the corners of the room. She checked inside to find they were full of old household items.

She moved across to the sitting room. There was no camera

on the sideboard, and she pulled open the drawers. The right-hand drawer revealed a pale blue folder and she flipped it open. Inside were the press cuttings from Lola's disappearance.

The main photograph was Lola, with a request for information from the public, and a smaller inset image showed Nancy and Ray Holland, the latter not looking at the camera. Frustrated that they hadn't done more eleven years ago, she shut the folder and slammed the drawer with unnecessary force.

The bedrooms provided nothing of interest, other than a few clothes in the wardrobe of the double room. Again, there was no camera.

Returning downstairs, Stephanie picked up Nancy's purse. A couple of receipts were scrunched into the slip pocket – one from a restaurant in the nearest town. She recognised the date as the night Nancy had seen Quinn, and it appeared she had paid by card. Stephanie took a note of the last four digits printed on the receipt to pass on to the team.

'All done, Sergeant,' the locksmith said. 'What do you want me to do with the keys?'

'I'll take them. Thanks.'

'I'll get off, then. It's a better lock than the one that was here before, anyway.'

Stephanie took a last look round but couldn't see anything of interest. She needed to lodge a key with someone in case Nancy came back, and it seemed there was little choice but to ask Mrs Roskilly. As Nancy's phone was inside the house, she wouldn't be able to call anyone to come and unlock the door, so the key had to be left with someone local.

Shutting and locking the door, Stephanie pinned her business card to the wood with a brief note to Nancy, should she return. The storm from the night before had turned the sea wild and for a moment Stephanie stood and watched the waves pounding on the shingle beach, breakers throwing plumes of white foam towards the shore.

She tore herself away and hurried to Mrs Roskilly's house, hoping to get in and out without being diverted by either gossip or an interrogation. The woman had clearly been watching from the window and had seen her coming, because the door was opened before she had a chance to knock.

'I saw the policeman outside, and the locksmith this morning. You had to break down the door, they said.'

Stephanie groaned. She didn't really want to get into this, and quickly explained that Nancy's lock had been changed, but they hadn't been able to get hold of her to give her a key. Mrs Roskilly smirked.

'I bet she's with a man.'

'Maybe. No doubt we'll find out soon enough.'

Any further speculation about exactly why the police had to break in was interrupted by Stephanie's phone ringing.

'Steph, it's Effie. Look, this is a complete and utter stab in the dark, and only a guess, but I think that when Nancy was here before she might have had a brief thing with a guy.'

Stephanie signalled to Mrs Roskilly that she was going to have to take this outside. The last thing she wanted was for her to hear, and Effie's voice wasn't the quietest.

'Do you know who?' she asked as she stepped into the front courtyard.

'Liam Riordan. Do you know him?'

The name didn't ring a bell, but then the town was only a small part of the area she covered as a detective, and although Stephanie had gone to school with Effie's sister, they hadn't lived close to each other.

'What can you tell me about him?'

'Fancied himself rotten when he was younger, but I gather he's settled down since then. He used to prey on young holidaymakers who were here and gone in a flash. Married one of them about fifteen years ago. She left for a while, but came back. Monique, she's called. Someone said they have kids, but

I don't know if that's true. They keep very much to themselves.'

'And do you think Nancy will have tried to contact him again?'

'God knows. Sorry, Steph, I have no idea. She caught a glimpse of him the other night and seemed a bit spooked, but she didn't say much.'

'What makes you think she was seeing him eleven years ago?'

'I could tell that she recognised him, and when I talked about how he used to lure young female holidaymakers into his evil clutches, Nancy looked very uncomfortable. I'm guessing, Steph. I just thought it was worth letting you know. He broke a lot of hearts when he was younger. Hers might have been one of them.'

Stephanie felt a tingle. 'Do you know where he lives, Effie?'

'Somewhere on the coastal path, going west from town, and I'm told it's hard to find if you don't know it's there – hidden below a cliff, I think, with a path through the hawthorn. I don't know anyone who's ever been there. I don't think he welcomes visitors.'

Stephanie thanked Effie and ended the call. The tingle had built to a full-on shiver of excitement.

Was this finally a lead?

SEVENTY-FIVE

It's starting to make sense to me. At least, some of it is. As soon as Liam knew I was here, in Cornwall, he suspected I would come to the clifftop, and he was right. He had to make sure I saw nothing of what he was doing – that I wasn't there, watching, when his boat returned.

Showing Cal the photos was a mistake, but I had no choice. I thought they were merely evidence of my relationship with Liam, and even though I'd seen the young men – not much more than boys – who were in the cabin of Liam's boat eleven years ago, I'd assumed they were his friends. I thought nothing of the fact that they appeared to be Asian, and I'd discounted the photo because I was only looking for Monique. But now there's no escaping the fact that I really have seen too much.

I huddle up against the driest part of the wall, knees drawn up, head bent, breathing out through my mouth into the tiny cavity I've formed between my bent legs and my body, trying to generate what little warmth I can. I can still hear crying from the other cage, and I wish I could shout to them, say something positive, but what? They must be cold, damp, probably hungry, and I can't imagine how scared they must feel. It helps me to focus on their fear rather than on my own – at least for a moment or two.

There's a sudden change in the sounds from the other cage. I can hear a rustling as if they are moving, then they are rattling the bars, calling out.

Someone must be coming, but no one answers their calls. The darkness lightens slightly, but no one speaks.

I don't know what's happening. Are they coming for me?

It takes me a moment to realise that the person holding the light has passed the main cage.

Is it Liam, coming to take me to the boat and to dump me out at sea?

My heart is hammering, and despite the freezing cold, I start to sweat. He's getting closer. I can see nothing because he's holding the lantern in front of him, and it's blinding me, then I glance down at the feet and realise it isn't Liam. It has to be Lola.

I push myself to my feet and hurry towards the bars, grasping them in my hands.

'Lola, help me. Please!'

'I've brought you a blanket and some water,' she says, her voice abrupt and unfriendly. 'The tide will be back in soon, and you'll be here until tonight, when it's dark enough to move you. But don't expect anything else from me. I told you – I'm with Liam now.'

I want to say that I heard how he spoke to her, that it's hard to believe she's happy with him, but if she becomes too defensive she'll leave and I need to understand what she said – what she believes I did wrong.

'I know you're with him,' I say, keeping my tone gentle as if I'm speaking to one of my oldies. 'I'd like to understand why you think I let you down so badly, Lola. Whatever I did, I'm so very sorry, but I genuinely don't know what it was, if it wasn't Mum.'

She's still holding the lamp aloft, and I can see a frown of puzzlement. 'How could you not know?'

'Know *what*?'

She shakes her head as if it's all too much, and doesn't respond. She pushes the blanket through the bars and places a bottle of water on the floor where I can reach it. She looks as if she's about to leave, but I am desperate for her to stay.

'Tell me about your children, then,' I call as she begins to turn away. 'I came one day to look at the cove, to remember that summer, and I saw them on the beach. You've got a boy and two little girls, haven't you? They're beautiful.'

She stops and turns back slightly. Talking about her children seems easier. 'The girls are twins. They're five.'

'And your son?'

She stares at me and doesn't speak for a moment. 'Josh will be eleven at Christmas.'

Eleven? She would have been barely sixteen when he was born, fifteen when he was conceived. 'Oh, I'm so sorry, Lola. He raped you, didn't he?'

I reach through the bars, but she backs away with a contemptuous laugh. 'So you *did* know!'

What does she mean? She's staring at me, her eyes flat, cold, shaking her head as if she is disgusted with me.

My head is spinning with all that's happened, but one thought suddenly bursts through the fog. Lola disappeared in the July before she was sixteen. Christmas was only five months away. *She was already pregnant.*

'The boy's not Liam's?' I don't know why I'm asking the question because it's obvious. 'Who's the father, Lola? I had no idea you had a boyfriend.'

Her eyes burn into mine, and suddenly they flood with tears.

'I thought you knew. He told me you knew, that you were jealous, so I wasn't to speak to you about it.'

For a moment I have no idea what she might mean. Then a slow, creeping sensation of horror crawls up from my gut to my throat. I try to find another meaning, but I can't, and although I don't want to ask, I have to.

'Who's the father, Lola? Tell me you don't mean what I think you do.'

She drops her head. 'Imagine the worst thing possible, and you'll get there eventually.' She sniffs and wipes her hand under her nose. 'I thought I'd cried for the last time over that vile bastard.'

I need her to say it. If I say what I'm thinking out loud and I'm wrong, I will hate myself for uttering the words. I reach through the bars to touch her, but she takes a quick step back again.

'Tell me.'

She raises her eyes to mine, and I see years of torment reflected in them.

'Josh is your brother, Nancy.'

SEVENTY-SIX

I can't speak. I ache for the pain Lola must have suffered, and yet my sense of revulsion at what she has told me has left me dumb. My mouth fills with saliva, but I mustn't vomit. My thoughts and feelings don't matter, and I try to imagine how life must have been for her.

I can't.

After a few minutes, it's Lola who speaks, and I'm ashamed of myself for not offering her any words of sympathy.

'I thought you knew.'

The tears have dried and her voice has hardened again. She's had years of dealing with this, but I'm certain that doesn't make it any easier to talk about. She's keeping her voice low so the people in the other cage can't hear, and it sounds as if she's hissing at me.

'It was always you, you know. You were his shining star. I was so jealous when we were younger because he always wanted *you* to be with him, not me. Then Mum made you do more work in the house, spend less time with him, and I was pleased because I thought it was my chance.'

My throat tightens, and I reach for the bottle of water that

Lola has placed inside the bars, twist the top off and take a huge gulp.

'I was only thirteen, and he'd never shown any interest in me, but when you were out of the way, looking after Mum, I did whatever I could to please him. More fool me.'

Her raw, bitter tone twists a knife in my heart. Lola was right. I was Dad's favourite, and for one shocking moment I wonder what might have happened if Mum hadn't had a stroke, if I hadn't been forced to sleep in her room.

'He started to come into my bed,' Lola says, and I want to beg her to stop. 'He said we needed to comfort each other while things were difficult. It didn't seem weird to me. It made me feel special, and he just slept with his arms around me. At least, to start with. I was his special girl, but it had to be our secret. And then...' She stops and swallows. She glances at me. 'I'm not going to paint any pictures for you, Nancy. They're too ugly, and I'm sure you can join the dots. It took me a long time to realise what was happening. It was a slow process, every touch carefully orchestrated.'

I want to tell her it wasn't her fault, that she should have told me – or someone – but before I can find the right words, she speaks again, so quietly I can barely hear her.

'The thing is, all I ever wanted was to hear him call me his *kochanie*.'

I feel my heart lurch. How cruel to single out one child from the other. She must have been desperate to feel loved by him. Why did I never see this? Moments come back to me of finding them together, cuddled on the sofa after Mum became ill. And I was jealous! Lola had suddenly become the one with the close relationship with Dad, and I had Mum – who could barely speak and who seemed to exist in a world of her own.

'I don't know what to say, Lola – except I am so very, very sorry. I promise you, I didn't have a clue. Why didn't you tell me?'

She gives a strangled laugh. 'Do you know how difficult it is to share something like that?'

The desperation in her voice, even after all these years, is raw with the ugliness of it all.

'I would have looked after you,' I tell her.

She shakes her head. 'It's easy to say now, isn't it? When it started I thought that if I told you, you'd hate me. And then, when it escalated, he must have sensed that I'd started to get uncomfortable, so told me you knew – and so did Mum. It was fine – normal in many families and cultures.'

'And did you believe that?'

'Of course! I thought you knew, and you didn't care. I was so ashamed. I felt it was my fault that it had gone so far. He said I'd encouraged him, and anyway, we were just loving each other. I felt sick every night when the door to your part of the house closed.'

'But I heard you laughing together.'

She shakes her head. 'Only in the beginning, when I was desperate to be his favourite. After the first few months you never left Mum's room in the evening.'

It's true. I'd given up trying to be a member of what I perceived to be the happy part of our family, filled instead with resentment for what my life had become.

'I would have helped you,' I mutter, ashamed of the fact that I didn't take better care of my sister.

'You say that now, but it's never that simple, is it? You'd have felt forced to tell someone, and social services would have become involved. I'd have been taken into care. Mum couldn't look after us, could she? What was I supposed to do?'

'You never came to Mum's room. It was as if you pretended she wasn't there.'

'How *could* I? I couldn't face her. Her husband was sneaking into my bed every night, and I thought she was okay with it.'

'Lola, she wouldn't have been. I know she struggled, and she was battling her own demons, but she would never have wanted you to suffer. She wasn't unkind. Only unhappy.'

Now I see tears running down Lola's cheeks. All her defences have gone, broken down, destroyed by memories of her own father.

'I'm sorry she died, Lola. I'm sorry I didn't do a better job of caring for her.'

'Of all the things I've blamed you for, I've never thought that was your fault. I knew it wasn't. Dad tried to blame you for everything – he even told the doctor that you'd been getting vodka for Mum.'

She brushes the tears from her cheeks as she looks at my horror-stricken face.

'I know it wasn't true, Nancy. It was Dad. It's why he visited Mum each night – to give her a huge nightcap to wash down her sleeping tablet. He didn't want her to be well enough to start wandering around the house when we were all suppos-edly in our own beds. He manipulated us. We both had to feel guilty for something, so he didn't need to.'

SEVENTY-SEVEN

I am in a daze, overwhelmed by everything I've heard. Lola keeps glancing over her shoulder as if she's expecting Liam to appear, but she can't leave now. We need each other. She looks at me, her expression still wary, as if she's not sure whether to believe that I knew nothing about Dad.

'Lola, please. Just let me touch you,' I say, praying that I can break through the barriers she has spent years erecting. 'I want to know that you're real; that I'm not dreaming.'

I try to offer her an encouraging smile, and she takes one step towards me. I wait, and finally she leans towards the cage and grabs my hands. I want to kick down the bars so I can hold my little sister, but all I can do is wrap my fingers round hers.

She drops her head. 'Maybe I should have trusted you, but by the time Mum died, I had nothing left, no emotional strength. I suspected I was pregnant and I thought you didn't care that I was being abused by our father. I was fifteen. I thought it would be my word against his, so I said nothing. My only option was to run away.'

'That's why you were so difficult, isn't it? I couldn't understand why you were being so disrespectful, but now it makes sense.'

'I'd wanted it to stop for so long. Something had to give. I didn't know what to do, so I acted like a wild thing on the beach with all the other kids. But Dad was always there – sitting at a café, watching.'

She's still holding on to me, but I think of what she said to Liam about how she blamed me for everything.

'I feel as if you hate me, Lola, but if I'd known what was happening to you, I would have done something – I promise you.'

Her lips tighten again, and she eases her hands out of mine.

'Hating you was the only thing that kept me sane. If I thought about missing you, how I was desperate to see you, to feel you hug me like you used to before it all went to shit, I would have fallen apart. I nurtured that hatred; fanned the flames.'

I try to reach for her again, but she's too far away now, as if her moment of weakness has passed.

She glances nervously over her shoulder again. 'I can't stay. Liam's drunk a load of whisky and he's asleep right now, but if he wakes up and finds I'm gone, I'll be in trouble.'

'Does he hurt you?' I ask.

She drops her head. It seems it's her automatic defence mechanism when the questions are tough. 'No, but he's in charge. He controls my destiny. When I came looking for you that night, I ran down to the beach and saw him taking people from his boat. It was dark, and I could only make out body shapes, but there was a sense of defeat in the way they were walking, and I stood and stared, horrified. Liam saw me. I ran but he chased after me and grabbed me, nearly strangled me. He was working on his own back then. It was his first shipment, and he was terrified that you'd seen something when he arrived back in the boat, when you were watching from the cliff. Then I turned up. He had no idea what to do, so he ferried everyone into the cave, and threw me in with them.'

I close my eyes and imagine how it must have been for her, locked in this cold, dank hole in the side of a cliff. I've been here for no more than a few hours, and already I feel chilled through to my bones.

'If only you hadn't been planning to run away! The police would have looked much harder for you. Liam was a lucky bastard.'

Lola shrugs. 'No, I was the lucky one. He couldn't let me go after what I'd seen, but everyone believed I'd run away so no one looked very hard. If the police had been scouring the countryside for a kid who had disappeared with no explanation, they'd have searched every nook and cranny – including the caves. Liam would have taken me out in his boat, weighed me down and tipped me into the middle of the English Channel. Even I can see it would have been his only option.'

I feel sick as I realise this is what he has planned for me tonight, but however terrified I feel, a whisper at the back of my mind is telling me that I brought Lola to this.

'I...' is all I can muster before she interrupts again.

'You didn't make me come here, Nancy. I've always blamed you, but I was an impulsive, angry, damaged girl. Liam didn't know what to do with me, especially when I told him I was pregnant. He didn't believe me at first. I was barely showing – nothing more than a slightly round belly.'

I think back to the photos I took, and how surprised I was at her curvy body. She looked more like a woman than I did.

'He fed me, gave me a camp bed and some bedding,' she says. 'He kept me here until he was certain the police had given up looking for me and were unlikely to call at his cottage. He smuggled in another two groups of young men and women. They came and went, but I stayed here, locked in this awful cave. Liam wasn't as evil back then as he is now, and whatever else he is, he loves the kids. But these days he's part of a bigger organisation. He was competing in their market and they didn't like it. He had to choose whether to let them control him, or risk all our lives. They're the worst of the worst, Nancy, into every kind of crime, and Liam has to do as they say. But their demands are getting more and more dangerous.'

'Is Cal one of them?' I ask.

She makes a *pfft* sound. 'He's not important. He works for Liam, so does Dan. The real bosses stay well hidden. I don't know who they are, and he doesn't want them to know about me. Sometimes he goes off to meetings with them, and when he comes back his face is ashen for days. Even the children know not to speak to him, and if the bosses knew the police were looking for me, they'd make Liam kill me.'

I know very little about organised crime – only what I've read or seen on the television. But I know human life is cheap to them. I can't dwell on that thought or I will fall to pieces.

'What changed?' I ask. 'What made him decide to let you out of the cage?'

'He wanted people to believe he was married – that Monique was back. No woman was likely to venture to the cove if he had a wife living there, and once he started people-smuggling he couldn't have a relationship – and he likes women. He gave me a straight choice. I could live with him as his wife, or he would deliver me back to Dad.'

'And if he'd done that, how could he have squared the fact that he'd had you locked in a cage for two months?'

She shrugs. 'I was fifteen, pregnant and terrified, so I never questioned it. By the time I realised I could have run, it was too late. The thought of having to face Dad, live with the shame, was too horrific, so when Liam said I could stay here on the beach with him, it seemed the better option. He saved me, Nancy. Whatever else he is or was, living with him is so much better than the alternative.'

I can't even think what to say. Anything I suggest that she *could* have done will sound like criticism, and Liam had all the power, given everything that had happened in Lola's short life.

'What about since then, since you had the child? You've had Liam's children now – did you never think of leaving?'

'For the next five years, I stayed locked in the cottage. I wasn't allowed out during the day in case someone saw me and recognised me, and he held the threat of Dad over my head. The thought of ever having to see that man again repulsed me far more than anything that Liam could do. Whatever happens here, Nancy, I can't face Dad.'

I stare at her through the bars. It had never occurred to me until this moment that she might not know.

'Lola, he's *dead*! He died two months after you went missing.'

She stares at me, then her eyes flood with tears and she wraps her arms around her stomach.

'Did you see his body?' she asks, her voice so low I can hardly hear her.

'No, but...'

'Then you're wrong. You must be. Liam says he's seen him. He says he comes here every year. He's looking for me.'

SEVENTY-EIGHT

When Stephanie got back from Nancy's cottage, the incident room was buzzing, and she hurried across to where Gus was talking to a young female officer whom Stephanie didn't recognise.

'Any sign of the camera?' he asked, turning towards her.

'No, it's not there. But Effie called.'

Stephanie quickly recounted what she'd been told.

'Interesting,' Gus said, turning to the officer at his side. 'Ayaneh, this is Detective Sergeant King.' He nodded to Stephanie. 'Ayaneh has been drafted in from Major Crimes to help with the Lola case and has some interesting information to share. Ayaneh, can you repeat what you told me a couple of minutes ago?'

The young woman nodded. 'Yes, boss. We'd retained all the information on Lola Holland as her case hasn't been closed. We have the cell-siting records for the days before she went missing. She took a couple of walks along the coastal path in the days leading up to her disappearance, but there didn't seem to be any significance. We never found her phone, but we now have

Nancy's, recovered from the cottage, so in addition to cell-siting we've been able to check her location history. Yesterday, around the time we believe she disappeared, Nancy made a similar journey to those her sister made eleven years ago. Lola's data is less precise due to fewer masts locally at the time, but it's enough to show a strong correlation. Yesterday wasn't the first time Nancy had visited the location. According to her history, it's the third time since she arrived in Cornwall.'

'Do we know where the common point is?' Stephanie asked.

The officer nodded, tapped the screen of her phone and turned to the large monitor on which a map showing the coastal path and the sea beyond was displayed.

'This is the area where they ended up – both of them,' she said, pointing to a highlighted circle on the map. 'In Lola's case, she went there, stayed a while, and came back the same way – along the coastal path. On the day of her disappearance, she had her phone switched off unfortunately, so we don't know where she went. In Nancy's case, on Thursday, she took the same route Lola had taken and stayed about forty-five minutes. The day before yesterday – Sunday – she followed the route to the same spot, but didn't stay and turned inland.'

'Hang on a sec,' Stephanie said. 'What time was that?'

Ayaneh checked the records. 'Piecing it together from the data, she left home at around 11.50, walked through town and out onto the coast road to the south-west. She reached the point we're interested in at 12.33 before she turned inland. She reached the road twelve minutes later.'

'There was a man following her that day,' Stephanie said. 'She told me, but said she thought she was imagining it. I called her and she sounded worried, but then said it was nothing. What happened yesterday, Ayaneh?'

Ayaneh touched her phone and up came a list of dates and times. She pointed to those headed *Monday*.

'She went into town from her cottage and was there for over an hour, then she took the coastal path, reaching the same point, and was there for fifty-three minutes. Then she turned inland again and walked along the same track back to the main road. She went home that way. Since then, her phone has been in the house.'

'What time did she get back?'

'At 6.07 p.m. It's a longer walk that way.'

'The weather was vile,' Stephanie said. 'Why didn't she come back the quick way?'

No one had an answer to that, and they stared at the screen and the timings until Gus broke the contemplative silence.

'The man who saw Lola the night she disappeared said she was heading out of town along the coastal path in that direction.'

'Yes!' Stephanie said. 'And when Lola left the beach to follow Nancy home that night, Quinn says Nancy was coming *from* the coastal path.'

'Good work, Ayaneh,' Gus said, then turned to Stephanie. 'Nancy's computer was accessed just after six, and we heard from the tech team earlier. They've not finished yet, but apparently around that time her photo library was wiped. So what's interesting about this spot, then?'

'I told you Effie Dawson called about this guy, Liam Riordan. She thinks his cottage is somewhere on the coastal path,' Stephanie said.

'Can you switch to a satellite image?' Gus asked Ayaneh.

'Of course, boss.'

Gus glanced at Stephanie and raised his eyebrows. She could read his mind. This young officer exuded confidence and capability.

They stared at the screen as Ayaneh manipulated the image until it was enlarged to the maximum.

'A cottage,' Stephanie said, 'and a lovely tiny cove. What an incredible place that must be.'

'Indeed. And if Nancy was there in the early evening yesterday, it's possible that Liam Riordan saw her,' Gus said.

'Then let's go and ask him,' Stephanie said.

SEVENTY-NINE

Ayaneh had checked the best route to reach the Riordan property by car and sent it to both Stephanie and Gus's phones.

'I think we should drive there separately,' Stephanie said, grabbing her bag and her keys. 'If something crops up, one of us might have to get back.'

'Good idea. There's a track that leaves the main road. Go as far down it as you can, then we'll continue on foot. If you get there first, wait for me, Steph. *Steph!* Are you listening?'

She was, and much as she wanted to go barging in there, convinced that there were too many coincidences and Nancy had to be connected to Liam Riordan, she knew two heads would be better than one.

Stephanie was first to arrive at the track. It didn't look as if it would do much for her suspension, but she took it slowly and pulled her car into the yard of a derelict barn. A grey van was parked inside. If this was the closest parking spot to the Riordan property, it could be Liam Riordan's van, and as she got out of the car she quickly took a photo of the van's plate.

She was about to send it off to check the ownership when she glanced up the track to see Gus speeding along, clearly unconcerned about the ruts and any damage to his own car. He pulled in next to hers.

'Have you run a PNC check?' he called as he got out of the car.

'About to send it to the team. Do you want to wait for the results?'

'No, not important enough yet. Let's go and talk to the man.'

He strolled towards her, picking his way around the worst of the puddles caused by the previous night's rain.

'You ready?' he asked.

'I am. I'm sure this Riordan must know something about Nancy, but it occurred to me he might not know her by name, so I asked Ayaneh to send a photo of her. It's an old one, but her hair is very distinctive.'

'Good thinking. Come on,' he said, setting off at his usual fast pace.

Gus was staring at his phone, following the directions to the property, but when they reached the path that led to the cottage and the cove, they were faced with a gate. Not only was it closed, it was locked.

'Who the hell locks their gate with a padlock?' Stephanie asked, her suspicions further aroused.

'Someone who lives close to a remote public footpath that's used by plenty of strangers, at a guess. You know tourists often ignore keep out and private property signs. You're deciding about this man before we've even spoken to him, Steph.'

She grunted in response. He was right, but she had a feeling, one she couldn't ignore.

A metal postbox stood on a wooden plinth to one side of the gate, but there was no means of communicating with the cottage or its occupants.

'I get the idea of security, but what happens if they have legitimate visitors?' Stephanie asked, looking at the gate and hoping Gus wouldn't suggest climbing over. She didn't like the look of the spikes on the top.

'Hmm,' was the only answer she got, as Gus looked around to see if there was another way past the gate. 'Steph, could you take a walk along the clifftop and see if there's another way down?'

Stephanie stared at him. 'What? You know there isn't.'

'Nevertheless, go and take a look. That's an order!'

'For God's sake, Gus, whatever you're about to do, I'm hardly going to dob you in, am I?' With a sigh, Stephanie made a pretence of wandering away along the clifftop.

'We're in!' She turned back to a beaming Gus. 'It seems the padlock wasn't properly closed. Careless, I'd say.' He opened the gate wide to let her through.

'Just tell me how you did that – for future reference. And don't say "Did what?"'

Gus chuckled. 'If you didn't see me do anything, you won't have to lie if you're asked. But, for the record, look up "how to open a combination padlock" online. It's a useful technique to have, and surprisingly easy.'

They didn't say any more as they strode down the narrow path in single file. The only sound was the thunder of the sea, and Stephanie imagined living here, listening to the moods of the ocean, from the gentle swish of waves washing over the sand on a calm day to the roar and crash of the surf on a stormy day like today.

As they turned a bend, they saw the tiny cove below them. The tide was fully in, and there was little more than a sliver of fat pebbles and a thin strip of sand between the end of the path and the ocean. A boy was building an intricate construction out of the larger pebbles.

Gus dislodged a stone with his foot and it tumbled down the path. The boy looked up, shocked to see two people he didn't recognise walking towards him.

'Dad!' he shouted, getting to his feet to run towards a cottage that had just become visible. White painted, it nestled in a hollow two thirds of the way down the cliff. The red front door opened, and a man stepped out. Even from where they were, Stephanie could sense his anger that they had invaded his land, and after observing her and Gus for no more than a second or two, he marched towards the path to meet them.

'This is private property. The gate was locked. How did you get in?'

He stood below them, fists on hips, legs spread. Gus ignored the question.

'I'm Detective Chief Inspector Brodie, and this is my colleague Detective Sergeant King. We'd like a word, please?'

'You are trespassing.'

'Are you Liam Riordan?' Gus asked.

'I repeat, unless you have a warrant, I don't want you on my land.'

Gus raised his eyebrows, clearly unimpressed. 'And why would that be?'

'We value our privacy.'

Gus nodded. 'Then we won't keep you long. A few questions, if you don't mind. Otherwise we'll have to go through the tedium of organising some paperwork. One of us will have to wait here, of course, until it's sorted. Is that what you want us to do?'

Stephanie had been watching Riordan's face. She was certain they didn't have enough for a search warrant, but hopefully he wouldn't realise that. She saw him glance out to sea, then back at Gus.

'Fine. What do you want to know?'

'Can we please go down to the shore so we're on firmer ground?' Gus asked.

Without another word, Riordan turned and walked back

down as far as the pebbled edge of the beach. The blond boy was still there, staring at them.

'Josh, go back to the house. Tell your mum we have visitors. Two police officers.'

Josh looked at his dad for a moment, his eyes wide, his lips parting in surprise, then turned on his heel and ran towards the house.

Stephanie glanced into the bay. A boat was sitting at anchor, quite a long way out, and a RIB bobbed about in the water closer to shore, tied by a rope to a ring set in a rock. She couldn't make out the boat's name from this distance, but it seemed Riordan saw her looking.

'It's the *Monique III*,' he said. 'Named for my wife. Registered fishing vessel.'

'Was there a *Monique II* and *I* as well?' Stephanie asked.

Riordan's eyes narrowed slightly. 'A *II*, but not a *I*. That name was already registered in Penzance.'

'What do you catch?'

'It varies. I use tangle nets, so recently it's been monkfish mainly. But I'm sure you're not here to talk about fishing.'

'We're here to ask about a woman called Nancy Holland. Does the name mean anything to you?'

Riordan's brow furrowed. 'It kind of rings a bell, but I'm not sure why. Should I know her?'

Neither detective answered, but Stephanie pulled out her phone and showed him the photo Ayaneh had sent.

'Does that help?'

Again, he looked puzzled. 'There's definitely something familiar about her. Is she local?'

'No. We believe you first met her eleven years ago,' Gus said. 'She's back in the area, and we think she may have come here to speak to you.'

That wasn't true, but Stephanie knew Gus was pushing a few buttons.

'No one comes here unless they're invited, and I've not seen her.'

'In that case, we'd like to speak to your wife, please. See if she knows Nancy Holland.'

Riordan stood still for a while, staring at the ground. 'Look, this is delicate. But now you've shown me the photo, there's a possibility that this Nancy Howard—'

'Holland,' Stephanie corrected, although she felt certain he knew her name perfectly well.

'Sorry, Holland, might be a girl I saw for a while when she was on holiday here. It only lasted a few days, and it's a long time ago. My wife was away – she knows nothing about it.'

'That's fine, sir,' Gus said. 'We don't need to give her specifics. We know that Nancy has been in this area a few times in the last week, and we wondered if she'd paid you a visit. We'd like your wife to confirm if she came here, to your cove or your cottage, perhaps when you were fishing.'

'Hardly. The gate's locked, which rather begs the question of how you got in.'

Gus ignored the implied question yet again. 'Can we please talk to your wife?'

'If it makes you happy, you can search the whole fucking house. Be my guest, but please don't disturb my wife.'

'Is she ill?' Stephanie asked.

'Depends on your definition. I asked Josh to tell her you were here because she can't deal with visitors. With people, in fact. She has a fear of anyone she doesn't know, and she'll struggle to breathe if she has to speak to you. She never leaves the house and we don't welcome callers. If you're concerned that she's hiding this woman in her room, I'll take you in to check. Monique can take the kids into the garden.'

EIGHTY

Liam Riordan turned towards the cottage, and as Stephanie and Gus followed, she nudged him and raised her eyebrows.

'*Wife?*' she mouthed. It seemed a bit convenient that she couldn't talk to them. Was Riordan concerned they would blurt something out about his previous relationship with Nancy? Or was he worried that the wife might reveal something he didn't want them to hear? Either way, it seemed more than a little dodgy to Stephanie.

Gus shook his head. She knew it meant he had a theory, but he couldn't say anything without Riordan hearing.

Stephanie took the opportunity to scan the beach, but there was nowhere to hide. A fishing boat was thrashing around furiously in the bay, rocked by the stormy seas, but Riordan didn't seem to be worried.

A thought occurred to her. *The boat!* If Nancy was here, could he be hiding her on the boat?

Riordan was in front of them, so she nudged Gus again and inclined her head towards the bay. Gus gave her a brief nod, as if he'd already thought of that. Of course he had.

At that moment, the front door opened and the boy came out again.

'Josh, tell your mum to take the twins into the garden.'

The child stopped, gave his dad a quizzical look, then turned and ran back into the cottage.

'We won't distress her,' Gus said. 'We don't need specifically to speak to her.'

Other than to check she's not Nancy, Stephanie thought.

A moment later, Stephanie saw four figures emerge from the far side of the house into a small garden. A woman, the boy Josh, and two little girls with dark curly hair like their father's who ran up a path towards a wooden swing seat.

The woman was wearing a hoodie with the hood up and jeans, but even from this distance Stephanie knew this wasn't Nancy Holland. She was shorter, for a start, and she carried more weight than Nancy. She didn't raise her head to look at them and clung on to her son's hand as if her life depended on it.

'Come in,' Riordan said, ignoring his wife and children.

They followed him into the dark cottage. Despite its proximity to the shore, the small windows allowed little of the wonderful bright ocean light into the room, and there was something depressing about the space. It was clean enough, but it felt unloved. Not that Stephanie was the world's greatest housekeeper, but there were no personal touches – no photographs, paintings, or even flowers in a jam jar.

It was a bigger property than it appeared from the outside, stretching back into the cliff face, and the rooms at the back felt dank with limited natural light.

Riordan's attitude made it perfectly clear that he wasn't worried about anything they might find, and he told them to 'feel free' as he leaned against the kitchen units, legs crossed at the ankles, and waved his permission for them to roam.

Stephanie wished she could talk to the wife, but accepted

that they had no grounds to do so, especially if she had mental health issues. But there was one thing she wanted to try.

'Mr Riordan, I appreciate your wife isn't strong enough to speak to us, but as we mentioned, it's possible that Nancy Holland came here when you were away fishing. Would it be possible to ask your son if she came to the cove at all? It would be very helpful.'

Riordan narrowed his eyes. 'You can ask him, by all means.' He went to the side door and shouted into the garden. 'Josh, come here a moment.'

Stephanie watched through the window as the little boy turned, flashed a quick glance at his mum and scurried towards the cottage.

'These two people want to ask you some questions. Okay?'

The boy looked at his dad and shrugged, as if to say *Whatever*.

Stephanie bent towards him, her phone in hand. 'Josh, the woman in this photo is missing, and we wondered if she'd been here to look at your beach. Do you think you've seen her?'

The little boy looked at the phone for all of about three seconds. 'No. Nobody's been here in ages, except Cal and Dan. No women.'

Gus looked at Riordan. 'Cal and Dan?'

'They work for me from time to time – they come fishing, help me haul in the nets, deliver the fish, that kind of thing. It's all very casual.'

'We'll need their contact details. If they've been here in the last few days, we can check if they saw Miss Holland.'

'Fine. I'll dig them out and send them on to you.'

Stephanie pulled out a card with her email address and handed it to Riordan. 'As soon as you can, please. We don't want to have to come back unless we have to.'

She glared at him, letting him know mutely that she would

love an excuse to come back. But there was no sign of Nancy, and there was nowhere to hide her on this beach.

They thanked Josh and he ran off, back to his mother and sisters.

Turning towards the door, Stephanie noticed something hiding behind a washing basket on the worktop. She walked over and picked it up.

'Nice camera,' she said.

'Yes, it's my wife's. She likes to take photos of the kids.'

'I'm a bit of a fan of a good camera myself. Mind if I take a look?'

Riordan smiled and Stephanie knew instantly there was nothing to find. 'Knock yourself out, but you won't find any pictures. Monique wiped the card yesterday. She uploads the photos so she can reuse the memory card. Very frugal, my wife.'

As they left the cottage, Gus stopped and pointed out to sea. 'One last thing, sir. To make sure we've covered everything and we don't have to pay a return visit, could we take a look at your boat?'

Riordan grinned. 'Once again, be my guest. You'll need to take the RIB, but if you fancy beach-launching it in these seas, you're a better sailor than me.'

Stephanie glanced towards the spectacular waves that were breaking in the bay. Riordan was right. Sailing the small RIB from here to where the boat was moored would be perilous. As a minimum they would get a good soaking, even if they could prevent it from capsizing, and transferring from the RIB to the boat would be beyond hazardous.

'It doesn't have to be now. Maybe we could come back when things are calmer. I assume you're not planning on taking the boat out any time soon?'

'Nope. I've no trips planned for at least a couple of days.

Given last night's storm, the sea will be like this for the next twenty-four hours or so, but if you come back tomorrow, I'll happily take you out.'

There was nothing else they could ask Riordan, and so, thanking him for his time, they made their way to the path.

Stephanie didn't speak until they were halfway up the steep hill.

'He's involved in Nancy's disappearance, Gus. I can feel it. I don't believe him about his wife, either. Scared of strangers? Really? That's a bit bloody suspicious if you ask me.'

'It's an actual condition. I came across it once before – I think it's called anthropophobia. And anyway, you could see it wasn't Nancy. I was watching to see if the boy interacted with her, and he seemed perfectly comfortable. Whether Riordan wanted to make sure we didn't ask about an ex-lover in his wife's presence or she really does have some mental health issues, it seemed pointless to make a big deal out of it.'

'Hmm, that's as may be, but I'm certain he's involved in what's happened to Nancy. I bet that's her camera, not his wife's. There wasn't a single photo in that house – on the front of the fridge or in a frame. And anyway, most people use their phones.'

'That's an assumption, Steph. She may not have a phone if she never leaves the house and has no friends, and even with the best of phones, a proper camera can do things a phone can't.'

'Even so...'

'We don't know the make of Nancy's camera. It could be entirely irrelevant. We know Nancy isn't in Riordan's cottage, and there was nowhere else – other than the boat. We can monitor that – make sure he doesn't sneak out to sea in it. It's bigger than fifteen metres and that means he has to have AIS installed.'

Stephanie knew the Automatic Identification System was a

legal requirement so boats could be tracked and identified, but would that be enough?

'He could turn it off.'

'Theoretically, but if he went dark and was discovered, he'd be in trouble.'

'Yes, but realistically if he's got Nancy on the boat and wants to get rid of her, I guess it would be worth the risk.'

Gus grunted. There was no reply to that thought.

He turned round and pulled the gate behind them, clicking the padlock closed.

'Why did you do that? We might want to get in again, in a hurry!'

'If the padlock's open, he'll know we picked it and he'll change the combination. It'll slow us down. This way he might think we climbed over and leave it. The code is 9630, in case I forget, and in case we should need it again.'

In Stephanie's mind there was no 'should' about it.

EIGHTY-ONE

Stephanie felt her mood turn black as they trudged along the muddy track from Riordan's cove to their respective cars. They had shown their hand, and if Riordan knew anything about Nancy's disappearance, he would know they suspected him. Lola and Nancy had walked to this exact spot several times. He *had* to be involved.

'Should we put someone out here on the headland, Gus, in case Riordan takes his boat out without switching on his AIS? He wouldn't have to go far if he was planning to dump a body over the side, and if he came straight back no one would notice he'd gone.'

Gus sighed. 'I know how you feel, and it's frustrating. But we don't have any serious grounds to suspect Riordan, and you know it. Nancy apparently had a fling with the guy when she was nineteen and hasn't seen him since, as far as anyone knows. It's possible her sister went with her to the cove a couple of times, which is why it's showed up on the cell-siting information in our initial investigation. Nancy probably just wanted to take a peek to see if the man she'd been shagging was as gorgeous as she'd thought at the time. You'd want to check him out if it was you!'

Stephanie was saved from the need to respond by the vibration of her phone. She listened to the caller and turned to Gus. 'We were right about the grey van. It's registered to Riordan.'

'Let's check it out, then, while we're here,' Gus said. 'No harm in taking a look.'

They peered through the front windows, but there was nothing of interest. If anything, it looked cleaner than Stephanie would have expected.

'Can you see into the back?' she asked Gus.

'No, but hang on and I'll get my torch from the car.'

Stephanie tried to angle her head so that she could see between the driver and passenger seats and deep into the dark area at the rear where there were no windows.

Gus returned and shone his torch through the windscreen. All they could see was a thin metal grille separating the front seats from the rear storage area, and beyond that nothing other than shadows.

'It looks empty,' he said.

'If she's in there, she might be lying down, or tied down.'

Gus gave her a look, but he knew she wouldn't be satisfied if he didn't do more.

He banged hard on the side of the van. 'Police!' he shouted. 'Kick or shout if you're in there.'

There was nothing.

'You're assuming that if she's inside she's conscious – or even alive,' Stephanie grunted.

Gus switched off the torch and rubbed the back of his neck with his free hand, frustration at Stephanie's persistence written all over his face.

'Can we have a reality check, Steph? We have zero grounds to suspect there is a dead body, or even an injured one, in the back of this van. As for Riordan, you might not like the guy and perhaps he led Nancy a bit of a dance years ago, but it doesn't make him a killer. Let's get back to the office and work with the team to see what we can discover. And then, if we need to, we'll come back. But don't be blind to other options.'

There had been nothing she could add to that, and it didn't help that she knew Gus was right, so without another word they got into their cars to head back to the station.

Stephanie had only been driving for a couple of minutes when her phone rang.

'Sergeant King, it's PC Jafari – Ayaneh. You wanted someone to follow up on the debit card. I've got information on a couple of places where Nancy Holland shopped yesterday. Would you like me to send you the details now, or wait until you're back here?'

'Send them through, please, but can you give me a quick summary?'

'Of course. Nancy bought a few items from a small hardware store for a total of £37.95 and she spent £11.30 at a photographic shop. I gave both shops a ring. She bought some door bolts and a couple of tools from the hardware shop, and she had some pictures printed at the photo shop.'

'*Really?* That's interesting. Can you ping me the location of the shops, please? I'll call in on my way back.'

The bolts and tools suggested she wanted to increase her security – which was a concern. But more than anything, Stephanie wanted to know what was on the photos.

EIGHTY-TWO

After Lola left, I had nothing to do but think. There was so much to absorb, and my head throbbed – not just with pain, but with endless questions.

Why hadn't I seen what was happening?

Why didn't I realise that Dad was giving Mum vodka, feeding her addiction?

Why did Liam say he'd seen Dad? How would he even know what he looked like?

There were too many questions, and no one to answer them.

I could hear the sea again. The tide was in, which meant Liam couldn't get to me, but it was only a matter of time.

Eventually, exhaustion overtook me, and as the brutal crashing of the waves reached its crescendo I must have drifted into an uncomfortable sleep, safe in the knowledge that no one could come for me for a few hours.

It's only the aching of my head, my knee and every other bone in my body that tells me I'm awake, because I'm surrounded once again by an impenetrable blackness. The last of the lanterns must have died and I can no longer hear the sea. The tide must have gone out, or at least ebbed away from the entrance to the cave, and my muscles give a sudden jerk as I realise that once again I'm vulnerable.

It's not quite silent; there are whispers and rustles from the other cage, and I wish I could offer some comfort. But what can I say?

As I try to frame some words of encouragement in the hope that they will be able to interpret my tone of voice, if not my language, I see a glimmer of light, growing in strength as someone moves through the cave.

I push myself up and stagger towards the bars, weak from hunger, my legs stiff from being curled under me for so long.

I can see Lola pushing paper bags through the bars of the other cage. I hear her speak quietly, although I'm not sure if she will be understood.

'I've brought you food. We'll be back later to move you. There's nothing to worry about.'

The people all begin to speak at once, but Lola ignores them and glances my way. Is she going to come and speak to me?

It seems she is undecided, but finally, with one bag remaining in her hand, she heads towards me.

'I've brought you a sandwich,' she says, unable to look me in the eye. She's withdrawn again, her barriers back in place.

I push my face close to the bars and try to keep the panic from my voice. 'Lola, I understand about your children, but you have to get me out of here. If you don't, this can't end well.'

She stares at the floor. 'You don't know what you're asking,' she whispers.

'I *do*! I know Liam will be furious, but I won't say anything to anyone.' I feel a stab of guilt for the people in the next cage, but I push it aside. My death isn't going to help them, and at least if I escape I can think of a way to save them

– a way that doesn't hurt Lola. 'I'll do whatever you need me to.'

She finally lifts her eyes to mine and takes a step forward. I could reach out and touch her again, but I'm terrified that she will turn and run.

'There's only one thing I want – for my kids to be safe. I want them to have their mother, who will die herself if that's what it takes to protect them against evil bastards like our father. If that means staying here, if it means turning a blind eye to whatever Liam does, then that's what I'll do.'

'Dad was evil, you're right. What he did is unforgivable. But what kind of a life is this for your children? How long before Josh understands what's going on here?'

I take a risk and reach through the bars for her hands. She tries to pull away, but I hold on. 'And what about *your* life? Do you ever leave the house? Do you have any friends?'

I see her eyes fill with tears, and I know the answer. I don't want to hurt her, but she has to see what's happening to her and to those poor souls locked in the other cage. 'Do you approve of what he's doing with these people? Do you know where the hell they are destined for when they leave here? What do you think happens to them?'

She finally jerks her hands away from mine. 'They're scared, that's all. They don't understand we're only keeping them here until it's safe to move them. They think now we've got their money they're going to die, but they're not. It's always like this until they're in the van and on their way. They *want* to come here. Liam and the men he works with find them jobs. They *help* them.'

I bark out a laugh. 'Can you *hear* yourself? Do you really believe that Liam and his bosses are doing this out of the goodness of their hearts? I bet these people have been lured here with a promise of a better life. They'll have paid money that to them must be a fortune, and arrived with no documents. I bet the promised fakes never materialise, do they? Do you know how many trafficked people become slaves – women forced to become sex workers, men forced to work for nothing, or even made to commit crimes? The news is full of it right now. They're controlled, given no freedom. Look at them, Lola.' I jab my finger towards the other cage. '*Look at them!* These are *people* – real live living, breathing people.'

She can't look at me again. She knows this, but she can't see a way out. And perhaps she believes their lives won't be so different from her own.

'What would *you* do, Nancy, if you were me?' she hisses. 'If I were the one locked in the cage, would you let me go, even if it meant that you might be killed as a result? I've told you, Liam does as he's told these days; he doesn't need a conscience of his own. He might control me, but someone else has power over him. If we get arrested, my children will go into care, and I won't be able to keep them safe. They too could be abused – because it happens, you know.'

I have no answer to that. I'm sure it's rare and most foster families are kind, but Lola wasn't safe with her own father, so I can't guarantee what might happen to her children.

'The police will be looking for me,' I tell her in a last-ditch attempt to make her do something. 'They'll know I'm missing because they're looking for you again. They've reopened the case, and they'll try much harder if we're both missing. They're bound to track me to here. And what will happen if they see you?'

She shakes her head slowly. 'They've already been – hours ago.'

I feel my stomach flip as if I've just fallen from a cliff. '*What?* What do you mean?'

'They came this morning. Liam let them look round the house. They know you're not there, but they don't know about the caves. The tide was in.'

'Didn't they see you?'

'Only from a distance. They think I'm Monique.'

'What happened to her, Lola? What did Liam do to Monique? Whatever it was, don't you worry that he might do the same to you when he's had enough of you?'

She tuts, as if I'm being dramatic. 'Monique's in France, with her parents. She was never coming back – he made that up to get you to stay away from the beach.'

'Do you know that for sure?'

I can see in her eyes it's what she has to believe. 'Why the hell did you come here, Nancy? Liam knew from the moment he saw you in town that you were a danger, and then Cal caught you spying on us, taking his photograph.'

'Is that why he took my camera?'

She gives me a strange look. 'Cal took your camera?'

'Someone broke into the cottage on Sunday night when I was in bed. He was in my room, Lola. Standing by the bed. I pretended to be asleep.'

I remember the feeling now, the amount of flesh that was exposed, and the thought of Cal looking at me brings acid to my throat.

'It won't have been Cal, then,' Lola says, her lip curling with disgust. 'I know he was in your house one day when you were out. He said he did something to spook you, but it won't have been him on Sunday night. If he'd seen a woman who looks like you in bed and vulnerable, I'm afraid you'd have come off much worse than you did.'

'Liam, then. Or Dan.'

'Liam was at sea, and Dan's too stupid.' I don't have time to think about what this might mean before she starts talking again. 'You made yourself a threat to us all, Nancy. You'd been to the headland before. They knew that, and they didn't know what else you'd seen.'

'What else *could* I have seen? These poor guys –' I point towards the other cave with my hand '– hadn't arrived by then.'

Lola sighs and looks away. 'No, but it's two-way traffic. Sometimes people need to go the other way.' I've no idea what she's talking about.

'They've been watching me since the day I arrived, Lola!'

'We just wanted you to go back to London. If you stayed, it seemed like only a matter of time until you found out about me, and that would have brought the police to our door. Liam told Cal to keep an eye on you, to see what you were up to. Then the cottage became a crime scene, so of *course* he had to watch you. He needed to know what you'd found.'

I am suddenly hit with the sickening realisation that if I had chosen to make Cornwall my home, I would have been a constant danger to Liam and Lola. She wouldn't have been able to set foot outside her front door in case I was watching, and with or without Lola's knowledge, Liam would have found some way of disposing of me.

I must find a way of getting through to her. I don't know how much time I have left.

'I understand how difficult it is for you,' I say, trying to keep my tone gentle.

'You don't.' Her voice is sad, the anger spent. 'I've hated you for so long, Nancy. I don't hate you now, but it's time for me to say goodbye. I tried to persuade him to wait a few days, to give us some time. But now the police have been, he won't risk it.'

She turns away, head bent. She looks as defeated as I feel. She's leaving, and I can't think of a single thing I can say to make her change her mind. And then in the glimmer from her lamp, I see my bag lying just beyond my reach on the floor of the cave and I feel a tingle of hope.

'Can you at least pass me my bag, Lola, before you go? They took my phone, so don't worry. I can't call anyone.'

She turns back, looks at me and at the bag, and to my relief, she goes to pick it up. It's my last hope.

She lifts it, and then lowers and lifts it again, as if feeling its weight.

Her eyes lock on mine and she opens the bag. Holding the lantern high, she looks inside. Her hand goes in, feeling around.

'Pass me the bag, Lola. He can't blame you for that.'

She drops the bag back on the floor, well out of my reach. She looks at me, her mouth a tight line, tears streaming from her eyes. I reach through the bars, trying to touch her, my little sister, but she backs away, pushes her hands into her pockets and shakes her head.

'I'm sorry, Nancy. My children come first. They always will. I won't see you again, but for what it's worth, I wish it hadn't come to this.'

With that, she turns and walks away.

EIGHTY-THREE

Stephanie ran up the stairs to the incident room, her head full of thoughts and ideas about Nancy. Gus looked up as she swung through the doors.

'Nancy told the guy in the hardware store that she was concerned about the security of her cottage.' Slightly breathless, she plonked herself on a chair next to his desk. 'She asked about getting a new lock fitted. And her next visit is even more interesting. She emailed some photos to a local print shop and called in to pick them up. Fortunately the man who runs the place archives all emails for a month, so he was able to retrieve them.'

'And...'

'He showed me on his computer, but he's also forwarded them to me. I think some are photos of Liam Riordan – from years ago. I need to get them up on the screen here, to be sure. There was one of a boat – not the *Monique III* – and of another man by a gate. I'm certain it's the gate down to Riordan's place.'

'What are we waiting for?'

Stephanie smiled and connected her phone to the large monitor as they both walked towards it.

'The photos were date-stamped by her camera, so the guy's

put the dates in the filename. There are three from eleven years ago, two from this week.'

She pulled up the first image - a young man in shorts and a T-shirt on a beach, pulling a RIB out of the sea.

'That's Liam Riordan. Different hair, much younger, but definitely him.'

'Taken from the clifftop without him knowing it, by the look of things. It could be the cove we left over an hour ago, although it looks different with the tide further out.'

'Here's the next,' Stephanie said. 'It's him again, this time taken at beach level, but it looks as if he was asleep and they'd been having a picnic. Seems Effie was right about them having an affair.'

Neither detective bothered to comment on the fact that Liam was naked.

'Okay. Up to now these haven't told us anything we didn't already know,' Gus said, his tone exasperated. He was clearly hoping for more and Stephanie's excitement was abating.

The next image was of a boat. 'His fishing boat, I guess – to be honest, it doesn't look like much of a fishing boat. Looks more like a cabin cruiser with a box at the back. For the tangle net, I assume, and there's a small hauler.'

'Let's have a look at the next one,' Gus suggested.

This time it was a picture of a man they didn't recognise, but they certainly recognised the location.

'That's Riordan's gate! And that man looks like he's fiddling with the padlock. Who is he? This and the next one were taken on Sunday. Perhaps this is the guy she thought was following her.'

'He might be one of the men who helps Riordan with the fishing. Josh mentioned a Cal and a Dan, I think. Has Riordan sent through their details?'

Stephanie confirmed he had, and that she'd forwarded them

to the team to be checked out. As yet, they'd failed to make contact.

'Why would Nancy take this man's photo?' She clicked to the next image. 'Here he is again. Obviously, this place was of significance to her, and she had these photos printed for some reason. I wish she'd spoken to me, so I'd have known what was in her head.'

'What time did all of this take place? When was she in the shops?'

'Between 2.50 and 4.10.'

'Okay, so if she left for Riordan's place after that, she would have got there at around 4.30 p.m. Yes?'

'Agreed, and that ties in with Ayaneh's timings too. But how does it help?'

'Let's get historical AIS data for Riordan's boat for the last day or two. We know it's there now, but we don't know where it was yesterday.'

Before Stephanie could answer, her phone rang.

'Stephanie, it's Dave Trebbith. Got a bit of news on the OCG I was telling you about – and possibly a lead on your skeleton.'

EIGHTY-FOUR

It took Stephanie a moment to remember that she'd spoken to Dave Trebbith from the Regional Organised Crime Unit about Lek and the boys who were searching for their brother.

'What have you found, Dave?'

'I put out a general enquiry in West Cornwall. It seems Helston CID have had their eye on a possible cannabis farm for a while, but were biding their time because they wanted to discover how the finished product was distributed. It's grown in a polytunnel on a legitimate wholesale plant nursery site. Most of the staff know nothing about it. It's strictly off limits and they've been told to keep away as it's being used to grow experimental plants. As you can imagine, the more savvy among them probably suspect something's going on, but they don't report it because if the place closes down, they lose their jobs. Same old story.'

Stephanie had some sympathy. If a report to the police meant you lost your livelihood, it couldn't be an easy decision to make. 'What changed?'

'A couple of months ago, one of the staff was sacked. That was all it took. He no longer had anything to lose, so he reported his suspicions. On the basis that it looked like a sizeable operation, the local CID team were sure there'd be bigger fish to fry so they waited. A couple of days ago, a van was loaded with the product and they followed it to Sandygate Services outside Exeter, where another vehicle was waiting – one that's already been associated with the OCG in Bristol.'

Stephanie shuddered at the mention of the OCG, but said nothing.

'This is where it gets interesting,' Dave said. 'The goods were transferred from one van to the other, as you might expect. But then a man got out of the Bristol vehicle and climbed *into* the van Helston CID had followed from the plant nursery, which promptly turned and headed straight back to Cornwall. It stopped briefly at a spot about twenty miles from the nursery, and the same man got out and swapped to a *third* van, which sped off towards Penzance. CID couldn't tail both, so with no intel on who this man might be, they stuck to following the van from the cannabis farm.'

Stephanie was at a loss to think why this might relate to Lek, but Dave no doubt had his reasons for telling her.

'We checked ANPR for the third van, but I guess it didn't stick to the main roads for long. However, we've now identified the man they were moving: Charles Curtis. He's been wanted for murder for three years. Our Bristol colleagues were getting close, so at a guess Curtis was being moved to either a port or a private yacht to be shipped out of the country.'

'And did you identify this van – the one that was heading our way?'

'Nope – false plates. We've informed DI Harris-Cooke because Curtis is probably either holed up in your area waiting to be shipped, or most likely he's already gone.'

'Did you discover how this might tie in to Lek? Were the two Asian boys I told you about working at the farm – the ones who had turned up at the Buddhist retreat?'

'They were, yes. As soon as we had evidence of where the cannabis was going, the farm was raided yesterday morning. There were several migrants – all illegal, and consequently my team have taken over the interviewing. I asked them to check if any of the men have been looking for their brother, and two of them said they had – so I guess these will be your Lek's brothers.'

Stephanie felt sorry that they were going to have to find out about their brother this way, but it still didn't explain what had happened to him.

'Did they get separated?'

'They came together by private boat from France about three years ago and travelled halfway across on a French boat. Then, when they were in the middle of the Channel, they were transferred to a RIB which took them to a fishing boat waiting about a mile away, and sailed to shore. It seems clear this is to avoid detection on AIS. If a British boat and a French boat are seen effectively touching each other mid-Channel – almost as if they've collided – it could ring warning bells, particularly if it happened regularly. But a fishing boat and a pleasure craft a mile apart wouldn't raise too many eyebrows.'

'So what happened to them? And what happened to Lek?'

'If we've got the right guy, I think you'll find your Lek is actually Hanh Phan, a seventeen-year-old Vietnamese. He arrived in the UK with about twelve others, and they were held in a cave for a couple of days. When some men came, ostensibly to transport them to their new and exciting lives, Lek ran into the sea and started to swim away. He was born and brought up next to the ocean, and his brothers say he was a brilliant swimmer. Two of the men pushed the rest of the migrants up a hill and into a van. The other guy got into a RIB and went in pursuit of Hanh. They never saw your Lek again.'

· · ·

As Stephanie hung up, she spared a thought for poor Lek – or Hanh, as she guessed she should now call him. There was no evidence that he had been murdered by whoever was in pursuit, but if he tried to get out of the sea and scramble over the rocks to escape the boat that was chasing him, it could explain his broken leg. She thought of his pain as he clambered up onto the ledge, only to fade slowly away as he suffered the effects of dehydration. What a way to die.

'Not good news?' Gus asked, correctly interpreting her mood.

'Yes and no. I think I know what happened to Lek, but I can't bear to think about his last few days.'

'Unfortunately, I've got some more bad news for you. We got the AIS data, and yesterday at the time Nancy went missing, Liam Riordan was fishing. He was way out at sea.'

Stephanie stared at Gus. She had been so sure it was him.

'Perhaps one of his goons – who we have yet to track down – took the boat out. Maybe it wasn't Riordan.'

'You're trying to fit the evidence to your theory, Steph. He wasn't there.'

Stephanie rested her chin on her hands and looked at the photos on her phone again. Why had Nancy printed these pictures off?

She opened them on her computer screen and enlarged them, looking for anything that might be relevant.

She looked briefly at the photos of Liam, and could see how a young girl might have been attracted to him. She enlarged the photo of the boat – the *Monique II*, the forerunner of Riordan's current boat. The focus of the image seemed to be on the cabin window, and Stephanie looked closely, her heart suddenly beating a little faster.

'Gus, come and look at this.'

Gus got up from his desk and walked round to stand behind her. She enlarged the screen as much as possible without losing all definition, and swivelled round to face Gus. She didn't need to see the screen any longer.

There were two faces close to the window and at least one other in the background. All of them appeared to be young Asian men. Gus looked at her and raised his eyebrows. Words weren't necessary.

Without losing eye contact with Gus, she reached for her phone and pressed to recall the last number.

'Dave,' she said, before her ROCU contact had time to even say his name. 'Do you have a description of the van that was used to transport the OCG guy in our direction?'

She listened as he gave her the details, thanked him, and hung up.

Gus listened as Stephanie repeated her previous conversation with Dave about Lek and the boys at the cannabis farm.

'It all fits, Gus. Illegal immigrants brought in by private boat from France, held in a cave. If the OCG wanted one of their guys shipped out, maybe that's where Riordan was going in his boat.'

Gus was frowning, but she could see he was coming round to her way of thinking, so she carried on, her voice speeding up as it all came clear in her mind.

'Dave has just confirmed that it was a Vauxhall panel van – grey – that was used to transport Charles Curtis. Now, who do we know with such a van?' Stephanie pointed to the screen. 'If Nancy Holland had inadvertently taken a photo all those years ago of Liam Riordan bringing in migrants and they've just discovered she has this picture, there's no way she'll be allowed to live.'

'But if she'd known what he was doing, why wouldn't she have told us?'

Stephanie shook her head. 'Why would she think anything about it? He had a few guys on his boat. Why would it mean he was people trafficking? They could have been friends. Not everyone has suspicious minds like us.'

Gus was staring into space, and Stephanie could almost hear the cogs turning.

'Where the hell was she, then, when we went to Riordan's place? Where has he put her?'

'Lek's brothers said they were held in a cave. We couldn't see any caves when we visited, but the tide was in. Lek was an excellent swimmer. The cave he was found in was just over a mile from Riordan's cove. That must have been where he was escaping from.'

'Ayaneh!' Gus shouted.

The young PC looked up expectantly. 'Boss?'

'Can you get the location of Riordan's cottage back up on the screen, but use Google Earth this time?'

Ayaneh stood up quickly from her desk. 'What angle do you want me to view it from, sir?'

'From the sea, looking inland,' Gus responded.

'There,' Stephanie shouted, moving towards the monitor and pointing with her finger. 'A cave. We wouldn't have been able to see it from the beach, and it looks like it's flooded at high tide. Jesus, Gus – you don't think he's got Nancy in there, do you?'

Gus had gone very still.

'We need to think this through carefully,' he finally said.

He turned to face the room. 'Can I have your attention, please?' he shouted. The room instantly fell quiet, all eyes on Gus. 'We have reason to believe that Liam Riordan is involved in people trafficking, modern slavery and maybe more. It's possible that Nancy Holland knew more than Riordan was comfortable with – or at least, he thought she did. We don't yet know how, or even if, Lola Holland is in any way connected, although we do know from our witness that she was heading towards Riordan's cottage when she disappeared. Riordan has access to a boat, and if we're right about his activities, he won't hang about if he knows we're coming. He doesn't own the cave, but unless we approach by sea, we have to cross his land to access it. Let's get a warrant, and for his van and his boat. In the meantime, we need to call in the marine unit. They may have to enter the cave from the sea, or block him if he tries to leave by boat, and we need to alert the coastguard in case we have a rescue situation. Let's move, everyone.'

Stephanie looked at her watch. 'Gus, the tide will be back in again soon. We haven't got long.'

'I know. That's what I'm worried about.'

EIGHTY-FIVE

There's someone coming again. With every atom of my being, I pray it's Lola, back to say she'll help me, that she won't let Liam kill me. Without her help, I don't see what other outcome there could be. I know too much.

The people in the next cave must already be able to see who it is, because I hear the pleading tones in their voices, and even though I don't understand the language they are speaking, I'm sure they are begging to be set free. But they are ignored. Whoever is coming, he's coming for me.

The lamp is held low in his hand and I can only see his chin, the underside of his nose and his eyebrows glowing in the white light. Then he lifts the lamp higher. It's the first time I've seen Liam up close for eleven years, and he still makes me tremble. This time I recognise it's with nothing but fear, and I finally understand that even back then, when I thought I was so desperately in love, I was scared of him – scared of the power he had over me. He's still the one in charge.

I won't plead with him to let me go. It won't work, and I won't give him the satisfaction. I'm not the young girl he once knew.

I wait for him to speak, but he just stares at me. I can't help wishing that I wasn't damp, cold, grubby, with the smell of urine from both cages wafting in the air.

'You shouldn't have come back, Nancy. You should have stayed away. I told you I never wanted to see you again, and I wish I wasn't having to stand here looking at you now.'

I lift my head and straighten my back. I can't change the outcome, but I will not let him see me crumble again. I've begged him once before. I know what the outcome will be.

'Have you nothing to say?'

I still stare at him silently, without dropping my gaze.

'I don't remember every girl I've ever had, but I do remember you – how it was on those days when you came to the beach. You were so young, so innocent. I remember your thighs – soft and white – and you quivered every time I touched you. It was intoxicating.'

My eyes sting and I swallow hard. He's playing me, getting malicious pleasure out of my gullibility. I don't know why he's doing this, but I refuse to respond. Maybe he wants me to unleash my fury so that whatever he has to do will be easier for him.

He's watching, waiting for me to say something. There's nothing to say.

Liam shakes his head. 'You've left me no choice. Lola won't save you. She's tried to convince me that you'll disappear back to wherever you came from and won't say a word, but I don't buy that. Not you, Nancy.'

He's right. In spite of Lola, I would find it impossible to let him continue to feed innocent souls into a hidden world of exploitation.

I have a flash of recollection of a sign inside a ladies' toilet at a railway station. CAN YOU SEE ME? it read, appealing to people to help stop human trafficking by identifying the signs. I don't need any signs – the evidence is in the next cage, only yards from where I'm standing.

'As you don't seem to want to talk to me, we may as well get on with this,' he says, putting the key into the lock and turning it. I feel my legs start to tremble. I'm not sure they will hold me up. 'And don't think about trying to run. Cal and Dan are outside the cave ready to catch you if you do anything stupid.'

I don't know what he thinks I might do. If Lola had given me my bag I might have stood a chance, but I can see it now, lying where she dropped it. And what could she have done? If she'd tried to help me, what would have happened to her?

'Get back,' Liam says. I consider standing my ground so he'd have to push me, but he would kick the gate open and I would fall. It wouldn't help, so I take a step back, a tremor running through my body. I'm not sure I could speak now if I tried. My tongue is glued to the roof of my mouth.

'Turn round.'

I don't want to. I've no idea what he has planned, but as he places the lantern on a ledge behind him, I notice a length of rope hanging around his neck.

'Do you want me to call Cal? Because he would love the opportunity to hit you again. Hurting women is one of his favourite pastimes – something of a speciality. So do as you're *fucking told!*'

I can hear the anger in his voice. The fact that I haven't spoken is getting to him, and I'm certain he wants me to fight him, even with words, so he can let rip with his anger and justify what he's about to do.

At first I don't move, but if Cal comes he'll knock me unconscious and I won't know what they're doing to me. If I'm to have any chance, I need to be conscious. I can't win, so for now at least, I need to comply. I turn round.

'Hands above your head,' Liam says. I was expecting him to

tell me to put them behind my back and his demand unnerves me, but I do as he asks.

He walks towards me and wraps a length of the rope around my waist, then up my back and round my wrists where they're clasped above my head. I can't move my arms backwards very far, and the rope up my back is stopping me from letting them fall forwards. They are effectively anchored in position, outstretched, as if I'm reaching for the sky.

'If you think you can untie these ropes, think again. I'm a sailor. I know how to tie a knot. Now move,' he says, spinning me round and pointing me towards the open cage door.

I can't run. With my arms above my head like this, I wouldn't be able to stay upright. He picks up the lantern and pushes me forward, back down the steep slope of the cave. He holds on to the rope at my waist, and I have a sudden recollection of following Liam down the path to the cove, my fingers slipped inside the waistband of his shorts. My throat closes and I can't swallow.

The people in the other cage hear us coming, and they begin to call out again. But when they see me, hands tied above my head, their shrieks turn to silence.

I glance into the cage and see them for the first time. They're young – not much more than boys – and each of them has a blank look that I recognise as the face of fear. I'm about to shout my name, to ask them to tell someone what they've seen when they are taken to their destination, wherever that might be. But I realise that will put them in danger, so I keep quiet and don't look at them again.

We get closer to the cave opening, and I can hear the sea. As we round the final bend, the black mouth of the cave frames the ocean in all its glory. Today it's a deep azure blue, with pure white breakers. It's truly beautiful and seeing the sky again feels like a relief, but it's short-lived.

We are about five metres from the edge of the cave when Liam speaks again. 'Sit.'

I turn to look at him. I don't know what I thought he was going to do with me, but I hadn't expected this.

'Sit,' he repeats, and I know that if I don't, he'll stick a leg out and force me to the ground. 'There.' He points to a spot against the wall.

And then I see it. A ring embedded in the rock, and I know exactly what he intends to do.

I glance back out at the sea. The tide is coming in.

EIGHTY-SIX

Stephanie was losing her mind. She had checked the tide tables and they couldn't afford to wait. Why was it taking so long? Yes, it was after hours and that was never the best time to get a warrant signed, but Nancy could be in danger.

'Calm down, Steph. I know you want to get moving, but there's no reason to think anything has happened to her since we were last there. We don't even know she's there. All we have is the make and colour of a van that potentially links Riordan to the OCG, and a photo that looks suspicious from eleven years ago. The warrant will be with us shortly. We have to be certain we've done everything by the book and it takes time – you know that.'

'Gus, we turned up at Riordan's cottage. He knows we're on to him. He might think he needs to get rid of her now. He can't afford to wait.'

'If he's going to kill her, he would most likely take her out to sea, so we need to have everything in place to prevent that. The marine unit are on their way, but we can't move until they get there. And that's assuming she's there. I repeat, we don't know that.'

Stephanie didn't have the time to argue. She *did* know that. It *had* to be Riordan's van that had been used to transport that OCG lowlife killer. Riordan had sailed out to sea that very night, no doubt getting him out of the country. It was all part of the same set-up as the cannabis farm where the migrants were working – migrants who had been brought in by fishing boat. Riordan had to be at the centre of all of it.

Gus was right that everything they had was circumstantial, not one solid piece of evidence, but she wished she'd gone to get the warrant signed herself. She was sure she'd have been quicker. They had agreed she had too much to do here, so they'd sent a DC to the magistrate's home, but she prayed he understood the urgency.

She was on the point of saying she was going out to the cove with or without a warrant when the DC returned.

Finally, they could move.

EIGHTY-SEVEN

I understand now why my hands had to be tied this way. The ring is above me, high enough to secure a boat to. I can see the water mark on the wall of the cave, the height the sea reaches. It's above my head. Way above my head.

The tide is coming in fast. It's already over my legs, and each new wave takes it higher. The last one reached my chest, but ebbed back, settling below my waist.

Liam is long gone, together with any remaining hope, and I wish now that I'd stayed strong. But as he tied me to the ring, I had broken my silence.

'Why are you doing this, Liam?'

'I don't need to explain to you.' He pulled the knot a little tighter.

'Just give me another day with Lola, that's all I ask.'

'Not a chance. The police are circling, thanks to you. Once the tide's in they won't be able to get to you. And that lot –' he jerked his head towards the other cage '– will be out of here by morning. They'll find nothing.'

He was going to let me die. I scrabbled around in desperation for something to say that might change his mind.

'If I drown here, the police will find me. Even with lungs full of seawater, they'll see the marks on my arms from the rope. You won't get away with this.'

He shook his head. 'I never thought you were stupid, Nancy. Gullible, naïve, yes. But never stupid. They'll be watching to see if my boat goes out, but the water's deep enough in the bay. I know how to bury a body at sea.'

I knew what he meant. He plans for me to die here, then as soon as it's dark he'll swim out, dragging me behind him until the water is deep enough. He's a strong swimmer, and if I'm already dead, it will be so much easier.

I was running out of chances and couldn't keep the pleading tone from my voice. 'Don't you remember those days on the beach, Liam? Don't you remember making love to me, the feel of my body, the things you helped me to discover? You were my first, you know.'

'Of course I know. You were trembling with nerves, and it was my pleasure.'

'Doesn't it mean anything to you at all? You said before that you remember me, that I stood out from the rest. Don't let me die, Liam. I *loved* you.'

I saw his jaw stiffen. For a moment, I thought I'd won.

'You were the only one I ever allowed onto my beach, you know. There were other girls, other beaches, but no one else came here,' he said as he tightened the knots securing me to the ring. 'Sometimes, though, it comes down to survival of the fittest – and I intend to survive.'

With one last pull on the rope, he turned towards the cave entrance.

'Liam!' I called. 'Please – don't do this!'

But he didn't turn back.

Another wave surges into the cave, crashing against me, pushing my body sideways. Then it ebbs and drags me back to where I was. The water is cold, but not as cold as the cave.

I've shouted, cried, screamed, but no one has come. The people in the other cave shouted back, but we don't understand each other and no words will help me now.

I watch as a wave comes towards me. Some say that the seventh wave is always the biggest, but maybe that's a myth. Myth or not, I'm counting and this one is the seventh. As it heads towards me, breaking just beyond the entrance to the cave, I know it will engulf me. This time, it will ebb. But what about next time, or the time after?

Maybe I should slither down into the water as far as I can and let it take me now, because I no longer have any hope of survival.

EIGHTY-EIGHT

'Please, Gus – as fast as you can,' Stephanie urged as they made their way in his car towards Liam Riordan's home. She had wanted to drive, but he had pulled rank.

'It's no good if you drive like a maniac and we have an accident. Where are the marine unit up to?'

Stephanie picked up her radio and called through to the team on the boat.

'Ten minutes out,' they told her.

They would prevent Riordan from escaping by sea and arrest him if he tried to get away, but if Stephanie had anything to do with it, he wouldn't get a chance. The coastguard and lifeboat were standing by. They wouldn't intervene until there were no active risks from hostile suspects, but they were waiting for her signal.

Gus spun his car down the rutted lane and headed past the barn that housed the grey van, racing to the very end of the lane. Stephanie was out of the car before it stopped, running towards the gate at the top of the path to Liam Riordan's cottage and the cove. She could hear the sirens in the distance, but she wasn't prepared to wait for backup. She could see the sea, but not yet the cove, and didn't know how far the tide had come in.

With his long legs, Gus overtook her and crouched by the padlocked gate.

'9630,' she barked, but he hadn't needed a reminder. The padlock was off, thrown into the bushes, and he flung the gate open.

'Go steady, Steph. This path is tricky. You're helping no one if you fall and hurt yourself.'

Frustrating as it was, he was right, and she stared at her feet as she hurried down the winding path. Gorse and shrubs blocked her view of the bay, and it was only as she reached the second turn that she could see the beach. The tide was well past the entrance to the cave now. There was no way they could reach it from the shore.

Her attention was suddenly diverted as a woman came running from the direction of Liam Riordan's cottage, Riordan chasing after her. Her hair was streaming out behind her, and Stephanie gasped and stopped.

'What is it?' Gus called from behind her. 'It's not Nancy, Steph. Her hair's a much darker red.'

'No, Gus. It's not Nancy, but I think it might be Lola.'

'*Jesus!* You're right. The wife, Monique. What the hell's been going on here?'

Stephanie had started to run again. Riordan had caught up with Lola, and she was fighting him. The wind coming off the sea carried her voice up to where they were.

'Let me *go*, Liam! You can't do this to her. You *can't!*'

Riordan grabbed her roughly and spun her round. Stephanie couldn't hear what he said, but she saw him shake her, then reach back and slap her hard across her face.

Stephanie glanced down at her feet as she almost tripped, and when she looked up again, Lola had her hand bunched in a fist, and was aiming at Riordan's neck. There was no sound, but she watched as Riordan fell to his knees, clutching his neck, blood pumping through his fingers.

Stephanie and Gus hit the beach, Stephanie with her radio in her hand.

'Ambulance,' she shouted. 'To the cove. Man down – stabbed in the neck.'

Lola ran into the sea as Gus shouted: 'Lola Holland! Stay where you are! We're here to help!'

She turned briefly but didn't stop. She was up to her thighs in the water when a breaker crashed over her, knocking her to the ground. She picked herself up, but the undertow dragged her back down again.

'*Shit!*' Gus started running, kicking off his shoes and ripping off his jacket as he ran. Stephanie raced towards Liam Riordan, who was lying on the sand, moaning in pain, with what looked like a bradawl sticking out of his neck, the tip buried deep into his flesh, blood oozing from around the shank. Certain it would be a bad idea to pull it out, she pressed the fingers of her left hand around the entry point to slow the bleeding and used her right to pull the radio close to her head while simultaneously keeping her eyes on Gus, praying he did nothing reckless.

'We need backup. Now!' she shouted, as she watched another wave wash over Gus. It didn't knock him down, and he reached for Lola, grabbed her arm, pulled her upright.

Stephanie sighed with relief, but it didn't last long. Lola was fighting Gus, trying to break free. With her other arm, she was pointing towards the cave, and although she couldn't hear the words, Stephanie knew what she was trying to tell him. Her sister had to be inside, about to be engulfed by the tide.

She could have wept with frustration. She had known that Nancy was in danger. And now it was too late to save her.

EIGHTY-NINE

I can't resist the water any longer. I've managed to get to my knees, but I can't stand. The boat ring would be below my head, and my arms can't drop forward because of the rope tied to my waist and up my back, and they won't reach backwards any further.

With each wave, the water has risen further up my body. Now it washes over my head, then retreats to just below my nose.

I stopped screaming for help a while ago. I was swallowing too much seawater. The boys in the cage stopped calling back to me and became quiet, knowing what was happening but unable to help. The only sound has been the sea and my own choking as I try to rid my mouth and throat of the seawater. But I'm fighting a losing battle.

Suddenly, I hear something. It starts softly, but then it swells between each crash of a wave.

It's the boys. They are singing, and I know it's for me. It begins with one voice, then two, and finally all their voices are raised, and I can hear them clearly above the roar of the sea.

The song is gentle, melodic, and I don't understand a word,

but it doesn't matter. It echoes around the cave, and I know they're trying in the only way they can to calm me in my dying moments, to reassure me that I'm not alone. My eyes fill with tears.

I'm going to die, but I feel at peace as at last the water washes over my face. And this time it doesn't retreat.

NINETY

Stephanie was still struggling to deal with all that had happened the previous evening. Her fear that she might lose Gus as he fought to rescue Lola had brought everything in her life into sharp perspective. She had some thinking to do, but for now she needed to get over herself and focus on the case.

Liam Riordan had lost a significant amount of blood, although the bradawl had missed both the jugular vein and the carotid artery. If either had been severed, or if Stephanie hadn't managed to stem the flow, he would by lying in the morgue now, and not a hospital bed.

Much as she hated everything he had done and all he stood for, she was glad he wasn't dead. ROCU needed to know who Riordan had been working with and where all the migrants had been taken. In Stephanie's mind, every single one of them needed to be rescued. Trafficked by organised crime, they were probably living in some kind of hell now, working endless hours for little or no pay, forced to live in conditions that no one should have to endure. Even if they weren't physically held prisoner, they would have no obvious means of escape – no money, no documentation, no right to be in the UK. Poor buggers.

Riordan would be questioned when the doctors deemed him well enough, and she didn't care what happened to him as long as he was jailed for a long time.

Lola was a different matter. She had been brought in as a precaution having ingested far too much seawater, and had been formally arrested and cautioned. A policeman stood guard on her door, not entirely to prevent her from escaping. The ROCU team felt she should be protected against attack by the OCG, who would believe she knew too much. How the CPS would choose to deal with Lola's crimes depended very much on how cooperative she was. Her guilt was unquestionable.

Stephanie and Gus stood outside the door to her hospital room. She knew Gus blamed himself – unreasonably – for not getting to the cove sooner, and had they delayed by even a few minutes, the outcome would have been very different. There would now be three bodies in the morgue.

'You ready?' Gus asked, reaching down to squeeze Stephanie's hand.

She wasn't, but she had to be. Someone had to tell Lola what was going to happen to her – that she would be interviewed formally when she was well enough to be discharged, and that in every likelihood she would be going to prison.

They could see through the glass that Lola was sitting up in bed, pulling nervously on her fingers, anxious and upset. Gus knocked, then stood back to let Stephanie go in first.

'Where are my children?' Her face pale and blotchy from tears, Lola's eyes darted to the door, as if expecting to see them there. Stephanie took a seat by the bed, and Gus stood at the end, hands in pockets.

'Your children are safe. Social services have placed them in emergency foster care.'

Lola started to cry. 'You don't understand. Children *aren't* safe. Look what happened to me when I was a child.' Her gaze flicked between the two detectives. 'You know who Josh's father is, don't you?'

'We know from his date of birth that it can't be Liam Riordan. That's all we know for certain, but Quinn Asher came to see us. She hadn't thought it appropriate to tell us why you wanted to run away in case you had a new life and had put it all behind you, but she'd done some thinking and decided we should be told about your father – in case he was involved in your disappearance. Do you want to tell us about him?'

'No! I don't want to ever think or talk about what that bastard did to me again.' Lola dropped her head, her body heaving with sobs, and Stephanie looked helplessly at Gus, who signalled that he would leave the room. She was grateful for his sensitivity and waited quietly until finally Lola opened her swollen eyes. She looked at the space where Gus had been, glanced around the room, and her eyes rested on Stephanie.

'Please don't look at me. I can't bear for anyone to see my shame.'

Stephanie knew that Lola should bear no shame for what she was about to say, but dropped her eyes to focus on the woman's hands.

Lola started to speak, her voice bleak as she confirmed not only who Josh's father was, but how it felt to have found herself in such a position within her own family; how she had no one to turn to; how she felt it was her fault in the first place.

'I can't bear the thought that any of my children might have to suffer that way, and I won't be there to save them.'

Stephanie reached for her hand and held it gently. She wasn't shocked by what she'd heard. It was too common a story, and something she'd dealt with more than once. But each time the horror of it struck her all over again.

'Lola, I understand how bad things were for you and I wish I could say or do something to take away that pain. All I can tell you is that social services do their very best to ensure the safety of every child in their care.'

Lola made a sound that was somewhere between a scoff and a sob, but said nothing.

Stephanie was finding it difficult to speak. Lola had broken the law, but looking at her now, her green eyes brimming with tears, shoulders rounded in defeat, it was impossible to imagine how she had suffered since she was thirteen years old.

'You understand that you've been arrested and cautioned for committing crimes relating to illegal immigration, don't you?'

Lola didn't respond.

'Is it okay if I ask DCI Brodie to come back in so we can explain what will happen next?'

She gave a tiny nod of the head, and Stephanie went to the door, knowing Gus would be waiting outside. She didn't fill him in on everything Lola had told her. That could wait, but Gus recognised that she wanted him to take over, and he took up his position at the end of the bed once again.

'Miss Holland, when you're released from here, you'll have to be interviewed formally. You can have a solicitor present – we can organise that for you, if you like.'

The look of desolation in her eyes was almost more than Stephanie could bear.

'I didn't want to help Liam, you know, but I had nowhere else to go. Those men – women sometimes – were so scared, and they arrived with such hope.' She looked pleadingly at Gus. 'I know I should have tried to stop it, but I was petrified – not just of Liam and the men he worked for, but of my father finding me. And now I've let my children down, the very last thing I wanted to do. I thought I could keep them safe.'

Stephanie's throat felt tight. This entire catalogue of mistakes and poor decisions had started with one man who crept into his daughter's bed. Now Lola's children would be separated from their mother – more unnecessary suffering.

'What about Nancy?' Lola asked, her voice choked. 'I tried to save her. I thought I could let him kill her to save my children, but I couldn't. She didn't deserve any of this.'

'Neither of you did,' Stephanie whispered.

NINETY-ONE

In my head I can still hear singing, the lilting tune repeating over and over, the words in an unknown language: memories of the music I died to. Or at least, almost died.

No sooner had I closed my eyes and given myself up to the waves than I felt something on my face. Hands were grasping me, forcing my mouth open, pushing a solid object between my lips, gripping my nose between fingers.

I opened my eyes. The saltwater stung, and my first thought was that someone was trying to hurt me. A face was pressed close to mine – a face in a mask. Two eyes, blinking at me as if trying to tell me something. The man's mouth was clamped around a black mouthpiece and he bobbed up and down with every wave. He pointed to his mouthpiece and then at the one he had just forced between my lips, and I took a big gulp of air, choking on the water in my lungs. He held the mouthpiece in place and kept his eyes on mine, smiling eyes, encouraging me, nodding his head.

Slowly, my breathing came under control, and he let go of my face, pointing to the rope binding me. Then he showed me his knife. I felt a jolt of fear, but finally I understood.

It seemed to take an age for him to free me, but I could breathe and I knew I would live.

I was too weak to swim, but the diver – a member of the police marine unit, I've been told – turned me on my back and towed me to the mouth of the cave. The sea was too rough to get a boat close enough, so I was winched into a waiting helicopter.

It was a truly heroic effort, and I will be forever grateful.

More than anything, though, I would love to see the boys who sang to me. It was an act of pure kindness and my heart aches every time I think of them, knowing that even though they have been freed from the cave, for them the story isn't over. They will be processed, and I don't know what will happen. I wish I could rescue every single one of them.

The police have told me I'm alive because of Lola. They were looking for me, but she was the one who made them understand how close I was to death. She risked everything by fighting Liam, sticking the bradawl she'd taken from my bag into his neck, and now I understand she's likely to go to prison herself.

They're taking me to see her and I don't know what I'll say. Everything she feared is now happening.

I have some decisions to make. They're not easy, and I'm not entirely sure I'm up to the job, but I think I know what I have to do – what I *want* to do.

NINETY-TWO

I'm wheeled into Lola's room. She'll be leaving the hospital shortly, but I have to stay because of the water in my lungs. They're concerned about secondary drowning, so they need to monitor me until the danger is past.

Lola is dressed and sitting on the side of the bed, head bowed. Her shoulders are shaking, and I know she's crying. A police officer stands just outside the door. I suppose he's necessary but it's horrifying to think he's here for my little sister.

The nurse pushes me close to Lola, and I reach towards her.

'I'm so sorry, Lola – for everything that's happened to you; for being so wound up in myself and my own problems that I didn't see what was happening, what he was putting you through.'

She grasps my hands and lifts her tear-streaked face, but she no longer looks at me as if she hates me.

'None of that matters now. All that matters is my children. They've taken Josh and the girls into foster care.' She whispers the words as if she can't bear to say them out loud.

I realise that I don't even know my nieces' names, so I ask the question.

'Ciara and Shauna. They're good girls, a bit giddy, and Josh gets frustrated with their silent communication, but he's good with them. I hope they won't split them up.'

I say nothing, but I suspect they may be separated. Josh is an eleven-year-old boy. I don't know how easy he will be to place, but probably not as easy as the girls. Unfair as it seems, there will be more families happy to take care of pretty five-year-old twin girls.

'I wish I could keep them safe, Nancy. All I've ever wanted to do was protect them, so they never have to suffer the way I did.' She lifts her shoulders high and drops them in a hopeless shrug. 'And now there's nothing I can do. When I'm sent to prison, I'll be miles from here, and I don't know if I'll ever get to see them. Do foster carers travel three hours each way with children to see their parents? I don't know, but I doubt it. Do you think they'll let me see them before they take me away? How can I explain to them what's happening?'

She chokes back the sobs, and it's breaking my heart. What a dreadful life she's had. Two men have abused their power over her, and now she and her children are left to deal with the consequences.

'I don't know what to say, Lola. I'm horrified that this happened to you.'

'I don't blame you. I did, but not now. We've had a life of blaming each other for our unhappiness, but none of it was our fault.'

She's right. Dad was too clever. I should have tried to spend more time with my sister, but he created barriers: the resentment I felt because Lola never visited Mum; Lola's bitterness because she thought Mum and I knew what was happening to her and didn't care. He drove a wedge between us, and we never really stood a chance. Blaming me for Mum's death was his masterpiece – another way to breed distrust.

'When did it get so bad, Lola? I've been told Mum and Dad

were madly in love, but I never saw any sign of that. I never saw any affection between them and I remember hearing Dad say she was stuck with him, or something like that – but she seemed so despondent, hopeless almost.'

'I was younger and didn't notice so much. As a child you tend to accept life for what it is, don't you? Dad told me she'd started drinking a long time ago, and he only gave her the vodka because her body craved it.'

I scoff at the thought, knowing now precisely why he did it.

'I think Mum wanted to do better, but she didn't know how. I think he made her feel useless and she began to believe it herself.'

Lola gazes towards the window, as if she doesn't want to look at me as she speaks. 'He was good at that, wasn't he?' She's right, of course. One way or another, he did it to each of us in turn. 'At least Mum tried to keep you safe.'

I don't understand what she means for a moment, but then I realise she thinks that's why Mum wanted me to sleep in her room.

'Lola, that can't be right! If she thought he was a paedophile, she'd have wanted to protect you too!'

Lola scowls. 'Maybe, although I think calling him a paedophile is too simplistic. I don't think he wanted me because I was a child, although I'm certain that held some depraved appeal. It felt more complex, as if he needed more from me. It wasn't *only* because I was a young girl, if that makes sense. He'd never shown any interest before, and you were sixteen by the time you moved into Mum's room, yet he hadn't made a move on you.' She spins towards me, her eyes wide. 'Had he?'

'No, although I suppose in retrospect there were a few occasions when I felt slightly uncomfortable. I dismissed them as me being oversensitive.'

'Such as?'

I shake my head. I don't want to talk about it now because

I'm sure it will bring back memories for Lola, but I never liked it when he came into my room to say goodnight and thrust his hands under the bedclothes to tickle me – anywhere and everywhere. I asked him to stop, but he mocked me, saying he was my dad; it was just horseplay. Perhaps it was.

'God,' she mutters. 'It's no surprise we're fucked up, is it?' For a moment we share a sad smile. 'He talked about us having a future, you know, as if we'd be together forever.' She visibly shudders. 'I don't want my kids to end up like us, Nancy, and I'm not going to be around to help them.'

The thought of those children and the chain of events started by our father forces me to come to a decision that I've been considering since I heard Lola had been arrested. It's an enormous step and a huge challenge, but I can't ignore her pain.

'Lola, I've been thinking.' I take a deep breath. 'How would you feel about me taking care of the children?'

She stares at me, as if it's the last thing she was expecting me to say.

'*Seriously?* Please don't say it if you don't mean it, Nancy – it's a major commitment, and it might be for years.' She looks as if she's scared to breathe in case I change my mind.

'I *do* mean it,' I tell her without hesitation. 'I want to do it, Lola. They deserve to feel secure, loved. I'll keep them safe until you can be back with them.'

We have no time to say more, because there's a soft knock on the door, and Sergeant King – Stephanie – comes in.

'I'm sorry to interrupt, but you have a visitor – someone who would like to talk to you both.'

NINETY-THREE

I don't know what Lola and I are expecting as the door opens wider, but another wheelchair is pushed through and for one terrible moment I think it must be Liam. But it isn't. It's an elderly lady with a gentle face, and as Effie guides her to the far side of the bed, I realise it must be her nan.

Effie gives me a sombre smile that tells me she knows how I'm feeling, but for once she doesn't speak.

'Hello, girls. My name's Stella and I was a good friend of your aunt Helen's. I've been looking forward to meeting you, Nancy. Effie's told me all about you, and I was planning to ask her to bring you round as soon as I was well enough.' Her gaze moves to Lola, and she gives her a gentle smile. 'I'm so sorry circumstances have overtaken us, and for everything that's happened to you both. If Helen were alive, it would break her heart. She always wanted to have a closer relationship with the two of you, but that wasn't possible, I'm sorry to say.'

I'm tempted to ask why not, but I know from dealing with the elderly that it's better to let them talk – and at some point, hopefully, everything she is saying will make sense.

'I asked Stephanie – DS King, as I suppose I should call her

– if I could speak to you both, because there are things I can explain, probably better than anyone. My Angie told you that we knew your mum, didn't she, Nancy?'

I nod. Lola won't have a clue who Angie Dawson or Effie are, but now isn't the time to explain.

'She was a feisty girl, your mum, and your aunt did her best – until Janice met Ray Holland, your dad. Big mistake taking her on that cruise – I said so at the time, but Helen wanted to do her best by the girl. She tried to dissuade her from having anything to do with Ray, who was away on the ship for most of the year. She thought Janice needed a bit more stability, but there was no telling her. She was quite besotted with him.'

Lola and I exchange puzzled glances. Once again, a picture is being painted that neither of us recognises.

'It all happened very quickly after that holiday. Janice moved to Southampton to be near Ray when his ship docked, and she soon got pregnant with you, Nancy. Ray opted to work on longer cruises to bring in more money, and a couple of years later he won the smallholding where you were brought up in a game of high-stakes poker, believe it or not.'

Lola reaches out for my hand again. She's thinking what I am. Where is this going?

'By that time, your mum was pregnant with you, Lola, but Ray thought it would be a better life for you in Shropshire. There was no way Janice could manage the farm, even though it was only a few chickens and pigs back then, so your dad sent her a man called Karl Novik to help – Polish, but he'd been in the UK for a long time. Apparently he worked on the docks but was in trouble with some gang or other and had to get away, so Ray offered him somewhere to live in return for helping on the farm.'

'How do you know all this – about their plans?' I ask, unable to keep quiet any longer.

Stella puts her head on one side, a gentle smile on her lips.

'Your aunt was still close to your mum at the time. She stayed with you and looked after you often, Nancy, when you were tiny.'

I wish I'd not interrupted her now, and for a moment she seems to have lost her thread. She frowns and then her face lightens as she picks up the story.

'Your mum hadn't heard from your dad in a long time. She'd written to tell him about Lola, but he never replied. And then a letter was forwarded from her old address in Southampton. It was from Ray's brother, who lived in Norway. He told her that Ray was dead – an accident. The brother was his next of kin, you see, because he and Janice had never married.'

Stella stops talking for a moment, and turns to Effie.

'Do you want some water, Nan?' Effie pulls a plastic bottle from her bag, and we wait while Stella takes a gulp.

'It seems the brother knew nothing about you girls, or the smallholding – perhaps because Janice hadn't got round to registering the new ownership – but he wanted to be clear that there was no life insurance and nothing for Janice following Ray's death.'

'But he wasn't dead at all!' Lola says. 'He was with her, in Shropshire.'

Stella shook her head. 'The man living with you all these years in Shropshire was Karl Novik. Janice thought she'd be homeless when Ray died, but she had his birth certificate and the deeds for the property, and so Karl Novik became Ray Holland.'

I try to swallow, but my mouth has dried up again. I drop Lola's hand and reach for the beaker by the side of the bed, but Lola beats me to it.

'You're saying that the man who brought us up, who lived with us for all those years, wasn't our father?' Lola whispers. 'He stole his identity?'

'With your mother's help, yes.'

'So the man who abused me was Karl Novik?'

Stella nods slowly, her eyes soft with compassion.

No one speaks for a while to give us time to process this. I can feel Lola shaking, but after a moment or two she looks at Stella. 'Is there more?'

'That's most of it. It's the reason Helen couldn't visit you. Janice told her what they'd done, and Helen was clear with her that this was fraud – a criminal offence. Janice and Karl could both go to prison. Helen didn't want that, but she couldn't visit the house, knowing full well that the man calling himself Ray was actually Karl Novik. It would have made her an accessory to their crime, and Helen couldn't tell lies. It wasn't in her nature.'

'Did Mum love Karl?' Lola asks, hoping for some rational explanation other than greed.

'I don't know the answer to that. She was grateful to start with, I believe, and Helen continued to write to her, although she rarely heard back. On the occasions when she did, she was increasingly concerned about the power Karl had over your mum. The whole thing had been Janice's idea – she was the one who gave him the papers, agreed to marry him knowing he wasn't the man on the birth certificate, but she couldn't tell a soul that Karl wasn't really Ray, and she couldn't throw him out of the house. She became more and more depressed and unable to handle life. Helen felt powerless to fix the problems. Even after Janice died, and you – Lola – disappeared, Helen wasn't sure what to do – whether to tell Nancy or not. It's why she kept her distance. Then Karl died, and it would have been impossible for her to fake sorrow and offer sympathy at that man's passing. She felt she would have to tell you the truth.'

'So why didn't she?' I whisper.

'How could she? As far as she was concerned, you thought of him as your dad. She didn't like him, but she had no reason to believe he'd hurt either of you. It would have been cruel to tell you that the man who had brought you up wasn't who you thought he was. She watched you at your mum's funeral, Nancy, and you seemed to really care about him. How would it have helped you to know that your life was built on lies? I'm only telling you now because of everything that's happened to Lola.'

I remember the funeral, reaching for Dad's hand. I had spent the day trying to please him, because I thought he blamed me for Mum's death, and I was desperate for his forgiveness. Aunt Helen was right not to tell me who he really was. I would have been devastated. Now, I don't know what to feel.

Stella takes another sip of water. 'That's it, I'm afraid. I can't imagine how confused you must feel and I hope I did the right thing telling you. I'm a bit weary now, but if you have any questions, Effie will let me know.'

Before she wheels her nan out of the room, Effie moves across to the side of the bed, reaches over to gently squeeze Lola's arm, then bends her head to kiss my cheek.

'Call me when you're ready. Any time, Nancy.'

I lift a hand to cover the one she's resting on my shoulder, but I don't speak. My eyes are fixed firmly on Lola. I don't know how she must feel about this. None of it diminishes what happened to her, what he did to her, and perhaps it alters nothing, but she's crying.

Stephanie indicates that she'll wait outside the door and the room empties of everyone except the two of us.

I wait for Lola to speak. However stunned I might feel about everything we have just heard, for Lola it's different. It's not only about her life, it's about her son.

Gazing at her hands, she silently shreds a damp tissue. When she speaks, her voice is flat, drained of emotion. 'Do you know, I haven't cried since I was fifteen years old. Possibly before that. For the last day I've done nothing but, and it's time to stop. I'm staggered by everything Stella told us and I'm struggling to take it in, but it makes sense of Mum, in a way. She made a mistake, Nancy – a stupid mistake. She did it so we would have a home, and it's no different from what I did with Liam. I too broke the law to keep my children safe. I felt myself on a downward spiral as my disgust grew at what I was allowing to happen. Maybe I would have turned to drink as well. I forgive Mum – she was no worse than me.'

'You should forgive yourself too, Lola. We both should.'

She reaches for my hand.

'And Dad? Karl?' I ask.

Her nose wrinkles and her top lip curls. 'I hate that man for many things, but knowing he's not my father...'

She pauses.

'You're relieved, aren't you?'

Lola lets out a deep breath, one I suspect she's been holding in for a long time, and nods.

I don't know whether to be surprised at her reaction or not. My revulsion at the man and his deeds won't be diminished by knowing he wasn't my birth father. To all intents and purposes, he was my dad, and I had loved him.

'Don't look so confused, Nancy,' Lola says. 'It doesn't matter about me, but for Josh, this is the best news. I've spent years watching him for any signs of abnormalities that could have come from an incestuous relationship, but now he's just a normal healthy boy, despite how he was conceived.'

She sits back, and I watch as tears she thought she'd never cry again pour unchecked down her cheeks.

NINETY-FOUR

The train trundled out of the station, the carriage rocking slightly as Stephanie stared into the gardens of the houses they passed, as always wondering about the lives of the people who lived there – whether they were happy or sad, lonely, or surrounded by people who loved them. Soon the train would reach full speed, and the images would be nothing more than a blur across her eyes.

She settled back in her seat, knowing that before long she would be asleep, but for now content to look at Gus, sitting across the table from her, his eyes closed. She knew he wasn't sleeping either. There was a contained excitement in him; she could feel it.

They had both taken a few days off in the knowledge that the case against Liam Riordan and his band of merry men was now in the hands of the Organised Crime Unit, and Nancy and Lola were both safe. It would be weeks before Lola's fate was decided, and despite everything she had done, Stephanie hoped her sentence wouldn't be too long.

Gus opened his eyes. 'You okay?'

Stephanie nodded. She was fine, if somewhat apprehensive. They were travelling to London for an overnight stop, and then on to Norwich in the morning to meet Daisy's doctors. The results of Gus's blood test had shown him to be a suitable donor, although they didn't know whether the stem cells would be taken from his blood or bone marrow. Either way, they needed to be there for a few days.

Gus had spoken to Paula at length, and they had agreed that now wasn't the right time to take any decisions regarding his involvement in Daisy's life. They had to focus on the little girl getting better, and in the meantime both Gus and Stephanie were going to meet her, introduced as friends of Paula. Daisy was too young to understand or ask questions, and Stephanie was grateful that Paula had agreed she could meet her daughter too. Her apprehension was solely because she wasn't in control of the situation, a position she never liked to be in.

If the circumstances of Nancy and Lola Holland's upbringing had taught Stephanie anything, though, it was that honesty was essential. When Daisy became strong and healthy again, which she hoped and prayed would be soon, emotions wouldn't be running so high. A resolution could be found that everyone was happy with – especially Daisy, who deserved to know who her father was.

Gus was watching her. 'I've been thinking, Stephie – about a few things, really.' He reached across the table and grabbed one of her hands. 'We spend too much time apart. I don't like it.'

If he was going to ask her to move to Newquay, she didn't know what she would say. She loved her job – most of the time – and wanted to stay within easy reach of her mum and brother, who always seemed so isolated. She thought Gus understood that. She waited.

'With all the travelling, I don't have time for any of the things I'd love us to do together. You used to sail, didn't you? I want to learn – you could teach me. We could join a sailing club, meet other people who aren't bloody police officers. It would be fun – something we never seem to have much time for. What do you think?'

'I think I don't know what your masterplan is, so I'm waiting to find out.'

Gus chuckled. 'I don't have a masterplan – it's just a conversation. But I wondered if you might consider selling your house – I know you don't love it and you bought it because it was convenient – and I could sell the flat. We could buy a home for us both, together, something we both like that's close enough to your mum's and to work, but nearer to Newquay so I can be at home with you every night. What do you think?'

Stephanie's heart beat a little faster. Owning a house together felt like a huge commitment. At the moment they both had their own space, and if anything went wrong, like last time, she could kick Gus out without losing her home. Buying a house together would leave her vulnerable. Then she remembered how she had felt when Gus ran into the sea to rescue Lola. She thought he was going to die, and she never wanted to lose him. Perhaps it was time for her to take a risk.

'I think it's an idea worth exploring. Maybe we should think about buying somewhere a bit bigger – perhaps with a decent garden and extra bedrooms.'

Gus's eyes opened wide. He knew what she meant. Space for children – their children, and a room for Daisy, if ever that became a possibility.

Gus leaned back. 'Thank God for that. I was worried you would say it was a ridiculous idea, or that you were still worried about Daisy coming between us.'

Stephanie thought of Nancy and Lola Holland again, and how a lack of honest communication had ruined both of their lives. She was guilty of holding back – she always had been –

for fear of getting hurt. She couldn't change overnight, but she could at least try to give this man something.

'I'm in this for the long haul, Gus. You should know that. Your joys, your fears and your problems are mine too.'

He squeezed her hand. 'Same here, my love.'

NINETY-FIVE

I take a final look around the kitchen and decide there is nothing more I can do. I've been preparing the cottage for the arrival of three children, and I want it to feel like home to them. When the police took Liam's computer they found a folder of Lola's photos of the children, and I've selected a few – including one of Lola with the twins – and had them blown up. They are now hanging on the walls around the kitchen in bright frames.

There's a staccato knock and I hear the latch click as the front door is pushed open.

'Only me! Oh, bloody hell, the door's not sticking,' Effie says, pushing said door backwards and forwards to test it. She turns to me with a grin. 'I've brought you some flowers! Thought they might cheer the place up, but I can see it doesn't need much cheering. It looks great!'

She's still talking as if every sentence ends in an exclamation mark, and she brightens the room even further with her wide smile.

I take the flowers from her. 'That's so kind of you.'

'You excited?'

'Very, but slightly terrified too. It's going to be hard for the children. They've effectively lost both parents, and they've rarely left the cove since they were born. They must wonder what on earth is happening to them. And they were home-schooled – I suppose so they couldn't talk to other children about their mum, or about what they saw and heard in the cove – so I don't know how they'll cope mixing with other kids.'

'Will they go to school here?'

'Probably,' I reply, although to be honest, I don't know for sure. We have to wait to see where Lola ends up after her trial, and then decide if it's best for us to move closer so they can visit as often as possible.

'Look at all this food!'

I turn to look at the table heaving under the weight of the feast I've prepared. I know I'll have to take things slowly with the children, but to make them feel welcome I've made a bit of a party out of their arrival.

'You know, Nancy, I do hope you decide to stay here. I know it wasn't what you planned, but things are different now.'

She's a big part of that difference, and I am so glad the email she believed I'd sent the very first day hadn't put her off. Lola has admitted to sending it, saying it was phase one of a campaign designed to send me scurrying back to London. Her plans fell apart when the cottage became a crime scene. She feared I would report any strange happenings to the police, and their investigations would lead to her discovery. I understand why she did it, and frankly I would forgive her anything.

'You could be happy here,' Effie says, 'and this cottage is great. I've always loved it.'

She's right about the cottage, but it only has two bedrooms. Josh is nearly eleven and will need his own space soon.

I walk over to the kitchen units, open a drawer and lift out an envelope.

'Effie, when the police were searching the cottage, they found this under the bed. Do you have any idea whose it might be?'

I hold my breath. I need to know if she's really a friend or not.

She opens the envelope and gives a delighted whoop. 'Oh, that's brilliant, Nancy! I'm so glad you found it. It's Patsy's and she bloody loves these earrings.' I breathe out. She hasn't denied it, and I feel terrible for testing her. 'We stayed here sometimes, you know – just to get away from everyone back at mine. Your aunt Helen gave her blessing, but we only did it a few times because I didn't want her to think we were taking the piss. Patsy will be thrilled. Thank you.'

She walks over and gives me a hug, and I feel a burst of relief. She wasn't keeping a secret – she just hadn't thought it was important enough to mention.

'Right, Auntie Nancy, I'm going to leave you to welcome your nephew and nieces. As always, shout if you need anything, and when you think it's the right time, I'd love to meet them.'

With a wave of her hand, she disappears out of the front door, and I turn to hunt for a vase.

I've just finished arranging the flowers when I hear the snap of the letterbox and turn towards the door. There's a postcard on the floor.

I haven't given my new address to anyone yet, so who can possibly know I'm here?

As I walk towards the door and bend down to pick it up, the image on the front looks familiar. It's the beach in town, the one Lola hung out at every day.

I stare at it, unsure if I'm imagining it. But I'm not, because slap bang in the centre of the picture is Lola in her bikini. It's one of the photos I took, an image that was only ever on my camera or laptop. The computer's been wiped, and the camera has never been found. The pictures exist online in the cloud, but no one else knows that. Nevertheless, someone has had this photo made into a postcard.

How is this possible?

I turn over the card, then drop it to the floor as if it has burned me and race towards the sink. My coffee and this morning's breakfast come up as I vomit into the bowl.

I would recognise that writing anywhere, and I lean against the worktop, trying to get my breath, trying not to think the unthinkable.

I know now who came into my room. I know who took my camera, and why there was no sound of creaking floorboards or any sign of a break-in. He had a key – the one I thought was lost. He knew where the loose boards were. The thought of him being in my room, so close to my semi-naked body, leaves me gasping.

I gulp down a glass of water, spilling it down my chin as I try to force my throat to swallow.

I must read the words, although I don't want to.

Nancy, you're even more beautiful than I always knew you would be. But Lola, she's my special girl. I know where she is. I can't reach her now, but I can be there for her when she comes out. Tell her she's on my mind every day. I've been searching for so long, but now I can rest. All I have to do is wait.
Dad x

I don't know how long I've been standing hunched over the postcard, staring at the words, but slowly the sick feeling fades. I breathe deeply and lift my head.

He's not doing this to us.

Not to me, not to Lola, not to the children. He may have controlled us once, but he has no power now, and I know what I must do.

He's been here, in my cottage. The postmark is local, so he

must have been staying close by, and not for the first time – if Liam was telling the truth. Maybe he was. He could have recognised him from the local press photos after Lola's disappearance, so perhaps he's not the only one to have seen him.

I flip up the lid of my laptop and access my images from the cloud. I have far better photos than the ones that were published, and *someone* will have seen him.

I stare at the face of the man I always thought of as Dad, trying to see beyond the person I thought I knew and get under the skin. From this day forward I will think of him only as Karl, and there is no doubt in my mind that I have to find him. Knowing he is out there, watching, waiting, is more than I can bear.

Maybe he can't be brought to justice for all his crimes, but Josh is living proof of Karl's abuse of a fifteen-year-old child in his care, and he must pay for what he did. The photos won't be enough, though. I need more.

Seeing his face, knowing him as I had believed I did, a thought hits me. He will have needed a new name, because he can't be calling himself Ray Holland. I registered the death of Ray Holland myself, and although it's easy enough for a living person to change their name, it's much harder to create a whole new identity.

And why would he need to?

Karl Novik never died. As far as Karl is aware, no one apart from Aunt Helen even knew of his existence. She believed he died in the reservoir, and she's dead herself now.

Karl Novik will have a birth certificate. He worked at the docks, so he'll have a National Insurance number, maybe a passport or a driving licence. If I'm right, the police will unearth him from wherever he's hiding. And I *am* right. I know I am.

I smile as I switch off the computer and slip the postcard into a drawer. Any minute now the children will arrive and today will be all about them.

But Stephanie is due back tomorrow, and together we will find him.

A LETTER FROM RACHEL

Dear Reader,

Thank you so much for taking the time to read *Don't Look Away*. I always enjoy writing about feisty, vulnerable Stephanie and in this book, we learned more about her insecurities. I hope you feel you're getting to know her better with each story.

Writing about Cornwall is a sheer pleasure, with its rugged coast, wonderful beaches and pretty towns. I particularly like writing about the sea as I am fortunate enough to be almost surrounded by it. One day the rocks are battered by spectacular waves, the next I look out onto calm blue water, and it's the ever-changing nature of the sea that mesmerises me. I also know how cruel it can be, and try to capture the joy and the fear in equal measure.

I wanted to write a book about guilt; about how some people's lives are haunted by the thought that had they done something differently, the worst would never have happened. This is so true of my character, Nancy, who seems to have taken responsibility for every dreadful event that impacted on her family. As the plotting of the story developed, so many other aspects of human experience came to mind: the thought of a young girl, isolated from everyone because she was caring for her mother; the jealousy between siblings caused by thoughtless parenting; the need to feel loved. Although at its heart *Don't Look Away* is a thriller, I do hope that the emotional elements of the story had an impact. It certainly made me think.

I always love to hear from readers, and one of the best ways of keeping in touch is via my special Facebook group – Rachel Abbott's Partners in Crime. It's a place where readers can chat about everything thriller related and discuss books they have enjoyed from a wide range of authors. I know that many of you base your reading choices on recommendations from other group members, and I am delighted that it is such a success. If you haven't joined in yet, you can find it here: *https://www.facebook.com/groups/Partners-in-Crime-RA*

I send regular newsletters and share some of my own favourite reads, plus keep my readers informed of offers and new releases. Whatever the means of keeping in touch, it's always great to 'meet' people who have read my books and to have an opportunity to answer any questions, so if you've not already signed up and would like to do so, here's where to go: *www.rachel-abbott.com/contact*

And of course there is always social media – currently I'm on Facebook and Twitter. I am trying harder with Instagram, but there are only so many hours in a day!

I'm now settling down to write the next in my Stephanie King series, and looking forward to it. At the moment, it's no more than a germ of an idea, and it will take time to develop into a fully formed concept, but I'm excited about the thoughts I've had up to now. And of course, the Tom Douglas series has now reached its eleventh title. I can't believe how time has flown since I came up with the idea for my first thriller as I sat in traffic jams on my way to work.

I would be delighted to hear if you enjoyed *Don't Look Away*, so feel free to tweet me, or leave me a message on Facebook. And one very special request – if you have enjoyed this book, I would be thrilled if you would leave a review on Amazon. Every author loves getting reviews, and I'm no exception. And of course, it helps other readers to find my books.

Thanks again for taking the time to read *Don't Look Away*.

Best wishes,

www.rachel-abbott.com

facebook.com/RachelAbbott1Writer

twitter.com/RachelAbbott

ACKNOWLEDGEMENTS

Writing is something of a solitary occupation, and yet none of my books would ever be written without the significant input of a number of key people. This story required more research support than most and, as ever, I have been astonished and delighted by the willingness of people I have never met to share their expertise. Without them, *Don't Look Away* wouldn't be the book it is.

I have to begin by thanking one person whose help is invaluable. Mark Gray, an ex-detective chief inspector, never fails to respond to my numerous questions. I do my best, with his guidance, to represent police procedure as accurately as possible, but any mistakes in this regard are entirely mine. With each book I kid myself that I know enough about the workings of detectives to manage without his support, and I am invariably wrong. Not only does Mark respond promptly and in great detail to my queries, he also takes the time to read and comment on the final manuscript. My very special thanks to him.

With *Don't Look Away*, I was keen to include the discovery of a skeleton, and knew I would need help understanding the evidence. I am grateful to forensic anthropologist Dr Catriona Davies for kindly offering her expertise to a writer she had never met. I found her advice fascinating, although I should say that my characterisation of the forensic anthropologist in the book bears no resemblance to the real Dr Davies!

Some parts of the story take place in or around the sea, so thank you Nigel Shaw, Alderney's Deputy Harbour Master, for not only giving me information about communicating with ships, but also advising me on which services might be involved in a rescue operation. His advice led me to contact HM Coastguard, whose response to my questions was incredibly detailed. Andrew Follows, a Senior Maritime Operations Officer, provided me with no end of information – not solely about how HM Coastguard would operate in the rescue conditions I outlined, but also how they would integrate with the police marine unit and the RNLI. This took a lot of his time, and is much appreciated.

As most writers know, the first draft of any novel is unlikely to be the last! Input from others whom I trust is vital, and I am forever grateful for the fact that Lizzy Kremer of David Higham Associates is my agent and friend. Her guidance throughout the writing process – from first concept to final draft – cannot be underestimated. She pushes me to write the best book I can, along with the efficient and inspired Maddalena Cavaciuti, and their enthusiasm and encouragement mean everything. The entire team at DHA has been with me throughout my writing career, and a special shoutout to the foreign rights team and the finance department for their ongoing support.

Thanks also to the team at Bookouture. I am thrilled they are publishing the third book in this series and it has been a real pleasure to work with the editorial team – Ruth Tross and Sarah Gunton, together with the wider Bookouture team of Kim Nash, Noelle Holten and Jess Readett in publicity, and Melanie Price in marketing. I consider myself lucky to have found a copyeditor as brilliant as Hugh Davis, and thanks also to Alexandra Holmes in managing editorial and proofreader Rachel Rowlands.

I feel privileged to have such wonderfully loyal readers, and I am overwhelmed by their fantastic support. Thank you all for not only reading my books, but for reviewing them, talking about them to your friends, and for joining me online whenever the opportunity arises. You are the best!

A shoutout to all the book bloggers too. I honestly don't know where writers would be without you. So many of you work hard to get the word out about new books, and it's impossible to overestimate the help you offer to the writing community.

Finally, as always, a huge thanks to my husband John. He reads my books when they are at an early, rough stage, knows my characters almost as well as I do (because I talk about them all the time) and offers nothing but encouragement. Plus, of course, he keeps me provided with coffee, food, wine, and always a big smile.

Made in United States
Orlando, FL
06 April 2024

45528612R00252